Marcella has been s............
from her wild ways...............mp girl; Lisa is
Jewish and rich. Yet the three girls form a friendship
that will last beyond their Derry school days as their
interests turn to men, careers and The Troubles. Inevitably their beliefs bring conflict between them but the
bonds of their friendship hold firm as they fight for what
they believe in and the men they love.

Angela Doherty was born in Inishowen, Co. Donegal, and educated in Derry. Her writing career began at the age of seven when she wrote her first poem. Producing and writing school plays followed, and she later ran a drama group in London. She has written various articles, short stories and radio scripts. Married in her early twenties, she has four children.

CONSTANT FRIENDS

······································

Angela Doherty

ORION

An Orion paperback
First published in Great Britain by Orion in 1993
This paperback edition published in 1994 by Orion Books Ltd,
Orion House, 5 Upper St Martin's Lane, London WC2H 9EA

A CIP catalogue record for this book is available from the
British Library.

ISBN: 1 85797 436 0

Typeset at The Spartan Press Ltd,
Lymington, Hants
Printed and bound in Great Britain by
Clays Ltd, St. Ives plc

For my family,
the
Màire Óines

PART ONE
Donegal, 1958

Chapter 1

Marcella Adams wondered if it was an advantage to be born on the 17th March, St Patrick's Day. No school, but up early for Mass. And Father McGill at the chapel door always remembering it was her birthday but getting the number of years wrong, though it was himself who christened her in 1946.

'Isn't it grand to be only eleven years old,' he said that morning, trying to control the bush of shamrocks flowing down his shabby cassock.

'It's twelve I am today, Father.'

'It's great when you get older,' her mother said as they climbed into their old Austin car. 'He keeps deducting twenty years off my age, which makes it a bit of a miracle that I gave birth to you and your brother.'

'Maybe he forgets things because he's getting old.'

'He's not all that old. Your daddy says he's got a first-class brain and should be teaching at the college in Derry. Maybe his mind is becoming addled sitting in that Parochial House with the roar of the Atlantic in his ears all day long and the voice of that sharp-nosed housekeeper, Kitty the blacksmith's daughter, treating him to bits of parish gossip he could do well without.'

After Mass, Marcella took her birthday present – a new bicycle – out to the lane. As she sped away from the house the wheels sank into the moist peaty soil; they were immediately cleansed by a little stream gushing across the road that had lost its way on the journey from the hills. It must have rained heavily in the night because the face of Crockalough was ribboned with cascading streams. Below the mountain the fields, which were mottled with stones, had a freshness and sparkle in the thin morning sunlight. A savage beauty, her mother called this part of the land, where the tiny fields were bound together by loosely-built stone walls. There were no gates to be seen, just gaps in the walls which could be undone and built up again if animals were grazing.

Out on the road Marcella pedalled straight towards the sea. The last bit sloped steeply and was rocky. Only fit for donkeys, she thought, jumping off her bike, not wishing to damage it on such a hazardous descent. Perhaps it would be better to leave it at Brae Cottage at the top of the hill and walk on down to the shore? The cottage had newly-whitewashed walls and a trim blond-coloured thatch. Biddy in the brae had been praying for ages that a work-bug would plague her brothers to get the job done. Ned and Liam must have divided the work between them, for Marcella could see where Liam, the younger brother, had wearied of his task and recklessly dashed whitewash over everything in sight, including the fuchsia bells that tumbled across the walls.

She went to prop her bicycle against the gates then changed her mind. The gates had left their posts years ago and were now firmly rooted amongst the wild roses and fuchsia bushes, whose branches had entwined themselves around the rusty bars. Inside the cottage, Liam and Ned were bent over a creel of potatoes resting in the centre of the floor, a spud in one hand and a mug of buttermilk in the other.

'Ye'll have a bite, Cella?' Liam offered. 'A few praties.'

'No, thanks. Where's Biddy?'

'Working at Slievan.'

'Can I leave my bike here, Liam?'

'Surely to God. Stand it against the wall there.'

When Marcella wheeled the bicycle into the kitchen, Ned scuttled across the floor. He was curious about everything. ' 'Tis a powerful machine, Cella.' A finger ran over the mudguard. 'A wee bent there, begod. See there, Cella? A wee bent.'

Dismayed, Marcella examined the mudguard then burst

out laughing. The mark was barely noticeable and had obviously been done in the workshop. She had a sudden picture of her mother searching through the store in Carndonagh for a machine with a slight flaw so that she could demand a reduction.

'I'll be back in about an hour's time,' she told the brothers. 'If you go out be sure to shut the door in case the hens come in and roost on it.'

'We will so, Cella,' they promised.

Down on the beach she climbed to the top of the *tulach* – a great mound of earth and rock which stood near the old ruined church of St Morallagh, a medieval monk who had lived in the cave just a few yards along the shore. In penal times the cave had been used to say Mass. Up here, she was standing on the very tip of the Inishowen peninsula, Ireland's most northerly point. Lough Foyle lay along the eastern side, to the west was Lough Swilly and out there on this northern shore, the Atlantic Ocean. The blue Atlantic, people called it. From here it looked drenched with the colour of the land. On this *tulach*, Marcella had been the heroine of every fable and historical story that she had read – Deirdre of Sorrow, Grainne wife of Diarmait, and many others. She had also acquainted herself with Sir Cahir O'Doherty, Chieftain of Inishowen, whom her mother claimed to be an ancestor of their family.

A flash of red on the hill over by the wireless station made her start. Through the mists of her imagination she saw a line of Redcoats making their way down towards the shore. There was reality in this image, for the English soldiers had indeed marched down there, searching for the priest who was saying Mass in the cave. On this very spot the look-out man had given the warning and saved the priest's life. The figure in red began to wave furiously. It was Biddy in the brae. Her high-pitched voice sounded above the billowing waves. The tone of urgency made Marcella scramble down and race across the shore, where she fell over a pile of kelp waiting to be carted away by a farmer who supplied medical laboratories.

'Cella,' Biddy called, 'get up to the house quick and tell

the brothers to hasten to the field where the Slievan stirks are grazing. See that they bring a knife. A terrible thing has happened.'

Breathless, Marcella turned and raced back again and up the steep stony road to the house. By the time she reached Brae Cottage she was panting for breath with a stitch in her side. Liam's old bike was missing from outside the door. There was no sign of Ned either. She pulled a sharp knife out of a kitchen drawer, glanced regretfully at her shining bicycle and tore off again.

A short cut took her through the heathland above the cliffs, which were covered with tufts of coarse heather and gaping holes where white stones protruded from the dark peaty soil. At night it looked as though the heath was scattered with pieces of white linen. She sped over the ground, wind tearing at her hair and seagulls screaming their resentment at the disturbance.

'Ye took yer time,' Biddy shouted when Marcella was within hearing distance. 'And where's the brothers, for God's sake?' She grabbed the knife out of the girl's hand. 'I suppose drownin' their shamrock in Boyle's like all the other eejits. There's not a man to be seen around this land today. I hope one of them will be able to drown his conscience, the careless blaggard.'

'Biddy, what's happened?'

'The Slievan stirks were put in the field and the gate not fastened properly. The wee things have got out and are destroying themselves somewhere. There's one in the slough – I fear its leg's broken. By this time it's maybe got strangled with the rope that's caught around its neck. I'll never get it out by m'sel'.'

A coldness ran through Marcella. She wanted to run away from the fearful sight that would meet her eyes in a minute. 'I'll help you, Biddy,' she said reluctantly as they crossed the road.

'I'm comin', birdie,' Biddy shouted in answer to the pitiful cries from the terrified animal. 'Cella, you go on up towards the hills and try to round up the other stirks.'

Ashamed of her cowardice, Marcella raced past the

slough without glancing at the one which had met such a terrible fate. Maybe Biddy would have it out by the time she found the others. They were in a field of unripe corn, leaping about in joyful abandonment. Shutting her eyes briefly at the chaos they were causing, she picked up a heavy stick and drove the young cows down the road.

Biddy, with perspiration streaming down her face, had just managed to cut the rope that had got caught on a stump of tree jutting from the hedge, and which had become entangled around the animal's neck. It was lying on its side with three feet in the air, the other trapped in mud and briars. The young cow's large eyes were turned on Biddy, who was murmuring endearments as though it were a child.

'Come on, m'darling, sure ye've only to pull yer wee foot out and all's well. Wouldn't it melt yer heart, Cella?'

'Could we not pull it out?' she suggested.

Biddy put her hands on her hips and looked up at the heavens. 'Wid ye listen to her? "Pull it out," says Marcella Adams, as if we had the strength of them divils down in Boyle's toasting Saint Patrick. Me, an auld wimin and she only a skinny wean. I tell ye, child,' she said irritably, 'its entire body would have to be held firmly if we tamper wi' that foot.'

'Why don't you try tying the rope loosely around its neck and then coaxing it to move?'

The rope was tied. 'Now shift yersel',' Biddy urged. 'Sweet God, what a stupid beast.'

When the stirk let out another plaintive cry, Marcella shut her eyes and murmured, 'I'm praying, Biddy. Who's the patron saint of animals?'

'Deel a hate I care. I'm past praying for miracles in this godforsaken land. There, pet . . .' She took a step closer. 'I'll have ye out yet.' With a look of determination she took hold of the rope. The next minute she went flying into the ditch beside the animal with her skirt swirling around her waist. So, Marcella thought, it's true what they say about Biddy wearing long red flannelette knickers for her rheumatism. She had not believed it, but now here was the evidence before her eyes and within inches of the animal's face.

The expression in the stirk's eyes changed from one of alarm to sheer terror. There was a long drawn-out sucking noise as it wrenched its foot free of mud and briars, then with a surprisingly deft movement, it was on its feet and scrambling away from the ditch to the road, where it fled without any obvious sign of injury.

'Bedam to it,' Biddy swore furiously, dragging herself off the ground. 'If I'd known a sight of m'bloomers would've shifted him, I'd have had him out of there ages ago. After him, Cella – don't spare the stick!'

With tears of laughter streaming down her face, Marcella raced up the road and found the calf in the cornfield where the others had been. In no time she had him back safely with the rest. Tired after their ordeal, the old woman and the girl pushed the offending gate firmly against its post.

'There should have been a chain on that gate,' Biddy complained, bending down to pick up a length of rope. 'And . . .' Her words died away. She gripped the girl's arm. 'Almighty God . . .'

'What is it?' Then Marcella saw that the rope had been deliberately severed. They found a piece of chain amongst the high grass by the hedge; the iron ring attached to it held the other part of the rope.

Eyes wide with alarm, Biddy said fearfully, 'All my days I've lived in Iniscad and never heard or seen such a wicked action. Someone in this place has deliberately tried to injure the Slievan cattle. Them wee things could have wandered down to the cliffs.'

Marcella felt frightened and bewildered. The people living in this part of Inishowen were friendly towards each other. The Gilroys at Slievan were Anglo-Irish gentry but a Catholic family who attended Mass every Sunday. Yet in this small close community someone had raised a hand against them.

'I told them not to cut it down,' Biddy muttered, as they hurried up the road home.

'Cut what down?'

'The thorn bush growing in the middle o' that field. The master ordered it to be done and not a word wid he listen to. Sure doesn't everyone know that them thorns must be treated with great respect.'

'That was no fairies' work,' Marcella said slowly. Although the old superstition troubled her a little, she was convinced that this was a deliberate act against the Gilroys.

She couldn't wait to get home and tell her mother.

Chapter 2

'Mr Adams, the editor wants to see you.'

Conor Adams glanced across his office at the junior reporter, Joe Gallagher, who had just opened the door. He was a cheeky lad who, Conor felt, planned to get to the top without wasting any time. The boy grinned. 'Witchhunt on,' he said, and disappeared again.

What the devil did he mean by that? Conor gathered some papers from his desk and went downstairs.

'Sit down, man, I want a wee word.' Andy McCay was stockily built with a florid face, and still a ten days' wonder to the staff of *The Northern Press*. Though it was not apparent from his accent, he had been born in Belfast, then brought up by a Scottish mother, in Glasgow, where he had worked until he inherited the *Press* from his uncle, who was a Derry man.

'What have you got there?' he added impatiently, wanting to get other matters out of the way before he came to the point. Conor Adams was a stick-in-the-mud — typical of everything else he had come across since taking over his uncle's paper in this half-dead town.

Conor pushed the folder across the desk. 'That's Eoin O'Donnell's latest yarn and verse. The verse is written in Irish. I'll translate it if you wish.'

Andy McCay rolled his eyes. 'The man's mad. How many people in this city can read their own language, for God's sake?'

'Eoin's got a thriving Irish class,' Conor told him, smiling. 'He's trying to influence the Derry people.'

'Not at the expense of this paper. I'd rather have a good juicy story any day . . . and you can take that look off your face, Adams. We want to build up our figures. Don't want *The Derry Journal* to have things all its own way. About time *The Northern Press* made its mark on this town instead of dragging behind.' He tossed Eoin O'Donnell's work across the desk again. 'Don't waste your time on it – send it back. Gaelic's a dead language. Let the people have it in English, the language they understand. Now . . .'

Conor lowered his head and tidied the papers together into the folder. Merciful God, he prayed, let me hold my patience with this madman. He'll run the paper into the ground if he tries to make any more changes. Juicy story . . . Derry is a quiet, decent place. We haven't got a Gorbals around here, he felt like telling him.

'What I envisage,' the editor continued, 'is a series of features that will make our readers really sit up and take notice. Something that'll make them impatient to buy the next copy and, most important of all, increase our sales.'

'What have you in mind, Mr McCay?'

'The landed gentry.'

'There's nothing new or exciting to write about the aristocracy in this part of the world. They live quietly in their big houses without a whisper of scandal. No one tries to burn them out these days. The last flare-up was thirteen years ago – during the war, and it died down quickly enough. Not even the German spies across the border benefited from it.'

'I wasn't thinking of a Republican involvement. I'm not interested in that kind of political angle.'

Conor frowned. 'What have you in mind?' he asked again, puzzled.

Andy McCay drew himself up in the chair. He hated to admit it to himself, but the huge desk and the tall man sitting on the other side of it, made him feel slightly diminished. In time, he was going to have to do something about this monstrosity, and it would give him great satisfaction to do something about Adams, as well. 'Some stories involving the seamy side of their lives. I believe you've got one of these families living in your part of the world, at Iniscad?'

'The Gilroys of Slievan? I don't think you'll find any skeletons in their cupboard,' Conor said quickly. What the hell was McCay getting at? He felt uneasy at the smug expression on the editor's face.

'Haven't you ever wondered where they came from – the Gilroys?' When Conor did not reply immediately, McCay snapped: 'Where's your nose for news, man? You've lived in these parts all your life and worked on this paper for several years. Surely you must have ferreted around your district for stories when you were a cub reporter?'

Conor coloured with resentment. 'The Gilroy family have never been newsworthy. There have been no scandals, nor even garden parties. They are just quiet people who inherited an estate. They go to Mass on a Sunday morning and that's all I hear or see of them.'

'Oh aye, they are good church folk now, but it wasnae always the same story! There's a lot of dirt in that connection. You'll likely have heard of Lord Kindron, kin of the Gilroys?'

'Of course.'

'The whole damn lot of them living off the fat of the land without the right to own it.'

'Now you're talking like a Republican,' Conor said sarcastically.

McCay sat forward in his seat. 'I want you to go to Slievan and see Gilroy. Talk to him about his infamous relative. Let him know that we are planning to do a series of stories on Lord Kindron. Get his reaction – not that he can do much to stop us, if he had a mind to. There's plenty about Kindron's antics in old copies of *The Northern Press*.' He rubbed his hands with gratification. 'It seems the people murdered him.'

'They did. That was in the late nineteenth century. Where is all this leading to, Mr McCay?'

'We know that Kindron ordered young girls into service in his home and then seduced them. When they became pregnant he threw them out again, declaring that they were already in that condition when they came to work for him. Apparently, when some parents tried to prevent their youngsters from going into service at Kindron's, they were flung out of their cottages, losing their bits of land. Many ended up as beggars on the road. Christ, man, doesn't it make your blood boil to think that English upstarts — pilfering soldiers — could come to your country, take over the land and behave in that way?'

'Of course it does when one thinks about it, but we can't go on forever living with bitterness. The culprits are long since dead; their descendants can't be held responsible for their actions.'

'They could hand back the land that their forefathers grabbed.'

Conor moved impatiently on his chair and looked his employer straight in the eye. 'Would you? For God's sake, let's be realistic. Anyway, I can't believe you want to rake up that old story about seductions and murder. It'll make one article in a single issue — no more.'

'Quite so.' Andy McCay smiled, then leaned across the desk and folded his hands like a benevolent uncle bestowing some well-meaning advice. 'Have you ever given a thought to the present whereabouts of all those illegitimate children of Kindron's?'

'No,' Conor said shortly. 'There's enough going on in the world without trying to dig up the present location of the unfortunate offspring of one who was called in the House of Lords "A noble lord of the Realm". Huh!'

'Aye, quite so. A man who ruled his tenants after the feudal fashion and indulged in "le droit de seigneur".'

'So where does this leave us, then?' Conor asked, still not comprehending.

'Many of these by-blows went to an orphans' home in Derry,' McCay said smoothly, 'and afterwards into domestic service in the area. The lucky ones got away to America. Now . . .' He banged his hand on the desk, as though disposing of any further objections that Conor might make. 'I would like you with young Gallagher's help to track down their descendants. Interview them . . . each story will make fascinating reading.'

'But these people will be second and third generations!'

'There are a few elderly women around who could be the actual daughters of Kindron. I've got a list of names.'

'You know who they are?' Conor was amazed. How in the name of heaven had McCay managed to obtain that information? Kindron had always denied responsibility, and with everyone so terrified of him, his word was not challenged. Imagine suddenly finding out you were related to that power-mad pervert. And this was the information McCay expected him to impart to unsuspecting, decent people. What was he going to do? His editor was asking him to work on a job that was no better than gutter-press copy. It was unthinkable.

Andy McCay arranged all the pencils on his desk in a neat row as though their order had some importance. 'So, Mr Adams, first do the smooth bit, interviewing Gilroy. Then the dirty work, as I fear you're going to call it.'

'Do your own dirty work, McCay,' Conor said angrily, pushing his chair away. 'Your uncle would not foul his paper with the misery of decent people. I suppose you intend to use the information, whether these people agree or not?' Words were flying recklessly from his mouth. He stopped, suddenly appalled by his rashness. The man might throw him out. He thought of his wife Mary B, Brian and young Marcella – all dependent on his meagre wage.

He waited for the words of dismissal. His seniority on the staff would pull no weight with this man.

'I think, Conor Adams, that you're being unwise and imprudent. You are a fine journalist – readers like your work and I don't want to lose you. However, this job *must* be done. A lot of groundwork has already been sorted out.' McCay rose to his feet. 'Arrange an interview with Gilroy of Slievan. We'll take it from there.'

'Very well,' Conor said stiffly. For the first time in his life he had a feeling of intense dislike towards another person.

Conor climbed the stairs back to his office slowly, remembering with sadness the plans McCay's uncle had made for the future of *The Northern Press*. God, the old man must be turning in his grave! He sat down at his desk and began to read the historical article that Eoin O'Donnell wrote once a week for the paper. Sometimes Conor roared with laughter, while at other times he underlined a sentence with a question mark. Like many strong-minded Republicans, Eoin could go a bit too far at times.

'*James VI of Scotland and I of England, that mean-spirited whipster of Mary Queen of Scots and Darnley, decided to plant the north of Ireland with English and Scots farmers. Their plan was, and they succeeded, to turn the north into a solid Protestant colony . . .*' Conor's head shot up. Eoin – that was his man. He reached for the phone and dialled a number. 'That you, Eoin?'

'It is and I'm not going to alter a word of it.'

'Hold on. Something else. I need your advice. Speak in Gaelic – *an dtuigeann tu?* Do you understand?' Conor told him what McCay was planning to do.

Eoin said thoughtfully, 'Some people might be pleased to have the blood of such a notorious ancestor, depending on which side they want their bread buttered, if you know what I mean. It might not do any harm at all if a man was after a job in a local government department. A drop of blood from an English Protestant could pull a bit of weight with those in Stormont.'

'Ah, be serious, Eoin.'

'But on the other side of the coin,' Eoin said, mixing his metaphors, 'if you were one of our worthy theologians . . .'

'You know someone?'

'Canon Reid.'

'*Him*? God almighty!'

'Aye, the very man. He certainly would not be pleased to know that he came from such rotten stock and that his grandmother's brother was one of the men who shot the dastardly earl.'

'I'd not imagined that anyone in higher places would be involved,' Conor said quietly.

'Huh! Higher places, bedam. Show me the Irish cleric who didn't come out of a humble home. Aye, they do well for themselves in this world.'

Don't let him start on that old theme, Conor thought impatiently. His friend's agnosticism could be irritating at times. It fired his words and bored the hell out of everyone who didn't agree with his point of view.

'Conor, listen,' Eoin went on. 'Do what the wee Scottie suggests. Go to Slievan and see Gilroy, and leave the rest to me. There'll come a day when this kind of information might be put to good use.'

'What do you mean?'

'I'm not sure, lad . . . not sure at all. Right now. On with the work.'

Conor rose from his desk and looked out of the window. Below were the walls of Derry, with the lofty Doric column erected to the memory of the Reverend George Walker, who had led the defence during the Derry Siege in 1688–9 and who later died at the Battle of the Boyne. Lying beneath the walls, the houses of the Bogside were clustered together, spirals of smoke rising steadily towards the great height of solid grey stone. Away beyond the city were the hills. He'd get out there now, see Gilroy, then go home to Mary B, where he could finish his day's work.

He took the road across the hills with Slieve Snaght, the highest mountain in the Inishowen peninsula, lying to his left. There was a sweetness in the air that flowed through the window, and a musical tone to the little wind that soughed in the bushes along the way. He drew in deep breaths, relaxing now after the disturbing conversation with his new boss. He couldn't help wondering how the situation was going to resolve itself. Still, one step at a time. Gilroy had agreed to see him this afternoon, though the clipped alien voice on the telephone had left Conor in no doubt that it would be a difficult meeting.

Why, he wondered, taking a short cut across moorland, did he shut himself away in a newspaper office in Derry and deprive himself of a life in the country as a farmer, which was his natural inheritance? The turf-cutters were out on the moor, slicing into the rich brown bog with a sleán. They were cutting from the side of a bank from which a three-foot heathery surface had been pared off, then stacking the turf in small piles to dry and harden in the sun. On the hill above them came the sound of sheep and the call of the curlew. A sweet aroma drifted from a fire near the turf-bank, where a big tin kettle boiled on a pile of turf and bog wood.

Conor had happy memories of days spent on the bog during the annual cutting of turf. It was his job to help the young serving-lad to light the fire and prepare a pot of potatoes for the men's dinner. Afterwards the big tin bog-kettle, as it was called (made by the tinkers), went on the fire and was boiled with a fistful of tea thrown in. The dark brown tea was accompanied by slices of soda bread spread thickly with freshly-made butter, still glistening with beads of moisture from its making. Later in the season, when the bog was spangled with flowers and drumming with snipe, he would go shooting with his father. The echoing silence had not brought a feeling of solitude then, for the plaintive piping of the golden plover, the sound of grouse and other birds filled the air.

The road from the moor narrowed; ahead of him was a farm cart loaded with hay which left wisps hanging on the briar roses and hawthorns. Branches tapped at the car windows as though demanding their bounty too. Conor liked this friendly scratching at his old Austin, and feeling in a mood that tuned with nature, regretted that all he could bestow on the hedges was car fumes to smite the buds of the briar rose. Out on the main road again, he approached Malin Town in the parish of Cloncha; it was no more than a village with a grassy triangular green built near Trawbreaga Bay, which was supposed to have the highest sand-dunes in Europe.

Slievan, the home of the Gilroys, was situated in a sheltered valley not far from the shore. Few trees grew in this part of the land but a previous owner had made sure that the house and parklands were well sheltered by planting a woodland around the house. The building was unprepossessing; a wide-leafed ivy, unfamiliar to Conor, grew all over the walls and with greedy fingers crept towards the windows as though determined to encase the entire building in a green tomb. What's Gilroy thinking about, letting it take over like that, Conor wondered critically.

Biddy in the brae, looking unlike herself in a white apron, opened the door. 'God bless my soul, Conor Adams, what are ye doin' here at all?' she asked with indignant alarm, as though he had come to burgle the house. She had worked in Conor's home when he was a child, and frequently forgot that he was now a man with a growing family.

'Mr Gilroy, Biddy. Is he in?'

'He's not back yet. The missus is in the drawing room.'

'Will you tell her I've called?'

'Well . . .' Biddy was unsure so he followed her into the hall. He understood the situation. Her mistress was not at home to casual callers.

'It's Mr Adams, mam, from River House. Will ye see him?'

Conor, behaving with a touch of ruthlessness that was familiar to his profession and which he disliked, left Mrs Gilroy no option; he moved towards the room door. The woman, reclining on a chaise longue, was pouring tea.

'Do come in, Mr Adams. My husband's not at home. Would you like to call back later?'

'This is the time we arranged,' he announced firmly. 'I phoned from my office in Derry, Mrs Gilroy, and made an appointment.'

'Oh, in that case.' She waved her hand towards a straight-backed chair that had elegance but obviously no comfort. Biddy remained standing by the door, her mouth hanging wide open with curiosity. She got a sharp look from the chaise longue. 'You may go, Biddy,' her mistress said.

And that should have been 'Bring another cup, Biddy,' Conor thought, not entirely surprised by the Englishwoman's manners. He was probably just a country yokel to her way of thinking. Still, this was an opportunity not to be wasted. He explained briefly the reason for his visit.

The pale elegant woman, in the gracious room decorated in a neo-Classical style, stirred her cup of tea slowly; somehow the action conveyed indifference. Was she indifferent, Conor wondered. It was a hard thing to understand the English of this class. Sometimes their faces presented an inscrutable mask; even a smile did not always convey a glimmer of warmth. Still, he had a feeling that his carefully phrased explanation was beginning to ruffle the surface a bit.

Mrs Gilroy replaced her spoon on the saucer. 'Really, I know nothing about Lord Kindron. My husband's family are only slightly connected.'

The door opened and her husband came in. He moved quickly towards Conor and held out his hand. 'Come to my study, Mr Adams. We'll have a chat there.' The man threw a brief smile at his wife. Conor noticed that the spoon-stirring had begun again. This time it conveyed displeasure. She had been subjected to an unwelcome visitor and he was going to hear about it later!

'Will you have a drink, Mr Adams? Whiskey?'

'Yes, thank you.' Conor nearly added, 'Thank God.' The drink might make Gilroy more communicative than his wife. Conor had met him on two other occasions, both to do with church matters, and had encountered an impenetrable reserve. Yet now, as they sipped their whiskey and discussed the little fleet of fishing boats that went out from Malin pier in all weathers, Conor thought that the man was possibly just naturally shy.

'It was good of you to see me, Mr Gilroy,' he said when the amount of whiskey had lowered in their glasses. 'I mustn't take too much of your time.' He noticed the nervous movement of the other's hand. The long sensitive fingers began to fold imaginary pleats on the surface of the table, then to smooth over the rich patina of wood again. It was disturbing and oddly fascinating.

'I mentioned on the phone,' he went on, 'that the purpose of my calling to see you was to do with Lord Kindron. I would like to . . .'

'Why has Lord Kindron suddenly aroused interest? No one has mentioned his name in all the years I've lived here.' Gilroy's words were like an attack.

'My editor is interested,' Conor said flatly.

'And will this "interest" churn up the less attractive associations of Lord Kindron's name?'

'I'm afraid so.'

'It all happened years ago.' There was a perceptible drop in the pitch of Gilroy's voice. When Conor did not reply, he said snappily, 'That's the problem with this country, it *can't* forget . . . keeps churning up old history.'

The accusatory tone and the utter stupidity of such words spoken by an Englishman brought Conor's head up sharply. He stared at Gilroy until the man's eyes dropped and colour flooded the pale features.

'Forgive me. That was a damn stupid thing to say. You see . . .' he stretched out for the decanter and refilled their glasses, 'things have been happening on the estate. I feel we're being threatened.'

Conor stared at him incredulously. 'Here?'

'Yes, in this quiet beautiful place where I have always felt our Catholicism made us fit in better with the people.'

'What happened?'

Gilroy pulled out a drawer and tossed a piece of rope on the table. Conor could see where it had been cut through. 'This was the gate-fastening to a field which had several fine stirks grazing in it. Only for the quick action of Biddy with the help of your daughter, I might have lost the lot. I've been in touch with the gardai, and they looked as surprised as you do at this moment, Mr Adams.'

Children in the country didn't go around doing that kind of thing, Conor thought anxiously. His look of perplexity made Gilroy say quickly, 'That's not the only incident. My tank of oil was also emptied.'

'Some would steal anything.'

'It went straight into the ground – wasted. Also, an unsuccessful attempt was made to fire the barn. There's unrest here somewhere, and if your paper rakes up that old scandal about Lord Kindron, the outcome will be laid on my doorstep. I beg of you to do what you can to suppress it, Mr Adams. There's my son, who will inherit the estate. I must think of him.'

Conor sensed the man's fear and wondered how many of the landed gentry lived with this uncertainty in their lives.

As he drove home, clouds like dark shadows stole across the restless sky. Spots of rain began to fall; by the time Conor reached River House they were shivering off the laurel tree by the lane. When he got out of the car he saw Marcella gathering crottle for her mother. The grey lichen-covered rocks outlined her gleaming black hair and blue jersey. He was about to call to her when skeins of dyed wool on the line by the orchard caught his eye. Unpegging the wool, he thought how industrious his wife, Mary B, was. She knitted, sewed, spun and made lace. It was pleasant in the evening to sit reading by the fire with the rhythmic sound of the spinning wheel in his ears. Indeed, as far as he knew it had been a familiar activity in Ireland for over three thousand years.

He bit his lip anxiously, remembering that he had promised his wife that one day, when there was money to spare, he would fix up the old stable for a little craft shop. Many of their neighbours scattered around the parish produced needlework of a high standard, including shawls crocheted in traditional patterns.

'Come on inside, Conor,' she called from the dairy window. 'You're getting wet out there.'

He went into the long cool room that had served his family for generations. His wife was busy washing and salting butter. Regarding her contented expression, Conor decided not to burden her with his work problem for the time being. She knew well his dream to be editor of *The Northern Press* one day. Some hope of that happening now! Mary Bridget beat the butter with a pair of ridged butter-platters, then taking a round wooden shape out of a vessel of water, stamped it on top, leaving the impression of a swan nestling in a bed of seagrass. The butter, rich in colour, was placed on a crystal dish.

'Quicker to buy it down in Boyle's.'

She planted a kiss on his cheek. 'Philistine! Churning is good for my nerves and think of the taste, darlin'. You've got a visitor . . . he's sleeping at the moment.'

'Who?'

'That cod, Eoin O'Donnell.'

He made a dash for the door again. 'The very man I want to see.' He paused. Of course he couldn't talk to Eoin here with Mary B around.

'There's mortal sin in his eyes every time he looks at me. And he could be m'grandfather.'

'He thinks you're the most beautiful woman in Ireland.'

'Blarney!' A gleam of mischief lit up her face. 'He's got a mistress. Imagine an old man like that.'

'I'll take him down to Boyle's for a drink.'

'Bring him back for supper. He always looks half-starved.'

'Mary B, did you ever know he's a Doctor of Philosophy as well as everything else?'

'I know he's a doctor of . . .' she rolled her eyes '. . . amour, amour.'

Conor threw back his head and laughed. She was always plucking words out of the air and tossing them casually into a conversation. Over in the kitchen, which was also the room in which they lived, Eoin was helping Marcella with her homework.

'Eoin, what about a jorum down in Boyle's before supper?'

Eoin raised his head and looked at Conor who nodded at the door, indicating that he wanted him away from the house so that they could talk. They settled themselves in the snug-bar at Boyle's, each with a bottle of stout and a glass of whiskey.

'Did you see Gilroy, Conor?'

'I did.' He told him what had taken place. 'Gilroy may be able to shoulder the publicity about Lord Kindron, but the stealthy attack on his animals and property is another matter. It's being done by someone who could cause destruction and trouble at any time.'

'Well,' said Eoin, tossing back his whiskey, 'as you know I haven't much time for people like Gilroy and his like, but I detest the sly buggers who harm a man's property behind his back. And as for interfering with stock . . . it's deplorable. However, don't let's waste our time feeling sorry for him. Now, listen to me. I've been around to see some of the people concerned. They understand and will refuse to discuss it with anyone.'

'What about young Gallagher? He's got the gift o' the gab.'

'He won't get far. They'll be tight-lipped and they're going to make sure that every member of their family does the same.'

'How did they take it?'

'Utterly shocked. Horrified.'

'How many were there altogether – families, I mean?'

'Eight, including the cleric. I've seen six. The Canon is away in Rome at the moment and the other one I'll be seeing this evening. You know, Conor, someone must have had the hell of a time getting that information for the wee Scottie.'

'How did you manage it?'

'Did I never tell you? I grew up near Lord Kindron's estate. Even to this day the old folk never stop talking about him. Of course the names of the families from which young girls were taken and abused were familiar to them. Some years ago, when I became well-known as a local historian – through writing in your paper, mind you – I went to the orphanage and began my investigations. Naturally I gave some story about being interested in old registers, which was true. It went on from there.'

'What a brute of a man Kindron must have been. I'm surprised someone didn't finish him off sooner.'

'Many's a time they planned it, Conor, and something always went wrong. Another thing, he knew that his life was threatened and he always wore a protective jacket.' Eoin drained his glass. 'I'd better be on the road and heading for Derry.'

'Mary B is expecting you back for a meal.'

'Ah well, give her my love and say I'll be down another day. To tell the truth, Conor, I'm not looking forward to number seven on my list.'

'I'm sorry, Eoin. All this can't be easy for you.'

'It can't be helped. It's Prisca McDaid, the girl in my Irish class. About the same age as your son, Brian. The kind of child I'd have liked if I'd a daughter of my own. Ah well, she's a tough wee thing.'

When Conor dropped Eoin outside Bridge House and the other man drove off in his car, doubt began to nag at him again. With or without the co-operation of the people on that list, McCay could still publish something. He'd find a way. In a place as small as Derry it would not be difficult for young Gallagher to snoop around and get some sort of story together. Perhaps it would not have the same impact without readers being able to identify the characters, but still, it could arouse a lot of unhealthy interest.

'Where's Eoin?' Mary B asked when he went into the house.

'On the way to Derry.'

'That's the first time I've known him to turn down a meal. Conor, I forgot to tell you what happened this morning. Biddy and Marcella . . .'

He went to the fireplace and bent down over the creel as his wife repeated the story about Gilroy's cattle.

'Yes, that's what happened. I had to go to Slievan to see him. He told me about it.'

'You were right inside the house?' Her voice rose in excitement. 'What's it like at all?'

Conor piled some turf on the fire and smiled. 'You'll die of envy.'

'Indeed I will not. Who'd want to live in an old barrack of a place like that?' Her eyes slid down mischievously to meet his. 'Don't you dare leave a word out!'

He dusted his fingers and frowned, trying to recapture the picture of that beautiful room. The words he spoke were inadequate, yet he could see in his mind the pale green ceiling delicately scrolled in white, as were the mouldings and frieze. Green damask curtains with a deep pelmet matched the wallpaper. Balancing this predominant colour were fine pieces of old furniture and a few pictures. Also a collection of blue porcelain. Opposite the chair where he had been sitting, was a rococo gilt pier-glass which had reflected an unusual-shaped chandelier at the other end of the room. The chandelier looked like a young tree hanging upside down from the ceiling, sparkling with a multitude of raindrops touched by sunlight.

'What was she like to talk to?'

'Talk? Her ladyship reclined on a chaise longue sipping tea while your man here sat on an uncomfortable chair.'

'Mother of God, didn't she offer you a cup? You'd think that Cockney upstart would have learnt some Irish courtesy after all these years of living in this country. Did you know she's been presented at Court and is distantly related to a member of the royal family? Biddy says the royal face smiles in every room – the same photograph reproduced.'

'Ah, I didn't notice it. I couldn't take my eyes off the fascinating mistress of Slievan!'

Mary B took the white linen cloth that covered the newly baked scone of bread and dropped it over his head. They were still laughing when Marcella came running down the stairs.

'Listen,' Conor said quickly in a low voice to his wife. 'Don't make too much of that story about Gilroy's cattle. You know what the youngster's like . . .'

Chapter 3

The bells of St Eugene's Cathedral rang out across the Bogside, not like other church bells with their measured doleful sound, but melodiously playing a soft Irish air. The music of their movement lifted Mrs McDaid's heart, lying in bed recovering from a miscarriage.

'Mammy, I've brought you a cup of tea.'

'Thanks, Prisca, put it down on the chair. I'll have it in a minute, pet.'

'Would you like something to read? The newspaper?'

'No, I'm content looking out the window. There's a ship coming up the Foyle. Such grandeur in its movement.'

Content, Prisca thought grimly. I'd be screaming if it was *my* third miscarriage, not to mention six weans under the roof.

'Are you managing downstairs?'

'Aye surely.'

'Don't forget to give your uniform a good pressing for school on Monday.'

'School? Well, we'll see how you are.'

'You're not to miss another day at school, Prisca, after getting that scholarship,' her mother said firmly. 'I'll be a proud woman when you're a schoolteacher.'

And prouder when Dominic is a doctor, Prisca decided, running downstairs. God, what would the poor in Ireland do without American relatives? Better still if one was your godmother, like Dominic's, who sent a regular money order for his education. Parcels of clothes came for his sisters — cast-offs from the well-to-do family in New York where Aunt Maggie worked as housekeeper. Under God, were they all film stars in that family? The parcels contained the same daft kind of garments the English had dumped on the starving Irish during the famine. A joke in their hour of need.

Her brother Dominic pushed his bicycle into the hall and unstrapped a pile of books from the handlebars. 'Half-day in honour of Saint Somebody.'

'Lucky you. I'm missing all those Saints' Days at the Mount Academy.'

'Maybe the Protestants have got a few of their own. Or do they commemorate them all on the Twelfth of July?' His expression changed. 'How's Mother?'

Prisca paused before replying. 'She's fine now.'

'What did the doctor say? What's the matter with her?'

'Miscarriage.'

His face flushed with anger. 'Christ!'

'Don't go on about it, Dominic.'

'How many more children and miscarriages is she supposed to stand before she lands in her grave?'

'Mammy's strong.'

'Her body is worn out. Don't you see that's why she's had three miscarriages?'

'I suppose it's because she hasn't the time to rest.' Prisca didn't feel close to her older brother as she did to the others in the family, but the tears of frustration in his eyes at that moment moved her. She touched his arm. 'There's nothing we can do about it, Dom. Go on in and I'll make a cup of tea when I've finished this hall.'

His lip jutted out rebelliously. 'She should sleep in the front room with Granny.'

'You mean Daddy should sleep upstairs on his own? What do you think he's going to say to that?'

'Who cares what he thinks.'

'Right enough, they're going to listen to our suggestion. Me, only fifteen years old and you only a few years older, planning their lives for them.'

'Aye, fifteen, with the cheek of an old woman and as bold as brass.'

'Cooking and washing, not to mention studying, has stunted my youth. Move away from that door, Dom, I'm

27

trying to wash off all the sticky fingermarks. That Granny fills the wee ones with sweets before they go to school every morning.'

'It should be stopped. It'll ruin their teeth.'

'God almighty, where do you live – on another planet? You've got a tongue in your head too.' Prisca wrung out the cloth, enjoying the pungent clean smell of carbolic soap. 'If there was an Englishman around he'd be offering to do this work for me. They say they're great housewives!'

'If there was an Englishman around he'd be out working.'

'Dominic, leave our father alone. It's not his fault that he can't find a job. Don't you ever take a look at the dole queue? It's miles long. Away in and cut some bread for the tea, standing there against the wall as if it needed holding up. Do plenty for Granny, she's got a new appetite with her second childhood.'

Her brother's lips moved in a smile. 'All right, I'll do that.'

'Did you remember to ring the Academy early about my not going to school today?'

'Of course.' As Dominic walked through the kitchen to the scullery he thought anxiously about his sister Prisca. She was the clever one of the family. It wouldn't do if she kept missing days off from that school. The fact that she had got a scholarship to Mount Academy – the first one from a Catholic school in Derry – was incredible. Thank goodness there were a few Catholic teachers in Derry who could see the possibilities for a girl of her ability.

Prisca carried the bucket of water down the hall, knelt and began to wash the lino. The work gave her a feeling of satisfaction as the gold and white mosaic pattern bordering the brown lino sprang to life under the hot soapy cloth. This was a brute of a house for her mother to look after, not to mention the McDaid clan who crowded every corner of it. The hall washed, she went out to the front door and scrubbed down the steps.

Mrs Kenny next door opened her window and called, 'How's yer mammy now, daughter?'

'Fine, thanks.'

'Wid she like me to do the washing for her next week?'

'No thanks, I'll manage.' The last time you did the washing, you old bitch, a towel and two pillowslips disappeared, Prisca thought savagely. My mother is too gentle to ask you about them.

'Wait a minute, love, I've got a wee present for her.' The neighbour came out of the house again with a fat chicken dangling from her hand.

'Mrs Kenny, that's too much.' Prisca's stomach leapt in anguish at the sight of the bird, and tears of longing started in her eyes. There were poundies for dinner and tomorrow a few salt herring with boiled spuds. She had been counting frantically over the housekeeping money, wondering what she could manage for the Sunday dinner. This big bird must have cost at least ten shillings.

'Sure it's too big for us with Kenny on the drink again and no appetite for a bite o' food. Drinkin' hisself to death he is, the divil take him. Sure maybe I'd be better off . . . Jesus! Look what's coming out through the door over there.'

Prisca's head spun in the direction of Mrs Kenny's gaze. The Merry Widow, as she was called, posed on her doorstep for a minute, so that everyone in Brawn Street could have a good look, then she walked slowly away from her house, the tight silk dress revealing every line of her perfectly shaped body.

'The divil visits that streetwalker's house,' Mrs Kenny said very loudly, and using her door as an instrument to convey indignation, slammed it shut before Prisca could say a word of thanks for her benevolence.

At the window of the Merry Widow's house sat a young girl, some years younger than herself. Her eyes, through the glass, seemed wide and haunted. They stared across at Mrs Kenny's door with a strange longing, then followed her mother's oddly elegant figure swaying down the street. Prisca saw and felt the girl's loneliness, and paused for a moment to consider her own deprived but happy home. She smiled and waved. The gesture was not returned.

29

Granny McDaid was sitting in her special chair munching a piece of bread and jam when Prisca went indoors. 'Have you had enough to eat, Granny?'

'A brave wee wheen.'

'Huh! That means too much, I bet.'

'What's that under yer oxter?'

'A chicken for Sunday dinner. Isn't that grand?'

'Divilabetter.'

Prisca bent and picked up a piece of knitting. 'Lord alive, what's that supposed to be?'

'A sock for my daughter's husband.' This was Granny McDaid's way of referring to her son-in-law when he had displeased her. News of the miscarriage had drawn her mouth into a tight line of displeasure since early morning, and her sitting here on her backside, weary-woe, not able to give a helping hand.

'Granny, dear, it's twenty inches long. What about turning the heel and making a foot? Daddy hasn't suddenly become footless or lost the use of them.'

'Pity he hasn't lost the use of other parts,' the old woman said crudely.

Prisca's face flamed in anger. The old woman closed her eyes and dozed off until the next meal. When Prisca went out to the scullery, Dominic was peeling a dish of potatoes. She made no comment about this unusual gesture; the same instinct made her push the fowl into the broom cupboard, out of sight. Her brother might not like the idea of taking food gifts from Mrs Kenny. To accept such a gift in Derry meant that you were on the lowest rung of society. Whether he liked it or not, that's where the McDaids were at the moment. Perhaps when a plate of roast chicken was pushed under his nose on Sunday he might not be able to show the same indignation.

To cover her movement, she asked, 'Have you been upstairs yet to see your mother?'

'She's sound asleep.'

'Good. Let's have a quiet cup of tea before the wee ones come in from school.' Prisca sat on the edge of the table and swung her feet. 'I've just discovered that I enjoy scrubbing floors. Maybe I should go in for charring.'

Dominic did not consider that funny. 'You're going to work like blazes at that school and go on to university, aren't you?'

'God willing.'

He stretched his legs across the little scullery floor. 'However does our mother cook for the crowd of us in this poky place?'

'Sure I can tell you down to the last minute detail. Number one rule, no one is allowed into the scullery except the helper on duty. Honestly, Dominic, you keep on as though Mammy is a badly-done-by wife and mother, too gentle to complain about the poverty in her life. There's a strength in her and ... happiness.' Prisca faltered over the last word, remembering the scene at five o'clock that morning in her parents' bedroom, when her father tore downstairs and out of the house for the doctor. The pain on her mother's face, and the helpless tears when she realized that nature was terminating her pregnancy ... Prisca clenched her hands and bit her lip.

'It was his fault that we lost everything and now live in a slum in the Bogside.'

'Who? What are you talking about?'

'Our father. His parents established a good business and when they died, he let it run down.'

'There were hard times after the war they say, especially in the drapery trade.'

'He gave tick to everyone and didn't bother to chase the debts. And he gambled on the horses. When I think of the good home we had then. Everything went down the drain.'

'He probably hated serving behind a counter and wasn't strong-willed enough to do something about it.'

'When it's your bread and butter,' Dominic said impatiently, 'you have to like what you're doing.'

The sound of children's voices came from the kitchen. Relieved, Prisca hurried away from her brother.

'Where's Mammy, where's our Mammy?' the little chorus cried, disbelieving that she wasn't in the kitchen, waiting for them as usual with a plate of pieces.

'Having a wee rest,' Prisca told them.

'Rest?' they chorused again, incredulously. Mammy never rested in the daytime.

Dominic came in with a plate filled with wedges of bread and jam. No butter or margarine – that was a Sunday treat. As the four children scrambled for their piece, Prisca slipped upstairs.

Patsy, aged eleven, came after her. 'Pris, that wee clashbag Deirdre is going to tell Dominic that I got slapped at school for not doing m'sums right.'

'She's only a wee thing, pet. I'll help you later with your homework.' Tell Dominic. Even the baby in the family ran to her elder brother instead of her father. Poor Daddy, stripped of authority by his children.

Phelim McDaid was sitting on the side of the bed holding his wife's hand. He dropped it guiltily when Prisca made her presence known, and a pinkness spread across her mother's face as a shaft of sunlight lit up the shining red hair that fell to her shoulders. Their daughter could feel the strength of love in that room. You poor things, she thought, with the oldness that was part of her nature. You've no idea what your two hard-skinned children were planning for you: instant separation to protect Mother from another pregnancy. A bed in Granny's musty-smelling bedroom where it was forbidden to open a window. And an old woman's mutterings instead of quiet conversation and shared love and laughter.

'God, we've got the bloody nerve.' The words ran out of her mouth before she could stop them.

Phelim rose to his feet. 'What is it, Prisca?'

'Nothing.' Embarrassed, she hurried from the room saying, 'I'll bring you up some tea, Mammy.'

'Prisca,' her mother called after her, 'make sure Maeve gets down to her practising.'

'Surely.' Her eight-year-old sister did not need prompting to practise the piano, nor help from her father who came immediately and took a seat beside the instrument. Deprived of a musical career himself, when he was pressed unwillingly into the family drapery business,

Phelim's greatest joy in life was teaching his children to play the piano. Little Maeve was the one with talent. Now, incredibly, she was called a child prodigy after several major awards at the Feis Doire Colmcille, where she competed with performers years older than herself.

Feeling a bit tired after a long day on her feet – and with the thought of work still to be done – Prisca carried a neatly laid tray up to her mother, containing thin fingers of toast and a pot of strong tea. Toast, made before the fire, was a great treat in the McDaid household.

'Don't go, Prisca. Put your feet up pet, for a minute,' her mother suggested. 'You look whacked out.' Prisca stretched beside her mother on the bed, feeling waves of tiredness drain through her body.

'Was there some trouble downstairs?' the quiet voice beside her asked after a few minutes.

'Dominic worrying about you.'

'Ah.'

'I think he would like the money order Aunt Maggie sends from America to be used for running the house, instead of paying his fees at the college. He's bitter because he didn't get a scholarship.'

'There's no question of his godmother's money going into the housekeeping. Apart from everything else, it would be dishonest. It's his money and,' Nora McDaid added firmly, 'he's going to be a doctor.'

'Never mind. How are you feeling, Mammy?'

'Grand now,' Nora said quickly, as though her health was of no concern because there was something more important to discuss. 'Prisca, before I met your father I had nothing. Granny and me lived in a damp wee cottage in Donegal, where I was born. Every day I walked four miles over the hills to a shirt factory in Derry because we would have starved without the money. They say a heavy purse makes a light heart but my heart has always been light and I never in my life had a heavy purse. Dear knows, maybe a body is as well without too much money.'

'How can you say that?' Prisca burst out impatiently.

'Yer father's mother had plenty, and didn't she go soft in

the head and take the notion to draw it all out of the bank over months, then had a bonfire in her bedroom one day. That's God's honest truth. A poor woman in spirit, who looked as though she had a permanent bad smell under her nose!'

'Bad scran to her! Think how it would have helped Daddy.'

'Arrah, it was lamentable, but she went witless and you can't even yer wit to a wean. Anyway, child, going back a bit . . . By the grace of God, something unexpected happened to me when I was eighteen years old. The manager at the factory where I worked asked me to take a box of sample shirts to yer grandfather's shop in The Diamond. When I signed the delivery chit, yer grandfather thought it was one of the world's wonders – he'd been at the bottle, you see – because the poor wee factory girl had the same grand name as himself – McDaid! He bellowed for his wife, and she being a nosy body as well as a sour one, took me inside into the living room for some tea and questions. Ach, she was curious to know how many pairs of shoes I went through walking all that distance every day to town. And I, being a great innocent, told the truth and said I didn't put my shoes on until I came in sight of Derry.'

'She must have had a fit when Daddy fell in love with you. How did it happen?'

'He came in from college that day I was being interrogated. And that's how it began. Ah, it was great luck entirely. I was a lucky girl and, my love,' she tapped Prisca's head lying below her shoulder, 'I still am.'

As Prisca went downstairs, she felt her mother had been trying to show her a gift – the gift of contentment. With all the poverty and struggle to bring up a large family, Nora McDaid seemed to be completely happy.

Prisca opened the kitchen door to a burst of music, which faded to a gentle exploratory movement of exquisite beauty as her little sister's tiny fingers raced across the piano keys. 'Dominic,' she said softly, 'I must get some homework done before tea because I have an Irish class this evening.'

'Haven't you enough to do without trying to learn Irish?'

'It happens to be our language. Anyway, I enjoy it. We always have a discussion group afterwards.'

'What about, for goodness sake? What do you discuss?'

'Dreams, Dominic. Our dreams for a united Ireland.'

Chapter 4

Prisca rode Dominic's bicycle up the Brandywell Road around to the side of Eoin O'Donnell's house. She could hear shouting coming across from the football field where the Derry City players were practising for their next big match.

'Wasn't that a grand day, Prisca Mary,' Eoin said, opening the door. 'Thank goodness there's a good appearance on the weather at last. Mind you, there was a bit of wind and rain over by Malin Head. There's no mercy in the wind by the Head.'

'Sorry I'm late, Eoin.'

'Divil a bit of difference it makes this evening for the others won't be here.'

'Where have they gone to?'

He walked down the hall towards the living room without replying. A tall man, he bent his head to enter the room, then turned his grey eyes, considering her thoughtfully. 'Perhaps you might join them another day?'

'Join them? You mean the group meet apart from the lessons and discussions we have here?'

'That's right. We conduct our meetings in another member's house, entirely in Gaelic.'

'Would I be able to keep up with them?'

'We're all very impressed by the way you express yourself, Prisca Mary.'

It wasn't the answer to her question but Prisca was satisfied.

'I wonder why your parents gave you that name?' he mused.

'When I was born, Mammy was in a hospital ward

where the other mothers called their babies after important saints or aunts and uncles in religious orders. She said
she felt ashamed by her lack of knowledge and worthy
connections and startled the life out of them by calling me
Prisca.'

Eoin laughed. 'The name suits you. Saint Prisca was a
strong-minded Roman lady who died triumphantly by the
sword.'

'I never knew that. I bet Mammy doesn't. She probably
saw the name in her prayer book.'

'First, let me see the work I set you.' The door opened
abruptly and a woman with cropped grey hair came into
the room. Eoin rose quickly to his feet. 'Ah, Rosheen. This
is Prisca McDaid.'

'Hello,' the woman said shortly, her heavy black brows
shooting down to link with the frown that formed from
her mouth. Eoin took her arm and they left the room,
speaking swiftly in Irish which Prisca had a job to
understand.

Out in the hall Rosheen Quinn said, 'Not Phelim
McDaid's daughter?'

'It is.'

'I remember him in nineteen forty-three. Spineless.'

'Gentle . . . unsure, Rosheen. That's different.'

'Huh!'

'Don't be a targe, aillean. Go and join the others and
come back later.'

Rosheen held his gaze for a moment. 'Where else would
I go?' she said softly and left the house.

'Prisca,' Eoin called through the door, 'there's a sign of
rain coming. I must get my tools in from the yard.'

She sat on the chair by the window that looked out on
the back yard. Like their own yard, it was small and
whitewashed, with pots of geraniums splashing colour
against the walls. Limbs of variegated ivy crept from a
black iron pot and grew rampantly around a bird-table. To
one side of the yard was a workbench where Eoin worked
at his woodcarving on fine days. Prisca watched him
gather up his tools, the colour of his skin and black hair

37

giving truth to the claims that his ancestors were Spanish.

There was an ascetic look about the room in which she sat. A delicately carved crucifix hung on one wall. On another were pictures of Irish revolutionaries. As usual, Prisca went over and studied the face of Michael Collins, Commander in Chief of the Free State Army who signed the peace treaty with the British government in 1921, after the War of Independence. And who was reported to have said afterwards, 'I have signed my death warrant.' As indeed he had. Then on his last breath as he lay dying on the road of Bealnamblath, the great general whispered, 'Forgive them.' Who did he mean, Prisca wondered – the English who had occupied the land for several hundred years, or the anti-Treaty Republicans who had ambushed his party? In the alcove above the fireplace hung a portrait of Maud Gonne. Prisca had never heard of her until she met Eoin O'Donnell.

'Like Yeats,' he said now, coming into the room, 'I was hopelessly in love with her.'

'Did you ever meet her?'

'Once, when she was growing old ... "Old and grey and full of sleep".' He looked at the portrait and added, 'Time was gentle on her. Shaw said she was the most beautiful woman he had ever seen. And didn't Yeats himself write the play *Kathleen ni Houlihan* for her.'

'Eoin, she wasn't really Irish, was she?'

'No, Maud had English blood but a great love for Ireland. You should read about her, my dear.'

Prisca rolled her eyes. 'Haven't I read nearly every book on your shelves under my bedclothes by torchlight.'

'Well now, didn't the books about Maud Gonne inspire you?'

'Indeed. But if she had come out of the Bogside and was the daughter of a poor shirt-tail hemmer working in a shirt factory, like my mother, I might have been more inspired. Apparently Gonne had pots of money, not to mention amazing beauty and height. Look at me. I'm no size.' Her eyes twinkled. 'Who, for heaven's sake, could *I* inspire?'

He laid a hand on her head. 'You're a grand girl, Prisca

McDaid. That's one thing you've got in common with Maud – spirit.' He drew up a chair. 'I want to have a talk with you.'

The sound of his voice and expression made her move uneasily. He got up again and stood by the window. 'What is it, Eoin?' she asked.

'Prisca, have you ever heard of Lord Kindron?'

'I think there's an old book about him in the house. I haven't read it.'

'Where did the book come from?'

'My father must have picked it up somewhere. He's got a collection, not that he can afford to buy any these days.'

'Your grandmother . . . she's a Donegal woman, isn't she?'

What's he going on about, Prisca wondered impatiently, wanting to get down to the lesson she had prepared. 'Granny's parents died and she was brought up in an orphanage in Derry. I believe she went to work on a farm somewhere and met my grandfather. He was a thatcher.'

'A thatcher, was he? A fine old craft. And that's all you know about the old people.'

She gave him a cheeky look. 'Isn't that enough? He was dead before I was born and Granny's still sitting in our corner plaguing the life out of us!'

Eoin laughed and thought, God almighty, how am I to get around to this story. He had come quickly enough to the point with the others, almost brutally so – perhaps because he didn't know them. This girl was different. He was unsure how she would react. Prisca was proud of her Irish blood and always had plenty to say for herself during the discussions they held on identity, culture and language. How the hell was he to tell the poor youngster that she was descended from a soldier adventurer, who'd come over here in the seventeenth century with the Parliamentary Army, and in recognition for his services had received grants of land in Ireland and eventually a title?

He saw her impatience mounting and plunged into the awful story. When the worst part was told, he turned from the window. 'Prisca, Lord Kindron was the rotten one of that family. There were good men before and after him. One opposed the Act of Union because he thought it was wrong for Ireland. And he did his best for the people during the famine in eighteen twenty-two.'

'How can you be so sure that that devil out of hell was my grandmother's father?'

The note in her voice made Eoin move quickly towards her. He was appalled by the look on her face. Her skin had a white-greyish tinge and the brown eyes were dark and listless. They were her best feature, always sparkling as though life had given her bountiful happiness. He would have put a glass of whiskey in her hand if she were not so young. He explained quickly about the orphanage and his personal knowledge of the area where she was born.

'Why did you find it necessary to tell me all this?' she asked with bitterness.

'Because, my dear, the editor of *The Northern Press* intends to publish a series of articles about the illegitimate children sired by this man, and their families. He has traced most of those concerned and it is his intention to interview them by any means. Apart from yourselves, there are several other families involved.'

'*Mammy*,' she said with a sound of desperation. 'She *mustn't* find out about this.'

'If McCay goes ahead with it, Prisca, she'll find out in a most unpleasant way. Someone from the paper may land on your doorstep. Wouldn't it be better now to tell her and your grandmother? I've been to see nearly all the other people concerned and it is firmly agreed that everyone will maintain a total silence on the matter, absolutely refusing to discuss it with anyone.'

Her eyes had a haunted look as they wandered around the room, as though seeking some familiar object to reassure her.

'Mr Adams, a senior member of the newspaper's staff, was on the point of resigning over this affair, he found it so distasteful. I probably shouldn't tell you this . . . Canon Reid is also one of Lord Kindron's offsprings.'

'No! He's so . . . so distinguished.'

'Well, a proud and clever theologian. Silence will defeat McCay in the end. We'll all stand together as the entire countryside did when Lord Kindron was murdered. Hundreds of pounds were offered for information about the identity of the three assailants, and not one of the poor people in that area was tempted to betray them.'

Nora McDaid was sitting by her bedroom window sewing one of the shirts from the pile stacked by her bed. It was a huge bed, leaving scarcely any space for the chair between it and the window. On the wall there hung a large picture of the Blessed Virgin and another of the Sacred Heart. A statue of the Child of Prague rested on a chest of drawers. Nora thought its coloured robes gave the room a touch of elegance. She hoped the layers of glue used to repair its frequent 'beheadings' would not diminish the graces which were attributed to its spiritual power. The weans loved the cold plaster image and she hadn't the heart to deprive them from embracing it. She smiled, remembering when one of them ate off the head – or part of it. Deal a bit of harm it did the child. Phelim made a grand job of patching it up again.

The pictures and statue were wedding presents, cherished because the givers were long since dead. Their colours gave a warmth to the room that they could not afford to supply by way of an electric fire. She watched Prisca down in the back yard hanging out the washing. Ever since last night there had been an expression on the girl's face that troubled her mother; it was so out of character. I'll bide my time, Nora thought, and wait for an opportunity to have a chat. Soon the three girls will have finished their Saturday morning chores, received their penny pocket money, which they'll take to their Aunt Cassy's sweetie shop up by Bishop Gate. Thank goodness they always bought strips of liquorice from Cassy. It saved Nora from having to dose them on Friday nights, the way her mother used to dose her.

Prisca looked up at the window. 'Would you like a cup of tea, Mammy?' she called.

41

'Bring one for yourself as well, love.'

When Prisca came into the room carrying the tray she placed it on the floor, as far from the pile of shirts as possible. She watched her mother sew on a tiny pearl button, then with the expertise acquired from years of practice, fold the shirt and put it aside.

'The price of that shirt would keep us fed for a week, Mammy, wouldn't it?'

'Indeed, it would be a grand spread at that! Look how the silk threads run through the linen. Isn't it a miracle how they achieve such things? I often wonder where my shirts will land. I imagine a grand bedroom and the back of the man it'll cover. It's never a skinny wee article, but a fine man, broad-backed like your father. Funny, I can never put a face to him. I often say a wee prayer for that man. Sure money isn't everything.'

'If I thought it was going to land on the back of Lord Brookeborough, I'd sew a few fine needles into the seams.'

Nora McDaid laughed. 'Now Prisca, stop that wicked talk!'

'Of course he'd never wear it if he knew that the hand of a Catholic had touched it.'

'So they say. Ach, he can't be right in the head, dear help him. When his time comes to meet his Maker, he'll surely see that the Catholics were not so bad.' There was silence for a moment. 'Prisca . . .'

'Yes, what is it?' Her mother had a low musical voice, unchanged by the years she had been living in Derry. It was amazing, Prisca often thought, how soft the Donegal accent was compared to the harsh consonants heard in the speech of the north, yet Donegal was only a few miles across the border.

'Tell me, dear, what's troubling you. I want to know, otherwise you'll be laying a worry on my shoulders.'

Prisca fidgeted with her fingers, pulling at each one as though trying to give them equal length. Her mother stilled the movement with a touch of her hand, then bent her head and continued to sew. Now she was convinced that there was something seriously troubling her daughter. The girl was always so direct, never hesitating when anything had to be said.

'It's terrible, Mammy. I feel sick at the thought of having to tell you.'

Nora threaded a needle, trying to give an impression of composure. The heart was frightened out of her. 'What is it at all? Surely it can't be that terrible? The one thing that bothers me in this life is that sickness might strike one of you. Now child, get it off your tongue and whatever it is won't seem so bad.'

Prisca glanced at her mother, sitting there working, frail and weak after a miscarriage and all that troubled her was that one of them might be taken ill. Without hesitating for another second, she plunged into the story that Eoin O'Donnell had told her. 'Granny always said that her father was lost at sea. It's not true. She was the illegitimate daughter of that Lord Kindron. Eoin said it was important that I told you because the editor of *The Northern Press* is planning to do a series of articles.'

'What about?' Mrs McDaid asked quickly.

'About all the families they can trace here in Derry and Donegal that were connected to Lord Kindron.' Prisca glanced fearfully at her mother and noticed how pale her face was, yet her fingers applied the needle steadily as though drawing comfort from the action. The holy pictures hanging around the room looked down with frozen compassion.

'That was a kind action Eoin O'Donnell took,' she said quietly. 'I expect he had to go to see all those poor people . . . dear knows, the knowledge might not trouble some of them over-much.' Her voice trembled. 'But others . . .'

This was not the reaction that Prisca had been expecting. Then the startling realization came that her mother already knew the story. Before she could say another word, the quiet voice went on, 'Your granny told me about her father years ago.' She put aside the needlework and joined her hands as though preparing for prayer. 'All this time I've lived with that terrible story at the back

43

of my mind. As long as it's not brought out in the open, I'll live with it until I die. Dominic, the others, they must never be told.'

'Granny knows? How could she?'

'Something happened at the orphanage. I couldn't get the story out of her. She told me before I married your father. He was a good man, she said, and should know that we had tainted blood.'

'Tainted blood?' Prisca's mouth twisted with bitterness. She clenched her hands and bit her lip as tears of rage started in her eyes. 'Christ, they came to Ireland, took over our land and raped our women.'

'Prisca! I won't have that talk. They were not all like that. Some were good caring men.'

'None of them were good men. They had no right to be in our country.'

Nora McDaid shook her head impatiently. 'It's in the past.' Her voice died away, losing its ring of conviction. 'Your granny has forgotten the true story about her birth and talks about her father being lost at sea. Wherever did she get that story from, I wonder?'

'Maybe that's one good thing about growing old, you can shut your eyes to the past.' Dear God, Prisca thought, how I wish I could go back to yesterday and feel again the peace and happiness of that day. And not to have the knowledge that my blood is corrupted by that of an evil man who died an ignominious death at the hands of the people.

Chapter 5

Conor Adams spoke to the receiver in his hand as though it had taken life and could reply to the questions which the caller had not been able to answer in their brief exchange of words. Questions like, why was McCay going to Belfast Airport with the intention of flying to Heathrow? What urgency had compelled the man to do something that was wholly out of character? McCay rarely took time off. When he did, preparations were set in motion days ahead as though he feared the paper would fold in his absence.

The housekeeper had told Conor in a nervous high-pitched voice that Mr McCay had been involved in an accident on his way to Belfast Airport. He was now in Derry Infirmary. Would Mr Adams attend to everything in his absence?

Well, Conor thought, going down to the editor's office, I'm glad he has the grace to acknowledge that I *am* a senior member of staff. The office with its big glass windows had a panoramic view of the city spread below. Unsettled, and unable to concentrate on his work, he went over to the window and gazed down on the Apprentice Boys' Hall – one of the finest buildings in Ulster, he considered. The 'Boys', some of them looking as though they were in their dotage, went out marching every August to commemorate their forefathers who had shut the gates in the face of James II's army, in what was surely one of the most gallant defences in the history of siege warfare, Conor had always thought. Eoin would not agree!

After a phone call to the hospital to enquire about McCay, he went to see his colleagues and view the work situation. When he was there, someone asked for informa-

45

tion that was in the safe in the editor's office. He went to fetch it, first collecting a set of keys from a locked drawer in his own room. The folder, with yesterday's date, was at hand. He took it over to the desk and, as he was going through it, came on an envelope marked *Delivered by hand, most urgent.*

He knew immediately that the typed message on the envelope had been done on Eoin O'Donnell's typewriter. There were three defects in the lettering: the *r* slipped slightly, the letter *n* had a barely discernible flaw and the tip of the *h* was missing. Conor also knew that he had absolutely no right to read the letter inside the envelope. Nevertheless he was going to do so.

Sir, I understand that you are planning to use the medium of your paper to publish certain facts about the life and death of the late Lord Kindron. You must be aware that the details of that sordid and tragic story will affect the lives of decent people living in this town. I must ask you to reconsider your decision. Otherwise, action will be taken which could seriously affect the future of The Northern Press.

We are a peace-loving people in the city of Derry and in all conscience I cannot allow a stranger in our midst to destroy the happiness and peace of mind of my fellow citizens.

I do not make this threat lightly.

The letter was unsigned.

Conor rang Eoin immediately and arranged to meet him for lunch.

They sat in a corner of Duffy's pub near Craigavon Bridge, with a plate of hot pies and two glasses of Guinness between them. 'What exactly happened to McCay?' Eoin enquired.

'Skid. Travelling too fast. He's lucky to be alive.' Conor put one of the pies on his plate. 'I've read the letter you sent him – the unsigned one.'

Eoin took a long drink from the glass as though he were giving Conor's words careful consideration. 'Aha . . .'

'What the hell were you planning to do?'

'So that's why you asked me out to lunch?'

'It was. God, man, I didn't like the sound of that letter. There was a threat of violence in it.'

'Ah, not violence, *a chara*. Just a little threat.' With precise movements Eoin cut one of the pies. 'And what the blazes are you complaining about? A wee Glasgow scut comes among us, thinking he can do what he likes to make some quick money to feather his own nest. Look, the British took over our town during the war . . .'

'Don't exaggerate.'

'. . . and we're gradually slipping back again to our old ways. The Orangemen still beat the hell out of their drums on the Twelfth of July and we're still laughing our heads off at their antics. And why the divil shouldn't the Orange Billies have fun playing with their drums?'

Conor waited, wondering what Eoin was getting at.

His friend moved the plate and glass, leant across the table with folded hands and said earnestly: 'We want to keep things going quietly until the right time comes to take some action.'

'Action?' Conor bolted up in his chair.

'I don't mean the way it has been in the past. A peaceful movement, with a political appeal. On a higher level altogether where intelligent people – a younger generation – will speak out for the atrocious situation Catholics have to put up with here in Ulster. I've seen the violent side of politics. It must not happen again.'

Conor sank back in his chair. 'Ha! Are you thinking of a miracle?' He was not going to get involved in that dreamland discussion. Greater men than Eoin, down through the years, had had the same idea and it never worked.

'And that's why,' Eoin added, picking up a piece of pie, 'we don't want wee Scottie McCay stirring up a nasty pot of trouble.'

Before he could reply, Eoin's friend Rosheen Quinn came striding into the pub. She saw them and waved her hand in an aggressive manner, indicating that she was well able to buy her own drink.

'What about young Prisca McDaid?' Conor asked quickly. 'How did it go?'

Eoin's sensitive face clouded. 'It didn't go well. She took it badly.'

'I'm sorry to hear that.'

'She's bitter, resentful and very angry. What a pity this had to happen. You see, I would like the members of my Gaelic group to keep their ideals high, in the way I've been explaining. Prisca was one of my greatest hopes. Now I'm not so sure. I don't think she'll forget her connection with Kindron.'

'She's young. She'll get over it.'

'Young in the number of years, that's all. She's old and matured beyond her age. Old because of poverty and her mother's frequent pregnancies. The burden always falls on Prisca's shoulders.' He sighed, then said thoughtfully, 'I can't say though that I agree with Samuel Johnson about poverty being a great enemy to human happiness – as far as the McDaids are concerned, anyway. They're a happy family. You can get a great feeling in that house. I've been there a few times and I'd say it was a house blessed with – '

'Surely that's not Eoin O'Donnell talking about blessings?' Rosheen Quinn sat down at their table, picked up a piece of Eoin's pie and put it in her mouth.

'Well, I must be going.' Conor rose quickly to his feet. He couldn't stand this woman. What the hell did that nice man see in her? 'Eoin, thanks anyway.'

They smiled at each other. It was a smile of understanding.

'I don't know what you see in that Conor Adams, apart from the job,' Rosheen said when Conor was out of the door. 'Typical Freestater. We're all right Jack over there. We don't want to hear about your problems in Ulster.'

Eoin did not reply. He was thinking about Prisca McDaid.

Chapter 6

'A grand haul altogether, Mrs Adams, praise be to God,' Liam in the brae said, pointing to the luminous pool of fish lying at the bottom of his boat. 'Finest pollack I've ever seen. And begod, look at the codlin'. Widden they tempt the mouth of a dead man?'

Marcella, sitting at the edge of the pier, slanted her eyes in her mother's direction. The fish were a gift, like most things that came from the family in Brae Cottage. Liam and his brother Ned cut the Adams' turf on the hill, carted it to River House and supplied as much milk as they could use. All this generosity because Marcella's grandparents had helped the widow in Brae Cottage when she was struggling to bring up a family of four children. Two boys and two girls. Katie, the eldest, went to seek her fortune in America and evidently came back with great plans to improve the family home. But the Returned Yank, as she was called locally, found a force of opposition when she attempted to modernize Brae Cottage. An extension was built for a bathroom. Somehow the brothers missed the spring (Marcella's mother said it was deliberate and the word was 'avoided') so the bathroom suite sat unused in lonely splendour in the extension. Disgusted with her family, Katie hurried back to Boston. Biddy and her brothers were greatly relieved, preferring the money orders that came through the post occasionally.

'I won't be needing many fish today, Liam,' Marcella's mother protested as their neighbour threw fistfuls into the bag. 'Biddy will be glad of a few.'

Liam, wearing his cap back to front to defy capricious winds, tugged at the peak which lay on the neck of his guernsey. 'Bad cess to that one, ye might as well try to turn back the tide with a pitchfork as to get her to put a bit of fish on the pan.'

'Thanks, Liam,' her mother called across her shoulder, as they went to move away. 'Tell Biddy not to bother bringing me any more eggs. My own hens are laying again.'

'Aye, I'll do that now,' he replied, bending down to tidy the nets. At that moment a volley of shots sounded across the strand, sending floods of agitated birds sweeping out to sea. 'Wid ye listen to thon eejit trying to shoot on a day like this wi' the voice of the wind rising like a scoldin' woman. Here,' he tossed a few more fish at their feet. 'There's a couple for the wee cutty. It'll put the brains in her.'

'Haste now,' Mrs Adams urged Marcella as she flung the extra fish back into the sea when Liam bent down to drink from a whiskey bottle. 'The clouds are gathering for a storm and the sea looks troubled. Listen to the hiss in the wind.'

They hurried off the pier, pausing occasionally to grab blades of dulse that lay against the rocks like ribbons of satin. As they scrambled up the cliff path, Marcella munched it with pleasure, enjoying the salty-sweet flavour. Later, she would hold it over the peat flames until it toasted to a nutty crispness. Her mother said that was what the people did during the famine when they fled to the shores of Inishowen. Old drawings showed wraith-like creatures cringing against the wind.

They were not far off the road when a horse went cantering along in the distance. They watched its elegant movements in silence; the dainty steps barely disturbing the resinous fragrance of wild herbs growing above the cliffs on the heathland.

'Mrs Gilroy. Huh! Wouldn't I just love to be her riding along on that fine horse.'

Seagulls began to wheel and scream around the cliff tops, then a stillness came as clouds fell across the blue hills. With heads bent, they climbed steadily towards the road. They paused when a single shot shattered the silence, followed by a drumming echo. The animal down below balked in fright, then in a terrifying rush, bolted across the heather towards the cliffs. The rider pulled helplessly on the reins. The animal, unable to stop, accepted the inevitability of death and soared majestically through the air, carrying its rider down to the foaming sea below.

'Run, child – run quickly to Slievan. Tell them, Mrs Gilroy – '

As Marcella raced along the road, her eyes turned in the direction of Hell's Hole, a great chasm over two hundred feet deep, where the Atlantic surged in with a roar and rumble sending up spray like clouds of smoke. Nearby was a natural sea arch called Devil's Bridge. She was sure the sound of shots had come from that direction.

The tall iron gates of the big house were always kept shut. Sheila Farren, who lived in the lodge, came around the gable-end of the house. Marcella told her what had happened. 'Mammy!' the girl shrieked and tore indoors, words flying piercingly from her lips. Her parents ran out of the house.

'I'll get the men,' Mr Farren said, tearing away towards Slievan. 'Find the young lad,' he shouted over his shoulder. 'He's around by the orchard.'

At that moment, Kiaran Gilroy, a tall fair-haired boy, came into sight accompanied by Sheila's brother John. Kiaran was tossing a ball indolently between his hands. It fell away unheeded when he saw the expression on the three faces before him.

'It's your mother, dear. There's been an accident. Best get on up home quickly.'

'My mother . . . where is she? What happened?' He looked from one to the other.

'Mama and I were coming along the cliff road,' Marcella began.

'Never mind,' Mrs Farren cut in sharply. 'You git along home now, Marcella Adams.' There was resentment in her voice as though this harbinger of bad news must be silenced and got out of sight as soon as possible.

Without another word, Kiaran picked up his bicycle

from the grass and sped down the drive towards his home. Marcella went to move away when Mr Gilroy walked through the gates with a gun slung across his shoulder; a gun-dog was at his heels. Scarcely realizing what she was saying, her eyes went to the gun and she blurted out, 'It was a shot that frightened the horse.'

He stopped and frowned. 'What's happened?'

Mrs Farren stumbled through the terrible story, and as though the telling of it increased the tragedy, her face aged and crumbled in grief. 'It's your wife, sir. Her horse bolted on the cliff and I'm afraid — '

The man looked in horror at the gun in his hand, as though it had suddenly been defaced by some evil image, then with a violence that distorted his features, he threw it into the long grass away among the trees. Marcella stared at him. The action was like an admission of guilt. And as though condemnation was written on her face, he winced and stumbled down the drive towards the mansion.

The woman tugged at her arm. 'Ye look like death, child. Come in and have a sup of tay. There's the doctor away down to the shore. I hope to God he's sober.'

As Marcella ate a piece of soda bread with the cup of strong tea that had been stewing on the hearth, she thought of the elegant woman who had sat through Mass every Sunday, an expression of boredom on her face. Everyone's eyes were riveted on her beautiful clothes. Now, Marcella thought sadly, the poor woman was dead, her body broken on the rocks below Slievan.

Conor and Mary Bridget would not let Marcella and her brother Brian accompany them to the Requiem Mass for Mrs Gilroy. People were coming from all over the world and there wouldn't be an inch of space to spare, they told them. Marcella wondered what the strangers looked like. As soon as her parents drove away she jumped on her bicycle. At the cross-roads near the church she hid it behind the hedge, then tore across the field to the churchyard. Concealed by a laurel tree growing near the wall, she had a perfect view.

The church doors were wide open. A coffin made of rich stained wood stood near the altar surrounded by tall brass candlesticks. The front pews were still unoccupied. Members of the staff, including Biddy in the brae, stood near the door waiting for the mourners to arrive before taking their seats.

'Sure money is all a body needs in this world,' Biddy announced to her friends. 'It can even keep ye out o' the grave a wee while longer. That body's been waiting for a whole week. Father McGill couldn't get the likes o' us under the soil fast enough so that he can get off to Buncrana for a game of golf.'

The solemnity of the scene struck Marcella forcibly when the Gilroy family began to arrive. She forgot to notice the spectacle of grand mourning clothes that Biddy had promised, when she saw Kiaran Gilroy and his father. They looked dreadful, walking apart as though they did not belong together. A tall woman strode behind them, her movements impatient as though she had interrupted something of importance to attend the funeral. Stricken, Marcella slipped away again. That was the last time her curiosity would bring her anywhere near a church when there was a death.

She and Brian were sitting by the fire reading when her mother ran into the house pulling off her hat. 'Dear God, my heart bled for that poor man. And the boy, pale as death.'

'He'll be all right, Mary B, when he gets off to his prep school in England,' Conor told her.

'Imagine sending that boy off to an English school,' she complained.

'It's the same one his father went to,' Brian told them enviously. 'Someone said he's coming to our school for the rest of the term.'

'The village school? His mother will be turning in the grave . . . poor soul, to die so young.' Marcella and Brian looked startled when she clasped their father's arm. 'Conor, you'd never give way like that if anything happened to me? You'd think of the children, wouldn't you?'

Conor smiled as though indulging a child and nodded his head.

Biddy in the brae can't wait to report the day's events at Slievan, Marcella thought later that day when their neighbour came scurrying down the road. Tall and thin, the woman always moved sideways as though a perpetual wind was striving against her. But Marcella was wrong; their neighbour had come on a most urgent matter.

'Mrs Adams, I'm in a desperate state. What with the death, I'd clean forgot it was my turn to have a house-Mass in the morning. Ned whitewashed the big room but I need candlesticks and vessels . . . Ach, sure, 'tis an auld bother, may God forgive me.'

'Don't worry, Biddy. Marcella and I will bring a few things up later.'

'That's grand. Bring some holy water too for that Liam put the last drop of it in his . . . drink.' Biddy's lips were drawn tightly together in disapproval.

'You don't mean his whiskey?' Mary Bridget glanced at their neighbour whose eyes were directed towards the window and beyond to the bogland as if throwing a clue. 'Not poteen?' she asked in a horrified whisper.

''Twas the night of the high wind and us wi'out a sup in the house and me not able to venture down the field to the well, for the force o' the wind wid have sent me flying like a banshee.'

'That brother of yours would drink the ocean dry.'

'Aye, with the other one licking up the drops.'

When they arrived at Brae Cottage that evening Biddy led them into a room containing a table laden with a rich selection of cakes, soda bread and duck eggs. In the centre was a jam jar full of fuchsia. This was the room which had been cleared for the Mass.

'You and Marcella have a bite afore we start,' she said, offering the customary hospitality as a way of showing her gratitude. 'The fancy cakes came from Slievan. The staff were told to take them away. I'll just pour the tay and lay

54

the pair of you in peace.'

Marcella knew that their neighbour would not eat with them because she had been a servant girl at River House years ago. No matter how friendly they were, Biddy would not presume to share their table.

'God, child,' her mother said irritably. 'Look what that eejit has given us. Duck eggs can poison you.'

'What are we going to do, Mama?' The look of the big green eggs made Marcella feel sick.

'Throw the brutes in the fire.' She grabbed the eggs and dropped them in among the pillars of turf burning in the hearth. Immediately there was a terrible explosion. Horrified, they looked at each other and went into fits of hysterical laughter.

Biddy hovered anxiously outside the door. What in under God were the pair of them doing in there?

Mary Bridget whispered to Marcella, 'Hope to God she doesn't give Father McGill that dose tomorrow morning.'

'Tell her, Mama.' Poor Biddy, she had done her best. The tablecloth was white damask and the china very fine. Gifts from the sister who fled back to America.

When the two women began to get the room ready for the Mass, Marcella wandered off. She had never been in the extension and was determined to see it. An unexpected door from the kitchen led into a bedroom where she caught sight of the freak bathroom. Geraniums grew out of the toilet bowl and potatoes were sprouting in the bath. The window had pretty sprigged linen curtains, made by the Returned Yank to occupy her during the long hours of boredom she had suffered admiring the view when her heart began to long for the hot crowded pavements of Boston. The curtains were kept pulled across in case neighbours peeped in at the catastrophe. Marcella pushed them aside and looked out on an acre of potatoes in flower. They seemed like a thousand butterflies: pale mauve, shades of pink – a glory of colour that danced before her eyes.

A figure came over the headland. It was Kiaran Gilroy. Every step he took, he whipped at the heather with the cane in his hand. There was a look of anger and desolation about him. Unseeingly he walked on, ignoring the tiller in the field who was throwing handfuls of seeds from a bag slung across his shoulders, and who had paused to bid him a courteous good-day.

She pulled the curtains across again and went into Biddy's large stone-flagged kitchen where two pictures hung over the wide ingle-nook fireplace. One was of the Sacred Heart and the other of John F. Kennedy. She studied the handsome Irish-American and the little red lamp which was normally placed before the holy picture, and now rested halfway between the two, giving the future American President equal reverence with the deity. Five years later, in 1963 when John F. Kennedy was assassinated, and afterwards doubt was thrown on his morals, Biddy was to pull that picture down and pitch it into the midden.

The bedroom adjacent to the aborted bathroom was bright and gaudy. Curtains of various hues clashed with the soft vista beyond the window. On the bed a thick eiderdown was covered with colourful stitching and a glass globe containing a snowbound saint, stood on a table. Bored with inspecting Biddy's things, Marcella threw herself on the bed; the next minute she was grabbing desperately at the eiderdown which was slipping off the silk undercover.

No sooner had she landed on the floor when a shower of money fell across her face. One-pound and five-pound notes flew around her like the snow in the globe. She had never seen so much money in all her life. At that moment her mother came into the room. Horrified, Mary Bridget shut the door, clutched Marcella's hand and hauled her up, then began to scurry about gathering the money.

'It's Biddy's hoard. Liam says she sits up every night counting it, feeling rich because it's hidden in the bed and her hand can touch it any time . . . what's this?'

Marcella watched her mother pick up a piece of folded jotter paper which had been glued down at one time. She flicked it open. Curious, she looked over Mary Bridget's shoulder and read the few words written on the lined paper. '"*Your Honour, pardon my forwardness but your gun would be as well at home when there's a wind about to blow the horns off a cow.*" Liam's writing, the devil take him! He must have given this note to Biddy to slip in with Mr Gilroy's mail and she had the sense to read it.' Mrs Adams put the note in her pocket.

'Mama!'

'You don't think I'm going to let the poor man see that spiteful scribble at a time like this? Away now. She'll be wondering what's happened to us.'

Biddy was outside talking to Liam who was inspecting a calf which he said had taken a founder. Marcella studied Liam's good-natured expression. She wondered if there was some terrible threat behind those written words in the note. Everyone knew that Liam resented the Anglo-Irish family in their midst. Intruders from another land, he called them, as though they had just landed.

'How did the Gilroy funeral go, Biddy?' she asked, following her into the kitchen.

'Was just telling yer mother that it was a sad do, not even a wake to console themselves. A drop of whiskey and company would have shortened the night. It would have been as well for them if they'd placed the coffin on the keening rock by the shore and howled their heads off, the way folk did in yore. All stuffed up wi' their grief, they were. How can they live in a country for so long and not take heed of our ways?'

'Mama says they're sophisticated.'

'They're stuck-up and you should see the auld crow comin' to look after the master and the boy. Thon wan wodden ask if ye had a mouth on ye. Not a drop of whiskey for the kitchen staff, and himself past caring. The saddest death-house I've ever seen. Thon wan will bring changes, mark my words! She'd begrudge ye standing room in heaven.'

A few weeks later Marcella was up in the cashel lying on a flat rock covered with a lace of grey and white lichen. The cashel, her favourite place where she played childish games, was a wide expanse of high ground covered in rocks of various sizes. In the grassy area, saxifrage, roseroot and cushion pinks grew; also, willowherb and fool's parsley. Nearly every stone in this place belonged to her make-believe world. One was the Big House where the gentry lived. Another, the school where she taught recalcitrant children. For this game flat stones were laid out in rows. Each one had a face and name chalked on it. She taught these imaginary pupils with a bamboo cane, giving Shelia Farren from the lodge-house the heaviest whacking.

She had always felt a deep happiness here, where her brother was not allowed to play; and where her mother could not talk to her as if she were a grown-up or, at other times, as if she was a young child. In the cashel Marcella had found her own world until her brother began sneaking around and shouting, 'What's going on in Cloud Cuckoo Land today?' She had discovered only recently that he used to lie in the heather below the cashel for, as he put it, a half-hour's entertainment.

When she was a little girl, her special part was down by the mulberry bushes where she ate berries and prayed that the fairies would appear. The small rocks there were covered with a lemon-coloured lichen and surrounded by masses of tiny wild flowers. This involvement with the fairies ended when her father found she was neglecting her lessons, and conversing with the invisible world of tiny green men and dainty creatures of unimaginable beauty. Some time after that she discovered a far more interesting spectacle down on the shore – the old boat with a hole in its side.

Every evening Liam in the brae and fat Rosie who worked in the hotel, crept through a hole in the upside-down boat and remained there for a long time. Marcella pondered continuously on this meaningless activity and decided to investigate. Inside, there was a bed of fresh straw; she crept in, lay down and in this snug little place listened to the sound of the sea. Then one day, before her startled gaze, two guards surrounded the boat. Big Rosie and Liam crept out, shamefacedly. They were marched up the road and down past River House to Rosie's home.

'Now he'll have to marry her,' Biddy said delightedly to Marcella's mother. 'He's been courting her for ten years — a soiled bargain, the divil serve him right! He could have done better for himself.'

'Deal a bit, doesn't she inherit her father's farm? And who was responsible for soiling the girl anyway?'

'Sweet Virgin, yer right, I'd forgotten the farm. I bet the old man spites the grave to keep Liam's hands off that bit o' land. He can't stand my brother.'

'The old man can't live forever but they say his father before him went on to nearly a hundred.'

'Don't pour vinegar on my hopes, Mrs Adams dear,' Biddy said anxiously. 'I'll be glad to see the back o' him. Well, he'd better wash down the cart, for Rosie will never make it to church on foot.'

Colour had flooded Marcella's face then and still did when she recalled that conversation. All in the course of a few weeks fairies had been replaced by the bewildering world of sex. Soon it was known far and wide that Liam in the brae was in grave trouble if he didn't marry fat Rosie.

The sound of a footstep rattled against a stone, disturbing her thoughts. 'Go away, Brian. There's nothing to jeer about now, I no longer talk to the stones, you rotten sneak.'

'I'm sorry to disturb you . . .' The voice was hesitant, unfamiliar.

Mortified, she sprang off the rock. 'You're welcome,' she mumbled, using her mother's manner of greeting people who called casually at the house. He wasn't a bit welcome, this tall grave boy, who walked out of church every Sunday, looking neither to right nor left. His mother's death had changed him, she thought with a stirring of pity. Marcella remembered the Easter Sunday, years ago, when he dropped a pile of marbles at Mass. They had bounced down the aisle like butterflies' wings passing through a blade of sunshine. She had shot out of her seat and gone after them, whipping off her new hat to gather the stones as they flashed to freedom through the church door. Kiaran Gilroy had smiled warmly as he received the rainbow flow back in his hands. The boy before her seemed like a different person, as though a mask had fallen on his face.

'There's something I must ask you,' he said with a nervous outburst of words. 'The day of my mother's death . . . you saw what happened.'

'The horse bolted.'

'Why did it do that?'

She tore at the lichen. 'I don't know.'

'Marcella . . .' The use of her name surprised her until she remembered Brian saying he and Kiaran Gilroy had become friends. 'My mother was a skilled horsewoman and the animal – well, it would not've taken off like that unless something had frightened it badly.'

'Maybe it was a stoat or a weasel, or . . .' Anxiously, her list of possibilities increased, so determined was she to convince him. When he turned away abruptly, Marcella knew she had overdone it. She saw him battling with words, then they came in an anguished rush.

'It's my father, something's troubling him. He walks around the grounds at night. The servants tell me he sometimes doesn't go to bed.'

'He'd still be upset about your mother.'

'It's not that . . . I think he's going out of his mind.'

'Oh, no!'

'He never goes out shooting or fishing any more. He just – ' As Kiaran spoke he turned to her and she saw his unhappiness. And on that instant, Kiaran realized that this girl knew what he desperately needed to find out. 'You do know, don't you?'

'I promised my mother never to speak about it.'

'I see.' As though he accepted the impossibility of making her break that promise, he looked away defeated.

Determinedly, she took a step towards him and said: 'It was a shot over by Hell's Hole that frightened the horse. Mama said your father must've shot downwards to have created such a terrible noise. Afterwards, I saw him fling away his gun before he went up the drive to Slievan. It was a terrible accident. Not a soul knows, only Mama and me.' Please God, she prayed, try and make that be the truth of it.

He looked at her for a moment and frowned. 'I think someone else does know. That's one of the reasons why I've come to see you. An unstamped letter arrived at the house. Fortunately, as I was helping my father to sort out his mail, I came on it first. I couldn't make head nor tail of it.'

'To do with your father shooting that day?'

'Yes, something like that.'

Cautious now, for that fool of a Liam with his spite could get Biddy sacked from Slievan, Marcella said: 'Don't take any notice of it. He's a dunderhead who wrote those notes. I'll get my mother to do something about it.'

Kiaran paused, about to speak, then his words came quietly. 'All right. I wouldn't like any more notes like that to come. I might not have the same chance. Father wasn't aware my mother had left the house on that day.'

'A sudden notion to get out in the air, it would be that now,' she said eagerly, trying to mend his sorrow.

'I suppose so.' He held out his hand and smiled at the young girl looking at him so earnestly. She pulled at the green silk ribbon holding back her long black hair and gazed at him with a strange maturity.

Hesitantly, Marcella put her hand in his. She had never shaken hands with anyone in her life before. Somehow, he no longer seemed so aloof and distant, or even strange. She watched Kiaran Gilroy disappear out of sight, then tore down from the cashel.

'Mama,' she shouted, running indoors. 'I must tell you something dreadful.'

'Dear me,' her mother replied, scraping a bowlful of cake mixture into a large iron pan. As she flattened it out to the edges with the back of her hand and marked the top with the sign of a cross, Marcella told her about the conversation with Kiaran Gilroy. Placing the pan on the iron crook over the fire, Mrs Adams said quietly, 'Liam and Ned are in the orchard cutting down a tree for your father. Tell Liam I'd like a word with him.'

Marcella ran eagerly out of the house and delivered the message. Liam came reluctantly. He looped himself around the front door as if he resented the interruption and wanted to be off again.

'Bring the rest of yourself into the house, Liam. I want to talk to you.'

'I'm in a fearful hurry, missus.'

'You'll be in fearful trouble if you don't listen to me and mend your ways,' she said sharply.

'What is it at all?'

'You're persecuting a man who has suffered a grievous loss. I mean Mr Gilroy.'

Liam looked down sullenly at his feet in the heavy boots, as if they had made the comment.

'You've been sending him notes, haven't you? Letting him know you were around that day when his wife's horse bolted on the cliffs.'

''Tis the likes o' him that hasn't a thought for anyone and gits away wi' murder,' he said angrily. 'Didn't I lose my foal last spring through the same stupid action. Himself shooting anywhere he pleases as if he owned the land entirely.'

'You were well compensated for the loss of the foal,' she retorted. '*Very* well. The animal was dying on its feet and it's yourself that knows it.'

'In the name of God, Mrs Adams, are any of us safe when that man has a gun in his hands?'

'Aren't you man enough to go up to the house and see him instead of writing stupid notes? Sure he must be nearly out of his mind after what happened. There's only a boy of fifteen years old around to talk to.' From the look of the pair of them, she thought, there's not much of that going on either.

'He widden listen to the likes o' me,' Liam said defiantly, tossing his head with an unusual display of spirit. 'And I don't care a tinker's curse about him. I'll bliddy well do as I like if ye'll 'cuse the language.'

'I'll excuse nothing,' she snapped. 'Nor the fact that

you've got your store of poteen hidden down our old well in the orchard.'

Liam's head bounced up as if someone had pulled strings.

'You'll give me your word now that there'll be no more notes or,' she went to the door and pulled her coat off the hook, 'I'll go this minute and fetch the guard.'

His eyes widened in alarm. 'Jayus, woman, ye widden do that and me 'bout to be wed?'

'I will unless you give me your word. You silly man, do you think poor Gilroy will ever touch a gun again?'

'A'right, we'll let it rest like that then,' he muttered, slouching out of the house.

'That's his word,' Marcella's mother told her. 'He'll keep it.'

Marcella knew that Liam was a bit in awe of Mama, and called her 'the schoolmarm' behind her back, because she had been a teacher before she was married.

'There's your father, dear. Go down to the room and get on with your books. Conor, I'll have a cup of tea ready in a minute.'

'Sit down, Mary B. I'll get it.' He had shortened her name the first time they met and she loved it. 'I need to stretch my legs,' he added.

She saw that her husband was in a restless mood, and picking up a piece of knitting asked, 'How did things go today?'

He poured water from the big iron kettle into the teapot. 'I went to see McCay in hospital. He's had a slight stroke.'

'That's bad, on top of his injury. Was his speech all right?'

'Fairly good.'

'Any more talk of that Kindron story you were telling me about?'

'He never mentioned it.' Conor poured two cups of tea. 'We'll just have to wait and see. He seems grateful enough about the way I'm handling things at the office. Did I tell you his solicitor has been going through the contents of his desk and the private safe? And . . . ah, I've just found out, the police took a great interest in McCay's car brakes. Apparently there was a notion they might have been tampered with.'

Mary Bridget bit off a piece of wool. 'Are you surprised, after that letter of Eoin's?'

'Eoin said the worst thing he would have considered doing was to get someone to remove the copies of *The Northern Press* that go to the bus depot for distribution in Donegal. The paper would soon find a financial pinch if that went on for long.'

'Conor, I know Eoin would be incapable of interfering with a man's brakes but I wouldn't put it past that Rosheen Quinn he goes around with. She's a tough nut.'

'It was simply a case of a man driving too fast in bad conditions,' Conor told her with a touch of impatience. He didn't voice his other fear, that McCay might have been going to London in connection with the Kindron file. Maybe he was going over there to pick the right man or men for the job? Noticing Mary B's worried expression, he changed the subject. 'I had a letter today from a Mr Schenber in London. He wants to come to Derry and start a business and buy a house. He's ordered copies of the paper to be sent to his address in London.'

'Wants to come to Derry? What kind of business?'

'Clothing trade.'

'He must be crazy. With no work in the town it's taking people all their time to buy food, never mind clothes. Anyway, there are enough shops.'

'Schenber is a Jew. They are good at business and I think he's got money. Wish I had a house to sell him. Bet he won't quibble about the price if he sees what he wants.'

'Conor, just think how we frittered away the money when you sold the farm. We should have invested it by buying a house in Derry.'

'We had the time of our lives travelling before the children were born.'

Mary Bridget rolled up her knitting. 'We're just spendthrift Irish!'

'There's a bit in the bank for a rainy day.' God almighty, he thought with a moment's panic, I hope I won't need to draw it out when McCay gets on his feet again.

Chapter 7

'Now Momma, Lisa, what do you think of the house, eh?'
Mr Schenber asked his wife and daughter. 'It is very fine, is
it not?'

Jacob Schenber could not believe how well everything
was going for him. When copies of *The Northern Press*
arrived in London, he soon realized that the city of Derry
had a very cheap property market. He rubbed his hands in
glee. In one issue he saw just the type of house he wanted,
and praise the good God, business premises too, for sale
right in the middle of the town. A phone call to his Cousin
Joseph, who had lived in Derry since before the last war
and . . . He nodded his head sagely. Everything was going
well for old Jacob.

Lisa Schenber, with a disinterested shrug, played her
fingers along the stone balcony above the terraced garden
that looked out across the River Foyle. Her father,
delighted that his family had arrived in Derry to join him,
began excitedly to throw out bits of information that he
thought would arouse Lisa's interest.

'Down there, little one, by the docks, ships have
travelled to many parts of the world. Many poor Irish
emigrants went on sailing ships to America from this port.'
He lowered his voice with customary caution. 'During the
war it played a vital part in winning the great Battle of the
Atlantic.'

'Poppa . . .'

'And you know,' his excitement grew, 'sixty German U-
boats surrendered out there. Urrr,' he growled, 'I wish I
could have been there to spit on them.'

'Darling Poppa, I cannot take everything in at one

moment.'

'Yes, yes. I get excited in this peaceful place. No bad people here. A few hotheads make a little noise sometimes – nothing much. No robbers like in other places to break into my stores, so my Cousin Joseph tells me. And, little one, never forget – when Hitler tried to kill our people, this little town opened its doors to the Jews. Look at happy Joseph. He has an Irish wife. Now they have an Irish-Jewish family.'

Brimming over with goodwill and happiness, Mr Schenber marched down the terrace to find his wife. It was good the cousin had persuaded him to come to this green and pleasant land. So peaceful, part of it would not join in the war with Germany . . . well, something like that. Mr Schenber's eyes narrowed shrewdly. A big house for a singsong and a fine shop to be opened when he got things organized. After that, he would think about a factory. No more moving. This time it was for ever. All this he wanted for dear Hannah and little Lisa – ah, not so little now. Please the good Lord she would meet a nice Jewish boy and settle down. A frown crossed his face. Joseph's sons – he must take a look there.

Jacob stopped for a moment to admire his wife who, weary after the inspection of the house, had flopped on a padded sunchair. A smile flitted over his face. She would fill the house with warmth and everywhere her Chanel perfume would float to remind him that he could give her all the good things she desired. Every flash from her diamond rings was like a signal reminding him that Jacob Schenber was doing all right in this world, thanks to the good God.

Mrs Schenber's face was turned to the sky to catch the warmth of the sun. A well-built woman, his Hannah. Not always so. Before the war she was a slender girl, a girl of great spirit and courage. Only for her they most certainly would have died in a concentration camp after that night when, with a group of friends, they had motored outside Berlin to a restaurant where there was good food, wine and music. The restaurant had been very crowded, the floor a mass of movement as they danced to a Viennese waltz. When the men in uniform walked in unexpectedly, his wife had gone limp in his arms and fallen to the floor. Horrified, he picked her up and pushed through the dancers to the restroom. Mercifully, their departure had not been noticed by the soldiers. The first sign of movement from Hannah came when she hissed into his breast, 'Quick, the Fräuleins' room.' Once inside there she sprang to life and pulled him into one of the toilets where she bolted the door and with great caution raised the window.

They made their escape that night long ago, leaving everything behind them. All they had to sell to bribe their way to freedom was the jewellery Hannah was wearing. Mr Schenber shrugged. It was an old sad story now, and one that had been experienced by many people with the presence of mind to get out of Germany in time.

'Poppa, Momma,' Lisa called, 'listen to the music. Everyone around here seems to be practising the violin and piano. I hope they learn quickly!'

Mrs Schenber rolled her eyes expressively. Her husband gave a wide happy grin. His Cousin Joseph had told him that the Irish were lively and they loved music and dancing. In the country a fiddler sat in every cottage doorway. He was a blessed man to have chosen their new life so well. Derry was said to be a city of great talent. The people danced, sang and played instruments. Only people content in life took up such occupations, Jacob decided.

'Poppa.' Lisa walked into the drawing room, dragging the toe of her shoe across the rich carpet which had been laid that day. 'When do I start at my new school?'

'Do not torture the carpet so, little one,' he said sharply. 'Walk like a little lady.' Then, mildly, 'It is not possible until the beginning of the autumn term. Patience, my child.'

When her father walked away, Lisa looked around the room boredly. It was a replica of every house they had lived in. All the old sepia photographs that friends and relations had sent seemed to be shouting from the mantel-piece, 'We are still with you.' Lisa would have liked to pull them down and push them in a drawer out of sight.

Everyone in her life seemed to be elderly – parents, aunts and family friends. Maybe she would feel less isolated when she went to her new school. How was she going to fit in with girls who were half-English, though? That was not right. How did they explain it to her in Switzerland? Because of politics, some did not understand or speak their own language. Some resented this; others, not of the pure Irish race, rejoiced. Ja! It was too difficult to understand. Poppa said not to bother about these little things, but to work hard to fit in and achieve good academic results. It was a very expensive school, so therefore it must be a very good school.

She wandered outside again and went around to the front of the house to where her mother's new car sat in glittering splendour. A sound made her glance down the drive where a gallery of children's faces peeped over the gate leading to the street. In the wider spaces of the wrought-iron design, younger ones had pushed their heads through, reminding Lisa of a painting where bodyless angels appeared in the clouds. These 'angels' had grubby little faces surrounded by masses of dark curls and large blue-green eyes, fringed with long black eyelashes.

'What do you want, little ones?' she asked, walking towards the gate.

'Miss, is that your car?' The oldest boy stood up to his full height, towering over the others. 'Gie's a ride, will ye?'

'What?'

A little girl with two front teeth missing shot up beside him. 'M'brother wants a ride.'

'It is my mother's car.'

'Us too,' the chorus of babies lisped from the lower end of the gate. 'We want to come wid ye.'

For the first time in days, Lisa broke into laughter. All these children, where did they come from? She did not think from the other houses in the street; their exteriors had the same well-cared for look as their own, but passing through the district earlier on she had seen some very poor dwellings.

When Lisa put out her hand to open the gate, all the children withdrew in a flash, the older ones jumping down with an expertise that showed plenty of practice. Without the gate between them, there was an immediate reaction. The boy stood aside, a proud tilt to his head, the long stick in his hand held like a warrior. The others crowded bashfully behind him, while the tiny tots waddled down the street and around the corner, two with wet napkins flapping about their legs. At the corner they took up their stand again and peeped around cautiously.

'What's your name?' Lisa asked the boy.

'Micky O'Kane. That's m'sister, Mary Josephine, behind me. She's a dancer. Show her, Mary Jo.'

The little girl moved out promptly, threw back her head and let her arms fall in a straight line to the hem of her skirt. Lisa watched in amazement as the short slender feet moved through the intricate steps of a dance.

'Miss, ye wouldn't be knowing the hornpipe now, would ye – as it's your first time in Ireland. Jo, do the tap,' he ordered.

Micky O'Kane began to clack clack with his large white teeth as his sister let her body go limp in preparation for another dance. Then with crisp little steps, she tapped her way around the pavement, finally moving in the direction of the corner where she disappeared out of sight.

So, Lisa thought smiling, perhaps the old house with its lugubrious photographs won't seem so bad after all if I can be entertained like this at our own gates. 'How do you know it's my first time in Ireland?' she asked the boy.

'Sure m'ma's goin' to work in yer house. It's all fixed up.' Micky's eyes were riveted on Lisa's hair. 'Miss . . . is yer hair real? I've never seen that colour before. It's like hay.' He shook his head vigorously. 'Na, the other stuff – corn.'

Lisa let out a peal of laughter. 'It is real. Your mother is going to work for us? That is good.'

'She has to 'cause m'da died last year. He was a soldier in the British Army and got injured during the war. Sure he was always ailing.' This was said as though death was the only thing that could be expected. 'Ma's got a pension but she has to work to pay for my sister's dancing lessons and clothes. It's wild expensive, sure it is. Miss . . .'

'Call me Lisa.'

'Miss, can I go wid ye? I'll show you around the town, so I will.'

'If you ask your mother for permission.'

'Sure, she's out somewhere. It's Mary Jo's turn today to mind the weans.'

'The what?'

'Me brothers and sisters.'

Lisa felt a sudden rush of affection for the boy. She wondered how old he was but felt it might injure his pride to ask. 'Wait a minute, Micky, I must tell my mother that I'm going out.'

'Aren't you too big now to be doing a thing like that?' he asked in amazement.

Lisa rolled her eyes, threw out her hands and shrugged. 'I know.'

Micky O'Kane led her up the Strand Road. By the time they reached the ancient walls of Derry, she felt exhausted. But her companion was determined she should see every inch of the famous walls, and hear about the siege in 1689 when the Apprentice Boys shut the gates against King James and declared for William, Prince of Orange. When they reached Roaring Meg, one of the great guns, Lisa said they must stop and rest to eat the ice cream they had bought from a cart.

Micky felt in powerful form and couldn't stop himself talking to this receptive audience. His mother said he had a gift-o'-the-gab that would plague the very divil. Lisa protested then shrieked loudly when he went on to tell her about the people inside the Derry gates who, in their need for food, ate dogs and rats.

She threw away the ice cream. 'You have put me off. I do not eat any more.'

'Michael O'Kane, what are you up to?' The sharp unexpected question came from a tall dark youth passing by.

The boy flushed. Intrigued, Lisa stared at Dominic

McDaid. 'He is my guide.'

'Your guide?' Dominic looked disbelievingly at the girl with the startlingly coloured hair, dark eyes and foreign accent. Lisa stared back with frank curiosity. Embarrassed, Dominic mumbled, 'I thought he was bothering you,' and walked on.

Lisa turned quickly to Micky. 'Who is he?'

'Him,' the boy said derisively, 'he used to be a clod of a monitor at my school – the Long Tower. Now he goes to Saint Columba's College.' Micky felt deflated; his moment of importance had ended when Big Mouth McDaid belittled him before her eyes.

Lisa could feel his withdrawal. 'No more terrifying tales to tell me? Who is the stone man standing up so high?'

'Lundy,' Micky said flatly. 'The eejits burn him every year.'

'The eejits? Burn?'

'Ach, they stuff him up.' Micky was lost for words.

'I know. You mean effigy. Who are the eejits?'

'The Orangemen.'

'Ich verstehe nicht . . .' Lisa mumbled. The boy was becoming incomprehensible again. 'We will go now,' she said wearily.

Micky felt disappointed. 'All right.'

'And this time we ride.'

'The bus stop is outside the gates.' He hesitated, remembering one of his mother's warnings: 'If I ever catch you cadging, Micky O'Kane, I'll murder ye.'

'I haven't the fare, miss,' he admitted. Surely it wouldn't be cadging if someone *insisted*. 'So I'll say, so long now,' he murmured hopefully, looking down at his feet, frightened they'd make off in spite of him.

'It is only a little money. I take you.'

Billy the Man – as he was called by some Derry people – had an eye open for tourists. This one with the wee boy looked as if she had come from foreign parts, with her bits of gold flashing in the sunshine. 'Are ye needin' a taxi, miss?' he called out, his round face beaming, the cap in his hand like a begging bowl.

Lisa's face lit up expectantly. 'Ja.'

Micky tugged at her skirt. 'Not him. That's a Protestant wan,' he hissed. 'If I wis you I widden go wi' the likes o' him. He takes a drop and ye could land anywhere. Last Twelfth of July he nearly went straight into the River Foyle wi' a load of Orange Billies.' Micky remembered his mother saying, 'It was a pity he didn't make a good job of it and go the whole way.'

The incomprehensible words flew over Lisa's head. Her feet were aching and her stomach was disturbed. She scrambled into the car. 'Come, Micky. Please,' she said to the taxi driver, 'I go in that direction.' She pointed towards the Strand Road.

'Come on, son,' Billy the Man suggested. 'You ride wi' me and give me the right way. Ye look a right smart lad.'

Micky forgot about the Protestant cab and jumped in eagerly beside him. He just hoped his ma wasn't on the road anywhere. She'd gae him a right good clout if she saw him cocked up here beside an Orangeman.

'Are you on holiday, miss?' Billy asked.

'No, I come to live here and please, my father is anxious to have contact with a good taxi service for his business. May I have your card?' The car was spotless. She could smell the polish that had been rubbed into the old leather. Even Momma wouldn't be able to complain about this one.

Billy scratched his head briefly. 'I haven't got around to that yet, miss. I'm usually at the station picking up fares or around where we met a minute ago. Sure, everyone knows Billy the Man and couldn't ye send the wee boy here if ye needed me?'

This casual way of doing business astonished her. It certainly would not suit her father. 'You have a strange name,' she said, embarrassed now and wishing she had not made the offer.

Billy tossed his head back. 'Aye, right enough. I'm stuck wi' it for that's what everyone calls me. M'father came to Derry on a Twelfth of July march, met wi' an accident and dammit, the memory went. No one claimed him for the 'poor bugger came off the roads.'

'The roads?' It was all getting too much for Lisa. She wished she had not spoken.

'A beggar?' Micky spoke out in astonishment. Imagine a Protestant being so low! He thought only Catholics became beggars.

'Higher than that, son. He worked his way around the country wi' a trade. Anyway, the Derry people who gave him wee jobs called him 'the Man' for want of a better name. When the memory came back, the name stuck and dammit wasn't I christened Billy too and landed wi' the full title!'

Lisa leaned back on the seat choking with half-stifled laughter. These Derry people were strange and funny the way they tossed off the story of their lives after only a minute's acquaintance.

Chapter 8

I need never have known about Lord Kindron, Prisca
McDaid thought as she cycled up Brandywell Road on her
way home from Eoin O'Donnell's house. Eoin had just
told her that Mr McCay, the editor of *The Northern Press*,
had died in a nursing home on the previous day. The new
editor was Conor Adams, who had resented McCay's
intention to ferret out information about Kindron's descendants living in Derry.

Well, Prisca, she asked herself, do you feel any different
about the situation now? Since hearing about her grandmother's parent, a small flame of anger had been growing
steadily, consuming her with bitter resentment. Eoin
understood how she felt, but not her mother. As long as the
knowledge was kept from her brother, Dominic, and other
people, Mam felt it was silly to get upset about it. Over the
past few weeks every stranger who called at the door had
been a cause for alarm. He might be the one who had come
to quiz them. Up to now, Eoin had been blunt about the
possibility of it still happening. If the editor of *The
Northern Press* recovered, he had warned her, the whole
thing could be thrown open again. Now the man was dead.

She had been appalled by her father's reaction, too. He
who used to be a staunch Republican, and had actually
taken part in the abortive uprising during the last war,
could stand before her and say, 'If it's the English blood
you're worrying about, don't forget that there were plenty
of good Englishmen who fought and pleaded for Ireland's
cause. *They* were not proud of the fact that Irish people
were thrown off their land and it handed over to their
forefathers.'

One day when Prisca came home early from school she heard her parents talking out in the yard. 'Phelim,' her mother was saying, 'you must try to get Prisca away from Eoin O'Donnell's classes. I think he's got too much influence on her.'

'You could be right,' her father replied. 'Eoin has got ideals.'

'And that Rosheen Quinn he goes around with is known to be a fanatic. They say she was involved with the spot of IRA trouble at the border some time ago.'

'I've no use for Rosheen myself — as you say, a fanatic. I certainly don't want Prisca to get ideas from that woman.'

Annoyed, Prisca thought, They're talking about me as if I were a child with no mind of my own. I've had to grow up pretty fast when Mammy started having her miscarriages and left me to look after the family. Noisily, she made a pot of tea, carried the tray out to the yard and placed it on the coal-bunker beside their chairs.

'You're home early today,' her mother said in dismay.

Without a word Prisca poured two cups of tea, then raised her eyes. 'I was fifteen years old last week,' she said rebukingly. 'I am *not* giving up Eoin O'Donnell's Irish class.'

A silence followed her words. She went inside to the kitchen where her grandmother was unravelling an old jumper. 'Cup of tea, Gran?'

'Bless ye, daughter.'

Her mother hurried in with an anxious look on her face.

'Mammy, could I have a word with you in Granny's room?'

'Surely, dear.' Mrs McDaid's voice matched her expression. 'Is something the matter?'

'On the contrary.' They sat on the bed which was covered with an old patchwork quilt that Granny had made sixty years ago with scraps of cloth from the shirt factory. Briefly, Prisca repeated what Eoin had told her. Nora McDaid shut her eyes.

'Thank God. Now we can put the whole thing out of our minds. We'll never mention it again.' When her daughter did not reply, she said anxiously, 'You've got your whole life ahead of you, dear. There's no use bothering about what can't be helped.'

Prisca shrugged. 'Aye, I suppose I did get a bit carried away.' Choosing words that would satisfy her mother she said, jumping to her feet, 'Anyway, I've got my exams coming up soon. I must work.'

'Will ye bother going to the Irish classes then?' her mother asked in a voice that was humble, yet hopeful that the reply would be the one she desired.

'Look, Mammy, I don't do half the things other girls of my age do – dancing, parties and so on. Do you know several in my class are going to Austria in a few months' time. *Austria*. Just imagine?' She took one look at her mother's face and said quickly, 'It doesn't bother me a bit. France is the place I'll make for when I'm earning some money.'

'Dear, there's something I want to tell you.'

Alarmed, Prisca bent her head. She couldn't bear to hear that her mother was pregnant again.

Nora said quickly: 'I've got to go to hospital to have a hysterectomy.'

Now it was a feeling of alarm. 'That's serious.'

'Not at all.'

'How do you know you've got to go to hospital? You haven't been near the doctor. Daddy collects your iron pills, doesn't he?'

'I've been slipping away quietly, love. Sure what's the point of putting everyone up the pole with worry? Anyway, there's a bed available next week. Now,' she put a hand on Prisca's knee, 'everything's organized. Mrs Kenny is going to do all the washing. Kenny's off the drink because the doctor frightened the life out of him. And would ye believe it, Pris, he's bought her a grand washing machine. Does everything with a flick of a finger. Isn't the world a clever place? So, love, she says you're to send a pillowcase of clothes in every day with Patsy, and Pat can put them in the machine and wait till they've spun dry.'

'Maybe that way we won't lose anything!'

' 'Tis a wee weakness. She's got a heart of gold.'

'And a hand that picks things up in shops. Maybe she stole the washing machine!'

Laughing, her mother went on, 'She loves ironing and will come in and do a bit every day. Isn't that grand? Your father will attend to the breakfast in the morning as well as the washing up.'

'That'll please Dominic for a change.'

'You can make the tea in the evening and Dom with the others can do the dishes. I'm writing out a new list of work duties.'

Prisca felt moved by her mother's thoughtfulness in making all these arrangements to relieve her of endless chores.

'What about putting Dom down for another wee job like cleaning all the shoes in the morning! How long will you be away for?'

With reluctance Nora said, 'I'm afraid it'll be a couple of weeks. The doctor is arranging for me to go into a convalescent home for a week afterwards. Just think of it, two whole weeks when I'll be waited on hand and foot. I just can't imagine it.'

'That's the best news I've had for ages. It'll do you the world of good.'

Everything had gone peacefully over the two weeks of her mother's absence, apart from Granny forgetting occasionally where her daughter had gone to.

'She hasn't run away?' she asked anxiously one day.

'If she had any sense, Gran, my mother would do just that. Didn't I tell you she's in hospital and will be home soon. What gave you that idea about her running away?'

'Mrs Kenny was reading me an English newspaper. She said the English wimin are great wans for goin' wi' other men.'

'What are you talking about? Aren't we famous for our good Catholic marriages? Once the knot's tied it's there forever, love you.' We don't spend enough time talking to her, Prisca thought worriedly. We're leaving her to the mercies of our neighbour who is a mixed blessing. Granny's mind seems to be wandering. Lord, I hope she doesn't become senile and a burden on my mother.

Prisca placed a cushion behind the old woman's head. 'You didn't run away from your husband now, did you?'

'No, but he ran away from me, the divil take him. Away to sea and got hisself kilt. Left me a poor widda wimin wi' a wean to rear.'

'Away to sea? I thought Grandfather was a thatcher?'

'That was the second wan.'

'Where did you meet the sailor?' Prisca asked, humouring her.

'I was the skivvy in the house of an English captain. M'man was attached to him. He got me into trouble and had to wed me.'

My God, she's not dotering, she means it. 'An Englishman, Gran?'

'Aye, God forgive me.'

My Irish blood is getting thinner, Prisca thought bleakly, searching her grandmother's eyes again to find a sign of vagueness: they were as clear as her own.

'An Englishman to m'shame,' the old woman repeated.

'Granny,' Prisca said with sharpness, 'does my mother know this story?'

'She doesn't and don' ye tell her. It wid skunner the pure wee soul.'

'What about Mrs Kenny?'

'Tell Kenny? Are ye daft? She'd have the whole street tole in a minute.'

Prisca bent down and whispered: 'Our secret. Right?'

The old woman nodded her head shrewdly and whispered, 'The thatcher and me kept the story to ourselfs and wee Nora never knew the truth of it.'

Dominic passed through the kitchen to the scullery. Prisca's eyes followed him. My proud brother, if only you knew.

Across the street, Peggy O'Donovan or the Merry Widow, as she was nicknamed in Brawn Street, sprayed herself with a cheap perfume. Fascinated by her mother's daily toilette her daughter, Mona, watched.

'I want ye to take a present over to that nice Mrs McDaid, love.'

'Surely ye hardly know her, Ma.'

'She's the only one in this street that gives me a friendly word.'

'Why don't they like you?'

'Because I dress like a swank and they're jealous. That Mrs Kenny wid flay ye wi' her tongue. Who'd want to be friendly wi' the likes of yon wan?'

Mona looked away remembering the night, years ago, when her mother came home late and the wind had been howling pitilessly around the house. Terrified, Mona tore downstairs to the front door. Somehow the street beyond seemed less threatening than the empty house. When she wrenched the door open, the force of the wind knocked her down. Just then Mrs Kenny, who was waiting for her husband, peeped out and saw what happened. The neighbour beat her way across the street, picked up Mona in her arms and carried her into the warmth of her kitchen where she was wrapped in a blanket and given a hot mug of cocoa.

'What are ye thinking about?' her mother asked, applying mascara to her eyelashes.

'The night Mrs Kenny saved m'life.'

'Wid ye listen to her! Sure I was only detained a while by the high wind.' Aye, Peggy O'Donovan thought, and that was the night the same oul bliddy Kenny messed up m'life. Ever since I've been haunted by that Father Hay. Sent him on me, the bitch.

Mona dropped her head when she recalled what happened afterwards. When her ma came rushing in, looking for her, their neighbour screamed, 'You bliddy whore! That wean might've died on yer doorstep. Git over to that house, ye bitch, and make a warm bed to put her in. She's taken a founder. I'll have the priest on ye. He'll make ye do yer duty.'

The terrible words brought an angry flash to Ma's eyes.

'I'll take my daughter now, if ye'll kindly let me borrow the blanket.' Ma had spoken carefully, showing up their neighbour's roughness.

'Jaysus,' a voice had said from the doorway. 'Ye canna spake like that to a neighbour woman.' Mr Kenny, who had just come home, kept shifting uncomfortably, each foot rising slowly and journeying backwards as though preparing for flight.

'Shut yer gub,' his wife snapped. 'Look at the cut of ye.'

'There's a bit o' wind about the night, woman, or did yer voice drown it?'

Mona remembered giggling into the blanket until Mrs Kenny's glance sharpened when her husband eyed Ma, standing there, her beauty showing up the cheaply furnished room with its 'pairs of everything' as Ma put it later. All the men looked at her mother in that way, and if she caught them at it, their eyes went down and they made a wide sweep as though the pavement had suddenly split open. 'I'm on their conscience if they spare me a glance,' Ma had laughed one day. Mona didn't know what she meant but she was beginning to wonder.

'Change yer frock, Mona, and away o'er the street to McDaids'.'

Mona hated having to change every time her mother wanted her to look smart. Her clothes were another barrier between herself and the other children in Brawn Street. No one changed their dress unless they were going to Mass.

'Are ye listenin' at all ... standing there like an auld wimin. Don' let yer lip drop like that, love. Think yer simple.'

The words smarted Mona and she retorted, 'I'm not simple! The teacher says I'm smart if I work.'

'What do stuck-up teachers expect, and you only six years old.'

'I'm eight, so I am.' Ma hated her to mention age.

'Ye'll make me an auld wimin yet. Away ye go and walk down wi' me as far as Stanley Walk.'

As she slipped on a clean dress Mona's thoughts went

back to that night again, when Ma carried her across the street and laid Mona in the lovely bed with the wee heater under the sheet. Then with her arms around her daughter she had cried bitterly. 'They all judge me. If they only knew about my life.'

'Don' worry, Ma. When I grow up I'll look after you.' In their closeness that night she had found her mother.

Prisca was on her knees scrubbing out the hall when the knock came.

'Come in,' she shouted.

The prostitute's daughter thrust a box at her and fled across the street again. 'Thank you, Mona,' Prisca called after her. Inside the box was a large lilac-coloured shaped heart, made of silk trimmed with cheap lace filled with a bottle of cheap scent that reeked of violets, a powder-puff and lipstick. From one of her menfriends, she thought distastefully, and pushed it into the cupboard as though it were contaminated. Prisca spread the last piece of newspaper below the stairs when the hall was washed, then leaned back on her heels, satisfied that the job was done and smelling of clean carbolic soap. Idly she glanced down at the print on the paper and read the news with little interest, for the papers which Mrs Kenny brought over occasionally were days old.

Across the front page was printed: *Another sad death in Iniscad. Yesterday afternoon Mary Bridget Adams, wife of the editor of* The Northern Press, *was killed in an accident outside her home . . .*

Marcella Adams sat by the river listlessly trailing her fingers in the sparkling water. A bunch of watercress and a picking of mushrooms lay by her side on a leaf of wild rhubarb. She had made herself perform the simple task of picking them to defy the lethargy that had taken hold of her since her mother's death. The mushrooms brought back a poignant memory of Mama going out early in the mornings to gather the little creamy caps that nestled in the dewy grass by the river. Only a few weeks ago, when the freshly gathered mushrooms had sizzled on the pan with crisp slices of bacon, her life had been perfect and she had not realized it. This was the thing that haunted and bewildered her now, the casual acceptance . . . taking everything for granted, unaware of the transience of life. This word, used frequently by the nuns in the convent, began to have a meaning for her now.

Anger made her slash at the grass with a stick. She wanted to scream at God in heaven. How could she pray and think, His will be done, when her beautiful, gay mother had been destroyed by the hand of a drunken driver? Marcella felt a helpless rage tear at her. Yet it was to God she prayed in endless anguish, a torrent of words always ending, 'Help me please.' She snapped the stick in two and threw it into the river . 'I'll have to help myself,' she muttered, scrambling to her feet. 'Daddy and Brian are like automatons since the death.'

Liam in the brae was fishing further along the river. It was the divil's own luck, he thought, that the poor wee cratur came this way today – the first time he'd ever laid eyes on her down this part of the river. He bore an awful load of guilt. But how was he to know that stupid eejit of a lorry driver would take to the road after the wee jap of poteen Liam had given him? The power in it went to the man's head, taking away the few senses that he possessed. Feeling uncomfortable by the girl's staring gaze, he packed his tackle and went up to her.

'Sorry ye lost yer mammy, Cella. Sure she'll be in heaven now and the right place for the likes of herself. Begod, if she isn't, what hope will there be for the rest of us?'

Marcella had an urge to push the big mouth into the water. Without a word she swung around and went to walk away.

'Look what I've got for yer tay,' he called, seeing that his clumsy words had disturbed the girl, and anxious to make amends. 'The finest trout I've ever laid m'eyes on.' He threw the fish on a bed of cress, unconsciously garnishing it richly and causing her, for the first time in weeks, to feel a pang of hunger.

'How will I cook it, Liam?'

'Slap the bugger on the pan wi' a bittie of butter and ye'll be eating like a queen.' His knife snapped open and he quickly gutted it before her eyes, throwing the guts into the river, where voracious seagulls swooped down and gobbled.

By the door of River House Marcella paused, unwilling to enter. She turned and regarded the range of hills across the river, purple blue against the clear sky. In the valley freshly whitewashed cottages sparkled, their whiteness almost dazzling the eye. A thread of smoke rose in spirals from their chimneys, making a companionable link in the isolated countryside and revealing the knowledge that all was well in a neighbour's house. Never in her life had she seen a dead fireplace in anyone's house. A lifeless grate is like a coffin in the corner, her mother used to say. And here was her daughter letting the ash grow cold every day instead of supplying a little kindling and peat to warm the cinders.

When she came home from school every day, she reluctantly entered the house with its terrifying silence. Taking off her school uniform she pulled on an old dress and rushed away again from the home that used to give her a feeling of protection. Brian was no help. Morose and silent, he went straight upstairs to do his homework. At night she often heard the muffled sound of crying coming from his bedroom. She was deprived of the indulgence of tears; there was only pain like a band of steel across her chest. Just before her father was due back, she would rush indoors and lay the table for tea. In he came, smiling brightly and whirled her around the room as though she were a little girl. Marcella could see the forsaken look in his eyes, but it was a game he had to play – a joyless game because of the promise.

The girdle of her tunic was lying on the floor. She picked it up, and then for the first time allowed herself to remember that last day of happiness in River House. It was a Saturday. Her mother had said, 'We must get into Derry and buy you a new gym tunic. The shop in Carndonagh hasn't your size in stock yet.'

On the Monday morning when she was dressed for school, Marcella ran into the kitchen and whirled around to be admired.

'Smart,' her father commented over his paper.

'Too long,' Brian muttered.

'Yes, I think you're right,' Mama said. 'Mother of God what was I thinking about? No time now, pet. It'll have to wait until this evening.' Impish laughter filled her eyes. 'Keep out of Sister Joseph's way, as she always imagines that girls in long tunics have vocations. Bare knees and the immortal soul have a sort of connection in her mind.'

Marcella laughed and went off to school, indifferent to the dowdy uniform; only its freshness was important because the bishop was visiting the school that day.

The gym tunic was never altered, for that afternoon her mother was killed when she was cycling down the road to collect bread from Boyle's Hotel, which was also the village shop. They said the brakes on her bicycle must have snapped for when a lorry came along the main road too fast, she tried to throw herself into the hedge. This was told by old Mick O'Hare who clipped the hedges for the County Council. The driver panicked when he saw the bike out of control, swerved to the right and hit her.

Everyone had been shocked by Mrs Gilroy's death a few months previously; now they were completely stunned that a personality like her mother's could be snatched away in a second. Neighbours, full of pity, crowded the cottage before and after the funeral and exhausted them with kindness. They had no time to feel the harshness of their wound but, when left to their own company, they felt the lonely silence. Her mother's spinning wheel and all the other things she used for her needlework were pushed away into the dairy which her father had locked in case one of them should open the door and prolong the aching pulse of death with which they were trying to come to terms.

A knock on the door startled her. Neighbours just called out and walked in. Reluctantly she opened the door. Kiaran Gilroy stood outside with a bundle of books in his hand. He smiled.

'Hello, Marcella. Brian has gone to play football in Carndonagh. He asked me to bring these home for him.'

'Thanks.' She held out her hand to take the books, not knowing how to handle his unexpected appearance on the doorstep.

'They're heavy. Let me carry them inside.' Kiaran was shocked by her appearance. The childish roundness of her face had altered and the large sparkling eyes were dull. Her hair shocked him most of all. 'What happened to your hair?' he asked impulsively.

'Sister Joseph cut it off.'

'She cut it off? Why?'

'She thought I couldn't look after it properly. Indeed, it was a great deal of trouble to me.'

He put the books on the window-ledge and deliberately glanced outside. 'I was away when your mother died.'

Marcella knew words of sympathy were coming and didn't know how to stand them. And he wasn't going to leave in a hurry either, for he had now placed himself in the old oak chair, sitting back comfortably as though he meant to stay for a while. She moved nervously towards the fireplace, ashamed that there wasn't even the hospitality of a fire for the visitor. Fumbling with the small kindling that her father kept on the hob, she looked helplessly at the wide iron grate that filled most of the inglenook fireplace.

'Let me do it.' He rose quickly from the chair and picked up the poker, gently easing fine ash through the bars. Tiny sparks fell from the abundance of fuel that had been piled there earlier that day. 'Ah,' Kiaran said, 'that *was* a good fire and we're going to rescue it. Marcella, pick me out small pieces of peat from the creel there.'

'Are you sure you want to do it?' she asked anxiously, thinking of all the servants at Slievan and him dirtying his hands at their hearth.

'I'll let you into a secret.' He pushed a wing of fair hair away from his eyes. 'An ogre of an aunt now runs the house, most of the staff have gone and I have been made responsible for the fires.'

'You tell me that? Sure Biddy in the brae is still there.'

'Biddy is above fireplaces,' he said smiling. 'She assists the cook in the kitchen who, I'm afraid, is mainly my aunt because staff keep leaving.'

'Biddy cooking? Mama said she couldn't boil a kettle of water – ' Marcella broke off, dismay flooding her face and a knife of pain turning in her heart.

Kiaran took the peat from her hands and built it around the small flames fighting for life. 'That should do it.' He wiped his fingers on a handkerchief then turned to her. 'Marcella, grief is like an illness. Gradually with time it gets a little better. The healing begins – ' He turned to the door and said as he touched her hair lightly, 'Let it grow again. It was the most beautiful hair I'd ever seen.'

She watched him out of sight as he bounded over stone walls, taking a short cut to his home. Brian had told her that Kiaran Gilroy thought he wanted to be a priest and that he would be going to a Jesuit public school next term. That information now troubled her but she didn't know why.

A few weeks after Kiaran Gilroy had called at Bridge House, Marcella was in Boyle's buying bread when several gypsies crowded through the door. They were the ones that came every year to Briar Meadow, a piece of waste ground that lay just below the Gilroy estate and not far from the shore. She stood behind some rolls of material and watched them haggling over the price of things.

The village store was lit with the brilliance of their colourful clothes. The women, dark and attractive in long skirts, had shawls thrown over their shoulders in unconscious elegance. The children ran around them fighting and laughing with unrestrained happiness.

As she watched, Marcella remembered one of the few quarrels that had taken place between her parents some years ago. It had something to do with the gypsies. 'Tinkers,' her father had called them. 'The Gilroys should not have encouraged them to come around the place after the famine ended.'

Famine? What were they talking about, she had wondered. The potato famine was over a hundred years ago.

'Huh!' Mama said angrily. ''Tis well for them that the present gentry were not in the big house then. That Mrs Gilroy would begrudge you the time o' day. She's tried to chase them away from the meadow many's a time. Deal a bit of notice they take of her.'

'I wish you wouldn't go there,' her father insisted with an unusual firmness in his voice.

'I must visit Nanta. She's dear to me.' He shot a warning glance and nodded in Marcella's direction. 'The child —'

Which one was Nanta, she wondered now, and why had her mother liked her so much? In the weeks after her death, Marcella felt closer to the people Mama had liked, as if she were seeking something of her in them. She hurried home, threw the bread in the cupboard and set out for Briar Meadow.

Peering through the trees on the edge of the encampment, her eyes were stung by the smoke from a camp fire. Men were busy making things while women hung around untidily, small children clinging to their skirts. A tall woman walked down through the centre of the site. With a Carmen-like indolence, she flung a dead rabbit to a youth who had a small knife in his hand. This one, more than the others, looked like one of God's gentry. Nervously, Marcella made her way into the centre of the caravans.

'Who's 'ee?' a little girl murmured. Her jet black eyes and hair gleamed in the sunlight.

'Which one is Nanta?' she asked.

'Nanta,' the girl said vaguely, catching the folds of Marcella's cotton dress and examining it.

Some of the women wore scowling expressions which told her plainly that she was an intruder and had no right to be there. More in alarm than by instinct, she ran towards a richly coloured caravan set apart from the others. It was on the edge of the encampment, near a path through the woods. If the woman standing on the steps was unfriendly too, it would not take long to get away from the camp.

To Marcella's relief she smiled and nodded.

'My name is Marcella Adams. You knew my mother.'

'Who is it?' A man's harsh voice came from inside the caravan.

'The little wean – the mammy died. Come,' Nanta said, inviting Marcella to sit beside her on the steps. A slim brown hand swept back a wing of red-gold hair. Her large blue eyes were warm and consoling. 'So you are Marcella.'

As she looked at this strange, beautiful woman, Marcella felt a wave of emotions; grief, loneliness and something indefinable.

'Yer a handsome girl.' The deep musical voice left a lingering note in the air.

They sat together silently for a while, Nanta gently stroking her arm as though they had known each other for a long time and the caress was the sympathy she could not convey in words.

'Look yonder.' She drew Marcella to her feet and pointed a finger to where the meadow opened out to a sweep of land. 'See how the sun is lifting the gold from the earth.'

Startled, Marcella gazed at the fields in the distance: one was wild with clover and buttercups, the other full of movement as the breeze touched the ripening corn. The gypsy drew her around to the other side of the caravan.

'Look now, lovey, see yon little seedlings. Aren't they like emeralds nestling in purple velvet?'

Marcella looked to the west where the grazing land ended and on to the glen which stretched down to the firm golden strand. Then she noticed the tiny green pines scattered among the glowing colours of the heather and, as though a different part of her was brought to life, she saw Nanta's picture. In that moment, a sudden awareness of the countryside flickered to life and she knew that never again would she run through it without looking and searching out its beauty.

'You're like a poet,' she told the gypsy.

Nanta threw back her head and laughed. She went into the caravan and brought out a bulging red scarf. When the knots were undone, a variety of seashells and stones rippled to the ground.

'Don't touch them, Nial,' she said sharply to a boy who leapt across the grass and began tossing them around with long greedy fingers.

'They're lovely,' Marcella whispered. 'My mother used to collect stones down on the shore but none as beautiful as these.'

'I know she did,' Nanta said sadly. 'That's how we met. She came over and bade me the time o' day. Didn't hurry away like the others, dreading I'd try to sell them the very stones off the shore.'

Marcella laughed and thought of the rough jewellery sold in Boyle's and made from the semi-precious stones found beyond the pier. 'And tell me,' she said, one word tumbling over the other in a train of excitement, 'what happened then about you and Mama?'

Nanta explained how her mother had accompanied her back to the meadow that day to see how the stones were tumbled and polished. After that, they often met.

When Nial ran off to join a group of boys and girls, he said something which made them laugh and look at Marcella's feet. Suddenly she felt the weight of her strong laced shoes and felt ashamed, envying them the freedom of their bare feet. They were strange and wild, these people, but because of Nanta she did not want to feel so different.

That afternoon when she got home, she took off her shoes and socks. Slowly and painfully, her back bent like an old woman's, she tried to walk up and down on the pebbles in front of the house.

'What in the name of God are you trying to do down there? Preparing for Saint Patrick's Purgatory?' Brian shouted from the window. 'You look a right eejit.' He shut the window with a disgusted bang.

Every day after that she went to Briar Meadow. Before leaving the woods adjoining the meadow, Marcella took off her shoes and hid them under a bush. Her soles were hardening; walking was gradually becoming less difficult. She felt proud of this achievement. Nanta made no comment about her bare feet, only Nial gave them sly glances.

One day when she was pushing the shoes out of sight, laughter came from the direction of Slievan which was further along the road. Curious, she made her way towards the gates, climbed up a few bars and peeped in.

Sheila Farren came running over. 'What do you want, Marcella Adams?' she demanded.

'Nothing. Just looking.'

When Kiaran and Sheila's brother John walked over too, Kiaran said, 'Hello.'

'Hello,' she answered shyly.

For a moment he looked at her with a slight awkwardness, then quickly regained the sophisticated manner that made him so different from other boys. 'Would you like to come and play this ball game? We could do with another one.'

'She hasn't any shoes on,' Sheila said sharply.

Everyone looked at Marcella's bare dirty feet sticking out of the gate. 'My shoes are just down the road there,' she said hurriedly in embarrassment. 'I'll go and get them.'

The shoes were no longer there. She searched around frantically for a while, then noticed long narrow footprints on the muddy earth surrounding a pool of water. Nial's. The thief! Running back to the others, she said: 'My shoes are not where I left them. Someone must have taken them.' There was a tremor in her voice.

'Are you sure they're not there?' Kiaran asked.

Marcella gave an emphatic nod and to her horror, tears filled her eyes.

'Don't believe her,' Sheila taunted, pulling up her socks and tightening her belt to emphasize what a nice little girl *she* was. 'She probably hadn't any on — she's always hanging around them tinks in the meadow.'

'Let me come and take a look,' Kiaran offered. 'They may have fallen down the other side.'

He ran up the road bouncing the ball, while she trotted behind him. When he parted the bushes there was evidence of her hiding place. The long yellow grass lay flattened, and a dirty white sock was caught in the top briars of a bush. Kiaran walked around and searched. Her eyes followed him, noticing the strong shoulders that made the shirt taut as he bent down. She had a sudden urge to stretch out and touch his arm. The thought made her go scarlet with shame. And shame brought another thought. He was untouchable; he was going to be a priest.

'Not here.' He pushed the ball into his pocket. 'Marcella, why do you take your shoes off?' Then hurriedly, as though he had said something out of place: 'I know some boys and girls do go around in their bare feet but you're not used to it, are you?'

She shook her head, unable to explain the confused reason; her need to belong, anywhere – even with the gypsies. Kiaran looked at her thoughtfully. 'I'll take you home on my bike,' he said gently. He raced up to the gates and returned on a gleaming machine which he braked dramatically. They sped down the road, close to the hedge, through showers of dark red fuchsia bells. Marcella felt like the queen of England, even though the crossbar hurt her bottom and her dirty feet were sticking out like a pair of wooden legs she had once seen hanging on a bush beside a holy well, renowned for its miraculous cures.

Cattle coming out of a farm made them slow down and stop. When Kiaran put his foot into the hedge, she jumped off happily and clambered to the top. Down on the shore, green waves with white ruched edges crept teasingly around the rocks, then rushed away again, leaving dark gleaming plinths to display the beauty of the seagulls. She wished with all her heart that the uncomfortable journey could go on forever.

Just as they reached the gates of River House her fingers accidentally slipped in between the handlebars and the brake. She bit her lip to silence a cry of pain. Kiaran, realizing what had happened, carefully moved her bent white fingers. 'Are you all right?' he asked anxiously.

'Surely,' she replied.

'Brave little Marcella,' he said with a smile.

It was the most perfect moment of her life; only the word

'little' spoilt it.

The next afternoon Nanta handed her the shoes. Nial had taken them back to the camp to remove her name before going to Derry to sell them.

'What are ye going to do when ye grow up?' Nanta asked unexpectedly.

Marcella shrugged her shoulders. 'I don't know.'

'Yer father has a way wi' words. What about that?'

'No, my compositions at school are not very good.'

Nanta considered her for a moment. 'Coming here tomorrow, look at the shape and colour of the things you see on the way. I'll give you some paper and crayons and ye can make me a picture.'

When Nanta's people moved on to the south for the big fairs, Marcella found the days long and lonely again, though not as empty as before. She began to study the wild flowers and marvelled at the perfection of their beauty. She lay in beds of pungently scented ferns and noticed how the tiny ones opened like a baby's fist. Up to then, God had been Mass on Sundays, but now she looked and wondered about the beauty of it all. A new strength seemed to flow through her; she felt it came from the earth, the trees – even the birds. I wonder, she pondered, if this is the reason why travelling people find such contentment with the nomadic life?

When she tried to draw the wild flowers, her futile attempts made her cross. She longed to have the skill to reproduce these flowers which she loved, particularly when they nestled under green leaves damp with dew. One morning on her way to school she watched the blue hills coming slowly out of the mist. Coming back that afternoon, she sat at the foot of the hill with her crayons and worked for an hour. When it was finished she said crossly, 'Awful!' and wrote across the paper before she crumpled it in her hand, 'You're stupid, Marcella Adams. You can't draw a thing.' She threw it away into the wind that was rising from the sea.

Over in Slievan, Kiaran Gilroy sat at a tea table out on

the lawn with his aunt and a second cousin who had just arrived from Cork. The girl was a year or two older than himself and about to return to England to a finishing school. He suspected now that his aunt had gone out of her way to arrange this visit. She had often spoken about this cousin, her beauty and the wealth of her family.

A ball of paper came dancing across the lawn. He rose from his seat and pounced on it. When he saw Marcella's sketch and read what she had written, he began to laugh. His cousin spoke to him. He lifted his head and for the first time really looked at the girl. Something in him reacted to her beauty – the pale golden hair and perfectly shaped features. He opened his hand and let Marcella's drawing fly away again in the wind.

Chapter 9

It seemed to Conor Adams that the old inn, The Refuge, had earned its name on that day weeks ago when he fled from his home after Mary B died. Work was, he discovered, a solace but he began to realize with a feeling of guilt that it was not fair on the children to spend so much time at the office. He returned early this day to Iniscad, and in an act of cowardice, hurried away again. The silent house, without the children who were at school, had struck him with a feeling of unbearable loneliness.

He had tried to clean the place because it had become unbelievably grubby. Dust lay everywhere. The place was mouldering with neglect, he felt. Dishes were casually washed and the linen basket overflowed. Biddy in the brae, who was supposed to be giving a hand, was as reluctant as himself to enter the lonely house. She fussed around on Saturday mornings with a lick and a promise. At least she saw to the washing in a haphazard fashion, and made a bundle of linen ready for the laundry man who called on Monday mornings.

In that state of mind he drove away from River House and went along in the direction of Derry again. Without any sense of purpose, he turned off on an unfamiliar road, trying to forget the times he used to come home early and he and Mary B would unashamedly lock the front door and go to their bedroom. Suddenly he saw before him an inn lying on the shores of a lough. It was a low white building with beamed roofs inside. Everything was fresh and clean, smelling sweetly of the peat and wood burning in the grate. Vases of flowers, simply arranged in copper containers, added their own charm.

'Were you wanting a drink?' a young woman of about thirty-three enquired as he stood there looking about him. She had long brown hair arranged neatly at the top of her head. Her eyes were dark blue and a smattering of freckles lay across the bridge of her nose.

'I don't know what I want,' Conor said. 'I saw the name of the inn and decided it was the place for me.'

Oonagh Toland smiled. 'Have a drop of whiskey. They say around here it's the cure for everything. That, and a Guinness.' She told him that she owned The Refuge and with the help of a small staff, ran the inn. When a few customers came in they all chatted companionably together, and for the first time since Mary Bridget's death, Conor began to find himself relaxing and feeling reasonably happy.

He was just about to leave when someone mentioned a cave up in the hills which had been used as a hide-out during the Troubles. The old man telling the story looked at Oonagh and said: 'You've got a wee place tucked away here, Oonagh, haven't you?'

Conor noticed immediately how reluctant she was to discuss it and how quickly she turned to serve another customer.

'It's in the taproom—a priest's hole,' the man told Conor in a low voice. 'A passage runs down to the lough. The priests had to swim across the icy waters to an underground cavern on the other side, where dry clothes were at hand.' He puffed at his pipe for a minute, then added, 'As soon as the coast was clear they made for the hills or down to the shore where a boat was waiting.'

That evening when Conor and the children were eating their supper, he was pleased to have a topic to talk about. Since Mary B's death an unremitting gloom seemed to hang over the table every time they sat down for a meal.

'Could I go there some time and see this priest's hole, Father?' Brian asked eagerly. 'I'm interested in places like that.'

The unusual sound of enthusiasm in his son's voice pleased Conor. 'Surely, Brian, when I get a chance to ask

Miss Toland.'

A few weeks later Conor decided one afternoon to take a break from the office and go out to The Refuge for a quick drink. Perhaps the bar would be quiet and give him an opportunity to ask Oonagh if he could bring his son along to see the priest's hole. He called frequently now at the inn, enjoying her company and that of the few regular customers. It was a wet day in Derry. The streets glistened with rain and the puddles where drains were choked, looked like busy waterways. Empty cigarette and matchboxes sailed along while choppy little currents, caused by passing cars, tipped them over precariously.

When he walked into the bar Oonagh drew him a Guinness. 'Conor, did I tell you that cousins of mine are arriving from America today? You'll understand if I dash away in a minute to make sure their rooms are ready.'

'Surely, Oonagh. I can't stay long anyway – I've got to get back to Derry again. Look, there's something I've been meaning to ask you.'

She smiled. 'What is . . .' The question was left unfinished and her expression changed. 'Mrs O'Donovan,' she called with an unusual sharpness in her voice, 'I don't think your friend's coming today. He rang earlier on. Would you like me to ring for a taxi to take you back to Derry?'

'Someone needing a lift? I'll take them in,' Conor offered. He was surprised to see the look of alarm that raced across Oonagh's face. He turned. A young woman was standing behind him who, he thought, looked rather lost. She moved quickly to his side.

'I'd be ever so grateful, mister. There won't be another bus for an hour.'

'That's all right,' he said kindly. 'No need to go to the expense of taking a taxi either.' Conor drank up quickly and they left the inn together. When he opened the door of the car Mrs O'Donovan slipped in gracefully. For the first time he really looked at the woman. She had a kind of ethereal beauty: pale fine skin with a faint blush on the high cheekbones, large blue eyes, short fair hair. Perfectly shaped legs and slender feet.

'What about your friend?' he asked, just to make conversation.

'He's a Belfast man. That's the first time he hasn't turned up.'

'Would it not be more convenient to meet in Derry?'

She did not reply. For all her beauty there was something about the woman that jarred on him. She wore a fine Donegal tweed suit in a heather mixture that suited her colouring. He liked her scent; it reminded him of something long ago.

'Isn't the weather shocking,' she kept murmuring, as though she found the silence unbearable and spoke for his entertainment or in token payment for the lift. 'I've never seen such weather.'

As they came into Derry, he asked: 'Where do you live?'

'I'll show you.'

Just tell me, he wanted to say, and felt irritated. When they approached Brawn Street, Peggy O'Donovan said quickly, 'Turn up this wee lane. You'll be right at my back door. It's the neighbours, you see mister. They're ever so nosy 'cause I'm a widow.'

Conor drew in at the door she indicated in the secluded little lane. Damn nuisance, he'd have to back down again. Surely it wasn't a crime for a widow to accept a lift?

She jumped out. 'Would you be ever so kind and bring in my bag?'

'Oh, very well.' The request surprised him.

She opened the back gate, which was set in a high stone wall, with a large key. 'Look what I've gone and done, got you all wet. Come on in for a quick cup of tea.'

He glanced down at his feet standing in a pool of muddy water, then wiped the rain off his face and handed her the bag. 'I must get back to my office.'

'At this time?'

'It's that kind of office.'

'Sure it won't take a minute and look at the grand fire my wee girl has got on. I bet the kettle's boiling already. It'll be a wee thank you for the lift.'

Through the window he could see the cheerful glow of a well-backed fire. By heavens he could do with a hot cup of tea. Mrs O'Donovan was holding the back door open for him. He felt he had no choice but to enter. A shy young girl was laying a tray in the scullery as they passed through.

'You go on down to Stanley Walk, Mona, and do that message,' she told her daughter.

The room was tastefully furnished. A picture of St Antony giving a motionless blessing hung on the wall.

'Sit down over there, I won't be a minute.' When the tray was brought in, she placed it on a low table beside the divan. Then she slipped off her jacket and kicked her shoes into a corner. 'That's better.' Her beautifully shaped arms reached out. 'Let me take yer jacket and I'll give it a good shake.'

'It's all . . .' A scent rose from the low neckline of her blouse and her hair as she moved about him. Against his will the jacket was slipped from his shoulders, given a good shake then placed carefully over the back of a chair. Conor began to feel hot and unsure of himself. Peggy O'Donovan curled on the floor beside him and poured the tea. She looked up and smiled, her lips soft and moist. Pleasure that had lain in abeyance for a very long time, took hold of him. She held his eyes, knowing that she had got through to him at last. Her hand slipped up and lay lightly on his knee; holding his gaze in case she lost his attention, Peggy withdrew her hand, moved the tray and rested both hands against his thighs.

Blindly he reached out for her. She withdrew again and pulled the heavy curtain across the window, then removed her suit and walked unhurriedly across the room towards him. Peggy knew just how seductive she looked in a bra and panties. 'Don't worry,' she whispered, coming closer. 'No one will know. The front and back doors are locked and bolted.'

Worry? The only thing worrying Conor at that moment was she might change her mind. He was desperate for her. Some time later, he swore that was the last time he would commit this sin. It was the first time in his life that he had done so. Like many men of his upbringing with a happy marriage, he had wondered idly at times how these casual incidents came about. Now he knew. He had been in the hands and bed of an expert. Ah, correction! On the hearthrug by firelight.

After the love-making and cups of tepid tea, Peggy ran out to a shower-room off the scullery which had been built by a 'friend', switched on the wall heater and gave him an armful of large fluffy towels.

'Now shower yerself and take yer time,' she told him broadly.

The smell of grilled bacon shortened his time under the shower. The sandwiches were delicious with a fresh pot of steaming hot tea. Before he left Peggy O'Donovan's house, Conor's lack of experience made him fumble awkwardly with his wallet.

'No, it's all right,' she said quickly. 'Not you . . .' She came over and laid her head against his chest. His arms went around her and he experienced the same feeling of fondness he felt for his daughter, Marcella. 'You see,' Peggy whispered, 'I've fallen for ye. That's why . . . no money.'

Good God, Conor thought in alarm, what the hell do I do now? He put her away gently. 'You must need money. You've got to live like everyone else. I mean . . . you don't go out to work – '

His clumsy words trespassed on some chord of sensitivity. The perfectly shaped mouth tightened and hardened, and in a second he saw the other side of her nature. 'That's my business,' she snapped.

Her toughness did not repel him; it had the opposite effect. He opened his wallet again and said firmly, 'Children are expensive. I've got two myself. Your little girl . . . buy her something.' Conor placed more than he could afford on the table.

'Ach, it's too much.' She caught his hand. 'Ye know where I live. I'll be here this time every Wednesday if ye want to see me again. Come in by the back lane. Nobody will know.'

By this time some of the euphoria was passing. 'I don't think so, Peggy. You've been very kind.'

'It's that wan at The Refuge,' she retorted, hurt by the sound of finality in his voice. 'I've seen you there before, when I was with m'friend.'

Her words startled him. 'Yes, of course I'm friendly with Oonagh.'

'Oh aye, thinks she's too good t'speak to the likes o' me.' Peggy's voice was becoming increasingly hard. 'She and me came from the same rotten cabbage, ye know.'

'What do you mean? What are you talking about?'

'The reporter from *The Northern Press* came to see me. Said it was all goin' to be written up or somethin'. Told me I'd get money. 'Twas some story about this Lord Kindron's badness and all the weans he was responsible for. I said I'll be shown up, and he sez t'me there's a lot of important people in the same boat. Just tell me one, sez I to him and sez he t'me, well I've seen ye at The Refuge. The same Lord bought that house for a mistress of his and them that's in it now descended from her.'

Christ! Conor thought angrily, that young bastard Joe Gallagher must have been sneaking around while McCay was in hospital. Just wait till he saw him.

Peggy looked at him anxiously. 'Ye'll come back again, maybe?'

He was silent for so long that she repeated the question. In spite of himself Conor felt moved by her expression: it was childish, crafty.

When he put the car in reverse and crawled awkwardly down the back lane again, he thought, that's the last time I'll do this ridiculous manoeuvre. He was wrong. His need for Peggy O'Donovan got the better of him and every following Wednesday he crawled up and down the back lane in Brawn Street.

'I haven't seen you for ages, Conor.' Oonagh Toland's voice was crisp with a hint of accusation which surprised him.

'I've been very busy.' And indeed he had; getting rid of

and replacing Joe Gallagher. First, Conor checked in the presence of McCay's solicitor, who was also one of the trustees of the estate and mainly responsible for getting Conor the editorship of the paper, all the papers relating to the Kindron affair. Gallagher had not been given permission at that time to represent *The Northern Press* when he went probing into some people's lives. Nor could it be said, from the information Peggy O'Donovan had given, that Joe Gallagher had handled the story with the delicacy and discretion that were necessary in this case. He had done it to impress McCay, of course, but the poor man did not live to appreciate his action.

'You went with that woman, didn't you?'

'You saw me go, Oonagh.'

She picked up his glass and moved it to a quiet corner of the counter. There was something proprietorial about the gesture that disturbed him, until he realized she was upset. 'You know what she is?'

'I know now. When I offered her a lift the last time I was here, I knew nothing about the woman.'

'Did you . . . stay?' Her eyes were commanding him to give an honest reply.

'Yes, I stayed,' he told her frankly, annoyed that she should question him.

Oonagh flushed, and tears of anger started in her eyes. 'How could you? I'm . . . I'm here alone. I care for you. I know how much you loved your wife. I would have understood.'

Conor dropped his head to hide a flush of embarrassment. God, this was awful. He was appalled by her words. How could he possibly tell her that to indulge in an affair with her would seem irresponsible and morally wrong. He cared deeply for her as a friend but could never consider a physical relationship.

'That Peggy O'Donovan,' she went on, 'the man she's friendly with has been coming here for years. That's the only reason I allowed someone like that into my place.'

'Oonagh, how can you talk like that? How do you know what anyone's like who comes in here?'

'I know she's a tart. In future she will not be allowed into The Refuge. He can find another hotel too, if he doesn't like my decision. I can't have that woman picking up my customers.'

Conor finished his drink and walked out of the bar. He was furious. So, he mustn't associate with Peggy, yet Oonagh was prepared to be just as obliging. What hypocrisy. Behind his anger he knew she was hurt. She had used words as weapons. Though it was his evening to see Peggy, he felt the need she satisfied was not there. Peggy's conversation was very limited. It would be beyond her understanding if he tried to tell her about that appalling scene with Oonagh.

Conor took the road home drowned in a feeling of overwhelming loneliness and self-pity. He decided to stop at Malin Town for a drink, and try to come to terms with himself. Somehow he must find a balance in his life. When he walked into the lounge-bar of the hotel, a voice greeted him.

'Well, if it isn't Conor Adams I'm seeing. Stranger! Where've you been hiding yourself this while back?'

'Hello, Eoin. What are you doing here?'

'Giving a talk to the Historical Society this evening. What will you have?'

'A stout and whiskey.'

Eoin frowned. 'Something wrong?' he asked, concerned, 'You don't look yourself at all.'

Conor drank the whiskey. 'Ah, that's better. I've got my life in a bit of a muddle, Eoin. Really, I've been very stupid.'

'Out with it, man. Your story is safe with me.'

With some reticence at first, Conor began to talk. All the time Eoin's eyes grew wide in amazement and his mouth fell open. Honest Conor, he thought, who never looked at another woman since the day he met his wife. Now he's gone and got himself caught between two smart little ladies.

'Man,' he said in wonder. 'You're not safe to be let out.' Before he could stop himself, Eoin's shoulders began to shake with laughter. 'Everyone the length of Ireland knows O'Donovan. And that Oonagh Toland is as hard as nails. That one's desperate to find a husband.'

The expression on Conor's face did not change, but something brightened inside him, like a finger of light striking the greyness of his mood. He felt the touch of his friend's hand on his arm.

'Conor, I think you should be a bit more discreet, you know . . . I mean, Peggy O'Donovan – in *your* position. It's a small town. Give Oonagh Toland a miss, too. It's not the only pub on the way home.' Eoin rose and held out his hand. 'I must be off now.'

Conor stood up and shook it in gratitude. 'You're a good friend.' He smiled. 'I'll be okay, Eoin. Did me good to have a talk with you.'

Chapter 10

Billy the Man drew up sharply at the Schenbers' house. 'You are twenty minutes late,' Lisa said impatiently.

'Better be twenty minutes late in this world than twenty years too soon in the next,' Billy replied, jumping out of the car.

Micky O'Kane, his hair slicked down with water and wearing a new shirt his ma had made for his birthday, grinned. The Man was great, always had an answer. Lisa, wearing a cream linen suit, scrambled into the back seat.

'We will be late for the film.' She pouted her lips with annoyance.

'Divil a bit,' Billy told her. 'Now, young sir, where does this friend of yours, Brendan McDaid, live?'

'In Brawn Street, Billy. Go up the Strand, turn right into William Street and I'll show you from there.' You'd never think a Protestant could be so friendly to a wee boy like himself, Micky thought. Mind you, he had never known a Protestant before. He'd as soon have Billy any day to that stuck up McDaid, Brendan's brother. God, he hoped Bren was all ready to go. Lisa was in an awful auld mood the day. Always making a fuss about time. Still, she was giving him a grand time of it. Even his ma was impressed.

A frown gathered on Billy's face as Micky's directions took him further into the Bogside. He'd never taken a fare here before. The last thing people in this part of Derry could afford were taxis, he imagined. Still, they had their own men and were hardly likely to call an Orangeman!

When Prisca McDaid arrived home after school, she put on an overall and began to rinse out the load of washing in the tub which her mother had scrubbed on the washing-board that morning, and left to soak in a sink of clean water for Prisca to rinse and put through the mangle. It was a chore the girl detested but it had to be done. Mam was not so strong since the operation.

'Brendan, Patsy, is that you? Come out to the yard,' she called.

The children came out and waited for their orders.

'Patsy, you and Maeve do the bread and jam. Brendan, turn the handle of the mangle and I'll catch the clothes to put on the line. Wouldn't it be marvellous to have a washing machine like Mrs Kenny? Do the whole lot in one go. Sounds like heaven!'

'Pris, Mammy gave me permission to go to the pictures with Micky O'Kane.'

'What with, Bren? Mammy hasn't a shilling to spare.'

'It's Micky's birthday. His girlfriend . . .' he chuckled, 'is taking us.'

'Girlfriend? You're codding. What kind of girl would that wee article pick up? Though he's got cheek for anything.'

'She's a fat German Jewess and they've lived in lots of places. Is that why they're called "The Wandering Jew"?'

'If you ask me, Bren, they wander in the right direction. No old Bog Road for them, like the Paddies! Surely you can go if she's paying. Where'd you plan to meet them?'

'They're coming here for me.'

'She'll have a fit when she sees Brawn Street.'

A car horn tooted outside the house. Brendan raced a sheet through the old mangle into the zinc bath on the ground. 'I must go, Pris. Micky says she looks like Elizabeth Taylor. Going to take a peep?'

'Elizabeth Taylor? In that case I must see the wonder.' Prisca followed her brother into the hall. The three younger children had their noses glued to Gran's bedroom window.

Lisa raised her eyes to the old battered house, noticing the flaking paint and spotless curtains at the window. It was as poor a place as she had ever seen, as were all the other houses in the street. She shot forwards in the seat when Dominic McDaid came along carrying a bundle of books.

Alarmed at the unusual sight of a taxicab outside their door, Dominic went to hurry into the house when he saw Lisa. They stared hard at each other, then he turned away quickly. Next time we meet he will know me, she thought, pleased. Dominic rushed inside where his young sisters gabbled excitedly about their brother going in the car to the pictures.

'Prisca,' Dominic said severely, 'I don't like to see our Brendan going around with that boy. O'Kane's sponging on the girl.'

'From the look of her, Dom, I'd say she was well able to cope with him. God, he must be a handful for that poor widow to manage. He's twelve years old today and already got the look of a gangster about him. Do you know he goes to the films every week and slips in through a toilet window? He must have bones of rubber. Our Brendan wouldn't do a thing like that.' Prisca began to giggle. 'Maybe he's got his crafty wee eye on her diamonds. I'll swear that was no Woolworth's flash I saw through Gran's window.'

'You won't believe it, Prisca,' Dominic announced with annoyance, 'but that girl's father has bought our old shop, and the one next door. He's starting a big drapery business with ideas to catch all the trade in Derry, so one of the fellows at college was telling me.'

So what, Prisca thought. If only Dominic wouldn't keep on harping about what they might have had. No wonder he had a feeling of bitterness towards their father. 'Someone's at the front door, Patsy,' she called. 'See who it is.'

'I think it's the old donkey at the letter box, Pris. He's come for his piece of bread.'

Prisca put her hand in the breadbin. 'As if we hadn't enough mouths to feed in this house without the four-legged callers. Who said donkeys were stupid? Crafty as hell. He knows well it's "piece time" in this house.'

When she opened the door Prisca began to laugh.

Standing beside the dirty-looking donkey was a tiny foal covered in a soft woolly coat of hair. 'He's cleverer than we thought,' she called. 'He's had a young one.' Something caught at her throat and tears started in her eyes. There was a look of nobility in the sight before her: the ragged donkey and its beautiful offspring.

Dominic came out and said quietly, touching the older donkey with gentle fingers, 'Can you spare the mother some milk, Pris?'

'Surely. Heaven help us, there'll be two to feed from now on. I just hope word of our generosity doesn't get around the hills out there, or wherever the donkeys hang out.'

Lisa sat between the two boys in the cinema. A box of chocolates passed continuously between them. She felt depressed. The Hollywood film was clever and colourful, but something about the story made her feel . . . she struggled for a word. Inadequate. The girls on the screen were slim, beautiful; their accents assured, careless. She was too fat and her English so limited. And she had no friends. Momma and Poppa were so strict, yet now they talked casually about old Joseph's boring sons as if she were a piece of merchandise to be presented on some kind of marriage market. Lisa's eyes narrowed. 'Verdammt!' she muttered.

Aware of the turbulence going on beside him, Micky touched her arm. 'You a'right now?'

The box of chocolates was dumped on his knee. 'You take these. I eat no more.'

'Aye, surely. Yer not feeling sick now, are ye?'

Lisa pouted her lips and thought, Yes I am sick. I am sick of life and you, my little friend, who comes to see me every day. You have shown me Derry – it is not a beautiful town. I do not understand why there are so many poor people and why they look so happy about it.

When they were outside, Brendan said, 'Thanks very much for taking me to the pictures, it was smashing. I'll say so long now. See you at school tomorrow, Micky.' He went to hurry away.

'One moment,' Lisa said quickly. 'Billy is coming for us. He will take you home.'

'Sure I can walk.' God, I've had enough of this one, Brendan thought. O'Kane's welcome to her!

'Tell me, Brendan, what does your brother do at college?' she asked, to his surprise.

'I'm not rightly sure. Everything. One day he's going to be a doctor.'

'Ah! What is his name again?'

'Dominic.'

'It is a very beautiful name.' Lisa repeated it slowly. The two boys looked at each other. Micky rolled his eyes and tapped his head. Brendan covered his mouth to stifle a giggle.

Billy the Man was eating a bag of chips when they reached the car, which was parked in a side street. All the windows were tightly shut. Lisa was furious.

'It is disgusting,' she fumed. 'The smell will linger on my clothes.'

The boys were startled by her fit of temper. 'Sure I can walk home,' Brendan repeated, wanting to get away from this tempestuous creature.

'No, we'll be taking you.' Micky opened the door and pushed him into the car. Every trip with Lisa was worth a few pence. The Man had made that quite clear.

Billy, frightened that he was going to lose a good customer, jumped out of the car and, though it broke his heart, threw the bag of chips into a rubbish bin. 'Yer right, miss. Sure a man stuck them in the window and how could I refuse such an act of kindness?' He gave Micky a sly wink, who at that moment was wondering how he could fish the bag of chips out later. Ma would tan his hide if she knew he did a thing like that. His mam was only a wisp of a thing, but she could clout you one that would send you spinning from today to the 'morrow!

'Miss,' Billy the Man said with a contrite expression, ''tis a lovely evening. How d'ye like a wee run down to the sea at Fahan?'

'No. Take Micky home and then we go to Brendan's

house.'

'Right you are, miss.' Billy knew when to keep his mouth shut. And so did Micky though he was furious. It wasn't fair. It was his birthday and now he was being shoved off. Lisa had forgotten her promise to take him home for a mug of chocolate and a slab of cake.

When the car drew up outside the McDaids', Lisa opened the door and jumped out. Brendan ran on ahead of her into the house. 'Mam . . . I'm home!'

Dominic, on his way upstairs with a cup of tea in his hand, walked down the hall towards the girl waiting expectantly on the doorstep. He coloured with embarrassment. You couldn't ask a person like this into your home. What with Granny using the parlour for a bedroom and the kitchen table covered with piecework his mother brought from the factory to do in the evenings . . . there wasn't even a spare chair.

Lisa sensed Dominic's discomfort, and with a feeling of unusual sensitivity, took a quick step away from the door. She looked at the lean, clever face and jet black hair. Smiling, she held out her hand. 'I am Lisa Schenber. I bring your brother home . . . pardon, my English is not so good yet.'

Feeling suddenly sorry for the girl, Dominic took her hand and gave a little smile. 'The English we speak here is not always acceptable either.' The soft plumpness of her skin as he touched it felt sensuous and gave him the startling urge to pull this beautiful girl into his arms. Dominic's body began to stir with a sensation that normally lay dormant. So many things in his life endeavoured to put a damper on any stray feelings that he might experience towards the opposite sex. He was disciplined by an upbringing that did not allow such thoughts. First, the teachers at the Long Tower School; then the Christian Brothers, and finally the priests at the college. All of them had tried to advise young men how to curb 'thoughts of the flesh'.

Prisca saw the taxi from the bedroom window where she was sitting doing her homework. Surely poor Mammy wasn't stuck with that foreign girl? With a feeling of exasperation, she pushed her books aside and tore down the stairs.

The girl was climbing into the taxi as Dominic closed the door. Prisca glanced at her brother's expression and raised her eyebrows. 'Fancy her?'

'Too voluptuous,' he replied untruthfully and dashed up the stairs, forgetting the cup of tea he had placed on the hall table.

Chapter 11

When Marcella returned from school one day, she found Brian and her father reading a letter.

'Well I'm blowed,' Conor muttered.

The letter from his sister, Sarah, shattered him. She apparently felt it was her duty to come and look after the family because someone had written that 'Marcella was running wild around the countryside'. She was arriving the following week. Conor recalled how Sarah had written after Mary B's death, suggesting she should come to Iniscad. He had replied by return, thanking her for the generous offer and saying he felt it was too soon to make any definite plans about the future. His sister had a difficult nature and at that time he could not bear the thought of her fussing around him. He had wanted to be on his own with the children. Somehow, that wasn't working out either.

He tapped his lips thoughtfully with the letter. 'Marcella, I wonder who told her that you were running around . . .' Conor's words faded when he caught sight of his daughter filling the kettle. 'Why are you in bare feet?'

'Just to see what it's like.' Her feet disappeared under the stool with the hope that out of sight would mean out of mind. She saw his worried expression increase as he looked at her unkempt hair and torn dress. Conor knew that Sister Joseph often sent his daughter home in an old gym tunic on Fridays so that the other one could be cleaned over the weekend. The convent tunic with its long boxed pleats, faded to a deep mulberry, looked like one worn in the thirties.

'You're like something out of a circus,' Brian said every time she appeared in it. 'If you took it off and went around in your bloomers, you couldn't look more spectacular.'

'Perhaps,' Conor said resignedly, 'it's for the best.'

Brian was upset about their aunt coming to live with them. At least, Conor thought, the news had stirred a bit of life into him. The boy had become so morose. 'She'll have us on our knees half the evening,' his son moaned, remembering how his mother referred to her as 'Holy Sarah'.

'You'll have to tell her that Mama shortened the Rosary by saying only five Hail Mary's a decade,' Marcella came out with promptly.

'She'll go mad. Bet you wouldn't tell Sister Joseph that.'

Sister Joseph was an awful weight on Marcella's conscience. The nun loved her in the long gym tunic and was sure she had a vocation. She claimed for her virtues which Marcella did not possess. Sister Joseph was certain that her pupil went home every afternoon, cleaned the house and cooked a meal. Worse, she called her a little saint. If only she could see the dirty house and her running wild around the gypsy camp, Marcella thought guiltily. She did not want to disillusion the old nun because all the love and kindness she gave were necessary for her well-being. Sister Joseph also misunderstood the reason for Marcella sitting in the convent chapel so often. To Sister Joseph it was a sign of great piety; only girls who had vocations did such a thing. To Marcella, it meant something different. She did not pray but just sat there, absorbing the quiet peace and the smell of incense. It brought a happiness that confused and comforted her.

This misunderstood act of piety ended when she found a note on her desk one day with a saint's crown drawn on it. Underneath was written, '*Dear sister's holy pet, you're a holy cheat.*' It was the large scrawl of Sheila Farren from the lodge house.

Aunt Sarah arrived the following week and changed all their lives drastically. Even Nanta became a warm memory. Marcella had no time to miss her because she was so busy using her wits to cope with Holy Sarah.

'She's a headcase,' Brian kept saying. He was now

attending a grammar school in Derry and had been chosen to play in the school's football team. When he came home tired and dirty on Friday afternoons, Sarah treated him like a leper and cleansed his clothes as though they were contaminated.

Their relative, Marcella decided, was really an empty shell filled with the echo of other people's personalities. The one thing in her favour was her cooking. For the preparation of the various dishes, Sarah dressed and behaved like an inhabitant of the country of their origin. American recipes brought out a colourful frock and a slow drawl: an air of gentility came with English food; a black shawl with Irish stew. Though the house had never been so clean, it lacked warmth. When their mother was alive they never knew how many would arrive and stay for meals. Now their only visitor was Ned in the brae. In fact, he was not a visitor; Sarah had engaged him to look after the vegetable garden. Biddy was furious about this arrangement. It was Ned she was losing and not Liam, whom she wanted, and expected, to lose. After Liam, dead drunk, had to be held up at the altar to get married (Father McGill was determined to make an honest woman of Rosie), Rosie's father would not allow him in the house.

'You know, Cella, I believe we've got a madwoman in residence,' Brian said one day.

'Maybe she's escaped back to Ireland from a looney-bin.'

'Maybe she's as crafty as hell. Dad says she's sold her flat in London, so we're good and truly stuck with her.'

After all the freedom following her mother's death, Marcella was not allowed to leave the vicinity of the house. One afternoon, when her aunt was being particularly irritating, she said to Brian, 'Come for a walk to the village. She'll let me out of her sight if you're with me.'

As they were passing Boyle's Hotel, Miss Boyle came to the door flushed and unsteady on her feet. 'Well, if it isn't Brian Adams in the long britches at last.' He had been wearing them for years. 'Come in and celebrate with a drink.' The little snug bar was very dark. When the woman poured two glasses of sweet sherry, she helped herself from the lip of the bottle.

'You're too young to be in here,' Brian whispered uncomfortably. 'She's far gone.'

'We're celebrating your manhood, dear,' Marcella giggled, looking at his terrible tweed trousers that made him resemble a dwarf. She took a long drink like a frustrated alcoholic and nearly choked. 'There's something in the glass.'

'Flies! The damn glasses were not washed.' While Brian disposed of their drinks in a pot of geraniums, Marcella chatted like mad to Miss Boyle.

'Come into the kitchen,' the woman invited. 'You must have a wee keepsake.'

Thinking she meant one of her ashtrays with *Boyle's of Iniscad* printed on it, Marcella followed. To her horror, Miss Boyle pulled out a huge willow-pattern meat platter and thrust it into her arms.

'Put it down somewhere,' Brian hissed, as they went through the back hall door. 'Don't you dare take it out of the Hotel.'

She wedged the platter down the front of her old blazer where it rested uncomfortably around her stomach. Looking like a well-advanced pregnancy, she scuttled through the door. Kiaran Gilroy was outside pumping his bicycle. Marcella's hands flew wide in surprise and the platter fell to the ground, breaking into a thousand bits on the cobbled stone. Kiaran looked absolutely astonished. Brian gave a groan of exasperation.

'It was a present,' Marcella said quickly, her face scarlet. The two boys burst out laughing and began to pick up the bits. 'She made me take it, didn't she, Brian?'

The added explanation seemed, for some reason, to increase their mirth. After all the pieces were put in the bin, Kiaran turned to Brian:

'Would you like to come down to the pier and see a yacht belonging to some people staying at Slievan?'

The invitation did not include Marcella. He probably thought she'd do something stupid, she decided, aware that she had looked a fool.

'You run on home, Cella.' Brian eyed her blazer impatiently, which still protruded as if a phantom dish lurked there.

She slapped at the bump. 'When it suits me,' she said, and walked away quickly.

Aunt Sarah was waiting for her like an avenging angel with a huge pair of scissors in her hand. 'You took your time, miss. Ned, place the chair outside. Here,' she threw a towel at Marcella. 'Take that blazer off and tuck this towel around your neck.'

'What for?' Marcella's eyes widened in alarm.

'To cut your hair; it's growing too long and untidy.'

'I don't want my hair cut.'

'Sit down or I'll skelp you.'

Ned in the brae, with a newspaper which he had not the ability to read, sat down and held it before his face like a shield. When Sarah spoke again, the right eye slid around the side of the paper. Marcella's voice from the other side of the kitchen made him move his head and the left eye appeared. Sarah stamped her feet. 'Go outside at once!'

'I'm *not* having my hair cut, now or ever. I'll tie it back,' Marcella shouted.

Defeated and furious, Sarah pulled a drawer open and tossed out a thick rubber band. 'Don't let me see that hair on your shoulders again.'

'Mama hated rubber bands. I'll tie it back with a ribbon.'

'Your mother's dead and it was God's wish I gave up my freedom and came here to look after my brother's family.'

'How could God be so bloody cruel!' Marcella shouted, and tore out of the house and up to the cashel. Tears of anger, frustration and knotted grief flooded the flat rock. After a while she felt calmer and went over to the stream and bathed her face. A piece of dark brown string tarred with oil was lying on the ground. She picked it up, tied back her hair, then walked down to the house. Brian and Kiaran were sitting on the bridge that crossed the river. She saluted them casually with a wave of her hand and walked on, her head held high. Kiaran's eyes followed. He called.

'Leave her,' Brian warned him. 'She's in a mood.'

Marcella had heard Kiaran and longed to turn back but the piece of tarred string, which she had used to spite Sarah, might make them laugh their heads off again. Sarah gave her hair a sharp glance, turned away and went down to the dresser where she filled a bowl with meal for the hens.

'Where's Kiaran?' Marcella asked casually when Brian walked into the house. 'Why didn't you invite him in for a cup of tea?'

'Invite a Gilroy here?' Sarah whispered in a horrified voice, as though he were a member of an enemy tribe.

'Mama would have insisted.' How casually I speak her name these days, the girl grieved. As though she were standing here, a buffer between me and this crazy woman.

It was Sarah's day to be poor Irish peasant. Marcella should have taken note of the shabby dress and tight bun of hair. With ill-humour Sarah threw the pounder to Brian and told him to get the potatoes pounded for supper. She pranced outside, clucking away in an alien voice that sent the birds scattering with fright. When fistfuls of meal were distributed around the yard, they pecked furiously as though death were imminent and it might be their last mouthful. No wonder they were laying so badly these days. Ned shuffled up from his chair by the door and sat peering into the pot.

'Man, them's grand spuds, like balls of flour.' The peaked cap that never left his head except when he went to Mass, shadowed the pot.

'Ned,' Brian said urgently, 'have you a spare fag?'

'Sweet God, I have surely.'

'Keep a watch-out, Marcella,' Brian said, frantically lighting a squashed cigarette.

Every now and then Sarah pushed a bush aside and scooped a few eggs into her apron. After a while, something attracted her attention out on the road. She walked backwards to get a better look, tripped over the feeding bowl and let go of her apron.

'Brian, quick, Aunt's dropped all the eggs. She's coming back to the house in a temper.'

'Jayus, git that fag out quick or she'll skin me.' Ned shuffled over to the table, grabbed *The Irish Messenger* and 'read' it upside down.

Brian went to flick the cigarette into the fire, but it flew right into the pot as his left hand brought the pounder down.

'Jayus,' Ned whispered, horrified.

Marcella quickly chopped an onion and threw it into the pot with a generous sprinkling of nutmeg. 'Mix well,' she told Brian. '*We* know what *not* to put in our mouths.'

'That dose will'ave youse wans in a bad way. I'm goin' up the road for m'supper.'

Sarah swept into the kitchen, driven by the fury boiling on her face. 'That gang are back in Briar Meadow. Seen them passing on the lower road.' Her sharp little eyes flashed at Marcella who kept her head bent. 'See that you keep away from them tinks.'

Marcella was frightened to lift her head in case Sarah could see what pleasure that news gave her.

Every day, as soon as she went out of the house, she sneaked across the fields into the back-end of the woods to reach the meadow. Aunt Sarah firmly believed she was up in the cashel. One day as she was struggling through a narrow path overgrown with brambles, Nial jumped out in front of her. His eyes were cunning and fiery as he pushed her to the ground. She kicked like mad. He stumbled and fell into the brambles. Running as fast as she could, she got away, but he knew the short cuts. When his legs suddenly shot out from behind a tree, Marcella tumbled to the ground again. His long fingers tore at the neck of her dress with a viciousness that bewildered and frightened her. When he pressed his lips against hers, she pushed him away, drawing her nails savagely across his face, leaving an ugly red line. Springing to her feet, she ran for dear life.

He went to follow, when the sound of a dog barking and Kiaran Gilroy's voice came through the woods. The gypsy turned and sped away in the opposite direction. Mortified, Marcella went to meet Kiaran.

'That gypsy, did he touch you?' he asked angrily.

'No,' she lied, 'but I marked him.'

'Marcella.' There was the sound of a rebuke in his voice. She lowered her head and dug the toe of her sandal into the ground. 'You shouldn't come into the woods when the gypsies are around. Get Brian to come with you.'

'He doesn't want to go anywhere with me.' There was a hint of self-pity in her words, which immediately annoyed her.

Kiaran folded his arms and leaned against a tree. He's so grown-up, she thought. Not like Brian and the other boys around here, who couldn't string a dozen words together when they talk to a girl. And the way he wears his clothes . . . it must be the English blood. She tried to imagine him dressed in restricting clerical clothes and failed. The Jesuits would soon make short work of that careless fall of fair hair which he continually whipped from his face. A hint of laughter crept into his eyes. She blushed and looked away.

Conscious that he was still staring at her, Marcella began to gabble to cover her embarrassment. 'I've got a friend over there in the meadow – Nanta. She's very clever, can read and write.' The defiant look she gave Kiaran was met uneasily. She had broken a conventional rule by associating with the 'travellers'. Apparently her mother had been excused because it was thought, quite incorrectly, that she was instructing the children in catechism. Her father had known differently; so did Marcella.

When she reached the meadow and told Nanta about Nial, the gypsy said casually, ''Tis natural for Nial to be attracted to you, lovey. Better meet me down by the pier when I'm collecting stones, for a while anyway.'

'What about my birthday next week? You said you were going to pierce my ears, didn't you?'

'Ah yes, that's true. And I've got the gold rings. Perhaps I'd better do them today instead.'

During the little operation, Nial hung around all the

time, indifferent to the mark that scarred his face. In fact, Marcella had the uneasy feeling that the injury had only aroused him more. And because of that, she would now have to meet Nanta on the shore instead of coming to this place which she loved. Why did everything in life have to change?

When she arrived home late that afternoon with her newly pierced ears, the entire family were shocked.

'Jayus,' Ned in the brae muttered, and scuttled out of the house.

After that incident, it seemed to Marcella that she was treated as an outcast by them all.

'Disobedient, deceitful.' Sarah's shots were harsh and vindictive.

'Old enough to have some sense.' Her father's words were not too strong but pointed, and they hurt. 'Did you know that your grandmother and a servant girl were attacked in this very house years ago by those people?'

Marcella rolled her eyes. 'That story gets worse, Daddy. I thought Granny frightened them off with Grandfather's gun. Anyway, it was *not* Nanta's people. They were tinkers, Mama told me, and drunk on poteen.'

'What's the difference?' he replied wearily.

'She can never be trusted again,' Brian said in his new adulthood, talking man to man, as if Marcella was not present. His sixteenth birthday had just passed unnoticed. 'Imagine a girl of her intelligence going over to that meadow. Honestly, Dad, she'll take to the roads with them if you're not careful.' Dead serious by nature, he was convinced by his own words. He was worried, too. Kiaran told him there was a bad one among that pack.

The discussion went on when she was not present. Marcella made a point of listening-in attentively, for she had a feeling that her fate was being slowly sealed, particularly when her father said one day, 'I believe your sister's mind has been disturbed by her mother's death. They were very close. Why hasn't she got friends? She needs girls of her own age to talk to.'

A new school away from Iniscad was to be the first step

in her rehabilitation. The Mother House of the local school was considered, then rejected. Conor said he suspected that some of the nuns were not fully qualified, and the last examination results were lamentable. 'I've heard of a good school in Derry. Marcella might be just as well away from convent life. Anyway, her art must be the first consideration.'

'In the name of all the saints you're not thinking of sending her to a Protestant school?' Sarah said anxiously, coming in from the kitchen.

'Dad's right about the convent,' Brian offered. 'If it's not the gypsies, it will be the Vows. That Sister Joseph is tightening the ecclesiastic net. She'll have her in there if we don't watch out.'

'And a proud day for us if she did,' Sarah said. 'But maybe you're thinking of a miracle!'

Conor said carefully, because his sister had promised to help financially, 'If she goes to the one I have in mind, Sarah, it will be less expensive as a weekly boarder. You know, coming home weekends. We'll be able to keep an eye on her that way.'

When Marcella read all the details about her new school, the Mount Academy in Derry, she thought it sounded pompous, then shrugged indifferently and hoped the time would pass speedily until she was old enough to go to Art College.

Chapter 12

Lisa Schenber leaned against the ancient Derry walls and thought, If I lift my eyes from the Bogside down there, and look towards the hills, it is better. Several times she had come on her own, hoping she might meet Dominic McDaid. 'Ich langweile mich,' she whispered to herself – I am so bored.

She made her way down to the big gun, Roaring Meg, propped an English study book against it, and began to read through the exercise she had set herself for today. The ice-cream van below the walls tinkled out its little tune, but Lisa ignored it. She was trying to lose weight. Every day now she walked along the River Foyle and into the town. She thought she was becoming slimmer. So, two things in life were good; this small loss of weight and an improvement in her knowledge of English. She felt unsettled, though, and lonely. Snapping the book shut she hurried down to Butcher's Gate. One day she and Micky O'Kane had walked nearly all the way to the McDaids' house in Brawn Street. A short cut, he told her. She would make an excuse to call on them. Maybe Dominic would be there.

People stared at her as she passed by. If she stared back they suddenly smiled. It was strange. And old men at street corners, smoking their pipes, said, 'A fine day, miss.' To strangers, so casually they talk about the weather, she marvelled. Mein Gott, this Derry is a funny place.

A tall, beautiful woman and a little girl approached. Unsure now, Lisa asked them the way.

The woman, flashily dressed and smelling of cheap perfume, said, 'If ye turn at the next street and . . . ach, sure m'daughter Mona here will show ye.' The little girl looked up at her mother. 'Go home, pet, and don' be late in gettin' to bed.'

'All right, Ma.' There was a note of quiet resignation in the child's voice.

'Will you go to bed early as your mother asks?' Lisa enquired as they walked along the street.

'I must. M'ma works very late. We're here now – Brawn Street.'

The sound of children's voices came from the McDaids' house at the corner. Mona O'Donovan stood at the edge of the pavement and looked at the door with a forlorn expression. Lisa stood beside her, suddenly losing confidence in her plan to call at the house. She turned to her companion. 'Thank you.' The girl did not move. She kept staring at the door as though willing it to open. Two of us! Lisa thought. 'Are you friends?' The other stared at her then ran across the street without a word.

Lisa knocked. A voice called: 'Come in.'

She hesitated. Perhaps they think I am a friend? She knocked again. A girl wearing a long cross-over overall opened the door. She was holding a tin of Brasso and a cloth which had stained her hands. Was she the maid, Lisa wondered. 'May I speak to your mistress?' she said tentatively.

'The what?' Prisca threw her head back and laughed. 'I'm the only maid here – daughter of the house, cleaner, child-minder, scholar – the whole bang-jang!'

'I am so sorry. You are Brendan's sister?'

'That's right. Oh, you took him to the pictures the other day? Come in.' There was something pathetic about the way the German girl shot over the doorstep, as though she were seeking refuge from some unmentionable fate outside in the street.

Come in, had meant into the hall. Prisca was tearing through the housework before her mother came home from the factory. Added to that, there was a load of homework this evening. She took a deep breath, noticing the expensive suit and fine leather shoes of the caller.

When Brendan's sister gave no indication that Lisa was

going to be asked any further inside, Lisa said, barely concealing her dismay and disappointment: 'You are busy. I am taking your time.'

An immediate pang of conscience because of her lack of hospitality, made Prisca say quickly, 'What's a bit of time? I was just cleaning some windows. If there's one thing my mother doesn't like, it's dirty windows.' What's this exotic creature doing standing in our hall and what in the name of God am I going to do with her? Dominic will have a fit if he comes in.

Lisa's face lit up when she heard someone playing the piano. Was it Dominic?

'Come in and have a cup of tea. By the way, I'm Prisca McDaid.'

'Lisa Schenber,' she said eagerly.

When Prisca pulled off her overall, Lisa stared at the uniform underneath. It was the same one her mother had ordered for the Mount Academy. How could a girl from such a poor home afford to go to that exclusive school? They were now in a large kitchen which looked bare and comfortless.

Noticing the puzzled expression in the girl's eyes, Prisca said laughingly, 'I should change when I come home but to tell the truth it takes up too much time, so I slip on one of my mother's overalls over my school uniform.'

'I am going to that school, too – the Mount Academy.'

'You are? Maeve . . . ' Prisca called, 'come and help me make some tea.'

Her sister slipped off the piano stool. Lisa stared at her incredulously. 'It was she who played?'

'Yes,' Prisca replied briefly, not wishing to talk about her young sister's ability. It wasn't good for Maeve to have too much adulation, particularly in her own home. Lisa's eyes were round with surprise. 'Come and meet my grandmother and my two other sisters. Granny . . . '

The old woman opened her eyes. 'Is that an angel I'm seeing or am I still in this world?' The old woman's eyes were on Lisa's cream suit and her hair.

'A visitor, Gran, from another land and would you

believe it, they've come to live in Derry.'

'Divilabetter place.' Her rosary beads fell to the floor and Lisa picked them up with a curious look.

'Granny's praying her way into heaven, aren't you?'

'Aye, 'tis time I prepared m'self for the next world.'

'Patsy, sprinkle the clothes ready for me to iron, like a good girl. Deirdre, I'll look at your sums later. Show Lisa the paintings you did at school today.'

'All this work you have to do and you spare me time,' Lisa said in a subdued voice, then it rose dramatically. 'I feel so ashamed. I am so idle.' Every eye in the room shot in her direction — what a way for a stranger to behave! 'I would love to have all these little sisters. One has so much and one is so poor.'

'God save us!' Prisca said laughing, taken aback by the outburst. 'You're surely needing a cup of tea.'

'But is there time for you?'

'Lisa, one thing you will soon learn about this country is that we are the greatest tea-drinkers on God's earth. The pot is always on the hob the minute a visitor sets foot in the house.'

Out in the scullery Prisca said to Maeve, 'Come on in to Granny's room. This is an occasion for the best china. We can't go on admiring it through glass for ever.' They opened the cupboard belonging to their father's mother and took out fragile blue and gold cups and saucers.

'I'll carry the tray and you bring that little case of spoons.'

'Pris, they haven't been used before. Not even for the priest.'

'Well, we're not going to let ourselves down before a grand visitor like Miss Schenber, are we?'

'Pris, do you think she's right in the head? Do you like her?'

'She's going to take a bit of getting used to. I think she plans to take us up!'

'Eh? Do you think she's taken a notion of our Brendan?'

'No, love, I think she'd like someone a bit older. Stand on the chair and hand me down the tin marked "Priest's

Biscuits".'

When a selection of biscuits was arranged on a china plate, Maeve tugged pleadingly at her sister's skirt. 'Pris — '

Prisca popped one into her little sister's mouth. 'Don't tell the others.' Her own mouth was watering. As sure as God, she thought, when I'm earning money I'm going to fill my cupboard with these biscuits. They were expensive, but her mother always said, 'Only the best for the priest.' And didn't Prisca know that the shy wee priest came out of a poorer home than themselves, where his parents hadn't a penny to bless themselves with! There was a pompous one too who called. She'd just love to know where he came from.

Lisa was down on the floor between Prisca's two other sisters when they carried the tea tray into the kitchen from the scullery. She was looking through their schoolbooks. Maeve, flushed with importance, handed round the biscuits. First to Lisa, then Granny while the other two sisters tried to will everyone not to choose the one they had their eyes on. Lisa took a biscuit without looking and nibbled it absentmindedly.

Granny, half-asleep, squeaked from the corner: 'The priest, and I haven't washed m'sel. Oh sweet God, I canna meet the holy priest wi' my auld duds on.'

'Granny, dear, wake up. It's only the biscuits *without* His Presence. Tomorrow's his day to call.'

Much to Prisca's concern, Lisa remained on the floor turning the pages of Deirdre's schoolbook while she sipped her tea. Please God don't let the teacup get knocked over, she prayed. It did not seem like good manners though. Maybe with the Schenbers' money you had no need to worry about things like that. And look at her placing the biscuit on the bare lino. Mammy would be appalled. For didn't we walk in from the street where dogs are known not to be particular, so it didn't matter how many times the floor was cleaned. Mam said she'd like to invite people to change their shoes on the doorstep like the Japanese, or was it the Chinese?

The door opened. Dominic walked into the kitchen,

then stopped abruptly at the sight before his eyes: the Jewish girl kneeling on the floor, her shoes lying under the table and her hair scattered wildly across her face. She looked younger now, and somehow vulnerable. Lisa was not aware that he was standing there until Prisca said, 'Cup of tea, Dom?'

Mein Gott! Lisa scrambled to her feet and ran a hand through her hair. There he was and she looking so bad. Prisca saw the girl's confusion and said casually, 'By the way, Lisa, did you say something about going to the Mount Academy in the autumn?'

Lisa pushed her feet into her shoes. 'But yes, I go there and you go too. That will be nice for me. Ach, I'm forgetting the reason for my coming. It was my intention to ask Brendan to take tea with me and Micky.' On impulse, she was about to include all his sisters, then thought better of it. That might be too much for Momma.

'Well, thanks,' Prisca said doubtfully. Her young brother said the Jewish girl was a headcase and even the free flicks wouldn't get him going out with her again. Micky was welcome to her! 'He's playing a football match today. I'll have a word with him.'

Lisa moved towards the door. 'Good. So you ask him.' She didn't want to go but Prisca was making brisk little movements towards the teacups.

'Would you like Patsy to walk down as far as the bus stop with you? You could get a bus to the Strand.'

Prisca watched the girl's eyes move to Dominic. Yes, I know you want him to go with you, she thought, but our Dominic hasn't time for girls. All he wants in life is to become a doctor and get away from the Bogside. Nothing is going to stand in his way. Anyway, he's starting a Retreat this evening, which means he has to prepare himself for meditation and devotion. Girls are *definitely* not recommended.

Then Prisca paused in her thoughts. What are you going on about, she scoffed to herself. Sure the poor girl only wants his company as far as the bus stop. She'll be back.

Chapter 13

During the long summer holidays Marcella spent a lot of time on the beach. Aunt Sarah had read in a health magazine that the shores around the coast were rich in shellfish which had abundant minerals. She was sent down twice a week to pick a bag of winkles, barnacles and mussels. Also dulse and carrageen moss. The dulse was dried for winter. When it resembled strips of fine linen, fistfuls were hidden in children's school satchels and nibbled cautiously during lessons. Sarah cooked the shellfish in a rich oatmeal sauce and made a creamy, lemon-flavoured dessert with the carrageen moss.

Unknown to Sarah, this thrift also benefited the woman she hated – Nanta. 'Why don't you fill a basket with some of this shellfish,' Marcella suggested to her friend one day. 'I'm gathering far too much. Stick a price on a card and leave the basket nearby while you collect the stones. People on a day's outing from Derry are desperate for it.'

'What if the auld wimin comes along and finds ye pickin' on the shore for me?'

'Don't worry, she says the sea air gives her rheumatism.'

'Ga!'

Marcella squatted beside Nanta's basket and ran her hand erratically through the stones. 'Have you got coral, jasper, opal and cornelian in here?'

Nanta frowned. 'What ails 'ee today, childeen?'

'Nothing.' That was not true; she was wondering with a feeling of sadness and a little excitement if her life was about to change dramatically.

'Ye've got the air of a hang-dog.'

Marcella threw back her head and gave a peal of

laughter. 'I don't think you mean what the English dictionary says it means.'

'We gave the English our words; it is our right to use them as we see fit.'

This surprised Marcella, for the English nun at school had told them one day that many Irish words and expressions had enriched the English language. How could Nanta know a thing like that? 'Would you believe it, Nanta, that old aunt of Kiaran Gilroy's at Slievan is supposed to be wife-hunting for him. Imagine – at his age!'

'Aye, some of the gentry are supposed to be forespeakers.'

'Biddy in the brae says she's anxious to keep the family tree growing – blue-blooded of course, with money to strengthen it. There's going to be a big party for his sixteenth birthday.'

'Perhaps ye'll be asked?'

'What a hope! Only the Cream of the County get into Slievan.'

'English Cream. Settlers,' the gypsy said harshly. 'God's ill-luck on them and theirs.'

That again surprised Marcella, for Nanta rarely expressed her feelings in this way. Her life was completely satisfying, she had told the girl one day. The small skill in using herbs to cure her people's ailments and the craft work that brought in money, gave great contentment to her life.

'Anyway, Nanta, I've got nothing to wear to a party even if such an impossible thing were to come about.' Marcella was beginning to feel very clumsy with her increase in height, and very unsure of herself. How much worse she might have been if Nanta had not taken her in hand. She washed her long black hair in rainwater, combed it dry and raved about its beautiful texture; she flattered her fair skin and odd-coloured eyes, small bones and even the big feet.

'Wish I had fair hair and lovely clothes like the Gilroy crowd, Nanta. Sunday Mass is like a fashion parade. I'm sure clothes would give me confidence.'

'Ga! Milk and water skitters,' Nanta said contemptuously. 'You wait, I'll make you a frock. Don't let the auld wimin see it.'

Leaving a hefty supply of winkles and barnacles for Nanta's stall as she called it, Marcella stowed her own bag in a hiding place and climbed over the rocks, stopping now and then to study the inhabitants of the rock pools which were like natural aquariums. She looked back across the shore to where her friend was bending gracefully, her slender brown fingers poking away among the stones to scoop another treasure into her bag. Fewer people came to that part of the shore, preferring the long stretch of golden sand, sheltered by tall rocks which gave bathers privacy for undressing. August was a busy month on the Iniscad shore because the Derry shirt factories had their annual holiday.

A freshwater pool, nestling in a crust of sharp-edged rocks fringed with leathery fronds of wrack, lay sparkling bright under a probing finger of sunlight. Marcella stretched out on her stomach and gazed into its depths. Miracles occurred here, it was said; the spring was blessed by St Morallagh himself and was reputed to cure people's ailments. Marcella remembered the day when Biddy in the brae went right into the pool to make sure of the cure, and her brothers had an awful job getting her out again. She declared that the rheumatism in her legs was completely cured. Shock, Mama had said. And wasn't she the lucky one not to be in crutches for the rest of her life!

Marcella leaned right over, holding firmly to the strong ropes of wrack. Her shadow darkened the water, making her reflection dance uncertainly like an uneasy spirit. A light wind stirred the surface and below, the will-o'-the wisp image darted to and fro. That's me, she thought, feeling an inexplicable sadness. Not sure of anything; wanting to get away from Aunt Sarah, yet dreading the thought of school in Derry and meeting so many strange people.

On the following week the dress Nanta had promised was ready, apart from the hem. 'Slip it on, lovey, an' I'll pin it up.' When that was done, Nanta said, 'We'll sit side by side and sew the hem. The skirt is wide enough to allow us the freedom.' After a while Marcella, who did not like sewing, began to feel bored.

'Nanta, do you ever wonder about your forefathers who came here during the famine?'

'They live in me.'

Unsure what she meant by that, Marcella tried again, not expecting much response. Her friend had a strange reserve regarding people. She talked about her work and the beauty of other parts of the country, yet she rarely mentioned her husband, who seemed to be away most of the time selling their wares, or the people in the camp. 'Nanta, you told me once that they came from near Cavan. Why did they come so far north at the time of famine?'

'I'll tell ye the story, child, as it was tole to me by the Old One who died last year. My family came, as some of the others did, from a little hamlet that was stricken by the famine. I say my family, but I mean on the side of the woman. My blood is mingled wi' that of the true Romany, on the side of the man.'

Trying to understand, Marcella stopped sewing and frowned thoughtfully.

'Hasten wi' yer needle child, as I tell the tale,' she was rebuked. 'The Donahues, for that was their name, had just a wee bit of land to live on, like most people. The cereal crops that they grew had to be sold to pay the landlord his rent. The family survived on a patch of potatoes. Then the curse of the Almighty fell on the land.' Marcella winced. She had always heard that the English were to blame for the famine. 'In our little hamlet people died daily. Donahue saw a terrible sight one day.' She paused.

'What was it, Nanta?'

'A dog wi' what looked like the arm of a child in its mouth.'

'Oh God –'

'And he decided to get away while the wife and weans had the strength to walk. Four other families went with him. Some had to be buried on the way. Ach, astoir, things were bad for them, not knowin' the way of the roads and very scarce were the green plants that might have nourished them. Indeed, the land was scalped in the great hunger. A blade of grass was nourishment to be cherished.'

Both needles were idle now as Nanta's large eyes went down through the years, searching time for her forefathers as they staggered along the roads.

'Well, they made it,' Marcella coaxed her on.

'Aye, eventually. They went into a woods to find somethin' to eat and rest themselves for the night. A long way in they went, for there was a smell in the air that they had not experienced in a long time.'

'Thank God!' Marcella wanted the awful story to have a happy ending.

'They came on a small group of caravans, rich to look at and in the contents of the pots hanging over the fire. Donahue and the others stumbled on their feet. It was the smell of food, you see; it took away the power from their legs. Donahue's eldest daughter was sixteen and a rare beauty. Proud, and still on her feet, she apologized for the intrusion and begged for a little nourishment. The Old One tole me that the son of the elder of the gypsy camp took wan look at her and it was love at first sight. They were well received and allowed to sleep in the shelter of the caravans that night.'

'And?' One of *those* stories, Marcella thought cynically – a gypsy wedding and they all lived happily ever after.

'The gypsies advised my people to make for Inishowen because the shores were rich in seafood. Provisions were provided for the journey and that is how they came to this place.'

'How did those gypsies have so much when the rest of the country was starving?' she asked, irritated.

'Money they had. The famine hit hardest those who had to live off a potato patch. The gypsies had all their crafts to sell which provided them with gold. They had the freedom of the roads wi' no landlord demanding his rent. Freedom and dignity an' beholding to no wan. Ah, childeen, the day is drawing in, let's hasten wi' the sewin' and the rest of the story. To cut it short, Donahue had to part wi' his lovely daughter. Willin' she was, so there were no hard words. The son of the camp put gold on her finger and around her neck and promised they would seek them out one day.' Nanta paused again. 'Time passed. It was ill-doin' that the son quarrelled wi' his elder but a blessing for the Donahues. The pair set out one day and found this place. And child that's how it was. I am of the blood of that pair and so is Nial. His foolish mother married a man o' the roads; that blood did a lot a'harm. Ah well . . . , Here's yer frock. Wear it well. Come, I'll see ye through the woods.'

As it was Sarah's sodality night at the church, Marcella decided to go down to her room and get a better view of Nanta's frock in the long mirror. It was flaming red with black spots, full-skirted and far too long – a dress for a gypsy. She felt guilty about being so critical. The stiff taffeta seemed to have a life of its own and gave little whines as though tormented by every movement of her body. When she opened the bedroom door, Sarah was standing by her bed dressed in a Franciscan nun's habit. For an awful moment Marcella thought it was a ghost because her aunt's face was lost inside the coif. She did not realize that people belonging to the Third Order could wear a nun's habit at home.

Startled, they stared at each other then Sarah screamed in fright, 'What's that you're wearing?' She grabbed at the material. 'Take that gypsy rag off you this minute!' The coarse cloth of the habit's wide sleeves flapped around Marcella's face, smelling like a room where the dead were laid out. Her aunt's anger was frightening; worse was her look of fear.

'It's only fancy-dress, Aunt,' she lied.

'And are the earrings fancy-dress too?' she screamed, stamping her foot. 'You're branded, that gypsy woman has marked you for life.'

Brian rushed into the room, took one astonished look at the pair of them and went for the brandy bottle. Sarah, clutching the bedpost, made a holy face before drinking a glassful, as if asking God to forgive her for breaking the pledge she had taken at her Confirmation.

In the morning post an invitation arrived for Brian to attend the party at Slievan. Sarah was so delighted with the honour that she actually forgot about Marcella's gypsy dress and went to pick ivy leaves to make a liquid for cleaning Brian's navy serge suit. Marcella watched all the preparations with a heavy heart. Not that she expected to be asked. Brian was an exception and the only local boy to receive an invitation.

'Any chance of me getting a job to help in the kitchen for the party?' she asked Biddy in the brae.

'Ach, don' be talkin'! There's that many extras already they'll be banging into wan another. Half the countryside came lookin' for a job so that they can fill their pockets from the Gilroy larder,' she added wickedly.

'Is it true that Miss Gilroy is seriously looking for a wife for Kiaran?'

'As God's m'judge. Sure she says the local men only cross the midden to pick their wives.'

'I thought he was going to be a priest?'

'I got a whid o' that rumour too. Divil a priest he'll make. He's got his eyes on the girls. I think one's caught his fancy.'

'I see,' Marcella said flatly.

After Brian left the house for Kiaran Gilroy's party, Sarah went to church for Benediction. Feeling restless and on a sudden impulse, Marcella decided to go and see what was going on at Slievan. If she couldn't get in with the Cream of the County, nor wash their dirty dishes, she would do the only thing left, stand on the outside and look in.

Dusk was falling when she reached the lodge gates. Slipping behind some veronica bushes, she crawled along the dew-drenched grass until she was hidden among the shrubs in the drive. The throbbing sadness of a Viennese waltz gave her a yearning feeling of loneliness. The wet hem of her dress clung uncomfortably to her bare legs as she climbed up the rough stone wall to look in one of the wide bay windows. Resting her arms on the ledge she gazed into a crowded room. Lovely girls danced around in delicate-coloured silks and taffetas. Pale skitters, maybe, but clothes make such a difference, she thought enviously. Brian, in his terrible ivy-cleaned suit, looked like a country bumpkin compared to the other young men. He was pushing a girl around like a ploughman tilling crops.

When the dance ended Kiaran, rubbing a handkerchief across his forehead, came into the alcove by the bay window. He looked tall and handsome in a light-coloured suit. As he battled with his unruly hair, Marcella gazed at his back view and felt it was worth all the agony of the stone cutting into her skin. A sudden sharp pull at her wrist sent fear racing through her. Long fingers began to tug aggressively at her ankle. She turned and looked into Nial's black eyes which seemed, in the moonlight, cunning and vicious. Her heart nearly stopped with fright because she realized she was at his mercy.

'Come wi' me,' he urged.

Lifting one arm off the ledge, she brought it back to swipe at the gypsy's face. The movement was too fast, and her hand crashed into the window pane. Kiaran swung round and saw her before she could drop to the ground. Nial tried to pull her into the shrubbery. She tore at his face and hair as they struggled furiously. It was the knife in his pocket that he always carried, which spurred her on to defend herself. The cruel knife that he used to skin rabbits terrified her. Kiaran would not come out, of course. She was just one of the locals peeping in at the window. If only she could scream but her throat was tight with fear.

Then Kiaran came running out of the front door, jumped the four steps and sped across the gravel. Nial shot into the undergrowth. Fear of the gypsy and the humiliation of being caught peeping in the Slievan windows made Marcella stand there, trembling uncontrollably.

'Marcella,' Kiaran said incredulously. 'It was you! What are you doing here?' Then he added quickly, 'You should have been at the party, too, with Brian.' He made it sound as though her absence was a mistake. 'There's no reason why you shouldn't come in now. Come along, we haven't had supper yet.'

She thought briefly of his father, who used to glance away when they met accidentally. Then, as though time was diminishing his memory, he no longer seemed to remember that she was the girl who had made the childish outburst of accusation when his wife was killed.

'No,' she stammered, 'I couldn't possibly do that. I'm not dressed.'

Moving his hand across her back he laughed. 'Yes, you are.'

Marcella thought of her worn-out cotton dress, its irregular hem hitched up at the side with a safety pin, and the old plimsolls with the holes in the toes. The 'pale skitters' would throw up their hands in horror and Miss Gilroy would send for Guard O'Neill.

'You're trembling. Something has frightened you. Was it that gypsy?'

'Yes.'

'You shouldn't be running around —'

'I don't usually,' she answered quickly. 'I was out for a walk and heard the music.' The pathetic lie lay between them in silence. 'Don't tell Brian, will you? He would kill me for coming here.'

He laughed. 'You're a wild one, aren't you?'

'I suppose I must be,' she said slowly, and immediately felt a burning shame about the way she was dressed and had behaved. What a despicable thing to do, spying through the window because she was envious of the people who had been invited to his party. 'I must go home.' There was an edge of bitterness in her voice.

'If you won't come in, I'm taking you home.'

'You'll miss the party.'

'Look, if you want to change your dress when we get to River House, I'll wait and bring you back again.'

Change to what? A black spotted dress made from one of the faded rolls of material lying in Boyle's window, priced five shillings a yard?

'I don't want to come back,' she said shortly. 'You may as well know I've got nothing to wear. My aunt thinks clothes are a vanity and that's a sin. My best dress is for Mass on Sunday and I'm ashamed to be seen in it.'

'Why are you ashamed?' he asked gently. Because, she thought with envy, I've got to sit in the congregation with your fine relations. When she did not reply, he went on, 'Thank goodness my mother left me some money. At least I don't have to beg from my aunt every time I want something. She'd mince the meatbones and serve them up if it were possible. No wonder we can't keep a cook.'

'We're a pair of orphans, God help us.'

Laughing, he led her across the yard to get his bicycle. In the barn, where it was kept, he bent down to point out something of interest about the machine. As he did so, his hair became caught in the wheel.

'Don't pull.' She knelt beside him. He wrenched his head away impatiently. 'That must have hurt.' Marcella touched the back of his neck lightly while her face remained severe at his foolishness. 'I could have eased it away.' He raised his head slowly and looked searchingly at her. She caught his gaze and knew it was different from the teasing, troubled look of before. Tossing back her hair she turned towards the shaft of moonlight streaming through the door. He put out his hand and touched the earrings.

'You look older.' There was quietness in his voice.

'Kiaran, inside me I am old. I was young, then the death . . . '

'I know.' He looked at the high cheekbones, wide dark eyes, and the perfectly shaped mouth. She was aware that a slender thread of feeling was growing between them, and blessed the moonlight for resting kindly on her tatty clothes. He drew her close. The bicycle got in the way. 'There's a scent of wild flowers and herbs on your hair.' The handlebar was digging into her ribs but she suffered it gladly to feel his touch.

'I'm being sent away to school, to become a weekly boarder in Derry.'

'That will be the making of you,' he teased.

'That'll be the end of me. At least I'll escape from my aunt.' She thought of Sarah's triumphant expression every time tabs were sewn on her school clothes, a task she was quite capable of doing herself.

'Don't forget me,' he said lightly.

Marcella laid her head against his shoulder and thought sadly, how could she? He gently bunched her hair, drew back her head and kissed her. In those few minutes, as their lips touched, she felt as though her childhood was being finally cast aside. She was in love. For all the difference that would make with the landed gentry . . . he might as well have become a poker-faced Jesuit. A 'ticker tape' began to snap through her conscience, tapping out its brief little messages of catechetical warning as his lips pressed down on hers. 'Occasion of sin'. Was this joy, sin? Father McGill began to interfere too. 'Dark lonely places . . . *temptation.*'

When Kiaran moved his head, she said innocently, killing his impetuous love-making: 'Kiaran, do you ever wish you were a Protestant? They must feel so free, not to be bothered about sin the way we Catholics are.'

'What?' He began to laugh. 'You're a scandalous girl!'

Sharp footsteps coming towards the barn drew them apart. His aunt's tall frame filled the doorway.

'Kiaran, are you there? How frightfully rude of you to go away and leave your guests.' She glared at Marcella. 'Who is that girl?'

'It's Marcella Adams. Brian's sister.' He sounded nervous.

'What is she doing here?'

'Well,' he paused. 'I went out for a breath of fresh air and found her at the lodge gates trying to pump her bicycle. It's punctured so I've offered to give her a lift home.'

'You can't possibly go away like that,' the woman said irritably.

The nervousness left Kiaran's voice. 'Marcella has to get home safely and I'm taking her.' He turned the machine and began to wheel it outside. Marcella could feel the woman's penetrating eyes glaring at her. 'Jump on quickly,' he whispered, 'before all hell breaks loose.'

'Will you get into a row?' she asked, giggling.

'Not as big a one as you, if your aunt catches you out.'

She wished they could cycle far away through the night. It was a calm evening filled with the scent of roses and that special smell of rich grass and earth that only a person brought up in the country can distinguish from the thousand other laced perfumes pouring from the hedgerows. The sea looked like a sheet of corrugated iron and the island, caught in the floodlight of the moon, was spectral.

'Look at the island, Kiaran. It's stretching its arms up to the moon, pleading to be noticed. What about rowing out there now? Ned's boat is down on the shore.' She was only half-joking.

'We'll wait for the spring, that's the best time for the island, when it's beginning to stir with life.'

'Next spring you'll forget.'

'I won't forget,' he said firmly and she believed him.

Chapter 14

On the Sunday before she started school in Derry, Marcella went to say goodbye to Nanta. The gypsies were about to leave for the south and would not return until the spring. During the long winter months high winds raked through Briar Meadow, beating the trees mercilessly until their skeletal shapes seemed to huddle together like ghosts of the famine victims who had sought shelter in this place.

'Yer eyes are sparklin', my love. Have ye seen that fella in the big house?' Nanta asked, to Marcella's surprise.

'Don't call him that, Nanta.' She smiled. 'He's a . . . Aeneas.'

Bewildered, her friend enquired: 'For the love of God, who's he? In the naked pelt every fella is the same.'

Marcella shut her eyes to the coarse words. The feeling that sprang to life that night in the barn was pure and could not be associated in any way with naked males. Her 'canonization' by Sister Joseph forbade such impure thoughts. They were a matter for the Confessional. She sweated at the thought of the ordeal, and could not help wondering if the sin was not multiplied by revealing such 'low behaviour'. Surely it would soil the ears of the priest by baring her soul in the hope of cleansing it?

The bus from Iniscad to Derry was very late because a cow in calf had slipped in the middle of the road. For a while Marcella thought the calving was going to take place before her very eyes. At last they reached Derry. Late, she dashed through the impressive entrance of the Mount Academy and down a corridor to the headmistress's office, where she had been on a previous visit with her father. At the corner she crashed into a girl carrying a pile of books. Embarrassed, she made a clumsy effort to help pick them up.

'Relax. What's the hurry?' Prisca McDaid said, laughing. 'You're new, aren't you?' Prisca had an immediate feeling of sympathy for this bewildered-looking girl.

'Yes, I am.'

'What's your name?'

Marcella told her. 'Mine's Prisca McDaid.' She rolled her eyes. 'I'm supposed to be bright. A year ahead of everyone else.' Her expression was full of mischief which made Marcella aware she was trying to put her at ease. The girl, who seemed so friendly and vivacious, was much shorter than herself but obviously older, because she wore the senior student's tunic, which was a harsh shade of burgundy, of indefinite design. Juniors wore a pleated skirt. Her hair, cut short with a deep fringe, was the same colour as her eyes — a sort of nut-brown.

While they were talking, a woman wearing thick-rimmed glasses flew past. 'Good morning, Miss Deary.'

'Good morning, Prisca.'

'That one teaches English,' Prisca whispered. 'I keep in with her because she gets me free uniform and things.' Marcella's eyes widened in surprise. 'I'm one of the poor, dear. A scholarship landed me here.'

'Well, I'm not very well off either.'

'You must be joking. I see you're wearing a boarder's pin. Are you a wealthy farmer's daughter?'

'No, indeed. I come from Iniscad.'

'Lucky. I live in a slum in Derry. Ever seen one?'

The question embarrassed Marcella. She shook her head.

'The Catholics are packed tight in one corner of Derry and the Protestants less uncomfortably in the other. What are you?'

'Catholic.' As she spoke, Marcella remembered her aunt's warning not to discuss religion because the Mount Academy was not a Catholic school and religion could be an awkward topic in Derry. She was soon to discover that

Prisca McDaid's thoughts were seldom far from the subject. And in a manner she had not experienced before, religion and politics seemed to be synonymous. 'I'm going to the headmistress's office.'

'It's the last door down there. See you later.'

She's only saying that, Marcella thought. Why should a senior girl be bothered with the likes of me?

The next student approaching Prisca moved with the eagerness and anxiety of someone trying to catch a last bus home. 'It *is* you,' Lisa Schenber said.

'Oh, hello, Lisa. Have you settled in all right?'

'I am in. I miss my own room.'

'Yes, there are a few disadvantages here,' Prisca said evenly.

'I get to know people though,' Lisa added quickly, detecting a critical note in the other's voice. In spite of her determination to make friends with Prisca McDaid, Lisa complained pettishly, 'I hate this uniform. It makes me so . . . '

God bless the mark, Prisca thought with sympathy, it makes her look like a mediocre actress who has not the talent to adapt to the character she's playing. The badly designed uniform fitted uneasily on the girl's figure, and the flat-heeled shoes thickened her ankles.

'Don't worry, Lisa, we all hate the uniform and you'll be off at the weekends.'

'Ach so — '

'Look, I've got a job to do for the French mistress. I'll keep an eye open for you later.' Prisca went on down the long beige-coloured corridor where the photographs of Old Girls hung. Those who had achieved distinction in the war were given places of honour. One, a Wren, had actually been responsible for catching an important German spy whom she had met at a hotel in Buncrana. Wish I'd been around then, Prisca thought fervently. I would have done a deal with that German if it meant clearing our town of English uniforms. Of course, there had been the uprising planned by the Republican Army during 1943, but before it got off the ground an informer had told the police. Prisca's father and others had to slip quietly over the border where they remained for a very long time. Where had all this fervour gone to, she wondered. Now her father laughed about those days, as though it were all part of growing up, forgetting the brave and wonderful Irishmen who had died for their country.

After lunch, Marcella was delighted when she found Prisca McDaid waiting for her with a foreign girl called Lisa. Walking in the centre, Prisca linked arms and led them towards the River Foyle.

'Come and see around,' she suggested.

On the way, they passed a girl sitting near the river manicuring her nails. She looked keenly at Marcella, then at Lisa, but ignored their companion.

'Flamin' Prod,' Prisca said. 'That fat lump's father owns the shirt factory where my mother works. Mammy sits for hours at a damn machine stitching the tails of men's shirts for a few lousy bob. That's the situation in Derry. The Protestants are the top dogs and the Catholics are the serfs.' Prisca's voice was harsh. 'One day it will change,' she said menacingly. 'It's got to. Did you know that big businessmen like old Fatty's father can get up to forty votes and people who haven't got a roof over their heads can't vote at all?'

Marcella told her that she did not understand about gerrymandering in Ulster, and in case her new friend began to go into a lengthy explanation, she asked quickly: 'Why does your mother work?'

'Why? Because there's eight of us and my granny. Someone's got to earn money.'

'Your father?'

'God's truth, you've no idea what it's like in Derry. He can't find anything to do.'

'Didn't he work at one time?'

'He used to have a drapery shop. It was doing well until the big stores came and killed the business.'

'Couldn't he find a job in one of them?'

'Those kind of shops bring their own trained managers from England. The staff are all young girls.'

'There are other shops in Derry. I've seen older men working in them.'

'Most of them are owned by Prods. Do you know what they asked when he went after a job? What school did he go to. When he said Saint Columba's, that did it. God almighty, you'd think he was trying to get a job in Stormont instead of a bloody Orangeman's shop.'

Over Prisca's head, Lisa glanced at Marcella, raised her eyes dramatically and shrugged. The two girls smiled and looked closely at each other. Marcella felt her heart gladden. She had made not just one friend on her first day at the new school, but two. Inevitably, Lisa, Prisca and Marcella kept together, and apart from the others. Their friendship gave Marcella a feeling of warmth and security, though she often became fed-up with their political diatribes.

'Old Sweinhünd Itler,' Lisa would say, making a savage cut with her finger across her throat. 'He tried to throw Momma and Poppa into concentration camps, so they had to get away.'

'And how did you get all your money, for goodness sake?' Prisca asked cheekily.

'Ach, Poppa and Momma work and work. He start in one little room, one little shop, then one little factory and . . . ' She threw her arms out expressively to convey how well they were doing now.

Marcella couldn't help comparing Prisca's background with the Jewess's. One man had inherited a shop and let it drift away; the other had started from nothing and was now a wealthy man. The two races of people had the same religious fervour but when it came to business, nothing in common.

On her way home from school one Friday afternoon, Lisa Schenber saw Dominic McDaid crossing the Guildhall Square. She tried to reach Shipquay Gate and hide, as she couldn't bear to be seen wearing her terrible school uniform, but a car raced out of Foyle Street, compelling Dominic to leap across the road and land beside her.

At that moment Billy the Man drew up smartly. 'Give ye a lift anywhere, miss?'

'No, no,' she said impatiently, her confusion increasing.

Billy drew his head back in the window. That little goldrush was over now the girl had got herself into that straitjacket. She was as bad as everyone else in Derry, wearing the pavements out or taking a bus.

Dominic's surprise at Lisa's ungainly appearance equalled her embarrassment. Whereas the uniform looked all right on his sister, it made Lisa Schenber look ridiculous. He was about to make a quick greeting and hurry on when something in her expression stirred his pity. He could see that the freakish gear was really demoralizing her.

'I've just been across to the Guildhall,' he told her. 'The feis is on at the moment.'

'The feis?'

'Irish festival. My sister Maeve's playing the piano.'

'She is very talented. I heard with amazement her music when I called at your home. Prisca told me she has a huge repertoire of memorized classical pieces.'

'Yes, she's an incredible youngster,' Dominic agreed.

'Lisa, my dear,' Mr Schenber came through the gate from Shipquay Street with a quick little trot as though there was not a moment to spare. 'Ach . . . and a friend.' There was a perceptible sharpness in the last three words.

'Poppa,' Lisa said quickly, 'this is my friend Prisca's brother, Dominic McDaid.'

Mr Schenber pushed his black wide-brimmed hat off his forehead. The small eyes behind the thick-rimmed glasses flashed over Dominic. 'Ach, so. And what work do you do, young man?'

'I'm at college,' Dominic said shortly, resenting the question.

'Ach . . . so.' With a movement that took Dominic by surprise, he felt his arm being gripped. 'We will have a little refreshment.'

'I'm afraid — '

'Poppa, nein!' Lisa spat out the words in a fury. Could

145

her stupid father not see Dominic's reluctance?

Crouched over the wheel of his car with a miserable expression on his face, Billy the Man gnawed at his knuckles. If business didn't buck up soon he'd be as hungry as his ancestors who had died behind those walls there. A little flurry of footsteps made him turn his head. He wiped his bulbous nose with the window cloth, straightened his tie and, shooting out of the car, bowed obsequiously to Mr Schenber.

'Sir, may I be of assistance?'

'Ja. Please, a good restaurant,' the Jew said, and hustled the other two into the car.

Sullenly, Lisa took the seat beside her father. Furious about the way he had been manoeuvred, Dominic sat beside Billy.

'There's a hotel over there,' Dominic muttered to him.

'Have a heart, son. I need the fare.' Billy whistled away as he swung the big old-fashioned car out into the stream of traffic. 'Somefin' better for his lordship, don' ye think?' he said out of the side of his mouth.

When the three of them were settled in the select little restaurant which Dominic had not known existed, he began to find himself relaxing before the lavishness of the food on the table. A three-tier cakestand held a large selection of rich cakes. There were scones, cream and strawberry jam and minute fingers of toast dripping with butter, 'straight from the churn' as his mother would say, and which she could not afford to buy.

The scowl eased from his face and he said to Mr Schenber, 'This is a pleasant place.'

Lisa relaxed too and tried to ignore the cakes which she loved, and nibbled a finger of toast. Dominic followed the movement of her hands as the white soft fingers touched and lingered on the tea service. 'Pour, Liebe,' her father said, when the waitress brought the slices of lemon he had requested.

A tremor of feeling rose unbidden deep inside Dominic. He glanced at the full lips and followed the movement of her hand again when she jerked the tie loose on her neck and opened the top button of her blouse. He tried not to look at her neck and how the material was drawn tightly across her breasts when she threw back her head and took a deep breath. Christ, I'm sunk, he thought and moved uneasily on his chair.

All the time, Mr Schenber kept talking about the great plans he had for Derry. Dominic tried to concentrate. A hotel on the banks of the Foyle, down towards Letterkenny Road, with the hills above. A place where people could relax and dine out in the evenings. Music, dancing.

The last words brought Dominic back to earth. 'Mr Schenber,' he said hurriedly, 'people living in Derry cannot afford that type of entertainment. This is a poor place, you know. Well, I'm speaking for the Catholic population anyway. Maybe the Protestants – '

'Why do we have to speak of Catholics and Protestants as if it were a colour segregation? Always I'm hearing of it,' the Jew said impatiently. 'You are all white. I have yet to see a black face in this town.'

'It's the situation in Northern Ireland, sir. You are of the Jewish faith and lived at one time in Germany. That made problems, didn't it . . . I mean the war.'

The expression on the other's face changed and hardened. Oh God, Dominic thought, I shouldn't have said that. He need not have worried. Mr Schenber was not going to allow himself to be sidetracked. He had a purpose in sitting here, drinking this appalling black tea of the Irish. 'Young man . . . ' he tapped Dominic's arm briskly. 'I have an offer to make to you. For my business, my shop, I want the right kind of men in the managerial area. If you have great brains like your sister, that Lisa tells me about, I will be happy to offer you a position when you finish college.'

What a bloody nerve, Dominic thought. Lisa saw the expression on his face and said quickly, 'Poppa, Dominic's going to be a doctor.'

'A doctor?' Schenber's eyes flew open. 'Ach so.' His head moved to and fro, as if he had heard of a bereavement. 'It is a great disappointment. I like the look of you, young man.'

So that's why I was hustled off to take tea. 'Chip on your shoulder,' he could hear Prisca's voice saying in his ear. 'Schenber isn't talking down to you. He just goes after what he wants without wasting time.' Suddenly a thought occurred to Dominic.

'Mr Schenber, my father is unemployed at the moment. Would you consider him for the job? He has all the necessary experience and –' this with a touch of sarcasm – 'a college education.'

'Experience, education . . . mmm,' Schenber muttered to himself. 'That is good. Most certainly I will consider him. Here,' he reached in his pocket for a business card. 'Please give this to your parent and ask him to contact me.'

Outside, Billy the Man was waiting – unrequested. 'Sure, it's no inconvenience at all, mister,' he came out with at the Jew's look of surprise. 'Get in there and I'll have ye home at the wink of an eye. And while we have this moment of leisure, mister . . . ' he produced a card from his pocket. 'That's my address. If it's more convenient for ye, sure I can be at your service all the time. Ye'll be needin' someone to run ye about now, won't ye?'

Dominic and Lisa looked at each other over the heads of the two short, stockily-built men and smiled. Maybe, Dominic thought, Schenber had met his match. Orange Billy was a fly one!

Back in Brawn Street, he found his mother and father sitting out in the small back yard. The large mangle, draped with a covering of brightly coloured oilcloth, looked festive against the whitewashed wall. His mother's pride and joy was the branch of a rosebush that crept over the wall each summer from the Kennys' yard. The roses growing on it were a pale cream with a delicate fragrance. Mrs McDaid felt that the branch was like an elegantly dressed stranger who had inadvertently strayed into this poor place.

'I'd love to know how that rose exists in the Kennys' yard,' she said thoughtfully. 'Herself would put a bunch of nettles in a vase for all that she knows or cares about things that grow. Poor soul, she's spent every day of her life in the Bogside. Up Northland Road in the Misses Thorns' house, where I do a wee job, they've got a garden full of roses growing all over the walls. More than anything, I'd like to live in a house like that.'

'One day,' her husband announced confidently, 'we'll manage it.'

Dominic gave a derisive laugh. His father looked away, unable to bear the enmity that his elder son showed towards him.

'Father, there's something I want to tell you; it's about a job.'

'Jobs seem to be flying around today,' Nora McDaid said gaily, putting a hand on her husband's knee. 'Tell him, Phelim, your good news.'

'I've just been offered a job at the convent. Sister Francis sent for me. I'm going to take the singing and music classes three times a week. The other man is retiring.'

'Convent? The nuns will pay nothing. You'd be better on the dole. Father, I'm talking about a real job.' He told him about Mr Schenber's offer.

'Work in the shop where I grew up?' Phelim McDaid said in dismay.

'I know you disliked the place but,' Dominic added realistically, 'with such a large family can you afford to be choosy?'

'Son!' Mrs McDaid said sharply. 'Don't speak to your father like that. For the first time he's got a chance to do what he really enjoys, teaching music.'

'And you, Mother, will have to go on working in the shirt factory to make ends meet.'

'Daddy, Dom's right,' Prisca said from the scullery door. 'Mr Schenber has got big ideas. He's really going to make things move in this town.'

Phelim McDaid looked at his two children and felt defeated. With unaccustomed bitterness in his voice, he said, 'I daresay you're right. The Jews never fail in business. Where does this man live?'

Dominic handed him Schenber's business card. 'I'll go

with you, if you like,' he offered.

'I think I can manage that on my own,' his father replied evenly. 'Why don't you cut along, son, and get down to your studies and make sure the end results achieve something worthwhile.'

Dominic brushed past Prisca. She followed him into the kitchen. 'You asked for that,' she hissed. 'Why couldn't you leave well alone? Go with him . . . as if he were a wee boy. Christ! You need your head examined. You know he's always been dreaming about getting that job at the school.'

'Dreaming? That's an occupational hazard with our father. People in this country have starved and died over their foolish dreams.'

Chapter 15

The months that Marcella had been attending school in Derry, enjoying the company of her friends, made it even more difficult than before to bear the long Easter holidays in the company of her aunt. Cold wet winds swept in from the sea and beat savagely around the coast; there were daily warnings of gale-force winds. Walking down the road one day when the wind had settled a bit, she looked out at the island, now cold, remote and hooded with a coil of mist. She recalled the promise Kiaran Gilroy had made last summer about visiting the island. Last summer . . . what a long time away it seemed now. She had been kissed for the first time and imagined a romance with, as Nanta put it, the fella from the big house. Apparently the Gilroys were in the south of France. Only a few servants remained at Slievan, where a spiral of smoke fought its way out of the kitchen chimney.

'Cella,' Prisca greeted her on the first day back at the Mount Academy, 'everyone in our house is dying to meet you. My mother says you're welcome to come and stay with us for a weekend soon.'

If only she'd asked her father's permission and made her plans, Marcella thought afterwards, but she was so excited by Prisca's invitation that she blurted it out on Friday at tea-time.

'You'd better bring your friend here first,' her aunt said. 'Hadn't she, Conor? Don't want her getting mixed up with the wrong sort of people in Derry.'

'Wrong sort? I don't know what you mean. Prisca's a Catholic.'

'Where does your friend live?' Conor asked.

'In the Bogside.'

'Bogside? What part?'

'Brawn Street.'

The name startled Conor. He wanted to forget about Brawn Street and Peggy O'Donovan.

'She's a scholarship girl.'

'Clever,' Brian remarked.

'Must be,' Conor said thoughtfully, 'to get into a school like that.'

Sarah Adams was not interested in clever girls, only nice ones. 'What's Brawn Street like?' she asked. 'I only know the main street in Derry.'

Brian and Conor looked at Marcella hesitantly. In their mind's eye they were seeing the poor shabby place huddled below the city walls where pregnant women, despondent and prematurely aged, stood around doorways or sat on the steps. And where men leaned against corners, wrapped in lethargy from lack of work.

'Is it a nice respectable street?' Sarah insisted.

'Oh, for heaven's sake,' Marcella retorted, jumping up from the table. 'I'll bring her here next weekend if that's the way you want it.'

Prisca was in Bridge House for only a short time before she had captivated all three of them, Brian most of all. She knew all about Marcella's awkward aunt and went to endless trouble to charm her. Brian and Conor were delighted with the girl's knowledge and witty remarks. There was something indescribably lovable about Prisca, Marcella thought. Though she was tough and sharp-tongued, she radiated happiness and good humour most of the time. Her delight in the countryside moved them all.

'To live so near the sea,' she cried, 'you're in heaven!'

Her friend did not rhapsodize about anything. She simply said the word 'heaven' to express happiness and perfection.

Before lunch the three of them went for a walk along the shore. It was a bright warm day with long green waves rolling in from the Atlantic. Brian pointed in the distance to Castle Fort.

'Prisca, away over there is where Ossian, son of Finn McCool, is supposed to be buried.'

'Wasn't he said to be the greatest poet of pagan times?'

'I wonder.' They walked on, absorbed in their conversation, forgetting all about Marcella. She had been looking forward to spending this weekend on her own with Prisca. The threesome at school was a bit trying at times, especially when Prisca went ranting on about politics; or when Lisa threw a bad mood. Worse, when she kept asking silly questions about Prisca's eldest brother, Dominic.

Prisca, against her will, refused a second helping of the rich roast beef. In all her life she had never eaten such good food. The choice of blackberry and apple tart with cream or lemon meringue pie, presented a momentous problem. She wanted both and lacked the courage to say so. Would it be good manners? Brian saw her indecision and said casually, 'Prisca, you must try both. Aunt Sarah makes wonderful pastry, light as a feather. Mother used to say a chisel was necessary to tackle hers.'

Sarah flushed with pleasure. It was the first time under this roof that one of them had compared her cooking with that flighty wife of her brother's. Marcella narrowed her eyes. Why was Brian all of a sudden sucking up to old Sarah? Mama used to give a peal of laughter at her hard pastry and then they would all laugh, not caring how it tasted. When did I last hear laughter in this house, she wondered. I'm getting like old Sarah, all dried up without a sense of humour. Thank God it's only for weekends now, and if Prisca could come down occasionally . . .

'Aunt, we'll do the dishes,' Marcella suggested. 'You go and have a rest. The meal was great.' That's right, you hypocrite, pay her compliments. Sweeten her up too. And hark at Prisca asking how to make lemon meringue pie. For God's sake, any eejit knows how to make that. You can buy packets in a shop.

When the dishes were washed, Prisca took Marcella aside and whispered, 'Brian and me are going for a walk. Three's a crowd!'

Marcella sighed resignedly. Her shy brother had obviously fallen for her cheeky friend.

Prisca stole a glance at Brian as they went down through the orchard, at his heavy brown hair, grey-green eyes and firm mouth line. Everything about Marcella's brother reminded her of the photograph of Michael Collins in Eoin O'Donnell's house. Even their build was similar. She liked his quiet manner too. He touched her arm.

'Here we are. Now see if you can find it.'

Laughing, Prisca ran down the side of the boreen. 'Like hide and seek?'

'Well, I didn't hide it. It's been there for centuries. Perhaps even before the Iron Age.' He sat down on a hump of ground and chewed a piece of grass.

Excitedly Prisca prowled around trying to find the souterrain that they had been discussing earlier on, which was part of a project Brian was doing. 'Are you interested in archaeology?' she called.

'Very. Only as a hobby though. Maths and science are my subjects.'

After a while she came back. 'I give in. Come and help me.'

He stood up. They were close, searching each other's faces then looking away. Girls had always overwhelmed him. Invariably they were too tall like his sister or short and fat. Prisca McDaid was perfect. Petite. Lovely – full of life. He thought of an old song his mother used to sing, *Nut Brown Maiden*.

She turned and looked at him with an impish smile. 'Shall I try again? Am I too old to play "getting warm"?'

'You'll never be too old,' he said gallantly and to his own surprise. To hide the confusion following his impulsive words, he caught her hand. 'Come on, I'll show you.' The hardness of her skin against his surprised him. He stopped, opened his hand and looked at her slender fingers. 'What do they make you do at that school? Scrub floors?'

'I scrub the floors of number one, Brawn Street, where I live.'

'I'm sorry.' He closed his hand protectively over hers.

'Of course, Cella mentioned you were one of a large family.'

'That's right,' she said brightly. 'Come on, show me where it is. Does Cella know?'

'She does not, and I have no intention of telling her. This used to be my refuge when storms were blowing up in the house. Now I never go near the place. It was a good hide-away at a difficult time.'

Bewildered, Prisca looked over the ground where they were standing. 'There's nothing here to see. Where's the entrance?'

'It's concealed. That's the way they were made. See how the ground rises towards the old mountain track there? Right. Now come through these whinbushes ... kneel behind me. I'm going to move that big stone covered with moss. See how neatly it fits into the lip of the ground?' He took a torch from his pocket and flicked it on. They dropped down to a wide step leading to a narrow passage roofed with slabs of slate; halfway through the passage one slab projected downwards, slowing their progress. 'I think this unexpected barrier was put here to stop unwary intruders.'

'Did you say the people took refuge here when the land was invaded?'

'That's right, and probably during Penal times when the Redcoats were around. See over there? That must have been used for an altar, so we can assume the people came here for Mass.' Brian lit the candles which had been placed in bottles on a previous visit. Prisca, with growing excitement, looked around the vast chamber which was divided into sections and listened carefully as he pointed out the perfectly curved roof and perpendicular sides. 'The people who made these places must have possessed a fair amount of culture. Look at those slate-lined apertures for allowing fresh air to flow down.'

'If the people sought refuge here, Brian, isn't it likely they brought their fiddles? Perhaps that's what gave rise to rumours of fairy music and the wee folk?'

'That's probably true.' He smiled. 'You think quickly!'

'Why did you show me this place? Didn't you say no one else knows about it?'

He was silent for a moment. 'I . . . don't know. I just wanted to.'

With the candlelight enclosing them in a little world of their own, their casual, easy manner slipped away. They continued to look at each other.

'You're very beautiful,' he said awkwardly.

Astonished by the compliment and knowing she was not beautiful, her hand went out towards him. He placed the candle on the altar, took her in his arms and kissed her. Gently at first, then with increasing feeling. Recklessly she responded until he reluctantly raised his head.

'Prisca, you're the best thing that has ever happened to me,' he said slowly. 'Will you come to Iniscad again soon?'

'I don't know how I'm going to keep away,' she replied simply, not sure how she was going to handle this unexpected happiness. Prisca's heart was racing. She wanted to slip into his arms again but for the first time in her life she felt shy and aware of the growing feeling in her body.

'I wonder how long we've been down here?' Brian said. 'I'm not wearing my watch.'

'I've never owned a watch in my life.'

There was a note on the kitchen table from Marcella when they returned to the house. '*I'm cycling to Lagg. If you wish to follow, Pris, borrow Sarah's bike. It's in the shed.*'

Prisca pushed the note away. 'Brian, would you show me your room? I'd like to see the place where you work and sleep.' Suddenly this seemed important to her.

'Better not,' he said cautiously. 'Sarah might not approve.'

She smiled mischievously. 'It's opposite the one I'm sharing with Marcella, isn't it? What about if I go upstairs to get something from my bag?'

Brian wanted very much to show her his room. He wanted to have the memory of her being there handling his things. Perhaps it would seem less like a monastical hide-away, as his sister put it. Quietly they crept upstairs.

'That you, Marcella?' Sarah called out. They crept down again and out of the house, smothering their laughter.

Late on Sunday afternoon Prisca knocked on Brian's door, then opened it. 'I'm away now.'

'I won't go to the bus stop with you. I'll leave it to Cella.'

'That's all right. I'd rather say cheerio on our own.'

They looked intently at each other for a moment. Brian felt like slamming the door shut and taking her in his arms. Instead, he said, 'Perhaps we could meet one day after school if I took a late bus home?'

Her eyes fell before the eagerness on his face. 'Brian, I never have a minute during the week. Helping my mother, homework and . . . ' she hadn't meant to mention it, 'I go to an Irish group.'

He frowned. 'Irish group?'

'You know, learning the native tongue!'

'Oh well,' he said lightly, trying to hide his disappointment, 'come back again soon.'

As Prisca went downstairs, Eoin O'Donnell's words were in her ears. 'Don't get involved with the boys yet,' he had warned. 'Keep to your studies and read about the things we discuss here.' A feeling of frustration made her think, 'You're an old man, Eoin O'Donnell, and you've got your hard-faced Rosheen Quinn.

Walking to the bus stop with Prisca, Marcella considered the weekend which had not worked out quite as she had planned; nevertheless, the atmosphere in the house had been very relaxed. Aunt Sarah had repeated an invitation for her friend to come any time she felt like it. Prisca had been in a strange mood during the weekend, but as they sat on top of the hedge waiting for the Derry bus, she became her old brisk self again.

'I don't know why you're always telling me that you and Brian shut yourselves away in your rooms.'

'Sarah's moods and tempers are awful, Pris. They depress me.'

'She's an old woman, Cella. Perhaps she tries too hard to

fill your mother's place. Possibly she dislikes housework and tries to do it better than another person would?'

'You may be right. She's very religious. Perhaps it would seem sinful to her not to do everything to perfection?'

'That's typical of a lot of Catholics, the way they mix up religion with superstition and fear. At school too much significance was given to theology, doctrine and Church Latin. Better to teach people to understand the simple message of Christianity. Prod schools and churches in Ulster are the same, 'cept instead they sing chunks of the Bible. It's funny, you know,' she said meditatively.

'What is?'

'We are so divided, the Protestants and Catholics of Ulster. You'd think there were two Gods up there.'

Years later, when the shadow of civil war fell across Ulster, Marcella remembered her friend's words.

During the previous weekend, it had seemed to Marcella that Prisca had been overdoing her enthusiasm about everything in River House to please Aunt Sarah, but after one hour in Brawn Street she realized that her friend had been quite sincere. The house in the Bogside was not merely humble; the finger of poverty lay everywhere and, surprisingly, so did a prevailing smell of carbolic soap.

It was the first house in a long row of dreary, grey-faced buildings. There were five rooms: three upstairs and two down – no bathroom. The furniture in the living-room consisted of a long wooden table, a battered German piano and several chairs of various designs lining the walls. On each side of the fireplace were two cupboards where the family's clothes were kept. Most of the time Mrs McDaid's mother sat in a rocking chair in the corner, her frail fingers moving around a pair of rosary beads which hung down the side of her long black skirt.

'Yer a strapping girl, Marcella. Not a bit like Prisca,' Mrs McDaid said when she arrived.

'All brawn and no brains, that one,' Prisca laughed. 'She's going to show us up tomorrow and sit in the Guildhall Square sketching the Orangemen beating hell

158

out of their drums.'

Granny McDaid came out of her reverie and murmured, 'Ach, they niver give over about that auld Saint William.'

'King William, Granny,' Prisca shouted in her ear.

The old woman nodded her head and said with laughter lighting up the faded eyes, 'Sure the Protestants canonized him years ago.'

'Let me have your things, dear.' Mrs McDaid opened a cupboard and placed her pyjamas on a shelf marked with Prisca's name. There were ten shelves, each with a name written on it in faultless copperplate.

After a cup of tea, Marcella went with Prisca into town to the pork stores, to get something for the evening meal. When she pushed the shop door open, the man looked up and started piling handfuls of bacon scraps on the scales, the little pieces that fall off the machine when bacon is sliced, which Marcella knew were thrown away in Boyle's because no countrywoman would belittle herself to buy them. On their way back they took a short cut through the Protestant area where streets were hung with Union Jacks for the Orangemen's parade the following day.

'Look at the children,' Prisca said. 'See how well-dressed they are compared to ours in Brawn Street.'

'They're cleaner, too.'

'They can limit their numbers, that's why. A woman with a big family can't be bothered to wipe her weans' faces every minute. You know what's just occurred to me?'

'What?'

'There are only half as many children here as there are in Brawn Street. We must be rapidly outnumbering them. Think what that means when the subjected Fenians wake up and protest; then there'll be blood shed all right.'

'Don't talk such nonsense,' Marcella said crossly.

'You needn't worry, the battle will be fought here in Ulster. You'll be safe over the border in Donegal.'

'What are you talking about?'

'Hello, daughter.' An old man was sitting outside a shop with a box of flags on his knee. 'Would ye like to buy a flag?'

Prisca ran her finger through the pile. 'Red, white and blue? That's the wrong colour. Haven't you got any green, white and yellow, the flag of Ireland?'

He flushed and cursed her. Prisca laughed and, catching Marcella's hand, hurried her down the street.

'It's not funny, Prisca, taunting an old man with political bigotry.'

Marcella found the young McDaids almost indistinguishable. They all had red hair and masses of freckles like their mother. One after the other they lined up in the yard to wash their hands under the cold water tap with a piece of hard carbolic soap. Afterwards they sat patiently waiting for their tea. Chips of bacon were poured into a huge iron pan with a pile of onions and fried crisply. A slice of bread for each person was browned in hot fat, then the bacon and onions were piled on top of it. Marcella thought it was delicious washed down with mugs of strong, sweet tea.

'Your father writes well,' Mr McDaid remarked, when they were eating their meal. 'He gave me a wonderful write-up once when I was doing a bit in a play at the festival.'

'What part did you have?'

'It was a serious, political play, and I was a sergeant of the police.'

'The trouble is, Marcella,' Mrs McDaid explained after everyone stopped laughing (Dominic was frowning), 'he wasn't content doing it on the stage. He had to go to one of them streets where the Union Jacks are flying and pretend he was sent by the Head Constable. He told them to take the flags down. Imagine codding around like that.'

'You didn't?'

'I told them . . . ' Mr McDaid choked with laughter, 'that there was a lot of tension in Brawn Street and it would be better not to aggravate the Catholics.'

'Wasn't that a risk? They might have seen you acting in the play.'

'Huh, not a chance; we don't frequent each other's halls of entertainment. It was odd. Not one of the eejits questioned it, just nodded their heads and said, "Ach, them silly auld Papists".'

'And that's the sort of nonsense that starts up trouble.' Dominic pushed back his chair angrily, and left the table.

Everyone was quiet for a moment, until Mrs McDaid said quietly, 'He doesn't see a joke like the rest of us.'

Marcella had a feeling their chatter and laughter was boring him. Dominic resembled his father, with his jet-black hair and brown eyes, straight nose and well-shaped mouth.

'But,' she insisted, going back to Mr McDaid's story, 'they might have seen you in the street some time and recognized you.'

'Oh, I never go down that way. Wouldn't dare, with all them Orangemen about!' Although he said it laughingly, none of them realized that there would indeed come a time when that street would be barricaded against the Catholics, and the two sides would fight each other across those barricades with stones and petrol bombs.

When Marcella and Prisca went for a walk in the evening, the children playing in the street clutched Marcella's skirt and chanted: 'Miss, ga's a wing (give us a penny).' Prisca shoo'd them away like hens and they went after a man collecting insurance who threw a few pennies into their midst. With excited cries and loud squabbling, they grabbed the money and then rushed to the tiny sweet-shop at the corner.

As they proceeded down the street, Marcella realized that the McDaids were well-off compared to some of their neighbours. Women with untidy hair dragged themselves around lethargically, some of them burdened with pregnancy. Others had their heads covered in large curling pins, heedless of the self-inflicted ugliness. Prisca said they dolled themselves up to watch telly in the evening and perhaps the little effort with their appearance made them feel that they could compete with the dream world on the screen.

'Tart,' Prisca whispered when Peggy O'Donovan passed them, with Mona by her side.

'Really?'

'For God's sake, muggins, don't sound so surprised. She's away into the city now, though the priest gives her money to keep off the streets. That bitch simpering to him says: "Ach, surely, Father, it was only starvation that drove me to it." The cow! Takes his money and goes her own way.'

'Starvation? With your welfare state here?'

'The priest doesn't take any heed of that story. He just gives her the money and prays that she'll reform.'

'He must be a very kind man.'

Prisca shrugged. 'I often think they should shut up their parochial houses and come and live amongst those souls they're trying to save.'

'You mean live in this community?' Marcella laughed. 'Aren't they entitled to some comfort?'

'It might give them a more realistic picture of a Catholic's life if they lived in this street with hordes of young ones screaming from morn till night. It just might make some of them do a spot of serious thinking about birth-control.'

'Birth-control? What do you mean? It's against the Church's teaching.'

'For God's sake, Marcella, if you lived all your life in this area you'd soon realize that something needs to be done about it. These women need help.'

That night they lay whispering in the dark, so as not to disturb Prisca's three younger sisters who were sleeping in the other bed across the room. The Guildhall clock was striking twelve when Marcella awoke feeling thirsty. She slipped out of bed and went downstairs. The sound of voices and the hum of a sewing machine made her hesitate by the kitchen door. Then she noticed another door further along the hall that led to the scullery, off the kitchen. In here, there was the agreeable smell of freshly laundered clothes. Picking up a glass, she went out to the yard where there were two lines of sheets. Her surprise was not entirely due to the fact that Mrs McDaid had done a washing so late in the evening, but because of the quality of the sheets. They were made of fine linen with pillowcases embroidered in rich handworked lace.

'Why in God's name, Mother, must you become a washerwoman as well as everything else?' Dominic's voice, heavy with bitterness, came through the kitchen window.

'Sure, I only do that wee bit for the Misses Thorn who live in the house with all the roses. The sheets hardly need washing, for the dear knows they're clean wee bodies,' Mrs McDaid said cheerfully.

Marcella moved up the yard and glanced in the window. Prisca's mother was sitting at the table before a pile of work. She was stretching the unattached cuffs of men's shirts over a tin shape. Three layers, two of material, one of lining, were damped down and placed together.

'Well, Miss Adams, what do you think of the way the other half live? Perhaps you imagine my mother is so enthusiastic about her work in the shirt factory that she is compelled to bring piles of it home in the evenings to keep her happy.'

Her face went scarlet with guilt before the look in Dominic McDaid's eyes. She realized though that he was angry and ashamed with the poverty that compelled his mother to work so hard, and angry with her because she witnessed his shame. He glanced at the glass in her hand.

'We have some modern conveniences,' he said sarcastically. 'There's a tap in the scullery if you want water. No need to come out here.'

He made it sound as though she had been deliberately eavesdropping. 'It's draped with teacloths,' she said quickly, touching one of the sheets. 'I hear that Derry men are great ones for standing around and talking while the women are always busy. Why don't you take these sheets off the line and help your mother? They're ready for ironing.'

There was a moment's silence. 'Well,' he said diffidently, 'let's do it together. It will add to your experience of slumming in Bogside. No doubt it is one you will have no wish to repeat.'

Her hand trembled with anger as she filled the glass with water from the tap set in the stone wall. For the first time in her life she felt an intense and instant dislike for another person. He had spoilt her pleasure in this unusual and perfect day. It seemed to her that, although the McDaids were poor, their poverty was cushioned with happiness. Unlike the frail dignity of another class of people, they accepted it robustly and made it seem like an enviable state. Dominic was the exception. They folded the sheets in silence, then Marcella turned away and without a word went back upstairs.

Next morning, Sunday, they all went to St Eugene's Cathedral for Mass – all but Dominic. When they crowded into the long seat that it took to accommodate them, Mrs McDaid's eyes passed over her children, neatly dressed in crisp cotton dresses and shirts; she abhorred nylon. There was a glow of happiness about her, a simplicity that seemed to convey strength and wisdom.

Patsy, who was dressed in an emerald-green skirt and gold-coloured shawl (to participate in a rehearsal for the feis after Mass) nudged her mother. 'Mammy, Dominic's standing at the back of the church.'

'Hush, love, don't let Daddy hear you.'

Marcella turned and saw Dominic standing apart from a group of young men who looked equally bored and impatient to get out of the door again. Before she could turn her head, he looked in their direction. A slight smile moved his mouth, while his eyes remained unfriendly and cautious. Dominic was furious about Marcella Adams. Why did his sister have to bring the likes of her to their house? One day, when he was qualified, he would get the lot of them out of this place in the Bogside to a district that would not shame him. Then there was Lisa Schenber. Any excuse and she was on their doorstep. It didn't take her long to charm his mother with bags of expensive fruit and gifts for the wee ones who clung around her.

Lisa. He didn't know what to do about that girl. She was a torment to him. And highly sexed, he was sure of that. Christ . . . Perspiration broke out on his upper lip; he was beginning to think he was that way inclined himself. Her exotic beauty, gold-tinted skin and the scent she used were like an aphrodisiac net, trapping him with forbidden desires.

Chapter 16

Prisca was delighted when Lisa told her she was having a birthday party. All the Schenbers' friends and relations were coming. 'Isn't that grand,' her mother said when she arrived home.

'Great. What am I going to wear though? That's the problem.'

'There's the dress Mrs Kenny got in the book club and took a dislike to. It's in the box out in the hall.'

'I'd look a show in that, Mammy. It's too long and far too wide.'

'She used to be a grand hand wi' the needle, Pris. Maybe she'd help us to alter it. Go and ask her to come in for a minute, if Himself's not around.'

The dress was a lovely shade of blue, Prisca remembered. She began to get excited. Lisa told her she must bring a friend – a boy, to even things out for dancing. That girl, Lisa, had no idea how scarce men were around Derry! She wondered would Brian be her partner? No manner of hints had made Marcella repeat the invitation to Iniscad. She loved it there, that wide blue sky and the amazing sunset where the sun seemed to sink into the sea, flooding the water with rich red-gold light. Marcella was spoilt. She refused to see how lucky she was living in that grand house.

Mrs Kenny came in with her sewing kit and one of the grandsons, a boy of about three years old. 'Surely to God I can fix it,' she said good-naturedly. 'Sit over there, son, and zip up yer gob.'

Prisca offered the little boy a large apple from the basketful that the Misses Thorn had given to her mother.

The cheeky little article grabbed it without a word of thanks. She stood perfectly still while their neighbour cut the hem and drew in seams with a mouthful of pins.

'You look a picture,' her mother said. 'Prisca, you must get Mrs Kenny to show you how to dressmake and get a bit of a wardrobe together.'

'Sure. In my spare time,' she said drily.

'What do ye think of it, pet?' their neighbour asked the little boy.

'Fuckin' good,' he said, and flattened his face against the apple.

Nora McDaid went scarlet in distress. 'Oh, Mrs Kenny dear, where did the wean hear that language?'

Prisca bent down quickly to pick pins from the floor to hide her laughter.

'Ye bad boy,' his grandmother scolded. And whispered aside, 'Kenny takes him down to the pub at Buncrana. That's what the fishermen say to wan another after a good haul.'

'An innocent tongue with a cruel word on it,' Mrs McDaid said severely.

Her neighbour tried to look abashed and began to chastise the child, but Prisca could see the gleam of pride in her eyes. The woman couldn't wait to tell her husband.

There hadn't been a sight of Billy the Man's taxi around the Guildhall Square for days and Micky O'Kane was wondering what was wrong as he ran up to Fountain Street. The old woman with whom Billy lodged came out of her room before he had time to dodge up the stairs.

'Hello, missus,' he called. 'Just goin' up to see Billy.'

'He's been in bed for days. Just hope he's bin savin' for his funeral.' She rocked back to her room, the worn lino and floorboards groaning under her weight.

Micky mounted the stairs slowly, his exuberance rapidly fading. There was no sound of the mouth organ playing *The Sash My Father Wore*. In residence, the Man always played his favourite tune. Micky loved the tune too. It wid be good enough for a hymn. He pitched himself at the door, acting like a cowboy and landed inside, feet apart, hands wide.

'Lord save us, Sheriff, be 'asy on an auld man,' Billy croaked. 'Can't you see I'm on m'last breath?' A craggy arm appeared from the sheet and tapped the chamber-pot. 'The gold's under the bed, mister.'

The room was in a desperate state, Micky observed. And Himself piled on the bed wearing his overcoat, looking half-alive. Billy's eyes were watering somefink awful and the nose, as usual, taking over the scene. 'What's the matter wi' ye at all? Sure the whole town's waitin' for yer taxi.'

'Them mean buggers,' Billy croaked again. 'I'm thinkin' of emigratin' to London.'

'Na, don' do that, Billy. Old Schenber will be keepin' ye busy soon. I've got an order as long as m'arm. Listen, they're givin' a party for Lisa's birthday and their friends wi' no cars will be needin' lifts to and fro. Isin' that grand?'

When Billy did not respond to this, Micky said sadly, 'Sure yer in a bad way. I'd be gettin' the priest for ye if you wis a Catholic.'

Billy groaned. 'Haven't I enough problems without the Popish one. M'auld mother was tortured wi' the burden of it all her livin' days . . . See if there's a drop of whiskey in that bottle, son – over in the cupboard.'

As Micky poured the whiskey, Billy eased himself up eagerly on the bed. Mickly stopped and swung around with narrowed eyes, hand going to his hip fingering an imaginary gun. 'Hey, mister, it wisin' the darn old bottle trouble that got ye in that bed there?'

The other blinked foolishly. 'Whiskey trouble? What are ye talkin' about, ye wee scut? I hate the stuff. It just puts a bit o' heat in me. I've had the 'flu. So c'mon, bring it over.'

There was silence between them for a minute or two while Micky's face fell into troubled lines. 'Billy, what did ye mean about yer mother being a Catholic?'

'Didin she marry a rantin' Orangeman. Him wi'out a name and none the wiser all their years together.'

'Do you mean she lost the faith?'

'Aye,' he said drily, 'until her an' me visited the place where she wis born in Letterkenny. Every time we got there, the conscience got the better of her an' she'd go away into the wee box at the chapel, jabberin' away in fright, not knowin' what she was sayin'. Tellin' the priest that she was disobedient to her parents. Her an auld wimin wid them ten feet in the soil years past.'

Micky thought he'd never heard anything so funny. He choked himself laughing. All the kids said that rigmarole – "disobedient to my parents". It was a handy wee sin to fill out the list. Billy eyed the boy with pleasure. Micky's crafty tough expression was dissolved in childish laughter. Och, he was a nice wee lad. Like himself he'd not had much of a start in life. Billy wiped his nose and eyes on the grey sheet.

'The confession box can get ye like that . . . in a real fright,' his young friend added. 'Not m'mam, though. Sure as God she'd show ye up if ye had the bad luck to be in the chapel at the same time. Shoutin' her sins out as if she wis proud of them. Never sparin' hersel'. Billy, I'll tell ye a secret – ' The crafty look was back again on the boy's face; the eyes sliding away in case he revealed too much. 'Every Friday at school we have to go to confession. It's a terrible penance goin' so often. I dodge it.'

'You surprise me,' remarked Billy, feeling a bit of life stirring in his bones after the drink and present company.

'I pretend I need to pee and go out o' the church holdin' m'sel as if I wis in real agony. Then I clear off like hell. The master hasn't caught on yet.'

Billy's shoulders began to shake with laughter. 'Lord, son, yer a tonic.'

'Well, I must go now. Okay to tell Lisa ye'll be on duty? It's a week from today. Tell you somefink, she's pantin' after that stiff-necked Dominic McDaid.'

'Thought ye fancied her yersel'?'

'I do. I've got a great notion of her.' Micky stuck his hands in his trouser pockets and sauntered towards the door. 'I can wait.'

The old man's laughter followed him downstairs.

*

'That's a fine day, Marcella.'

'Hello, Father McGill. What are you doing?'

'Taking a bit from the hedge. Paddy the Post was to do it but the lumbago's struck again.' The priest took out a handkerchief and wiped his brow. 'That's an awful frown. What's the matter?'

'I was just wondering who I could ask to a party in Derry. Half the school's been invited and there's going to be a desperate shortage of men.'

'Time enough for men, child. Take Brian.'

That's right, take your brother. He's safe. 'He's booked. Anyway, I don't fancy dancing with my brother.' Nor any of Lisa's fat Jewish cousins either. Marcella slouched across the road and picked a piece of honeysuckle.

Father McGill wiped the pair of shears he was using. 'By the way, someone was asking for you. Last Friday I think it was – young Gilroy.'

'Kiaran?' Marcella swung round in surprise.

'He went to the house – didn't your aunt mention it?'

'No, she didn't.'

'Wonder why she didn't now? Ach, she forgot. The boy seemed anxious to see you.'

'Why all of a sudden, Father?'

He looked up quickly at the tone of her voice. 'They're going off. He and the father.'

'Off where? Aren't they always doing that.'

'The man hasn't been right since the death. His grief is lasting a long time. Now they're going away to travel on the Continent. America was mentioned too.'

'They've gone then?'

'They've gone.'

The finality of his words left her with a sad, sinking feeling. 'It was deliberate not telling me,' she blurted out. 'I've been home for days and not a word.'

'She's forgotten, that's all.'

'Father, do you know something? I try *so hard* to like her, my father's only sister.'

'God save us, child! Come inside. The housekeeper's away somewhere, so you can make us a cup of tea.' What a sad business it was, he thought, storing the shears in the shed. This young girl with not a soul to open her heart to apart from the gypsy who comes with the good weather. Sarah Adams — God forgive me, I feel it difficult to like her myself. Father McGill washed his hands briskly under the kitchen tap.

'That looks like a good cup of tea. Take the tray into the room and we'll have a chat.' The girl was undoubtedly grieved about the Gilroy boy. That was an odd thing now.

'Every weekend when I come home,' Marcella began, pouring the tea, 'I can see she's been through my room. Not just dusting, really nosing in a sneaky way. Checking on what I've been reading. Usually she puts the bookmark back in the wrong place.'

'You could be wrong,' he began feebly. 'It's not a crime or unusual for an elder to be keeping an eye on a youngster she feels responsible for.'

'I'm not a youngster, Father. At the moment I'm blundering through *Ulysses*.'

'God save us!'

'The chapter I was reading was so obscure . . .'

'That's what I'd call the entire dreadful book.'

' . . . that I was reading it again. It was an awful bit. I hope it shocked her.'

The priest scratched his head, stuck for words. 'Pray for her, child. She's had a sad life.'

Marcella went up the road to Brae Cottage. The Source of all Information, as Mama used to call Biddy, threw a fistful of tea into a tin pot full of boiling water, then drew it away from the fierce heat of the fire and propped it against a bit of peat.

'Have ye heard the latest about Slievan?'

'No, what is it?'

'The lodge folk have gone to a farm somewhere. The daughter is off to nursing.'

'Sheila? Who's there now then?'

'Not a soul. It's shuttered up. No money to keep it goin'. Slievan's shuttered up as well.'

'They're not . . .'

'Deal a bit. They'll be back. The auld aunt's gone south and the father and Kiaran away on their travels. The master, poor cratur, was becomin' queer in the head. He was in Dublin for a while for treatment but he's not hisself at all. Did ye ever know he'd got a notion he'd kilt his wife? A long trip was advised. That's the very words I heard Kiaran tell someone on the phone.'

'Has Kiaran lost his vocation then?'

'I told ye before, 'tis the girls he's after not the round collar. When he comes back he's goin' to a cultural college.'

'Agricultural?'

'The very word.'

If only I had not gone to Derry that weekend, she thought. If only ... No! She had promised after her mother's death never to let those words cross her mind again. They were negative, destructive. 'Biddy, I'm going to cycle up to Carndonagh to buy myself a new dress and sandals.'

'A new dress is it? Maybe I could save ye the money. Come down to the room and see what the sister sent me from America. She must think I'm planning to get wed in m'old age.' Biddy tossed a white silk sleeveless dress across the bed. It was simply designed with a round neck and straight skirt.

'Can I try it on?' Marcella asked excitedly.

'Surely. Wait a minute while I pull the curtain across.'

'There's only the hills out there for goodness' sake.'

'The hills can have eyes. There wis a stranger out there the other day, tryin' not to be seen.'

'A stranger trying not to be seen?' Marcella frowned and slipped off her skirt.

The dress was such a perfect fit that she grabbed the surprised Biddy and danced her around the room in delight. 'Now I have only to buy a pair of sandals.'

Later, when she returned from Carndonagh, Marcella went back to Brae Cottage to collect the frock and was persuaded to drink a mug of tea with a piece of cake. Afterwards she made her way home through the fields because her bike had a slow puncture. The evening was falling in. Trees shadowed the ground and birds rustled noisily in the branches. No light showed from the back windows of Bridge House. Everyone must be out somewhere. She was about to jump down from the hedge into the orchard, when the sound of cautious footsteps came from around the west gable of the house. Then a murmur of quiet voices.

'Are you looking for my father or Brian?' she called out.

There was no reply. She ran across the orchard to the back door, opened it and put her shopping on the scullery table. Outside again, but there was no sign of anyone. It might be the gypsies. They were crafty enough to disappear into the treetops. She stood up on the hedge and looked in the direction of Briar Meadow, but no light came from there. Perhaps tinkers on their way to Derry? She hurried inside and shot the bolt across the door.

When a shuffling footstep fell outside the house again she knew immediately that it was Ned. He pushed at the door, expecting it to open at a touch.

'Cella,' he called, 'ye forgot the can o' milk. Auld Sarah . . . Miss Adams, will be bargin' ye wi' her tongue.'

She pulled back the bolt. 'Thanks, Ned. Come in a minute, I want to ask you something. Did you see any tinkers on the road? When I arrived a while ago I heard someone around the house; that's why I bolted the door.'

'Tinkers niver come this way, Cella. Wis there the sound of a conveyance? Tinks have auld vans these days.'

When she shook her head his eyes began to roll fearfully. 'There's supposed to be wee folk about this place – outside there.'

'Have you ever seen one, Ned?' she asked impatiently.

'There's them I know that has.' A car came up the lane. 'Be japers, I'd best be up the road or auld Sarah'll find a job for me.'

Too late. Sarah whisked through the door while Marcella's father put the car away. Ned looked at her sadly. It was beyond the understanding of God or man how a woman could change so powerfully. Her eyes behind the thick gold-rimmed spectacles reminded him of a pair of bluebottles battering around in the captivity of a jam jar. It was a desperate thing for a woman to dishonour her countenance so. Fine big eyes she had as a girl, softenin' wi' kindness to himself when the master at school declared him a dunce 'cause he couldn't get the hang of English words. How could she have changed so? Time was a tyrant. Look at her now. She would give a man the death-chill.

The excitement over the new dress and sandals kept Marcella awake. She lay listening to the waves crashing on the shore, then rushing back again, dragging pebbles to the sea in their greedy foraging. After a while the sea became gentle and the waves lapped mildly around the small rockpools. Her mind began to flit lightly over this place where she had been born. Paradise in summer, hell in winter, the local people said.

Every now and then the light from Inishtrahull Lighthouse came sliding into the room, striking her mother's smiling face in its silver frame. 'Ye can see she's as happy as the day is long,' Biddy in the brae said one day when she was in the room. There were times when Marcella suspected that Biddy was a bit strange in the head. Worse, that she took the odd drop of her brother's poteen.

A noise outside made her sit up quickly in the bed; it was like something being dragged along the ground. She went to the window and tried to look down but it was dark outside. When the light from Inishtrahull came round again, she pushed the window wide open and stretched out. There was nothing to be seen. Opening the door, she went and stood outside the other three bedrooms, listening. Her father, Brian and Sarah were in their beds and fast asleep. She shrugged and went back to her room.

Years later, when Marcella looked back on that evening and considered her unconcern, she remembered that was the way of life around Iniscad and in other parts of Ireland at that time. People did not lock their doors or be unduly bothered about unexplained noises in the night.

Chapter 17

Billy the Man and Micky O'Kane had been dashing around for the Schenbers since the early hours. Billy possessed only a tatty old suit and was togged out in one belonging to his friend, the undertaker. Sometimes when the undertaker was short of a man he engaged Billy to walk in solemn procession behind the hearse. The bowler hat worn on the Twelfth of July did duty on these occasions too.

The food laid out in the Schenbers' dining room was making Micky O'Kane faint with longing until he decided to look after himself. There wasn't a dish he hadn't sampled and now his finger was flaming hot from all the spices in the food. He stuffed his pockets with fistfuls of gherkins and when the doorbell rang, he went out to the hall. Micky stared at Marcella Adams. Not a bad bit of stuff, he decided. A bit standoffish maybe. He'd stick to Lisa.

Marcella was surprised at the dress Lisa was wearing for the party. It was black, cut very low in front and hugged her figure. She looked like Marilyn Monroe. Prisca, who came on her own because she said Dominic preferred to walk, looked younger in a pretty shade of blue.

When Lisa showed them up to her bedroom and dashed off again, Prisca said, 'Wish I could borrow a bit of what's under Lisa's bodice. It's no secret, is it? Look at me, flat as a pancake. Is that the Yankee dress you're wearing? A bit of Lisa's bosom would improve it no end, too!'

'Don't say that, Prisca.' Marcella looked anxiously in the mirror. 'I put a layer of cottonwool down my bra.'

'Another layer would have made all the difference.

Know what Lisa told me . . . ' Prisca giggled. 'She's on show tonight.'

'On show?'

'Momma hopes one of the wealthy Yids will take a fancy to her –Lisa's very words. Apparently that's what they call Jews in London. Some of the blokes coming are from Dublin and Belfast. Now's your chance, Cella! What about a wealthy Jew? Ah, there's Brian coming up the drive.' Prisca rushed out of the room.

Feeling very self-conscious, Marcella made her way downstairs. The music had begun in the drawing room where the carpet was rolled back. All the girls standing around were soon claimed. She liked dancing. Learning to do it properly was of great importance at the Mount Academy. She wandered on to the living room where older guests were gathered. All the women sat on one side, their husbands on the other. The men were discussing business matters in quick, excited voices. Off this room was a large sunlounge where a group of younger men were sitting around a table playing cards.

Dominic McDaid came through from the hall, well-dressed in a dark suit and a dazzling white shirt. She was surprised when he went across to Mr and Mrs Schenber and shook their hands. All three walked towards her. 'Do you know Marcella?' Lisa's mother asked and gave Dominic a little push. 'Now you young people go and enjoy yourselves.' She hurried away leaving Dominic and Marcella looking at each other with embarrassment. They strolled outside, pretending to be at ease.

'Some space in this garden,' he commented, looking about him at the shrubs and flowerbeds. They paused by a large stone urn overflowing with lobelia.

'Lisa was looking for you earlier on,' she told him.

'I suppose I should go and find her. This path leads towards the drive.' They walked on, then stopped involuntarily at a place where a tangle of yellow flowers gleamed through dark laurel bushes like a blade of light.

'I wonder what they are?' Marcella said, leaning over a low stone wall to part the bushes. The stone beneath her fingers began to move; the next minute it came toppling down, striking the side of her leg.

Dominic swung round. 'Are you hurt?'

'My stocking,' she said in dismay. 'It's ruined.'

'Never mind about that.' He bent down and dabbed at the cut on her leg with a handkerchief. 'You'd better go to the bathroom and bathe it with Dettol.'

'What am I going to do?' Marcella said with a sound of distress. 'Lisa was particular about us all wearing stockings.'

'Your legs are brown. You could go without,' he said, surprised at her reaction.

'Dominic, wait for me while I go behind these shrubs and take my stockings off, will you? Her mother is very fussy. We mustn't show her up, Lisa warned us.'

'A fashion parade. Will I do?' His eyes were twinkling with laughter.

'I couldn't believe it was you at first,' she told him, suddenly feeling more relaxed in his company.

He tapped the front of his shirt. 'That was a reject from a top grade batch which my mother got cheap. For best occasions only.'

'Your mother is a lovely woman,' she remarked, pushing through the shrubs. The ribbon around her head caught on a twig, letting her hair fall in a gleaming mass across her shoulder. Dominic watched her, noticing the touch of defiance in the way she held her head and the look of vulnerability in her eyes and in the set of her mouth. He felt a sudden and unaccustomed feeling of tenderness.

'Marcella, I'm sorry I was so churlish that night in our back yard.'

'Goodness, I'd forgotten all about it,' she said, appearing in bare feet and carrying her shoes. He noticed with amazement that she walked over twigs and sharp stones without flinching. When she slipped the shoes on her feet, she looked up and smiled. 'Honestly, I loved being at your house. It was – '

'Dominic, I've been looking everywhere for you.' Lisa came up a little path, picking her steps carefully in expensive black suede shoes. The toes were long and pointed, the heels narrowed to a point.

'Lisa, can I borrow a pair of your stockings? Mine are ruined.'

'How did you do such a thing?'

'Dominic threw me into the hedge.' Marcella twirled the stocking in her hand and walked away from them; she heard his surprised laughter. Another man claimed, she thought resignedly, and immediately stumbled into the arms of a young Jew with very distinct features and a strong Belfast accent. He's been sent to look after me, she decided, but it was Lisa his eyes were on. Not, the young man thought in confusion, this cool young girl who disconcerted him by being a head taller than himself.

In the part of the garden where they walked, Prisca came to the conclusion that Brian was the kind of person who spoke only when there was something positive to say. The silence that fell between them was not uncomfortable though. He took her hand and that felt marvellous. She wished it was soft and dainty but this lack of refinement was not going to bother her either.

'Are you still going to those Gaelic classes?'

'Yes.'

'Some of my lectures finish early these days. What about me going along with you?'

'It's not possible,' she said quickly. Eoin would be furious if she brought along someone like Brian, who had no interest in Irish politics.

'Why not? I've done quite a bit of Irish. Who takes the classes?'

'Eoin O'Donnell. Rosheen Quinn takes another group.'

'Don't know her. O'Donnell is friendly with my father. He's supposed to be a hot-headed Republican.'

'I wouldn't say that.'

'Wasn't he in prison some time during the last war?'

'He was unlucky enough not to get across the border in time like my father and others.'

'Your father?'

'His opinions are neutral now, cured by indifference –

like so many Irish people. Eoin O'Donnell has ideals. So have I. Let's leave it like that because I can see you're not interested.'

'Not interested? I've never given it a thought, Prisca. What's the point? Where have all the uprisings led to? There is no way the situation is going to change, so why worry about it?'

She felt bitterly disappointed. Brian would not speak so dismissively if he had to put up with the degradation of being a second-class citizen in Derry. 'If you lived here you might do a bit of worrying too,' she said severely, 'when you realized how difficult it is for a Catholic to get a good job.'

'Times have changed since the war, surely?'

'I haven't noticed.'

He smiled, trying to lighten her mood. 'You would scarcely remember. Prisca, let's change the subject. I'm not politically minded and I don't intend to change.'

She could have hit him. His complacency — it maddened her. He stopped and touched her arm, and once again she was struck by his incredible likeness to Michael Collins. I'm being unreasonable, she thought. Why should I expect Brian to agree with my political views? Still, it would have been perfect if he had done so.

'What about coming down to Iniscad for a weekend soon?'

'What about telling that sister of yours to invite me. No manner of hinting works.'

He laughed. 'I'm inviting you.'

'It would be better coming from Cella. Sarah . . . she might get ideas.'

'She might be right.' He drew her in amongst the shrubs and took her in his arms. For the first time in her life, Prisca discovered that the pleasurable thought of food had slipped out of her mind as Brian's mouth crushed hers in a long fierce kiss. After a while he said, 'I think we ought to be getting back to the house.'

'Are you hungry?'

He tilted up her face. 'Just for you . . . you can see that.'

Though his words made her smile with happiness, something held her back. It was happening too quickly. He was so earnest. Just as well he lived across the border – there were too many obstacles in her life to allow her to indulge in a serious romance, much as she would have liked to.

Lisa hung possessively on to Dominic's arm when the dance ended. She led him towards the bay window where bottles and glasses were standing on a heavy round table with claw feet. Dominic looked closely at the table. It had a thread of inlaid wood worked in a delicate pattern around the edge. One day he'd like to have a table like that. Tonight he was being introduced to the world of wealthy people. He was taking everything in, storing it up for the future.

Mrs Schenber came into the room followed by Billy the Man and Micky O'Kane who were both carrying trays. Dominic stared at them in surprise. Micky's face was scarlet with the exertion. I must make that table before I drop this, he was thinking. Stiff-necked McDaid's eyes were on him.

'I am missing Prisca,' Lisa said fretfully. 'Soon we drink toasts.'

'Ah, Dominic,' her mother said, 'be so kind as to help with the drinks. Poppa will come and pour, you hand around to the guests.'

Lisa hurried over to Marcella who was stuck with the Jewish boy from Belfast. The boy's eyes lit up expectantly at her approach. She ignored him. 'Where *is* Prisca?' she demanded.

'I'll go and find her,' Marcella offered eagerly, finding a way at last to free herself from his company.

Prisca and Brian were coming across the patio. The three of them joined the crowd in the room. After a while Marcella realized that the other two would be happier without her, so avoiding her previous companion, she drifted away.

'Why don't you try a drink?' Dominic, with one glass left on the tray, held it out. 'Come over and join me and

Lisa. The three of us can go in together for supper.'

'I would hate to spoil Lisa's evening.' Ignoring her protesting conscience, for she had the Pledge since her Confirmation, Marcella tossed the drink back, then picked another one off the tray carried by Micky O'Kane.

'Hey, steady,' Dominic protested. 'That's strong stuff.' She smiled across her shoulder and moved away.

Lisa was greatly relieved to see Dominic coming towards her again. For one awful moment she had thought Marcella was going to join them. She must keep him to herself. He was different tonight; friendly, warm. He held up his glass. 'Happy birthday, Lisa.'

She filled their glasses from a slender green bottle on the window-ledge. As she bent over, a wave of perfume flowed from the cleavage in her dress. Intoxicated by the wine and her scent, Dominic thought, Boy, this is living with a capital 'L'. He recalled a film he had seen recently in which sophisticated party guests strolled around a garden, glasses in hand. 'Let's take a stroll outside,' he suggested to her.

'Micky,' Lisa called, then whispered in the boy's ear, 'take that bottle of wine down to the summer-house. Don't let Poppa see you.'

'Surely, Lisa.'

'I meant just for a bit of a stroll,' Dominic said awkwardly, feeling somehow that the summer-house might not be a good idea.

'It is my birthday. I can do as I like. Come, we go now.'

As they walked down through the lovely garden, Dominic began to feel great again. This was Life! Lisa laughed at everything he said. She made him feel a man of the world, sure of himself. He stopped and picked a red rose, wrapped it in a leaf of scented geranium and thrust it gently in the V of her dress: he felt an electric shock at the daring intimacy. His other self watched with folded arms. Don't be an ass, he smirked. Get the hell up that garden again . . . you can't handle this sort of situation, Dominic McDaid.

Lisa went quickly through the summer-house door as

though she had caught a glimpse of his shadow beckoning him away. 'Pour the wine, Dominic.' She always dropped each syllable of his name, instead of clipping it in the way other people did. He wondered why he had not noticed before how expressive it was. They drank the wine quickly. He poured again, while Lisa told him about the other guests at the party.

'Some are refugees from the war. They could not face going back to Germany or Austria again . . . too many memories. They married into Jewish communities in Ireland, had sons and daughters, and so they spread, increased. Much business is done at these parties. Poppa has some big business on tonight . . . '

'It's getting late, Lisa. Perhaps we should get back now and have some supper.'

'It does not matter. Jewish people love their food. Eating will go on for hours. Oh, I feel a little drowsy.' She lay back on the padded seat. He felt intoxicated by everything – the wine, her perfume and the gentle tapping at the window of a curious branch.

'You're beautiful.' The words fell off his tongue, as the feeling of well-being increased by the minute.

She slid right down on the seat and stretched out tantalizingly. He put his glass down hurriedly, bent over and kissed her on the lips, neck, to the curve where the rose lay soft and fragrant. It fell to the ground when he put his arms around her. His lips moved on, seeking the source of the scent which she always wore. Lisa drew him closer. His hand slipped across the rich material of her dress, unintentionally brushing against the zip which, to his alarm, flew downwards and resisted his clumsy efforts to bring it up again. She gave a low laugh as the fumbling caused him to touch the bare skin of her back. He felt put out, wondering how he could cover her nakedness. Where was her vest, petticoat – all the undergarments Prisca and his mother wore and which were hung daily on the washing line?

Before he could collect himself, Lisa slipped her arms out of the dress. Christ, I'm sunk, he thought, as he had done on other occasions. He balked momentarily at the

Elysian state into which he was drifting, then gave up the struggle because he had neither the power nor the wish to do otherwise.

Micky O'Kane was getting bothered about Lisa when she didn't reappear in the dining room. 'Billy,' he said anxiously, as they were arranging another batch of baked potatoes on a blue dish, decorated with frills of parsley, 'that pain in the neck, McDaid, has got Lisa down in the summer-house. D'ye think she's a'right?'

'As right as rain, I'd be thinkin'. What are ye worrying about, son? She can't go far wrong wi' a good Catholic like McDaid. Now can she?'

When Dominic came down for breakfast the following morning, Prisca said, 'Mammy wants you to take down the curtains and move the beds up in our bedroom.'

'When?'

'Now.'

'I'm going out.'

She looked at her brother in surprise. Usually he fell over himself to do anything their mother asked. 'What's got into you? Hangover?'

'You could say that.'

'Our bedroom was to be papered this weekend. They're away into town to buy the paper.'

'All that work will kill him,' Dominic said cynically.

'So c'mon, we'll go up now and get it done before they come back.' What the devil's got into him, Prisca pondered. Last night she'd never seen him looking so happy. All the wine, of course. That cheeky article, Micky O'Kane, said he and Lisa had a bottle between them down in the summer-house. And they'd put plenty back before that. What a party. The bag of cakes she'd nicked for the wee ones made her feel a bit guilty now. It was worth it though to see the look of pleasure on their faces this morning when they scoffed the lot. What a pain in the neck Marcella Adams had been last night. Moping around like a lost soul with the wee Jew at her heels because he couldn't get Lisa. That was an odd thing Brian was telling her.

183

Marcella had a notion of Kiaran Gilroy from the big house – the Landed Gentry no less! As if the likes of him would look twice at someone out of a cottage.

When Dominic left the house, he cycled past the Cathedral and away down Lone Moor Road. He certainly wasn't going to confession in there, nor to St Columba's Church or the other ones where everyone knew you and wondered why you were taking so long in the confession box. You were either considered a sinner with a lot to confess, or a pious old bore taking up the priest's time and keeping everyone else waiting. Well, he had plenty to confess and that's why he was going out to the little church at Kilen where the young priest understood about things. Not like the old ones who didn't know what the word sex meant and would have a wish to ring a bell over a fellow's head.

Two children sat outside the confessional. Dominic said the Confiteor and prepared himself. He dreaded the ordeal, but at the same time was anxious to rid himself of sin. The little country church was filled with lightly scented flowers. Statues with benevolent expressions looked down on his bended head. He turned guiltily from the gentle Madonna to whom, encouraged by his mother, he had a great childhood devotion. When his turn came, the familiar dread gripped him. His throat felt dry as he stumbled to the kneeling pad. He lifted his head and blessed himself, then found to his dismay that the thin veil of concealment was no longer there. On the other side of the confession box sat a grey-haired man. Where was the young priest? He couldn't confess to this one. Dominic scrambled to his feet again.

'Kneel down, my son.'

'Father, I wanted to talk to Father O'Brien.'

A sigh came from the other side. 'Alas, he has gone to another parish,' the voice said gently, his face in profile. 'Won't I do?'

'It's . . . just that I dislike going to confession. Father O'Brien –'

'Made it easier?'

'Yes.'

'Sure don't we all dislike the thought of going to confession.'

'You mean – '

'Now you didn't think priests are free from sin, did you? Or that we're not tempted like everyone else. We go and humble ourselves before God just as you are doing now.'

Perspiration began to trickle down Dominic's face. His lips were frozen, lockjaw was setting in. He felt suspended in a vacuum as the dark, silent box pressed around him.

'You've been keeping bad company?' the priest suggested, his intuition being guided by a lifetime in the Church.

'Not bad. I . . . was weak. I . . . '

He mumbled some words of explanation, until the priest said with a compassion that did not go with his rugged profile, 'Tell me, son, what sex are you?'

The perspiration went cold on Dominic's face. 'What do you mean, Father? I'm . . . a man. Surely you can hear me?' God almighty, this one must be in his dotage.

'Exactly,' the voice said crisply. 'And you know now that a man's passions in a moment of intimacy are easily aroused. Have you got serious intentions towards this girl?'

'Serious intentions? Father, I'm still at school. I haven't even started on my career yet.'

'What are you planning to do?'

'Medicine,' he said proudly, the question calming him slightly.

'Ah, like priests, doctors see the rough side of life. When you come to my age there is nothing much left to learn.' Gently now, the priest asked, 'Hasn't it occurred to you that you may have got this girl into serious trouble?'

'She said that wasn't possible.' The words came quickly. Dominic immediately regretted them, but Lisa's words last night were ringing in his ears. When he tried feebly to withdraw from their hasty love-making in the summer-house, she had said, 'Don't worry, Momma has advised me . . . it will be all right. Momma says Jewish boys are passionate. I must try and be good. Should there be a little slip-up, though . . . '

Perspiration poured down Dominic's face again, and in the silence the old priest bowed his head with an expression of humility and eternal patience. Sensing that the penitent's distress was easing, he said: 'If the girl has had the experience and knowledge to protect herself from a serious development then, my son, she could be a continual source of temptation to you. Are you in love with her?'

'I think,' Dominic said with bitterness, the man taking over from the boy, 'that I am not in love with her.'

'You desire her?'

If only you could see Lisa Schenber, he thought. 'Yes, that's it.'

'Try and avoid all dangerous occasions of sin, as we must all do. Say three Hail Mary's to the Mother of God for your penance.' His hand came up and made the sign of the Cross. 'In nómine patris . . . '

When the prayers were finished and the priest removed his stole, Dominic said, 'Father, there is something I must say. I hate this embarrassment, humiliation. As a child, the confession box terrified me. I've never got over it.'

'Remember, my son, the teaching of the Church. It is not to me you confess, but to God. Go in peace.' Dominic stumbled to his feet. 'Listen,' the voice said from the other side, 'any time you're troubled about anything and feel like a chat, just come to the house. Sometimes it's easier. God bless you.'

As Dominic cycled down the hill from the little church where flags of wild rhododendrons fluttered along the way, a sadness came over him. He felt as though something belonging to his childhood had been irretrievably lost. Not his faith, but the part that he could no longer endure – the confessional.

'Where have you been?' Prisca demanded when he arrived home that afternoon.

Dominic looked at the three girls. Lisa's eyes were

sparkling with impatience. Marcella had Deirdre on her lap. 'I'll have to go now, pet,' she said to the little girl.

'Can't I go wi' you, Cella?'

'It's too far. We're going to Grianan.'

'What's Grianan?'

'The Grianan of Aileach is a prehistoric fort, built by the Druids about two thousand years before Christ,' Prisca told her.

Then Brendan added, 'Did you ever hear of Prince Owen, Deirdre?' She sucked her thumb, bored with the explanations. 'Well, Saint Patrick is supposed to have baptized him there in the year four hundred and forty-three. Grianan was the palace of the Northern Princes.'

'Hark at him showing off his knowledge. Come on, off you all go. I'm going to give a hand with the papering upstairs.'

'I thought you were coming with us, Prisca,' Marcella said in dismay. She followed her out to the kitchen. 'They don't want me trailing after them. Remember last night? They were inseparable.'

'You go with them. I went to no end of trouble to borrow that bike for you. That Lisa is as hard as nails. What a scene she created because Dominic didn't come back earlier. She's so possessive and spoilt.'

'You can be as hard as nails too. She'll be furious if they're stuck with me.'

'Right. You give her a bit of her own medicine. Look Cella, if Lisa wants anything she makes sure she gets it. At the moment she's after Dominic and it could make no end of problems for him. I think she's *fast*. I'll tell you something, Lisa's father had a lot of trouble buying that shirt factory. D'you know what he did? Made friends with a Protestant to pull a deal for him. Smart, wasn't it?'

'But the Schenbers are Jews. Why did he have trouble buying the factory?'

'Business people are frightened of someone like Schenber. Look at the great job he's made of the shop in The Diamond. All the other places must be getting alarmed.'

'Well, good for Schenber! Perhaps he works harder.'

'Are you two coming?' Dominic called impatiently.

Embarrassed, Marcella went into the kitchen. 'I'm afraid it's only me. Prisca hasn't got time.' She avoided Lisa's eyes which were saying plainly, 'You stay here as well.' Nevertheless, she wanted to see Grianan. She'd drag behind a bit, keeping out of their way.

They cycled along Culmore Road out of Derry, then took a side road that led to the hill of Grianan which rose to about 800 feet. The last part was too rough for the bicycles. They abandoned them and scrambled up a rough track to the ring fort that towered above.

'It is too far,' Lisa wailed, as a small wind got up and slipped through a honeysuckle bush, sending it swinging like a thurible dispensing incense.

The Grianan of Aileach had a complete amphitheatre with steps inset in the wall leading to the galleries. Marcella shivered with delight when they climbed to the top, where there was a panoramic view covering five counties, stretching as far as Benbulbin in Sligo. Then quite suddenly a soft rain began to fall and a grey veil of mist crept down across the Mountain of Errigal and Muckish over in west Donegal.

Dominic looked anxiously at the sky, then pointed south to the city of Derry lying in the curve of the river in an effort to entertain Lisa, who was obviously not enjoying herself. The mist was coming closer, rolling over the chequerboard of fields in the fertile plain. 'Come on,' he said, 'we'll shelter in the chamber down below.'

'You two go on,' Marcella suggested. 'I'd like to stay up here for a while. Look out for the ghost of the High King sitting on his throne at the end of the passage!' she called after them.

Disgruntled, the other two went away, ignoring her jest. She wanted to be on her own to think about this place, which had been erected for sun-worshipping by King Dagda of the ancient pagan Irish. Leaning over the wall, lost in the past, Marcella was not aware that a perceptible change was coming over the weather. When she lifted her head about ten minutes later, she gave an excited cry.

'Dominic, Lisa . . . come quickly.'

He was already clambering up the steps. 'She won't come. Marcella, your anorak's soaking.'

She smiled happily at him, moisture dripping from her face and hair. The rain had ceased and the mist was gradually lifting, then the sun came and speared through the low clouds, scattering them and flooding the valley with light. The Foyle below Culmore Point flowed through the land like a streak of silver. Tidy little parcels of fields across the plain had a freshness now, their colours making a bright pattern.

She clutched Dominic's arm. 'Can't you just imagine Saint Columba standing up here, his voice thundering down on the people, or gentle Saint Patrick?'

He smiled at her. 'I can just imagine a nice hot punch down in that little pub near Burt. Come on, you'll get your death.' He stopped and searched his pockets. 'God, I hope I've got some money left.'

'No problem.' Marcella whipped a pound note from her top pocket. 'Lisa keeps dropping these all the time. I was going to surprise one of the children playing in your street. We'll surprise Lisa instead with your generosity. Here, take it. And there's the ten-bob note Aunt Sarah removed from my dressing table because she thinks my father gives me too much pocket money. I retrieved it from the housekeeping purse.'

Dominic was surprised and amused by her candour. Marcella Adams was quite a character when you got to know her.

Chapter 18

Prisca visited Iniscad the following weekend. She and Brian were inseparable. When it was time for her to catch the Derry bus, Marcella left them on their own and decided to do something which she had been putting off for a long time – go down to the dairy where her mother had spent so many happy hours.

The place smelt musty. There were nets of cobwebs across the window and a layer of dust over everything. With a piece of rag she wiped the window, then looked around at the things which had been piled in here and had remained untouched since Mary B's death. She pulled the spinning wheel out of the corner where it had been pushed at an awkward angle, and put the old churn back in its place. One day she might spin, as Mama had taught her, but it was unlikely that she would ever turn her hand to making butter.

The long wooden table, bleached white from the scrubbing of past generations, was covered with her mother's unfinished work; the articles looked like a collection in a still-life painting. An Aran knit guernsey had a sleeve missing and was unlikely to be finished because the pattern was known only to her mother, as it had been handed down in her family. Its original purpose was to identify relations who were drowned at sea and eventually washed ashore. Apart from the knitting there was a piece of embroidery, a patchwork quilt, lace and crocheting. A small tablecloth with a cambric centre was edged with a wealth of lace. This Marcella put aside for her own bedroom.

When the door opened suddenly, she swung round with

a resentful expression, thinking it was Sarah who hated the dairy because everything in it belonged to Mary Bridget. It was her father.

'Hello, I've been cleaning up in here,' she said. 'Mama left such lovely unfinished work.'

He searched her face for signs of grief, and saw only calmness. 'Could you give it to one of her friends?'

'Later. Not yet.'

'What about making this into your den, darling? There's space here for your canvases and paints. Your bedroom's very crowded.'

She smiled. 'What a good idea. Sarah never lifts a duster to this place, I suppose because there's too much of Mama in here.' Marcella frowned. 'Why did she dislike my mother?'

Conor hesitated, then decided to tell her. 'Your grand-father, Mary B's father, shot the man Sarah was going to marry.'

'*What*? Why did he do such a terrible thing?'

'Your grandfather was an active member of the Irish Volunteers who took part in the Dublin Rising in 1916. In every political movement there are traitors or weak men. Anyway, the Volunteers discovered that the man Sarah was going to marry intended to betray them. The Irish rebels had their own courts and they say that condemned men were always justly tried. Death was the punishment meted out to traitors.'

'How old was Sarah then?'

'Twenty-two. The man was twenty-four. After his death she emigrated to America, went to nightschool over there and learnt typing and shorthand, then eventually got a job in London. She did her best to stop our marriage, you know. The bitterness was still there after all those years.'

'What a terrible story.' Marcella looked through the window at the sound of a car out by the lane. It had stalled on the turning to the hills. Sarah, who was down the lane carrying an egg basket, went over to speak to Kiaran Gilroy who had jumped out of the car. Marcella hadn't seen him for a long time. The gladness that came to her face died immediately when Kiaran's fair-haired cousin appeared too. They shook hands politely with Sarah and drove away again. Conor noticed his daughter's expression: the joy, then disappointment. Poor child. Gilroy's son. He moved towards the door.

'Prisca McDaid.' The unmistakable voice of Rosheen Quinn, Eoin O'Donnell's friend, made Prisca want to disappear into Watt's drapery shop in The Diamond. She turned slowly and faced her.

'Window shopping?' the woman asked briskly.

'Yes.' Prisca had been wondering whether she dare go in and buy herself one of the hand towels with the ten shillings Granny had slipped her. 'Squander it on yersel',' she had whispered. Since Prisca's visit to Lisa's home, where the hot rail in the bathroom was lined with soft colourful towels, she had longed for one. At home, the towels were either torn to shreds or hard and abrasive. She couldn't get over the fact that each member of the Schenber family had their own. That seemed the ultimate luxury. Maybe she should spend it on a necessary item of clothing, like stockings. The temptation was great, though.

'They are good value,' Rosheen commented. 'Come on in and help me choose some.'

That settles it, Prisca thought. I'm not going to show myself up before her by buying one wee towel. Inside the door they were greeted by a tall grave man. 'Can I help you?'

'Towels,' Rosheen said in her abrupt voice, ignoring the man's courteous attention. They were beckoned to a counter where an assistant greeted them as though they were old friends; she seemed to be under the impression that they required quantities to stock a hotel. A riot of colour rippled across the counter. The girl tossed the towels about as though her hand was possessed by some uncontrollable urge, and all the time imploring them to feel the quality. Prisca tried to slip the ten-shilling note into her pocket but it was damp with perspiration and clung to her hand.

'What colour do you like, Prisca?' Rosheen Quinn asked as the mound of towels heightened and the counter began to look like an end of season sale. Mrs Kenny would have a field day in this shop, Prisca thought, picking one off the floor. 'Are you tempted to buy some?' Rosheen asked.

Buy some, says Quinn. How are ye! Pride made Prisca look at the assistant and say, 'Really, what I want is a face flannel.' Surely no one ever bought more than one face-cloth at a time? Bits of old towel served in the McDaids' house.

'A face flannel?' the assistant repeated with an expression of disdain, as if Prisca had asked for a floorcloth. 'That's the other department, miss. What colour? I'll get you one.'

'Dark green to match our bathroom,' Prisca said, looking her straight in the eye. 'To match our water tap in the back yard,' she whispered to Rosheen, who actually strained her face and smiled. Quinn rarely smiled.

When the assistant returned with a face-cloth which was fringed and embroidered Prisca realized her mistake. The elaborate piece of fine towelling, which was not included in the sale, cost exactly the same as one of the reduced hand towels.

Subdued, she watched Rosheen Quinn hand the assistant two piles of different sizes and colours. 'Wrap separately,' she ordered. Outside the shop she turned to Prisca. 'Come and have a cup of tea. I live across the way in Linenhall Street. Take these.' She dropped one of the parcels into Prisca's arms. 'To match your face flannel.'

'Oh, I couldn't – '

Her protest was ignored. 'I hate that shop,' Rosheen retorted, striding across The Diamond square.

'It smells of wealth,' Prisca said, stunned and made uncomfortable by the generous gesture.

'Huh! Money certainly makes a difference. When my mother scrubbed their floors I was not allowed to wait for her inside. Had to stand outside in the cold with my face pressed against the window. Then they discovered she was a Catholic and, like all faithful followers of Lord Brookeborough, gave her the sack.'

'Why do you go in there now?'

'They've got one of the best selections of materials in Derry.'

'Material?'

'That's my trade. Making clothes for people, designing and teaching at the college.' She stopped outside a tall grey house in Linenhall Street. A thunder of sewing machines came from the room on the left side of the entrance, accompanied by chatter and laughter with a faint background of music.

'Eileen,' Rosheen called through the open door, 'make some tea.'

The girl, who was kneeling on the floor, had two pincushions slung around her neck on a piece of thick tape. In her hand was a magnetic bar which she passed slowly over the lino, drawing pins from it like insects to a fly-paper.

Prisca followed Rosheen down the hall to a long narrow living room with tall windows at each end. There were books everywhere. They spilled out of cupboards, shelves and were bundled on chairs.

'People come in here to read – members of my group – and leave them everywhere. I can't be bothered to tidy. Just push them out of your way and sit down.'

What a perfect room, Prisca thought. Dark green paper covered three walls; the other was painted white and crowded with Republican posters and photographs. Faces from Ireland's past history gazed at her out of time. A group of Bold Fenian Men looked down, clasping blunderbusses, garden forks, scythes and sticks to fight their battle. Parnell had a far-seeing look in his eyes; James Connelly a kindly expression and Pierce was looking fierce. There was a sad picture of Maud Gonne McBride being released from prison, her beauty gaunt with hunger. These and many others gazed down from the wall, fuelling the fire of Rosheen Quinn's patriotism.

'Did you know that we have some accursed blood in our

veins – Lord Kindron's?'

The unexpected and candid disclosure took Prisca completely by surprise. She could not imagine herself being so frank.

'You look startled,' Rosheen remarked drily. 'Surely Eoin has told you that there are several similarly afflicted families around Derry?'

'He did but – ' The door opened and the girl from the sewing room brought in a tray.

When the tea was poured, Rosheen said, 'I think you should know that members of those families have joined my political group. We meet here every Monday. Can you spare another evening from your studies?'

Prisca frowned. Rosheen Quinn must have gone to each house on Eoin's list and fired them with political fervour, made them feel it was their duty to take more interest and become involved. She said hesitatingly, 'I'll do my best.'

'I would like you here.' It no longer sounded like a request but a demand.

'I've always wanted to belong to a political group. Eoin O'Donnell promised . . . '

'The fight has gone out of Eoin. He has a dream of a peaceful ending, that some day Westminster will do something about Stormont. As if *they* cared.' She handed over a cup of tea and added, 'I hope you're not wasting any mental energy over Kindron – if I can put it that way. It's our misfortune. We must live with it.'

'It was a shock to find out. I felt . . . dirty.'

'It was a dirty business. Not enough was done about it at the time. As you probably know, he belonged to the House of Lords. They knew how that maniac was behaving, but who was going to worry about the welfare of the poor ignorant Irish?'

By the time Rosheen had finished talking about the injustice of Lord Kindron, Prisca felt her blood boiling with anger. She must remember these things. She must remember Kindron. She had become too engrossed in her studies. And in Brian, who constantly argued that her involvement in 'so-called Irish groups' engendered bitterness and would not solve Ulster's problems. The ideal thing, he said, was to live in peace. Prisca clenched her hands. *God, let me never forget. Let me never become complacent like my father.*

'Eoin tells me you're a clever girl. You must help to carry on the fight, Prisca McDaid. Prepare for the next time. Our numbers are growing. I'm depending on you.'

By the time Prisca arrived home, the only thing that troubled her was the parcel she held in her arms. Her mother would not be pleased if she realized Prisca had accepted a present from Rosheen Quinn. Present? She felt uncomfortable about the word and wondered if it should rather be called enticement – bribery. In the meantime she must find a hiding place for the towels. Later, when it would be possible to earn some money doing a holiday job, she would give the impression that she had just made the purchase.

Prisca found her mother in a state of perplexity. 'Do you know, Pris, Father Hay has been in to ask me to take the Merry Widow to the Retreat the Holy Fathers are giving at the church.'

'I don't think Peggy O'Donovan has ever been near a Retreat. She'll sway up the aisle and go out by one of the side doors. Why is he putting the responsibility on to you?'

'Daughter,' Granny McDaid said, 'ye don' want to be seen wi' the likes o' her.'

'God help her. Maybe she'll turn over a new leaf, Mother.'

'Turn over a new man likely.'

Nora McDaid flushed. 'Be quiet, Mother. If I can help to save the woman's soul, then please God I'll do my best.'

''Tis yerself, Father Hay. I was just goin' out,' Peggy O'Donovan said when the priest arrived on the doorstep.

'I won't be staying long. Hello, Mona. What a big girl you're growing.'

Mona, with her back against the wall, which was painted a glossy yellow, slid down towards the front door and slipped out. She crossed to Mrs Kenny's house but her eyes were turned to the McDaids'; that was the house she would really like to get inside, to be welcomed by that lovely woman. Mrs McDaid had a real mother's face. She didn't wear make-up like Mam. Real mothers didn't pretend either that their daughters were their sisters.

'That you, daughter?' Mrs Kenny peeped out the door, dread on her face in case His Reverence was going to give her a call as well.

'Do ye want yer floors scrubbed the day?' Mona looked guiltily over her shoulder in case her mam found out her secret.

'Do the parlour, daughter, the cat's got in again.'

'Can I?' Mona loved the lino in Mrs Kenny's parlour. It was covered with tiny coloured stars that twinkled like a starry sky when the wet cloth went over it. Mam would kill her if she found out about the floor-scrubbing and the threepence wages. Then there was a hot mug of tea and nice pastries.

'That the priest gone in yer house again?' Mrs Kenny would dearly love to know what went on in that house across the street. Not a soul in Brawn Street had been inside the widow's door.

'Aye.' Mona tightened her lips together, in case some detail of the mystery surrounding her mother might escape and feed Mrs Kenny's curiosity. Mam had warned her never to tell their neighbour a thing.

'I've told ye I've reformed, Father,' Peggy was protesting to the priest meanwhile. 'There's only one man now and that's the way it's goin' to be.' She gave a harsh cough which made Father Hay frown. He didn't like the sound of it.

'He's a married man, child. A good Catholic in a high position with a lovely wife and family. You're dragging him down to sin, taking advantage of his little weakness.'

Outraged, Peggy said cheekily, 'Is that what ye call it, Father? His little weakness. Begod, isin it well for men. All's forgiven 'cause they've got a wee weakness and wimin mustn't take advantage of it. Last time them Holy Fathers were in Derry I went to confession but they never called my sin a wee weakness.'

'Don't take advantage of a word, Peggy. You know what I mean. Now, will you go every evening to the Retreat if Mrs McDaid calls for you?'

Peggy's face fell into sulky lines. Mr R, her steady man, came two evenings a week when his wife thought he was at the Catholic men's club. All the well-off Catholic men spent their evenings there. Women were not allowed in. He expected Peggy to be sitting here doing her embroidery, waiting for him. Wish she'd never put on that act. She was incapable of threading a needle, never mind working all them coloured threads together.

Mona, who loved needlework, as her friend Mr R called it, had left it lying around and he thought it was Peggy's. It was early days then and she was not sure of him. The piece of linen with the wee squiggles seemed to make all the difference to his interest in her. Something about his mother . . . Now Mona had to do a piece for her every week, in preparation for his visit. Peggy shrugged. What was the harm if it kept him happy? Deep down, though, the deception about the needlework bothered her far more than anything else that took place between them.

The arrangement with Mr R suited Peggy. She seemed to tire easily these days and coughed a lot. He didn't like the cough, wanted her to go to a specialist. Money no problem. He was loaded. She liked him – that was all. No more falling in love for Peggy O'Donovan. She'd learnt her lesson. Ye're on top of the world one minute, next ye know it's all over. Not even a goodbye from Conor. Sitting waiting. A new dress for the occasion. Instead of him, a rattle at the letterbox. A fat envelope lying on the mat. Full of money and a brief note that broke her heart. Not even his name on it for her to treasure and remember. Just 'he would be unable to call again and thanked her for all her kindness.' Not even caring that she might be hurt. When men paid, that thought never entered their minds. And auld Kenny coming over and asking, 'What was that Mr Eoin O'Donnell pushing through your letterbox? What-ever was the likes of him doin' a thing like that?' Nosy bitch.

'A letter from a friend,' she had told her that day, and then went in and cried her eyes out. That was the last time Peggy O'Donovan shed a tear for any man.

'Are you looking after that cough?' the priest asked for the second time.

She heard the concern in his voice. God love him, Peggy thought, sure I'd go to the bliddy Retreat on m'knees if it pleases him.

'Aye, Father, I'm goin' to see a special doctor.'

'Do that, then get back to your work as a waitress.'

Waitress, how are ye! Mr R said no more black dresses and white pinnies for Peggy. Him thinking that was the only kind of work she did because she had met him at a special function. Doing a favour for a friend, that evening, and looking after her own interests as well. Only men with money ate out in hotels. Amazing how they could give you the eye – then look anxious in case you hadn't received the signal. And Mr R with the Bishop only a hair's-breadth away!

Conor was taken aback when Marcella asked him to drive her to Brawn Street. They met at lunch, then went to the Art College to keep an appointment with the Administrator to discuss his daughter's future. Afterwards she was calling for Prisca. They were going to a concert in the Guildhall and Marcella was spending the night with the McDaids. The priest was walking away from Peggy O'Donovan's house as Conor drew up at the corner. When he saw Peggy at the door, he leaned across, opened the car door for Marcella and said, 'Enjoy the concert. See you tomorrow,' and drove away again.

He did not feel at ease with himself for ignoring Peggy. The best part of his nature wanted him to go back, have a word . . . treat her like a human being. He shrugged. Peggy had probably forgotten all about him by now. Women like that did not really get emotionally involved, in spite of what they said at the time.

At the time. He turned away from that memory too. It

was Eoin who had suggested it, and Conor had gratefully accepted his offer. 'Be careful. No letter — only a few words,' his friend had advised. Now after all these months, he wished he had gone himself instead of letting Eoin O'Donnell push an envelope through Peggy O'Donovan's door.

PART TWO
Burntollet 1969

Chapter 19

As Marcella climbed to the top of the tulach a pair of gannets rose complaining in the air. They soared out to sea, their black-tipped wings dipped. She looked around anxiously for a nest, then remembered that gannets normally nested in large colonies. She had not been up here for years, yet time had not changed it. The tough little sea-pinks still flourished in the sandy soil and yellow saxifrage, stunted in growth, clustered under the grass like day-old chicks.

Over by the pier, a few fishing boats were preparing to go out to sea. She could hear Liam in the brae shouting orders to his one-man crew while his wife, Rosie, stood by firmly holding the hand of their five-year-old son, Patrick. One blustery day, behind Rosie's back, Liam had taken the boy out fishing to 'harden him'. When Rosie found out, she waited on the pier for their return. Bolder now, since the romantic days under the upside-down boat on the shore, she beat her husband around the head with a pair of dead pollack.

Snuggling into a hollow, Marcella took out a sketch-book. Her pencil lay idle as she considered her new life at the Art College in Derry. She had been impatient to leave the Mount Academy ever since the departure of Prisca and Lisa to a Teacher's Training College. Lisa had just scraped through her examinations while Prisca had done well but not outstandingly, considering her ability. Everyone was disappointed – some furious – at her decision not to go to university. Marcella could not understand it. Her friend's life at home had become considerably easier, yet she had turned down a wonderful opportunity. Brian was at

Trinity College, Dublin; it was thought that Prisca would try for Queen's in Belfast, like other students at the Mount Academy. A few years ago her decision might have been influenced by family finances, but now there was a steady income from Phelim McDaid's job with Mr Schenber. The family were even saving money to buy their own home.

'Cella . . . ' Prisca was calling from the shore. 'Come on down. We're going out in the boat to check the lobster pots and we need an extra hand.'

When Marcella arrived at the pier, Brian did not agree. 'Two are enough,' he said, so she went and sat on an iron bollard and began to unravel a fishing net to wait for their return. The voices of two people coming down the other side of the pier made her look up. It was Kiaran Gilroy with the girl with the ash-blonde hair, whose looks were spoilt by an expression of boredom. 'A useless fixture that wan will make at Slievan,' Biddy complained, 'a swanky gawk. 'Tis a pity now he didin cross the midden!'

Kiaran was wearing a navy-blue jersey. The girl had on a pair of well-tailored slacks and a silk blouse. 'What *are* they doing out there in that boat?' she demanded in an imperious voice. Brian was moving around the brightly coloured buoys that marked the pots lying on the sea-bed.

'He's pulling up each pot, taking out the catch and restocking it with bait then sinking it again,' Kiaran explained.

'No wonder lobsters are so expensive.'

'He's enjoying what he's doing,' Kiaran told her shortly. His voice had changed. It sounded flat, indifferent, without the touch of laughter that Marcella remembered. They turned suddenly, crossed over and began to walk towards the bollard. Alarmed at the thought of meeting them, Marcella picked up her Aran knit sweater, jumped off the pier and ran towards the shore. Scrambling up the tulach again, she felt glad to have this place where no one else ventured. Prisca had tried it once but had slipped down and hurt her leg. She and Brian invaded the cashel these days, sunbathing on the flat rocks and making it obvious that they wanted to be on their own. Prisca came quite often to Iniscad at the weekends now. Too often.

Marcella sketched until it became too chilly, then she stood up and stretched her arms. They dropped quickly when she saw the figure of a man standing near the edge of a cliff. Pulling a pair of binoculars out of her bag, she saw that it was Mr Gilroy; there was something uncertain about his movements that alarmed her. She scrambled down, ran across the shore and climbed up the cliff. He had moved further along and was now standing near the spot where his wife had met her death.

It was difficult to appear casual when gasping for breath, but fortunately the man was looking in the other direction, which gave Marcella a little time to say quickly, 'Good afternoon, Mr Gilroy.'

He turned. His eyes looked troubled, like those of someone who has lost their way. Standing well back from the edge, she held out her hand. 'I'm Marcella Adams.'

His instinctive courtesy made him move forward and shake it. She could see him wondering who on earth she was. Marcella smiled. 'Are you looking for something out there? I know the coastline well. Perhaps I can help you?' The words did not make much sense to her own ears.

'My dear young lady, no one can help me. I was responsible for an accident which occurred on this spot. It haunts me . . . day and night.'

'What kind of accident?' She unbuttoned the cuff of her blouse and pushed up the sleeve, deliberately avoiding his eyes.

'My wife. A shot from my gun distracted her horse.'

'Mr Gilroy, the shot came *after* the horse bolted. Something else caused the accident.'

'The little girl said — '

'She was just a little girl who made up stories.' God forgive me! 'I was there too that day and saw what happened.'

Confusion crossed the vagueness in his eyes. 'Are you sure?'

'I'm quite sure,' she said, gently and firmly.

It was then that she realized Kiaran was standing a little

distance off, listening. Their eyes met. He shook his head slightly.

'Hello, Father. Did you have a good walk? How'd you like a lift home? I've got the car up on the road.'

Mr Gilroy looked relieved at the sound of his son's voice. And walking on ahead he said, 'Yes . . . yes. I'd like to get home now.'

Kiaran came over and smiled. 'Hello, Marcella. You've grown tall – I scarcely recognized you.'

'I hope it stops. I'm getting worried.'

His laughter that came so easily, just as she remembered, made Mr Gilroy turn and look relaxed. 'Would you like a lift?' Kiaran offered. His eyes were asking her to accept.

'Yes, thank you.'

'Certainly she must have a lift,' the older man said vaguely.

At the gates of Slievan, Kiaran slowed down and stopped. 'Marcella, come in for a glass of sherry.'

Before she could refuse, his father said, 'Of course she must come in for a drink.'

The room they entered had been described to Marcella years ago. She was glancing around discreetly, taking note of its beauty, when the figure of Miss Gilroy sprang out of a deep chair by the fireside. She looked surprised and not very pleased when Kiaran introduced them. Over by the window, the fair-haired girl was leafing through a glossy magazine. When the introductions were made, she merely lifted a hand and let it drop again as though she were suffering from some restricting disability.

The grunt from the older woman and the indifferent gesture from the other, did not make Marcella feel at ease. These people felt alien and Kiaran, whom she had loved as a young girl, seemed restrained. He poured glasses of sherry and passed them around. When the two women began to discuss some detail about a regatta, Mr Gilroy said, to her surprise, 'How is your father, Miss Adams?'

'He's fine, thank you.'

'I have good reason to be grateful to him. It distresses me now that I did not write at the time.' He paused. 'Your father took steps at one period to prevent unfortunate information about my family being published in *The Northern Press*.'

Unfortunate information? Surely it was her mother, Marcella thought, who had tried to protect Mr Gilroy from Liam in the brae's bitter little note after his wife's accident . . . Kiaran was frowning thoughtfully, as if he too was wondering what his father was talking about.

'Have you taken any action about those gypsies in the meadow?' Miss Gilroy boomed out, as if her brother was sitting a mile away. Her voice was one that demanded immediate attention.

'No.' The brief reply from Mr Gilroy came with a withdrawal in his manner again, as if the responsibility of the question was more than he could cope with.

Marcella sat forward in her chair, alarmed at what might be coming next. Why was this woman, who was known not to like Iniscad, taking an interest in the gypsies?

'It *must* be done soon. You can't afford to have that land lying barren to accommodate a gang of layabouts. Kiaran, will you do something immediately now that you are helping to run the estate?'

'Do you mean Briar Meadow?' Marcella asked anxiously.

Miss Gilroy ignored her question and so did Kiaran; at least, he glanced away uncomfortably and avoided her eyes. The woman went on emphatically, 'We must be certain that they understand that they cannot return after this season. We want them out of there permanently. They're camping right in the middle of fertile land. We simply can't afford to waste it. The situation is quite ridiculous.'

Putting her glass on the table, Marcella rose quickly to her feet. 'The gypsies, Miss Gilroy, were given permission to camp there during the famine. Not one of your family, down through the years, has tried to reclaim that patch of ground – *not even* the notorious Lord Kindron, who rebuilt this house after it had been burnt down.'

Mr Gilroy raised his head and fear came to his eyes as he

rose slowly to his feet. His sister shot up out of her chair and for the first time looked directly at Marcella. 'I don't think this has anything to do with you, young woman.' She gave Kiaran a look which said plainly, 'Get her out of here.' Now they were all on their feet, all staring at Marcella, who could feel hot angry colour staining her cheeks.

'If you try to move them —' The hopelessness of the situation overwhelmed her. After all, it was Gilroy land.

If she had not raised her eyes to Miss Gilroy at that moment, and seen the supercilious smile which said plainly, 'The Irish', Marcella would probably have walked out of the house defeated. Instead, the injustice of the situation struck her. She thought of Nanta and her ailing husband; the older gypsies who were related to the Old One. Briar Meadow was their summer home, the shore rich in food to eat and sell. And Derry the place where they sold their crafts and hardware which they made during the winter months in the south. She felt like shouting in protest. Instead, she went on in a quiet, even voice.

'I think the gypsies have as much right to that piece of land as the descendants of a soldier of fortune.' What am I saying, Marcella thought, turning blindly towards the door. That's the way Prisca goes on. A stunned silence followed her outburst. She heard Kiaran coming after her. He doesn't matter any more, she thought dully. He had changed.

His hand fell on her arm. 'Marcella, I'll run you home.'

'No thanks. I'd rather walk.'

'What about the bike? You were the last passenger, you know. Ah, maybe you're too long in the leg to ride comfortably now!'

She gave him a quick glance and saw his warmth. Until that moment, he had seemed no different from the others in that room. Now, after all, she was not so sure. He kept looking at her, the smile fading from his eyes. This was the wild young girl who used to run through the woods in her bare feet — the girl to whom he had been so strangely attracted. He remembered that time when he was setting out with his father to travel somewhere, calling at River House, and the feeling of disappointment when she wasn't there.

'Don't worry, Marcella,' he said hurriedly. 'Aunt Ursula has no authority to make decisions about the land. She has been . . . taking over a bit while I was away at College. I promise you, the gypsies will not be moved against their will.'

'Thank you . . . thank you very much, Kiaran. Your father . . . he's still not very well, is he? He would need to get away from here.'

'I know. When I get married, he and my aunt are going to settle down south.'

Marcella held out her hand. 'Goodbye, Kiaran. I wish you every happiness.' Turning quickly, she hurried away down the drive, wishing with all her heart that she had not met Kiaran Gilroy again. The young girl who had been attracted to him, she thought bleakly, was still lurking somewhere in her nature.

Kiaran watched until she was out of sight, then turned with an unsettled expression towards the house and the woman who was to become his wife.

When Marcella reached River House she pulled her washing from the line and stuffed it into a canvas bag.

'What are you doing, Cella?'

'Think I'll take the early bus back to Derry, Father. I've got some work to get on with.'

Conor rested his spade against a tree where he had been digging. 'Are you happy living with Prisca's aunt?' he asked anxiously.

She smiled and nodded. 'It's heaven!' They laughed at her using Prisca's expression. 'The bell in Cassy's shop rings from morning to night. She calls the sweet bags, pokes.'

He picked up the spade again and shivered as a crisp breeze blew in from the sea; it reminded him of the day in Buncrana when he had bumped into Peggy O'Donovan from Brawn Street. She had come along the deserted street, staggering against the force of a blustery wind. All the guilt he had previously felt about the woman struck him at that moment. Not caring a damn if someone saw the editor of *The Northern Press* picking up a prostitute, as they would assume, he stopped the car and called her name. Peggy hesitated, not knowing whether he was going to snub her again or not.

Conor jumped out quickly, shook her hand and said solicitously: 'What are you doing by the sea on this cold day, Peggy? Come on in and have a cup of coffee – if you've got time.'

'Aye, surely,' she said eagerly, following him into the quiet little restaurant where the silence was relieved by the throb of *South Pacific* music coming from a distant kitchen. She was meeting a friend, she told him. 'Ach, sure, he doesn't matter at all.'

She looked into his eyes then and smiled. It was the coquettish smile of an aged vamp who tries to defy her image in the mirror. Christ, he thought sadly, how the poor woman has aged. It was incredible. She was still beautiful, though – a strained beauty. He asked about Mona, their health – everything he could think of. And that wasn't much, considering the months he had haunted her house and crept backwards down the little lane, scraping his car to blazes.

When he had finished his coffee, he put a pound note on the bill and a ten-pound note under it. 'That's for Mona – buy her something nice. Have another coffee yourself, Peggy. I must leave you. I've got an appointment.' He covered the hand that lay limply on the table and placed it over the pile of money.

'Ach, yer too kind,' she said in a low voice.

'Look after yourself. Don't hang around too long in Buncrana. It would chill a mountain goat today.'

When she gave a harsh cough, he noticed how shabby her clothes were. Distressed by a feeling of unreasonable responsibility, Conor hurried out of the restaurant and passed his own car parked by the pavement. At the top of the street he wondered where the hell he was going and remembered his appointment at the Lough Swilly Hotel.

He walked on. The car could be picked up later. This was something he would not tell Eoin about. He could not bear to hear his friend's laughter.

'I'm going now, Daddy,' Marcella called, breaking into his thoughts. 'Why don't you come and see my room one of these days? Climb to the second floor. It's so private, Cassy never comes up. I clean the room, cook my food — when I feel like it — and look after the sweetie shop when she goes down to devotions at the Long Tower Church. I don't know how many times she's told me that the church stands in the oak grove when Saint Columba founded his first monastery.'

Marcella loved the old fortress town on the hill with the Foyle curling around its banks. Derry had once been an island city, she had been told at the Mount Academy. She was enjoying the Art College, too, where tuition covered art in its various forms. The richness of colour fascinated her, as did the developing knowledge of mixing and applying paint. Fieldwork added another dimension to her studies.

'You're not going, Cella?' Prisca and Brian, looking flushed and tired after a long walk, came around the side of the house.

'Taking the early bus. Are you coming later?'

'Think I'll stay until tomorrow morning. The thing is, Liam in the brae has given me a big piece of salmon for my mother, and there's dulce for Granny. Do you think — ?'

'If you wrap it up well.'

'Don't let Aunt Cassy see it or it'll never reach our house.'

'She's hardly likely to see it if I go straight to Brawn Street from the bus depot.'

'You'll go straight there and not wait till the morning?'

Marcella sighed and tightened her lips. Prisca was so bossy. 'I've just said so, haven't I?'

Mrs McDaid was delighted when she arrived with the piece of salmon. 'I've been waiting for this treat for years, Cella. Sit down, dear, and I'll put the kettle on. Hope that Prisca isn't pestering your aunt.'

'She's the only person Aunt Sarah likes.'

Nora McDaid laughed, thinking it was a joke. They were chatting and drinking their tea when a terrible scream sounded in the street. 'Mary and Joseph, what is it at all?' Nora said, tearing out to the hall with Marcella at her heels.

Mona O'Donovan was standing in the middle of the road screaming, her hands beating the air helplessly. 'Marcella, take hold of the girl and get her into our house. Something must have happened to her mother.'

Mrs Kenny came running out. The two women went into the O'Donovans', where they found Peggy lying on the couch; a towel covered in blood was tucked under her chin.

'Oh my God, the poor soul. Mrs Kenny, go and tell our Brendan to run for the doctor and Patsy to get the priest.'

Marcella put her arm around Mona and drew her into the McDaids'. The street was now crowded with women and children wanting to know what had happened. In the kitchen, two cats which had come through the open window, were snarling over the piece of salmon which had been stripped of its paper. As Marcella darted across the floor, their jaws went into the fish. If they were going to be booted out, their defiant glares seemed to tell her, the salmon was going as well. She got the besom, chased them out and flung the fish after them. When she had cleansed the table she turned to Mona, who was cowering in a corner of the kitchen.

'What happened, Mona?' she asked gently.

'Mam's dead. I don't ever want to go back to that house again.'

Shocked, Marcella said, 'Mrs McDaid will look after things. I'll get you some tea.' She talked to the girl for about fifteen minutes; it was difficult.

When Nora McDaid came in with her neighbour, she told Mona that her mother had gone to hospital and that she was not to worry. Mrs Kenny took the girl by the hand and said, 'Yer comin' wi' me, daughter. I've got a gran' room all ready for ye.'

'Ye'll be fine wi' Mrs Kenny, love,' Mrs McDaid added anxiously. 'Come in here any time you like.'

As the two went towards the door, Mona looked back at Nora McDaid. The girl wants to stay here, Marcella thought. Just then, Dominic and Lisa hurried into the kitchen with anxious expressions. Lisa had 'happened' to meet him somewhere. Every time Dominic managed to get away from his medical studies in Belfast and Lisa was home from college, Prisca said, their friend was on the doorstep, as if she had a spy watching every train for his arrival. When Dominic's eyes rested on his mother he relaxed. Childish memories still haunted him about her health.

'Mrs O'Donovan's dying of consumption,' she told him. 'She was in a clinic. It was too late. She wanted to come home.'

'I didn't know,' he said slowly, angry that he had not been told, and maybe his mother taking some risk that he was not aware of.

'Mrs Kenny has been doin' for her.'

'But Mona,' Lisa said, looking around in alarm as though she was in imminent danger, 'she, too, will carry the disease.'

Marcella had a feeling that if Mona had been in the kitchen at that moment, Lisa would have fled from the house. She was always fussing about her health.

'No, Mona's all right, dear. The doctor has been keeping a check on her,' Mrs McDaid assured Lisa.

Two days later, Peggy O'Donovan died. Nora McDaid knew that there wasn't a penny in the widow's house with which to bury her. Mrs Kenny said she had been selling her nice things to bring in some money for food. On the following day, Nora was sitting wondering what to do, when her neighbour came in.

'I'm takin' a collection,' she told her. 'Wid ye come round wi' me? Kenny says I'm not to have charge of the money in case someone's bad tongue gets at me.'

'Oh, dear me,' Nora said, distressed. 'The people have little enough for themselves.'

''Tis what they want. They're pestering me to let them help, God bless 'em.'

'I'll go with you,' Prisca offered, coming in from the scullery.

Father Hay arrived when they were counting the money. 'Must've smelt it,' Mrs Kenny whispered.

The priest looked distressed. 'I've been trying to contact Mrs O'Donovan's cousin, her only relative. He's gone away from his last place in London and not left a forwarding address. What's to be done about Mona?'

'She'll have to go to the Children's Home, Father. I put it to Kenny and he won't hear of me havin' her.'

The sound of crying came from the scullery and Patsy's worried voice saying, 'Don't cry, Mona.'

'I don't want to go to that Home,' she sobbed. 'I want to stay in Brawn Street.'

The four adults in the kitchen looked at each other, troubled. Prisca was alarmed at the expression on her mother's face. 'Patsy,' she called, 'take Mona upstairs.' When the two girls passed through the kitchen, they saw the look of terror in the girl's eyes. Mona realized now that the little security in her life was about to be snatched away. She knew it would be impossible to stay in this house but had been sure Mrs Kenny would take her in.

'Well, I'll be away next door to see to Kenny's tea,' their neighbour said uncomfortably.

The priest shook his head sadly. 'The poor child's got no one. I'd better get up to the Home now and see if they can find a place for her.'

'No, don't bother, Father. We'll take her.'

'Mother,' Prisca protested, 'you mustn't. Dom will go wild.'

'It's got nothing to do wi' him,' Nora said sharply. 'I'd have liked a chance to discuss it with my husband, Father, but he's working late this evening.'

'Wait then,' Prisca said quickly.

Her mother turned with a cross expression. 'Under God, the wee girl's lost her mother and nobody cares about her. Well, we'll just have to see what we can do.'

'May God reward you for your kindness, Mrs McDaid,' Father Hay said gratefully. 'The girl needs the influence of a good home.'

'Prisca, go up and tell her. She can have your place in the bed when yer away during the week. I'll make a shake-down in Granny's room at the weekends.'

'The doctor has been most particular about the girl's health, Mrs McDaid,' the priest assured her hurriedly. 'There's no need to worry about – '

'You tell that to our Dominic,' Prisca told him shortly, leaving the kitchen. It was all right for the priest in his fine parochial house. His responsibility for Peggy O'Donovan had ended.

'Now, Father,' Nora said briskly, 'take a look at that money. See how far it'll go. I must get my purse and put in our contribution.'

After the priest left, Mrs Kenny was back in the kitchen clutching a few pound notes. 'You take that and put it away in yer purse for mindin' Mona.'

'Oh . . . Mrs Kenny, I couldn't.'

'You just take it. When that divil o' mine is drunk he niver knows what he's got in his pocket. I helped mesel'.'

'No, Mrs Kenny,' Nora said firmly. Imagine rifling her husband's pockets!

'Sure he's makin' good money.' Her neighbour's face fell in disappointment at her offer being rejected.

'Well . . . I'll tell you what we'll do. Mona needs a new pair of shoes, so why don't you take her downtown and get some. It'll cheer her up.' Mrs Kenny's face brightened again. Oh God, Nora thought in sudden alarm, the good-natured soul is supposed to have bad habits in shops. What if wee Mona got on to the same game? 'Patsy'll go with you,' she said hastily. 'Maybe a cup of tea in a restaurant?'

'God, aye. We'll paint the town red! I love weans' company.'

Dominic and Phelim were very shocked about Nora's decision to take in Mona O'Donovan. 'It's not fair on Prisca,' Dominic complained, so it was decided that Mona would sleep permanently in Granny McDaid's room. I hope to God it works out, Nora prayed. She was a great believer in prayer. In the factory women would say, 'Get Nora to do a novena for your request.' The main request was usually that one of the shirt-workers would not be pregnant. Unwanted pregnancies were one of the greatest burdens in the lives of the hard-working women, who were usually the breadwinners in the family. Sometimes she had to admit she was often overburdened with the prayers of others.

Prisca, who was impatient about it all, told her to cut down on the heavy novenas. Why not a few Hail Mary's? It was quality, not quantity, that counted when it came to praying, her daughter insisted. That Prisca was a wise one, Nora thought. How many Hail Mary's had flown from her lips over the tails of men's shirts, she wondered. Now there were no more shirts to be hemmed. Just the odd bundle of finishing work to be done at home, which brought a few more pounds to put aside for their dream home. They had never been so well off. Phelim was pushing money into a building society, depriving himself of a drink and a wee bet on the horses. Ah, but Nora knew what it was all about – Dominic! Instead of the son having to prove himself to the father, it was the other way around in their family.

As Nora hurried up Northland Road to return a parcel of clean bed-linen to the Misses Thorn, she thought about poor Peggy O'Donovan who had been a mystery during her life and now her death had revealed nothing. She and Mrs Kenny went over to look through the house before a man came to clear it out. The priest said it was important to try and find papers, documents or letters that might be tucked away somewhere. Important for Mona. They asked the girl to accompany them but she refused. After searching for an hour there was nothing to throw a clue as to who the widow was or where she came from. The Lord have mercy on her soul, Nora thought sadly, she was a woman from nowhere. A closed book. There was not even a sign of Mona's birth certificate.

With a secret little smile, Mona had watched the two

women going across the street that day. They didn't realize it, but she had gone back to the house, just once. Long enough to take away a little package Mam had given her before she died. 'Keep it hidden, love,' Mam had said. 'It's yours. Our secret. It'll safeguard you later on. Mrs Kenny said she'd take you in and Mrs McDaid will help ye too. No paupers' home for my Mona,' Mam had rambled on. 'Ye had a grand relation called Kindron – English, but noble. Remember the reporter from the paper? I tole him a great story ... did well for mesel' out of it!' Mona treasured that last conversation with her mother.

The Misses Daisy and Margaret Thorn were always delighted to see Mrs McDaid and to hear, as they called it, the latest bit in the McDaid saga. Nora felt upset about Daisy the younger one, who was laid up with a broken leg; her sister looked worn out trying to manage. As the three of them chatted and sipped a cup of tea, it occurred to Nora that they seemed uneasy today – fidgety, giving each other little glances.

'There's something we want to discuss with you, Mrs McDaid,' Margaret said finally. 'Our solicitor was here since your last visit. He and the doctor have been having words together and they think this house is far too big for us and we should consider moving into one of the new bungalows being built up the road.'

Nora was taken aback because they had always said that nothing would ever move them from their lovely home which had been built by their father at the beginning of the century. 'Daddy', as they referred to him when they were speaking to each other, still ruled the roost. Though the Misses Thorn were in their late sixties, they seemed to be still under their father's influence. If the man who came in once a week to do the garden happened to cut the hedge an inch too short, he was in trouble. 'Daddy always had it six feet from the ground. It must be kept that way.'

'Won't it be too much of a wrench to leave your memories?' Nora asked them. They often talked about the grand parties in the old days. Never mentioned boy-friends though, just Daddy who was a well-known Derry businessman.

Daisy folded the napkin on her lap into nervous little pleats. 'We can't bear to think of a stranger coming to live in our dear home . . . ' Her voice broke.

'Let me tell her, dear,' Margaret said briskly. 'My dear friend, all the years we've known you, you've been talking about your dream to save and buy a suitable home for your family. Well, our solicitor suggests that we have a valuation on this property and if you and Mr McDaid – '

'My dear souls, I'd rob a bank to get it. We'd never manage the price,' Nora said flatly.

'Well, just in case.' A pause followed. 'There's something we must confess,' Margaret said quickly. 'We think you ought to know . . . ought to hear it from us.'

'What is it?' Nora asked, alarmed by their uncomfortable expressions.

'If you could see a way to take over our dear home . . . ' Her face coloured with embarrassment. 'Our father, who was a member of the Orange Lodge, said that a Catholic would never be allowed to cross his doorstep. When he advertised for maids, it was "Protestants Only Need Apply".'

Nora glared at the photograph that dominated the fireplace. Ye auld Orange divil!

'You came here in kindness and . . . ' They both shot out the words as if they had rehearsed them. 'You're the best friend we've ever had in our lives.'

Nora didn't know how to react. What it must have cost them to say a bad word against their father! 'Times have changed, m'dears,' she said briskly. 'People in the sixties are more open-hearted and less bigoted.'

'A permissive age, the papers call it,' Daisy said severely, relieved to get away from the awkward subject of her father. 'Beatle mania and all sorts of strange things going on.'

'I'll tell you what we'll do,' Nora said to settle their agitation. 'Get your solicitor to see about the valuation and I'll have a word with my husband.'

'Your eldest son will soon be earning good money,'

Margaret said shrewdly.

'I think Dominic will want to live his own life, away from home.'

'The attic rooms, Mrs McDaid. Think of the space and the bathroom up there.'

'Bless you, ye've got m'head spinnin'.'

'Pick yourself a bunch of roses and come tomorrow with some news,' Daisy said mildly, feeling that her sister was pressing a little too hard.

Nora flew home, passing the Cathedral without going in to say a prayer, as was her custom. She put a good fry on the pan for Phelim. He enjoyed that. As she was filling the kettle, men's voices sounded in the hall. She couldn't believe her eyes when her husband and Dominic walked into the kitchen together.

'Another hurdle over,' Dominic said, giving his mother a big hug. 'I did well – '

'He called into the shop on his way home,' Phelim said, pleased by Dominic's unusual gesture. The enmity which had lain previously on their faces like scars seemed to have healed.

When the two men had eaten their meal, Nora told them about the house of roses. 'I know I'm wasting m'breath,' she added, 'but I promised the Misses Thorn to discuss it with you anyway.'

'It'll go for a good price,' Phelim said, 'and there'll be plenty after it.'

'If there's the slightest possibility of our being able to buy it, they'd hold on. Anyway, they've only just started to build them bungalows.'

Phelim took out his Building Society book and raced his finger down the column, rapidly working out the new interest rate. 'I doubt, Nora, if we could get near the value even with a hundred per cent loan.'

'Dad,' Dominic said quietly, 'I'll have no problem about getting a loan from the bank when I start working at the hospital.'

'You can't tie your future up with us, son,' his father protested. 'You'll want to get married, have a place of your own.'

'That's right,' his mother insisted.

'I'm going to need somewhere to live in Derry for a few years. If the rooms at the top of that house are more or less self-contained, then I can make it a place of my own.'

Nora thought of the way Mona O'Donovan hung around her eldest son every time he came home. Still, one step at a time.

Chapter 20

The following year, in nineteen sixty-three, Prisca and Brian became engaged. They planned to get married when he finished at university and Prisca her course at Teacher's Training College. As they both loved the country, they decided to live in Iniscad. Derry, where they hoped to get jobs, was within reasonable distance. Conor bought them an old cottage which had been empty for years. It was a couple of miles up the road, not far from Brae Cottage.

When the holidays began, Prisca asked Marcella to help them with the decorating. Marcella had been planning to go to France with Lisa, who had a summer job looking after children. Lisa thought there would be no problem about Marcella getting one too because *The Lady* magazine advertised numerous jobs every week.

One day when she was working at the cottage, Prisca said: 'By the way, Cella, I saw the young lord of the manor when I was down in Boyle's getting some cigarettes. Miss Boyle was trying to fill him with free drinks.'

'Who?' Marcella asked, absorbed in her task.

'The one you ran away from like a bog-eejit, that day when we went out to the lobster pots.'

There were times when Prisca could irritate Marcella. 'Was his fiancée with him?'

'Didn't see her.'

'Thought he would be married by now,' Marcella said with a casualness she did not feel. After that last time they met, she had tried very hard not to think about Kiaran Gilroy again.

'You mean you *hoped* he wouldn't be married by now. Lord, I'm dying for a fag.'

'Ask Ned when he brings along our lunch. He's got a tinful of butts. Maybe after smoking one of them, you'll be put off for life.'

Marcella had been very surprised when Prisca started the habit. Then one day she saw her in a Derry café with Rosheen Quinn, a woman years older than herself, who chain-smoked. What had she in common with that odd-looking character, Marcella wondered. There was something secretive about Prisca these days; it had been developing over the past few years. She had no time for Lisa now, whom she said was man-mad. It was all right for her; Brian had fallen into her lap before she was old enough to feel desperate. Some girls were not so lucky. Like poor Lisa – in love with Dominic and running around with anyone, hoping to get him in the end. Marcella and Lisa had remained close friends since that first day at the Mount Academy.

'Brian says you've always had a crush on Kiaran Gilroy.' Marcella ignored that and cleaned her paintbrush in turpentine. 'Cella, what about us going down to Boyle's one Saturday evening. Try your luck!'

'Try my patience. They're all old men over forty.'

'Just for a bit of fun,' Prisca suggested, the good nature in her trying to offer something. 'A break before you start slogging on that wall.'

Doing a mural in one of the bedrooms was a mad idea, Marcella thought. Prisca wanted her to mirror the scene from the window so that it could be remembered during the wet cold days of winter. Artistically, it was wrong in such a tiny cottage, but when Prisca made up her mind about anything . . . Anyway, it was supposed to be part of her wedding present.

Before she began the job, Marcella went over to see Nanta. It still delighted her to go into the woods. A fresh pungent smell mingled with smoke from the fires that smouldered in the meadow during the long summer days. She longed to take off her shoes – to feel the damp spongy moss under her feet. To paddle in the stream with its smooth stones, or sit on the bank among the violets that clustered in sheltered places. No time today.

Nanta saw her coming. 'Always alone, lovey?'

Marcella stretched herself on the steps of the caravan and gazed at the clouds tossed across the sky. They looked as though they had been flung out of the heavens for an airing.

''Tis not good. You should have a boy. What about that fella in the big house?'

'He's marrying one of the cousins from the castle in the south.'

'Castle? Ga!' Nanta said contemptuously. 'Old rack and ruin. I know it well.' She gave her a long searching look and said, 'Come.'

Marcella followed her into the caravan. Nanta lived alone since her husband's death. Flicking a pack of cards across the table, the gypsy raised one eye questioningly.

'Just this once,' Marcella said without interest, and to please her. She had no belief in such things.

Nodding her head, the gypsy began sorting and arranging the cards on the table. 'Good. Success in work. Ah . . . ' She gave a long contented sigh and looked at Marcella, her wonderful eyes sparkling. 'It is coming.'

'What is?' she asked, half-bored with the performance.

'A fella. Yes, 'tis good.'

Naturally she's going to tell me something like that, Marcella thought impatiently. Nanta turned the cards quickly. A look of incredulity crossed her face and her brow darkened. 'Jesus!'

It was the first time Marcella had heard her swearing. With a vicious swipe, her friend swept the cards away across the table.

'What is it, Nanta?' she asked anxiously. There was no reply. The gypsy's mood was now dark and withdrawn.

As she walked back through the woods, Marcella wondered about the little scene in the caravan. Nanta was such a complex character, sometimes pure gypsy and at other times the artist, creating. And often the philosopher – wise, kind and understanding. Despite her lack of interest or belief, the incident depressed Marcella, as though some weakness in herself accepted the foreboding in her friend's words. She shook the mood off and laughed. What could possibly happen in her extremely dull life?

The work on the cottage was nearly finished. The place had a great deal of charm. Though the extension and the two bedrooms were bright and modern, apart from tiny traditional windows, the living room or old kitchen was practically untouched. The old beams and stone walls had been treated, but the inglenook fireplace remained as it had been for hundreds of years. There would be plenty of fuel to keep the fire going because every cottage in Iniscad had a peat-patch up in the hills, a right that had been handed down through generations in most parts of Donegal.

When Brian went to the village to buy a paper one day, Prisca said, 'I'm probably going to move in here over the summer, Cella. A few bits and pieces will make it comfortable enough. I need to earn some money. I wonder if the hotel are taking on extra staff for the season?'

'Your mother will miss you at home.'

Prisca shrugged. 'It's dreadful since Mona O'Donovan came to live with us. I've nowhere to go. She's always hanging around our bedroom with the girls, or is in the kitchen when I want to talk to my mother. The house is just too small and I feel trapped in the space when I return from college at the weekends.'

'The girls all seem to get on well with her though, don't they?'

Prisca bit her lip thoughtfully. 'There's something sly about that Mona.'

'Her terrible life . . . '

'I know, Cella. I feel awful saying it, yet she looks like someone hoarding a secret . . . it's difficult to explain.'

'Don't forget she's just beginning to live a normal life. It's her first experience of being a young girl and not the confidante of a strange mother who didn't allow her out in the street to play with other children. What does Dominic make of her?'

'That's another problem. She haunts his room when he comes home, always taking up cups of tea when he's working. He has talked very bluntly to Mona about her mother.' Marcella looked shocked. 'Well, there's a good ten years' difference in their ages and he felt it might be necessary. The thing is, there was a suspicion that Peggy was dragging Mona into town with her.'

'Oh, no . . .'

'Mona said she only went as far as Stanley Walk where a friend of her mother's used to live. Dominic was convinced she was telling the truth.'

'Dominic is a very caring man as well as being attractive.'

'You don't seem to find him so attractive.'

'We're good friends.'

Prisca gave her a funny kind of look. 'He used to walk you over to Aunt Cassy's in the evenings from our house.'

'That doesn't mean anything. We discussed books because we both enjoy reading.' Marcella laughed, remembering the night Cassy tore downstairs in her nightgown when they came in late. Cassy had one rule only: Marcella was not allowed to take men into the parlour because the last girl who stayed in the house 'went astray' on the couch, she maintained. Only hard-backed chairs in the kitchen were allowed. They were sitting on this 'temptation to sin' drinking coffee when his aunt dashed in. 'No men in here, Marcella! Och, it's only you, son.' Her voice withered with indifference. Though she and Dominic had laughed, there had been something strained about his expression which made Marcella feel slightly discomfited.

Aunt Sarah always sent Ned over from Bridge House with their lunch so that they could work in the cottage without interruption. At one o'clock one day he put his head over the half-door and began sniffing and snorting.

'Sweet God,' he said, 'it smells better than it did when that auld wimin lived here. If I was youse wans I'd get the priest to bless this wee house. Mark my words, that wan was a she-devil.' The previous owner was known to have kept bullocks for pets, even holding a wake when they died. Ned put the basket down quickly and shuffled away.

The three of them carried it outside and ate their lunch in

the shade of the veronica bushes which surrounded the garden. The warm friendly silence, with the gentle humming of bees and seagulls calling, seemed to hold them in their different worlds of thought. A smell of wild thyme came from the hills and somewhere in the distance a church bell was ringing. Occasionally Prisca and Brian glanced at each other and smiled. Though Marcella did not envy them their happiness, she suddenly felt isolated, aware of a void in her life which she did not know how to fill.

Later that evening, when they were about to leave the cottage, Brian said with an assumed heartiness: 'Let's go down to the hotel for a drink. I've got an awful thirst.' Her brother was as natural as the wee spring well that had inconveniently asserted itself on their spare bedroom floor. Prisca must have put those words into his mouth.

The hotel bar was crowded, but they managed to find three seats on a bench. At the other end, a fiddler was playing. After a while, the barman shouted for someone to, 'Give us a song.' They got a never-ending come-all-you. After that, there was a lot of shouting for the man sitting next to them to give a verse or two. Shyly he stumbled to his feet, but as the words of his own composition brought forth a little chorus of, 'Great man. Boys, he's great,' he grew in confidence.

Prisca nudged Brian. 'For God's sake shut his gob with a drink.'

Brian shook his head. No one in Boyle's Bar was ever discourteous to a man who tried to entertain. If he had gone on all night, they would have had to sit politely to the end. After that there were shouts for Liam in the brae to give a stepdance. Liam came out on the floor like a matador and began a wild jig that made sparks fly from the soles of his heavy boots. Prisca started to clap her hands in time. He sparked his way over the floor and grabbed her; gradually others began to join in.

The poet said to Marcella with a look of panic, in case she refused, 'Dance, miss?' He was a skilful dancer. Unfortunately she had to endure the peak of his cap digging into her face, and the bottoms of his trousers whipping her ankles. Nevertheless, she began to relax and enjoy it; and as Biddy was fond of saying, 'It shook the starch out of her nature.' When the music stopped, everyone sat down and drank; then once again the poet was called to give another verse. The tall thin farmer shot out of the corner like a kite in the wind and hung over them with a long dreary tale about the potato famine.

Halfway through the recital there was a quiet shuffling down by the door as men moved aside to let someone enter. Kiaran Gilroy came in, hesitated, then went up to the counter where Miss Boyle began fussing. When she had served him he turned and looked in their direction. His eyes went past the poet to Brian, then fell on Marcella. He picked up his glass and edged his way towards them.

Marcella was so surprised to see him at the Saturday night hooley that she simply stared. He and Brian shook hands, and Prisca was introduced. 'Marcella . . . how are you?'

'Fine.' There was an awkward pause. 'You kept your word about the gypsies,' she said, stuck for words.

'I said I would,' he replied quietly.

The other two looked curious, not knowing what they were talking about. Marcella thought he had aged since that last day at Slievan. It surprised her now that she had spoken out so hastily, but she had to protect Nanta who, in a way, was like a surrogate mother. Biddy had told her only last week that there was no sign of wedding bells yet. The young master was working like a slave, and Himself (Mr Gilroy) was beginning to take more interest in the land. The daftness seemed to be gone . . . 'Pity the auld aunt wodden be gone too,' she had added. 'That wan would skin a flea.'

'Would you like another drink, Kiaran?' Brian offered.

'No thanks, Brian. I must be getting back. I promised to play a game of chess with my father. The house has been crowded with people for ages and we've scarcely had a chance to talk.' His eyes fell on Marcella again. To her astonishment, he said: 'Marcella, are you free tomorrow?

would you like to go somewhere for lunch – around the coast perhaps?'

The invitation was so unexpected that she remained silent for a minute. Then she noticed the expression in his eyes – anxious against her refusal. This was immediately followed by a look of determination. 'If not tomorrow, perhaps another day?'

'She's very busy at the moment working on a mural in our old cottage,' Prisca said briskly. 'She's trying to get it done before going off to France.'

'I would like to, Kiaran,' Marcella began, ignoring Prisca, whose toe came against her leg with a sharp, deliberate rebuke ' . . . though I am busy.'

'Leave the work, Cella,' Brian said firmly. 'Do you good to get out for an afternoon.'

When Kiaran smiled, Marcella knew that if he had asked her to accompany him to Lough Derg and go around bare-footed on a bread and water diet, she would have done so gladly. 'I'll be working at the cottage in the morning.'

'Can I come and collect you there? About twelve-thirty?'

After he had left, Prisca turned on her furiously. 'Why did you rush at his invitation like that? Isn't he supposed to be marrying one of them swanks from the south?'

Marcella stood up and pulled a cardigan around her shoulders. 'Perhaps,' she said coolly, 'the girl has gone away and he's feeling lonely. It's not all that unusual to invite someone out to lunch, is it?'

'Over here it is,' Prisca snapped. 'He just walks in and everyone practically bows to him. God, we're supposed to be second-class citizens in Derry, but at least we haven't got down-at-heel Catholic gentry to tip out hats to. It makes me sick on a Sunday to see the way people move aside to let that craggy old aunt of his sweep into church.'

'You're just bigoted,' Marcella said shortly, making for the door.

Something awoke her in the night. She turned in the bed and saw Prisca slipping out of the room. Thinking she was going to the bathroom, and suddenly realizing that she needed to go as well, Marcella waited for her to return. After a half-hour or so she fell asleep.

'Where did you go last night?' she asked Prisca in the morning. 'You were out of the room for ages.'

Prisca was obviously taken aback by the question. 'Where do you think? To Brian's room,' she admitted brazenly.

Shocked, Marcella said, 'I hope you were expected.'

'We're not waiting for the priest to say "All right, now you can sleep together." We love each other and that's all that matters to us. It would be hypocritical to wait, as far as I'm concerned.'

'Aunt would have a fit if she found out what was going on.'

'Well, we must protect her from the knowledge, mustn't we? Now that you know, it will make things easier. I won't have to keep on pretending and waiting until you go to sleep every night.'

It was typical of Prisca to be frank but her words shattered Marcella. Purity had been drummed into her by nuns, priests and Sarah who, she knew, prayed constantly that she would not do 'anything wrong'. At that moment she wished her aunt had spared a few prayers for Brian as well.

In the morning Marcella dressed in a pair of old jeans and a blue cotton shirt to work at the cottage. A dress of soft yellow Tricel was in a large plastic bag to slip on later. For two hours she worked on the wall, enjoying the peace and silence. About twelve o'clock she suddenly realized that Kiaran was standing watching her at the open door. He must have left his car on the road and come up through the field. She turned and looked at him, uncertain and shy. Prisca's words were beginning to eat into the frail fabric of her self-confidence.

He smiled. 'Hello, I'm far too early. Do you mind?'

'Oh, no.' She did mind, because she had planned to be dressed before he arrived.

'May I look at your work?'

'It's still a bit of a mess.'

'I like your choice of colours, though I don't know what they're doing on that wall.'

'Neither do I,' she said, and laughed as she wiped her fingers.

'Ah well, don't take any notice of me. I'm a Philistine.'

'No, you're right. They crowd the room.'

'I've got a confession to make, Marcella. It was such a lovely day, I decided to bring along a picnic lunch. What about having it on the cliffs and climbing the hills afterwards?'

She looked at her dress, its elegance as out of place as the pet bullocks that used to be cosseted by this hearth.

'I like you in jeans and shirt. They suit you. Wear the dress another time.'

There was cold chicken, soda bread and two bottles of beer. They sat on a bright green strip of grass, patterned with tightly closed pink daisy buds. Sheltering them was a ridge of yellow gorse. A silver and rose mist on distant cliff tops made ghostly shapes of yachts out at sea. Hungry, they ate in silence. Gusts of warm wind from the hill stirred through the grass, bringing the scent of heather and bog myrtle. It hummed away like a distant chorus.

Afterwards Kiaran hid the basket under the gorse and they walked up through the heather. As they climbed and chatted companionably, a stronger wind that smelt of the sea made the clouds sweep their shadows across the slopes.

'There's a holy lough at the top,' he said.

'I know. And you can make a wish. Race you . . . '

He smiled. 'Not a chance. You're a couple of stone lighter than me . . . watch how you go. Remember, three points on. A firm grip with your right hand.'

'Are you an experienced climber?'

'I've done quite a bit here and abroad. I prefer hill-climbing in Donegal though. It's gentle . . . heavens, smell that air.' He looked around him. 'The smouldering purple of those hills and the extraordinary blue sky must make this place an artist's paradise.'

'The subject could become boring.'

'You enjoy your work? Is it difficult?'

'Sometimes. But yes, I love it.'

'Not like mucking out byres!'

'You do that yourself?' she asked in surprise, sitting down on a little plateau that jutted from the hill. He was just below her, feet set firmly in a hollow, partly concealed by swags of heather.

'The old days at Slievan have gone – the "good old days" that my father enjoyed when he was my age. He wasn't cut out to be a farmer, nevertheless he's beginning to show more interest during the past year.'

'That would take him out of himself. Is he – ?'

'Yes, he's better. There was a plan that he might retire to the south with my aunt.' Kiaran looked towards the lighthouse. 'We were all making plans. They were not the right ones,' he added briefly.

Marcella rested her hand on the edge of the little plateau to raise herself up. Dried by the wind and sun, it suddenly gave way under her weight and she went tumbling down towards him. He went off-balance, but an instinctive reaction made him fling out one hand and clutch the wiry heather, grabbing her with the other. Somehow she found herself in the hollow with his arm across her shoulder, feet planted firmly on each side.

When she got her breath back, Marcella said, 'It didn't take me long to forget my first climbing lesson, did it?'

'That bit of overlapping ground was deceptive. You have to watch out for those sort of things at this height. The rain shifts the earth, reducing its firmness.' He looked down, searching her face, then away as though holding a memory. At that moment, Marcella knew for certain that some delicate emotion had been trapped irrevocably in their youth and, whatever plans they both made for the future, it would always lie between them.

'You first,' she said, feeling that the easy companionship of the last two hours was slipping away as his silence increased. She scrambled to the top of the hill and knelt before the deep green lough; some called it the pagan lough because of the strangely shaped stones surrounding it.

Others said it had been blessed by St Patrick himself. Woven into the ground was a tapestry of the emblem he had used to convert Ireland. She pulled out some of the shamrocks and threw them on the water. 'Take a wish, Kiaran.'

He came beside her, took her face in his hands and kissed her. The action was sudden, unexpected. She did not respond . . . not for a moment or two, then they were close in each other's arms. Blue shadows filled the hollows of the hill before they made their way down again. They took the easier path, a rough cart-track. Though their hands were joined, unspoken words lay between them. And through his silence, Marcella became aware that she had entered a troubled area of his life.

'Tomorrow?' he said, when they reached the bridge by River House.

She shook her head, against her will. All her tomorrows were the same, but she had to pretend to protect herself against her need for him. 'I'm too busy.'

'Next day, then?'

'All right,' she agreed willingly.

Lisa phoned that evening. Could Marcella leave for Paris immediately? There was a job for her in the house where Lisa was employed. The family were going to Perpignan for four weeks and wanted to know right away. When she hesitated and mumbled something about the cottage not being finished, her friend said crossly, 'But you promised and I *begged* Madame Terrasse to allow me to ring you.'

'All right, Lisa. I'll leave tomorrow morning then. My passport's all ready.' Perhaps it was just as well to get away for a while, Marcella decided. If Kiaran did not contact her when she returned, then she must accept the fact that the apparent uncertainty in his life did not involve her. Tomorrow he might even regret his day on the hill, she thought bleakly. Nevertheless she sat down and wrote him a note, explaining that she had agreed to work for a few weeks in France. She gave the note to Biddy. 'Will you give this to Kiaran Gilroy?' Biddy's eyes pierced the envelope but Marcella knew she could trust her.

Soon after she arrived in Perpignan, Marcella sent every-one a card with her address. She was disappointed that Kiaran had not written. It was near the end of the second week that his letter arrived. The entire family were just about to go into town to dine at the Place de la Loge. A table had been reserved outside the café where the Spanish Catalonians were performing their traditional dance, the 'Sardine'. Regretfully Marcella glanced at the envelope with the Eire stamp and the firm handwriting that raced across it.

When one of the twins became restless, she agreed to take the little boy for a walk. They went down past Maillol's bronze statue of Venus and found a quiet café. She ordered a coffee and a large chocolate ice cream, which the child had previously been forbidden. It was the only way to keep him silent.

'Marcella,' Kiaran wrote. 'Forgive me for not replying sooner to your letter. And thank you for your postcard. Perpignan looks as picturesque as ever. Must you wait until the end of the holidays before returning? After that you will be busy with your art studies in Derry. Please come back sooner if you can. There are things I want to say but find it difficult to write about. What I must say though is that the afternoon we spent in the hills made me very happy.'

She showed Lisa the letter that evening. 'I'm leaving at the beginning of next week, Lisa, when the maid returns from her holiday. I hope you don't mind?'

'I think you must,' Lisa replied thoughtfully. 'It is important that you do so.'

'You're my best friend,' Marcella said, hugging her.

'I hope so.' Lisa frowned. 'Prisca doesn't want to be bothered with me any more.' She shrugged. 'Brian and other things – '

'Other things? What do you mean?'

'You must not mention this, promise? Someone at college told me that she is the leader of a young Republican

233

group.'

'No!'

'It is so.'

'How, where do they meet? I didn't think anything like that went on these days.'

'It goes on. There are people at college interested in the politics of your country but not like Prisca.'

Marcella sent Kiaran a card saying '*Coming home on Tuesday*.' She couldn't wait to get back to Ireland. On the Thursday he drove up to the cottage door. She wiped her paintbrushes on an old rag and hurried out to meet him. 'Would you like to share my lunch, Kiaran?'

He smiled, kissed her and said, 'I would. Ah, a fire in the hearth. This looks cosy.' He touched one of the beams. 'It's a sound little place. Any land?'

'Just a half-acre around the cottage. That's why the place went so cheap. Kettle's on the boil. I'll make some tea.'

He took the heavy iron kettle from her. 'That's an old one.'

'Biddy gave it to them. Her brothers used to keep their poteen in it.'

He laughed. 'Tell me about France.'

'Hard work. Spoilt children. Spoilt, rich mother.'

'I'm glad you came back.'

'When your letter arrived I knew it was the only thing to do.'

He looked at her for a moment, as uncertain as she was, then crossed to the window and glanced out at the tangle of roses and veronica that crowded closely, scenting the room. Before his fixed gaze the years began to slip by in restless little scenes. Some wavering with uncertainty, like his time in the seminary. Ended quickly by his repulsion for the discipline and his unsuitability. Flickering love scenes. Helena. Love built on the foundation of her fragile beauty, sophistication and maturity – ah, how deceptive that word was. Certainly her eligibility had some importance too. His cousin's wealth would ensure the future of Slievan, his aunt said. Everyone was pleased. Now all were enraged about the broken engagement. All except his father, whose land would have benefited from her dowry. Then there was London which she loved. Her friends. The parties where it was fashionable to 'smoke' whatever it was they passed around. 'We're living in the sixties, darling . . . ' she had protested when he said he preferred a glass of whiskey. Kiaran turned abruptly from the window.

'Marcella, you've probably realized by now that the engagement to my cousin has ended.'

She poured the tea and handed him a cup. 'I hope it was not too distressing.'

'No,' he lied, trying to forget the terrible scene with Helena.

After that, they met once or twice a week. Sometimes Brian and Prisca joined them and they motored around the coast, calling in at little out of the way pubs where a fiddler would be found playing in the corner, or an old man with a tiny melodeon pressed between his hands. At first, Prisca resented Kiaran and showed it, but eventually his good humour and friendship with Brian broke down her belligerence. Even so, Marcella knew that Prisca was waiting for Kiaran to disappear 'back to the gentry where he belongs', as she put it once.

Several months later, when the windswept lands of Inishowen settled with the warmth of spring, Marcella came back to Iniscad for the Easter holidays. It was a busy time on the land for Kiaran. They had an easy arrangement. If he could get away at any time he would call around to River House and they would go walking. Like Prisca, Sarah often gave a disagreeable sniff, declaring that her niece was wasting her time . . . nothing would come of it. The landed gentry always married their own kind. It was only in stories that they married beneath them.

Marcella ignored her taunts, aware that there was a note of anxiety too, in case she was made a laughing stock of the countryside. One spring morning Kiaran rang early. He wanted to go and see a piece of Gilroy land that lay near the Free State border. Afterwards, they'd have lunch in

Buncrana.

'Huh! Off again at the drop of a hat,' her aunt commented drily. Marcella found it difficult to imagine this woman as a beautiful, broken-hearted heroine whose lover had been executed by a firing squad.

It was a quiet place they came to, nestling in a valley with a trout stream running through the land. Kiaran wanted to inspect the trees that were mostly gnarled with age. Sunlight touched them lightly, drawing colours from their crusted bark. Some had parasitic growths; others, tentacle-like roots gripping the ground.

'I used to camp here with my cousins, years ago,' he told her.

'It's a perfect place. There's shelter, water.'

'I wish we could –'

'Camp? No good! Aunt would have a fit.'

He laughed and turned away quickly aware, as she was, of the feeling that was growing rapidly between them. On the way home he said, 'Come and see the old barn. I've converted part of it into a workshop.' It was the first time he had invited her anywhere near the house. As they were going up the drive the car made a funny noise. 'It's the engine. Wish I could afford a new car. Go on into the barn, Cella, I'll be with you in a moment.'

The workshop part of the barn had neat rows of tools and pieces of woodwork on the bench. He was repairing a footstool which was covered with an exquisite piece of tapestry. The air was drenched with the sweet smell of hay. Marcella went over, flung herself on top of the stack and gazed up at the old walls which were filmed with a deep purple and green bloom, like the colours of Irish tweed.

'Kiaran.' The harsh voice of his aunt made her start. 'Do you realize how ridiculously you are behaving?'

'What do you mean?' Kiaran sounded surprised.

'That Adams girl you've been running around the countryside with over the past months.'

'Marcella? What about her?' His quiet casual question brought a flow of genteel vituperation.

'How can you associate with that type of girl? She's not

your class – not nearly good enough. And she's quite wild, I hear. Hangs around that gypsy camp. Practically lived there at one time.'

'I'd rather we didn't discuss this now. She's in the . . . '

'You know what she's after, don't you? She's going to make sure you get her in the family way and then you'll *have* to marry her!'

As the shrill words rang into the still evening, a feeling of shame swept over Marcella, leaving a blinding anger. She tore out of the barn and rushed at the tall woman clutching the delicate arms of jasmine which lit the wall in winter with their pale yellow flowers. Her hand flew through the air and crashed into Miss Gilroy's face.

'How dare you,' she shouted, and rushed away across the lawn to the woods.

At River House she went to tear upstairs when Sarah hurried out and barred her way. 'What's the matter? Why are you in such a state?'

'Kiaran's aunt, she . . . she talked about me as if I were a slut. And you know what I did?' Marcella shouted. 'I bloody well slapped her face, the virtuous old frozen hag.'

'You wicked brat. You dared to do such a thing.' Sarah's voice was one of amazed horror. Miss Gilroy belonged to lofty unattainable social heights. A smile of recognition in the passing car, or a 'Good morning, Miss Adams' honoured her. For her niece to have assaulted the woman was unthinkable. She stamped her foot. 'How could you *do* such a thing?'

'She insulted me.'

Sarah whacked her across the head. Pushing her aside, Marella leapt up the stairs to her bedroom, feeling that her happiness had been shattered by the tasteless words on the old aristocrat's tongue. What was Kiaran thinking now? There had not been any hint of anything serious in their friendship. After one unsuccessful relationship he certainly wasn't going to commit himself again so soon. Tears started in her eyes because she knew she was committed by a love that had begun in her childhood. His aunt's words were bound to cause embarrassment between them in future.

She heard Brian coming into the house, then talking to Sarah on the landing. He opened the door. 'Cup of tea, Cella?' He stood looking down at her, sprawled across the bed. 'I'd like to hear how you nearly killed that auld woman up at Slievan.' At that moment a car shot across the gravel outside. He glanced through the window. 'It's Kiaran Gilroy.' He hurried from the room.

Footsteps bounded up the stairs. There was a quick knock at the door and Kiaran came in. A feeling of lethargy seemed to have frozen Marcella's limbs. She could scarcely lift her head. 'Marcella.' He came over, sat beside her and gathered up all the damp hair, wet by her tears, as though that was the purpose of his visit. 'Marcella, will you marry me? To hell with not being able to afford it. We can always live on a creel of potatoes and maybe Biddy can steal a few bones from the Slievan kitchen!'

She covered her face with her hands and began to laugh helplessly and a little hysterically. He lay down beside her, took her in his arms and said, 'You know I'm crazy about you.'

Later, Brian poured sherry into the Waterford glasses which for years had been like holy relics – to be stared at and not touched. Marcella wrote a note of apology to Kiaran's aunt, who was leaving for a visit to Cork in the morning.

'I told my father that I was going to marry you, if you would have me.'

'What did he say?' she asked anxiously.

'Can she milk cows!'

'Oh, Kiaran!'

That evening they went to see Nanta. She wanted her friend to hear the news straight away. Nanta met them by the pond in the woods, a bundle of kindling in her arms. The expression on Marcella's face made words unnecessary. She held out her hand and gave Kiaran a long searching look. He had never met her before, and it was obvious he was a bit overwhelmed because the gypsy was still a beautiful woman. She led them through the woods to the caravan where they drank a glass of wine; then Nanta, losing some of her reserve, showed him a folder containing Marcella's childish drawings. Like a mother, she had kept them all.

On their way home he said, 'I think there must be something in that old Irish fable about the princess who was stolen by the gypsies. There's something regal about Nanta, isn't there?'

Chapter 21

Kiaran and Marcella decided to fix up the lodge house and make it their home. A large north-facing room upstairs would be ideal for a studio. Conor was very pleased about his daughter's future; however, he insisted that she must finish her art course before they were married. This meant she would have to go back to Derry during the week. Marcella wondered if Cassy would relax her rule and allow Kiaran to come up to her room, or even use the parlour.

'Now, daughter,' Cassy said piously, 'keep yerself right for your wedding day.' The sitting-room couch was still regarded as an instrument of sin and upstairs was certainly out of bounds.

'Cassy,' Marcella pleaded, 'all the students at college are allowed to bring their boyfriends into their rooms, never mind a freezing parlour like yours.'

'Now, daughter, the kitchen is the safest place for yer courting.'

A few weeks later Prisca came to Iniscad for the weekend. 'Brian and I are going to bring forward the date of our wedding,' she said abruptly.

'I thought you had to wait until you finished at the Teacher's Training College. I mean, what is the point? You're in Belfast and he's in Dublin, apart from the odd weekend and holidays.'

'We'll have to manage, that's all. Surely I don't have to spell it out for you.'

'What do you mean? Oh no!' Marcella said in dismay.

'Don't go worrying about what the lofty Gilroys might think,' Prisca said unfairly. 'I've got enough problems worrying about my own family and your aunt.'

'Prisca, are you quite sure?'

'I've missed two months,' she said flatly, then bent her head and began to cry. 'Oh God, Cella, what am I going to do? It'll break my mother's heart and my father will kill me.'

It was difficult to imagine the easygoing Mr McDaid killing anyone. Something prudish in Marcella held her back from giving Prisca the whole-hearted support she needed at that moment. Later, when she considered it, she felt ashamed. 'Finish your training then get married,' she suggested. 'No one will notice.'

'I'm showing already. Look how my blouse is strained across my breasts. And I've still got a couple of months at the college. I'm going to be one of those women who look like a mountain in four months.' For a few minutes Prisca looked trapped, then she became quiet and thoughtful. 'It's all right,' she said, springing to her feet. 'It's my problem. Why the hell should I worry about what everyone else thinks?'

Somehow her words didn't sound at all convincing. 'You're not going to do anything wrong, are you? For God's sake don't – '

'Whatever I do, Marcella, is my own business.'

Later that evening during the meal she was excitable and chatted away, even succeeding in making Sarah laugh. Brian had a strained, anxious look, and Marcella felt sorry for him. If a servant had not arrived that evening, bringing a note from Kiaran telling her he could not come because they had visitors, Marcella would not have discovered what Prisca was planning.

She was sitting by her bedroom window, working on a sketch, when she saw Prisca slip out the back door and cut up by the field towards the brae. About a half-hour later she and Biddy came down the same way and, to Marcella's surprise, went up the little lane and on towards the hill road that led to the dark pool – a deep pool in the peat bogs that was supposed to be haunted by a young girl whose lover fell in and was drowned.

What were they going up there for at this time of night? Marcella knew of only one cottage that way; the person who lived in it was called 'the witch'. She was a tinker woman who had become tired of roaming the roads and had a gift for curing ailments with herbs. There were strange stories told about her, though possibly all highly exaggerated. Feeling uneasy, Marcella pushed away her work and ran downstairs. Just as she was leaving the house, Brian and Sarah came round the gable discussing some repair that had been done to the porch.

'Have you seen Prisca?' he called.

Marcella shook her head. It was about fifteen minutes later before they went indoors. She pulled her bicycle out of the barn and made for the hills. The bicycle was a mistake. After a while she left it by the roadside and hurried on by foot. As she climbed, the wind began to whistle lightly, then gradually developed into a quick lilt which made the sparse trees along the way sway as though they had been waiting for this moment of the dance. The fanciful thought made her smile, but the old people called it the music of the mountain wind.

The cottage was a long way up and the wind was growing stronger, pressing against her as it strummed like a faltering hand on the deep notes of a harp. The little building came into sight as the wind gathered force and the full orchestration began. Pieces of twigs, moss and leaves swirled past as the sound mounted to a high-pitched note. She struggled on towards the trees and fuchsia bushes that surrounded the little property and stopped to get her breath. Not knowing what to expect inside the broken-down dwelling, she slumped against a mountain-ash, feeling exhilarated but tired.

As swiftly as it had begun the wind began to die away until it became like the gentle play of a wind-instrument. Rested, she approached the house, realizing that she had lost a lot of time because the other two had probably taken the short cut across the bog which would have enabled them to reach the cottage much faster. And of course, miss the storm on the mountain.

The door of the cottage was shut. She knocked. There was no reply. Marcella picked up a stone, went to the tiny window and banged against it. After a minute there was the sound of a bolt being drawn back. Slowly the door opened and Biddy in the brae looked out nervously.

'Cella . . . no need for all that,' she said sheepishly.

Marcella pushed past her. 'Where's Prisca?' she demanded and before Biddy could speak the denial that was plainly on her lips she said, 'You went up the hill together.'

'In here,' Prisca called.

The little room was off the kitchen. Against the wall a high featherbed stood; beside it was an old table and a chair. Prisca was sitting on the chair drinking from a glass filled with an evil-looking liquid. Marcella dashed it out of her hand.

'I've already had two,' she said wearily. 'And why the hell don't you mind your own business.'

'May God forgive the three of you,' Marcella said sanctimoniously. She walked out to the kitchen and glowered at the old crone stirring a black pot hanging from the crook over the peat fire; the fire was the only pleasant smell in that kitchen. Biddy shrank into the corner before the blazing look in Marcella's eyes, then she went into the room and tried to clear up the mess of broken glass.

'Cella . . .' Prisca was standing behind her. 'Don't tell Brian. *Please*. If you do, I'll jump into the black pool, for he'll never forgive me.'

Marcella turned slowly to look at her. 'You're trying to destroy your child, aren't you?'

Prisca winced. 'For God's sake . . .' Her face was deadly pale, eyes dark and shadowed. 'It's nothing – only an embryo.'

'That's true,' Biddy said.

'Shut up,' Marcella snarled at her.

'It has not been proved that – ' Prisca went on.

'You shut up too, Prisca.' Marcella wanted to weep for what had been done in this dirty hovel. A child in a woman's womb, from the moment of conception, was sacred. It had a soul. Between them . . . a simple old woman, ignorant Biddy and clever Prisca, they had killed it. 'Please don't try at this moment to give me any of your intellectual reasoning,' she shouted at Prisca, 'or I'll hit you.'

'There's no need to go on like that, Cella,' Biddy said meekly.

'You hadn't the moral courage to go through with your pregnancy, you were frightened of criticism, the anger of your parents.'

'You don't understand, do you, Marcella Adams?' Prisca accused her angrily. 'I have as much courage as anyone, but I could not bring such sorrow to my parents or Brian. He's breaking down under the strain of what's happened. Do you really think I wanted to come here? I would have gladly had the child but I am burdened with the pain of others.'

Marcella saw the despair in her face and the hardness left her heart. 'All right,' she said quietly, 'let me take you home.'

'I can't leave yet,' Prisca told her, a terrible weariness and despair in her voice.

'What's in that pot?' Marcella asked with fear and repulsion as the old woman built up the fire under it. The flames jumped greedily around as though hurrying on the potion that held death in its substance.

'Only a herbal dose – all that's needed at this early stage of pregnancy.'

'I'll go down and get Brian's car and come back for you,' Marcella said abruptly.

'The old woman said I must walk after taking the necessary quantity.'

'Nevertheless, I'll come. Just in case you need me.' Marcella turned to Biddy. 'You won't speak of this, will you?'

'As God's me judge. No one from the brae house ever told a tale on anyone.'

That's true, she thought. Biddy would protect them from gossip, if she could.

It was quite dark outside. Marcella walked down the

lonely hillside, glad of the light from Inishtrahull Lighthouse. Back at the house, Brian was getting anxious about Prisca. 'She went up to the brae house to see the patchwork quilt Biddy's making for your cottage,' Marcella lied. 'Brian, would you mind if I borrowed your car? I'll call in and give her a lift back.'

He looked surprised because he knew Marcella hated driving, particularly after dark; however, he raised no objection nor asked any awkward questions. She took the torch and went to the barn where he and her father kept the cars. Just as she was about to switch on the light, the sound reached her — the one she had heard before, as though people were somewhere near. She didn't move; the murmur seemed to float away in the night. Switching on the torch, she swung the light around. There was nothing to be seen.

The road up the hill was very rough and difficult. Marcella went cautiously, frightened to damage her brother's car. Near the cottage, Prisca and Biddy were coming down. No short cut this time, it was too dangerous in the dark. With great care, she turned the car and waited for them.

'It's good you're here, Cella,' Biddy said, 'for the dear knows she's had enough.' As she spoke, Prisca doubled over with pain. They helped her into the car and Biddy went in beside her. A bag containing old towels was in her hand. She pulled a bottle out of it.

'What's in that?' Marcella asked suspiciously.

'Poteen.'

'Poteen,' she repeated through her teeth.

'A wee jap will ease the pain.'

It was fortunate that Brian had walked down to Boyle's for a drink, because Prisca was in a bad way when they reached the house. They hustled her up the stairs. Sarah's sharp little voice called out: 'Who's out there?'

Biddy went down again into the living room leaving Marcella, who was really very alarmed and tried not to show it, to deal with the situation.

'The bathroom . . . I'll need to stay in there,' Prisca

whispered. 'Keep Sarah away.'

She was a half-hour in the bathroom; during that time Marcella put hot water bottles in her bed and made a pot of tea. The witches' brew has worked, she thought grimly when Prisca lay down on the bed, deadly white but calm.

'Thanks, Cella,' she said, touching her hand. 'Tell them all I've had one of my migraines and went to bed. Tomorrow, I'll tell Brian "my problem" was a false alarm.'

And what will you tell your conscience, Marcella wondered. No doubt Prisca would deal with that problem – if she considered it a problem – in the brisk efficient way that she dealt with everything in life.

The following morning she said to her, 'Prisca, why did you go off with Biddy after you spoke to me?' When she didn't reply, Marcella went on, 'You had it all planned, didn't you? Yet you sounded so uncertain at the time.'

Prisca fingered the bedspread then she raised her eyes. 'I *hadn't* planned to tell you. When I did, I wanted you to fight my conscience for me. I wanted you to protest vehemently, to threaten to tell Brian – something like that. I might just have changed my mind.'

'But I *did* protest,' she shouted at her, stunned by the unfairness of the words. Prisca was placing a part of the guilt on her shoulders.

'Not in the way I expected.'

Furious, Marcella walked out of the room and went downstairs to lie her head off to the other two.

When she returned to the room with a breakfast tray, Prisca said: 'There's something I would like you to do for me, Cella. Could you go into Derry tomorrow and see my mother?'

'Derry? Yes, all right.'

'Tell her I won't be home again before I go to Belfast.'

'What excuse will I give?'

'What do you think?' she said evenly. 'A bad period.'

'Should I not stay around to see that you're all right?'

'I'll be okay now. I'd rather be on my own for a bit. Apart from that, I'll lie better to Brian if you're not here.'

*

The McDaids' front door was half-open as usual. Dominic was sitting with his feet propped up over the stove when she walked into the kitchen. The stove was a big old-fashioned one and shone with care. Over in the corner, Granny McDaid was in her chair fast asleep. He rose slowly to his feet, a medical textbook sliding to the floor.

'Hello, Marcella. What a surprise,' he said coolly. 'I haven't seen you for a very long time.'

She stared at him for a moment. He had changed somehow; his face had lost some of the lean, almost gaunt look and the stark blackness in his eyes seemed less compelling now when he glanced at her. She thought of a comparison and said out loud, 'Franz Kafka. That's who you used to remind me of.'

The long, sensitive mouth moved in a half-sardonic smile. 'Good Lord, you don't read Kafka, do you?'

'Brian raves about him, but I don't like his books. It's the photo on the cover of *America*.' She shut up quickly, suddenly feeling a fool.

He raised his eyebrows. 'I suppose I must congratulate you on your engagement to Kiaran Gilroy. I wonder how you'll like living in the big house?'

'I'd be happy living anywhere with Kiaran,' she said snappily. His tone irritated her. It reminded Marcella of that first time they met years ago, that aloof manner with its edge of bitterness.

'Can I offer you something? My mother has gone out somewhere.' His eyes went to the clock.

'No thanks, I can see you're busy.'

'I am rather, trying to catch up with some work. Actually I should be up in my room but,' he nodded at his grandmother, 'I'm frightened she might wake up and stumble against the stove.'

'She's been around for nearly a hundred years, I'm sure she's safe enough,' Marcella said shortly, knowing that he wanted her to go.

'If you'd like to wait, my sister Patsy will be back in a minute. She's gone for some messages.'

'In that case, I'll walk down the street and meet her

coming from the shop.'

Dominic opened the kitchen door and they went out to the narrow hall. He went to pass her to pick up a scarf lying on the floor, but the old Victorian hall-stand, loaded with coats, jutted out and brought them close. He stopped and looked down at her, then his hand came up swiftly and curved around her chin. Bending his head, he kissed her hard and angrily. Marcella's surprise was mingled with a strong, unexpected feeling that raced through her body. 'Goodbye, Marcella.' She fumbled with the door and hurried away.

Patsy came up the street carrying a basket loaded with groceries. 'Hello, Cella. Are you looking for Mammy?'

'Yes, where is she?'

The girl glanced towards the house and lowered her voice. 'Don't let on because Dominic would be wild, but she's working in the shirt factory today. They sent for her because someone's ill and they've got a rushed order.'

'Would it be all right if I went there to see her?'

'Surely. I think so . . .'

She wasn't all that sure. Marcella was going anyway, for she was certain her message had a far greater importance than the few words could reveal. Prisca was very close to her mother.

At the factory, the noise of sewing machines mixed with loud chatter rattled down the stairs to meet her. There was a rich smell of linen and fine cotton. Inside the room, workers were sewing the piles of shirts placed on their benches by the cutter. Plain and striped colours flew through their fingers at an incredible speed. Many of the women had scarves tied around a headful of curlers. Nora McDaid was sitting by herself at a table doing, it would seem, finishing work. She looked up with surprise when Marcella spoke her name. Her hesitant smile was mixed with alarm.

Quickly, the prepared message passed Marcella's lips.

'Och, that auld trouble, I never knew she had it so bad. It was like that with me, after I got married,' she said with complete innocence. 'Ah well, I'll see her next time. How's yourself, Marcella?'

'Great,' she replied, looking at the wide blue eyes under the reddish glowing hair, and understanding why Prisca always said, 'My mother is so good, she couldn't think badly of anyone if she tried.' And certainly not her own daughter.

'Marcella, if you meet Dominic, never let on ye saw me here. They'll be all right for a few hours with Patsy to keep an eye on things.'

In the crowded workroom, the smell of perspiration from over-heated women mingled with the fresh smell of cloth. Marcella said, 'It's not a very comfortable place to work in, is it?'

'No, right enough. Sure they're lucky to have a job, dear. Their men are all on the dole.'

'I wish you didn't have to come here, Mrs McDaid.'

'Sure, dear knows, I don't like it one bit any more. But they sent for me. Anyway, Brendan wants to be a priest and that'll be another big expense.'

Brendan a priest? Marcella's eyes flew wide in surprise. Prisca hadn't mentioned it. Because she did not approve? The boy was like his sister in many ways. High-spirited, interested in politics.

'Och, I'm that happy about it. A bit of extra money will come in useful,' Mrs McDaid said. 'God has answered my prayers. I thought at one time it would be Dominic, now I have my doubts if he'd go to Mass if I wasn't around. I must get on. Give Prisca my love and tell her I'm only here to fill in for a while.'

It was not in Mrs McDaid's nature to ask Marcella to lie to her daughter about the factory work; for that she was grateful. She had done her share of lying for one day.

That evening when Marcella returned from Derry, Prisca was sitting downstairs by the fire with Sarah fussing over her. Brian looked relaxed and happy.

Chapter 22

The winter passed and the hedges began to brighten with spring flowers. All the fuss and preparations for Marcella's wedding had begun. How often she and Kiaran wished they could slip down to the church and be married quietly. His aunt had invited the Gilroy hierarchy to conduct the wedding service: a bishop, a canon and someone high up in the Vatican. Furious, Marcella told her that they could come as guests but as Father McGill had baptized and confirmed her, he was going to marry her as well. One night a few weeks before their wedding day she was about to get out of the car when Kiaran reached into the glove compartment and handed her a book.

'Would you like to take a look?'

Safe Period was printed on the cover. 'Ah, Prisca thinks . . .'

'Never mind what Prisca thinks, I know exactly how she feels about it.'

A few days previous to this they had all been in Boyle's Hotel having a drink when Prisca and Kiaran had had a heated discussion about the Pope's encyclical – *Humanae Vitae*. She was furious about his decision on birth control. Kiaran, who had a more conservative view, reminded her of various aspects of the Church's teaching. While the two of them thrashed it out, a silence fell over the customers. Their conversation petered away when they discovered that Miss Boyle and all the old men in the bar were listening too, their eyes round with shocked delight. Such a subject was never discussed openly.

That night Marcella sat up in bed and began to study the book. It looked complicated at first, then gradually the meaning of the rhythm chart became clearer. 'You'd better study this too,' she said when Prisca came into the room.

Prisca glanced through it briefly, then tossed it away. 'You're surely not going to bother with that?'

Marcella was taken aback by her complete rejection of it. 'Kiaran gave it to me. After all, the Church doesn't allow birth control and now there's this encyclical and you know what he thinks about that.'

'Oh yes, it's all right for Kiaran. How does he know you're going to have a safe period? Lots of people don't; that's the cause of a lot of trouble in Catholic marriages. Anyway, you have the right to plan your family and the Church has no right to interfere.' She emphasized her words and brought out all the arguments of the previous night. Marcella had not Kiaran's ability to weaken her ground. 'That's how I got caught, using a safe period that didn't exist,' Prisca admitted unhappily.

'If I haven't a safe period, I suppose I'll just have a child before I planned. That won't worry me very much.'

'If you have ten before you're thirty that'll certainly worry you,' she snapped. 'Have some sense, think of the women in Brawn Street.'

'What about your mother? Having a large family didn't bother her, did it?'

'Don't be stupid, of course it bothered her. When we were all young she didn't have time to enjoy us in the way a mother should. She was worn out. One miscarriage after another. My God, I can remember her standing very pregnant, ironing our clothes late at night.' Prisca bit her lip as though the memory still hurt.

'But you're such a happy, contented family . . .'

'Think of the poor things in Brawn Street: wretched because they have a child nearly every year, often because their husbands come home drunk, unhappy about their workless lives. Kiaran,' she went on, 'can argue about the authority of the Church, but he has no idea how important it was that the encyclical gave us complete freedom in our lives.' She banged her hand on the dressing-table. 'Another thing. Jews and Gentiles practised birth control from the earliest times by herbal treatment, yet neither Christ nor Saint Paul ever spoke against it, did they?'

'Father McGill . . .'

'Aye, the priests, it's fine for them to talk. What the hell do they really know about the anxiety and suffering that goes on in the minds of some women?'

'There's the confessional.'

Prisca tightened her lips in the way she had of showing displeasure. 'I for one would never take my bedroom into the confession box. Thank God there are priests who do understand and are wise enough to agree when doctors advise women to take the pill to regulate their periods.'

'What's going to happen now that people are getting worried about the effects of the pill? Honestly, Prisca, I would be frightened to take it.'

'There are birth control clinics.'

'Ugh!'

'Ugh, nothing. We're brainwashed against them. Look, Cella, why not go to Dominic and discuss it with him. He's very much against the safe period because it works for so few people, or so he says. Let me arrange a time for you to see him.'

'No!' The very thought of having such an intimate discussion with Dominic made Marcella hot with embarrassment. She had not seen him since the day he kissed her in the hall. He was not coming to their wedding. Work, he excused himself.

The weeks up to their wedding seemed to pass in a daze. She was worn out by Aunt Sarah's nerves, Miss Gilroy's voice and Ned in the brae chanting: 'As God's m'judge, I niver thought I'd see the day when I'd dance at Slievan.' There was going to be a party in the barn for the people who worked on the estate. Biddy was taking her brother to the celebrations.

Then their wedding day. After all the fuss was over, they climbed into Kiaran's car and drove away from Iniscad.

Prisca was appalled by the lavishness of Marcella's wedding reception. And to think that Conor Adams footed the bill! Pity he couldn't spare a bit to help her and Brian furnish their cottage. When was money going to stop being a problem? It was a continual embarrassment that she was unable to contribute anything to the Republican funds. It was amazing how well-heeled some of the Kindron descendants were. Now she could see the reason why Rosheen Quinn went after them. Prisca was sure that Eoin O'Donnell regretted letting Rosheen look at that list of names.

There was a bit of coolness between the pair these days. Of course it was caused by Eoin's interest in the Civil Rights Association. Eoin had a great dream that it would solve Ulster's problems. He said that a report on the Northern Ireland franchise had been drawn up and sent to various prominent people in the hope of awakening interest in the civil rights question.

Their first parade in Derry had been disastrous. It was planned to publicize the objectives of the movement in relation to jobs, housing and gerrymandering. Gerry Fitt, Hume and others had set out peacefully and unarmed but the police, under orders from the Minister for Home Affairs, baton-charged the crowd of marchers and drove them down William Street with water cannons. A few days after that, the students from Queen's University staged a sit-down outside the Guildhall to protest against police brutality. The government was actually showing some concern about the non-sectarian stance of the students.

Thank God her parents had now moved up to Northland Road and avoided trouble when the police invaded the Bogside. That place was becoming like a battlefield, particularly Brawn Street. They had moved to the house of roses, as her mother used to call it. What a grand place. And the generous Misses Thorn had left a pile of carpets and some furniture. The girls, if you please, had a room each. When Prisca thought of how she had had to struggle in that wee bedroom with her three sisters breathing down her neck . . .

Apparently Mona O'Donovan was going to move out and work as a live-in maid at Lisa's home. Prisca was glad that her mother was spared the worry of looking after her, particularly since the girl had started staying out late at night.

The house in Brussels, where Marcella and Kiaran were spending their honeymoon, was a few miles outside the city. It was an elegant house but one lacking in warmth. Mrs de Win, the housekeeper, reminded Marcella of the one in Daphne Du Maurier's *Rebecca*; with her colourless face and black hair swept severely to the top of her head. Kiaran said she had been with the family all her working life. There was a slight thaw in the woman's manner when she greeted him because he had spent holidays in the house with his uncle and aunt, who had been unable to come to the wedding because they were in America. When the woman's cold eyes swept over Marcella, they hesitated at her short pleated skirt.

Their bedroom was lovely: white Indian carpets, with silk curtains and bedspreads to match. In the alcove by the window, a group of delicate French-designed chairs was arranged. Outside the door was a spacious landing which looked like a salon. A floor of dark rich wood sparkled with a patina which reflected the Regency couch and chairs; these were covered in a green striped brocade. Ancestral portraits in heavy gold frames lined the walls.

'It's terribly grand,' Marcella whispered as they made their way downstairs for dinner. There was something about the house that made her whisper all the time they were there.

The dining room was long and dreary with a heavy mahogany table down the centre. Their places were set at each end. A glass of red wine beside the plates made a tiny welcoming glow in the elegant austerity of the room. As soon as the housekeeper went out, Marcella picked up her plate, cutlery and wine and went down beside Kiaran. When the woman returned again with the sweet, they were eating their food with a fork and holding hands. She gave a disapproving frown. The following morning, which was a Sunday, they planned to go to late Mass at the Dutch church. About nine o'clock Mrs de Win gave a sharp knock on their bedroom door, opened it and came in quickly.

'It's time to be up,' she said, going across the room and pulling back the curtains with a vicious tug.

Kiaran, with anger racing across his face, sprang up in bed. 'Mrs de Win, I might have been dressing. Next time please wait until we . . .' Before he could finish the sentence, she was out of the door again as though little wheels were attached to her feet.

'And that,' Marcella said, tapping him on the shoulder, 'is what she's going to do — pretend when it suits her that she doesn't understand what we're saying. Kiaran, that woman is going to spoil everything.'

When they finally came down to breakfast, the housekeeper was coming in through the front door from morning Mass. She reminded Marcella of an eagle: black and foreboding. Why was it, she wondered, that this type of woman always bothered her? Their piety seemed relentless, borne like a penance with no warmth or involvement with love, and yet how often they judged others, really believing themselves to be truly good.

After they had finished eating, Marcella carried their dishes into the kitchen. The housekeeper was protesting to a man at the back door.

'Non, non, they are here for just a holiday. They would not want a tent. Go away.'

'Ask them, ask them,' he insisted. 'It is a bargain. Ah, madame.' The man's face brightened when he saw Marcella. 'I have here a small tent. Would you be interested in buying it?'

When he mentioned the price, Marcella realized it was a terrific bargain. Ignoring her, Mrs de Win began to protest again. 'It is my affair,' Marcella said coldly. 'I must discuss it with my husband. Wait here,' she told the man who was enthusiastically setting up the tent and blocking the back door entrance.

At first Kiaran seemed reluctant when he saw the tiny tent and the excitable little foreigner jigging around it with a poking finger to prove its durability. 'I don't know that I want to spend my honeymoon in a tent that size.'

'If we stay on here I'll become frigid.'

At this the man began to fall about with laughter while Mrs de Win swept inside with an offended air.

'It'll make all the difference, Kiaran. We can get away from here and explore the countryside. Our money will last if we eat simple meals and there's old rugs in the back of the car.' She cleared the doubtful frown on his face by adding, 'Remember that noise last night? I think it was Mrs de Win walking in her sleep. And there's no key on our bedroom door!'

Next morning when they were leaving with their luggage, the housekeeper came out to the car, her arms loaded with rough red blankets, a tiny primus and a kettle. 'You keep them,' she said. 'They are no longer of use here.'

'It's her conscience,' Kiaran said as they sped down the wide tree-lined road. 'She's probably heartily glad to be rid of us. Wish she'd thrown in a few bottles of wine. I tried the cellar, but it was locked. However,' he grinned, 'I did just happen to lay my hands on a bottle of fine old brandy!'

They travelled as far as Luxembourg over the next few days. Marcella especially wanted to see it because it was her secret, magic place when she was a young girl. For some reason Sarah did not allow her to listen to the Luxembourg station so she used to hide her transistor under the sheets. It was a tiny escape route of brightness during those early days when Sarah came to the Adams' home.

On the way through Belgium they visited as many art galleries as they could manage. In one church, Marcella took so long studying a painting that Kiaran began to plait her hair at the back.

'Such irreverence,' a woman muttered angrily, which made them choke with laughter.

One day they were standing before Rubens' *Adoration of the Magi* in the Cathedral of Ghent, when suddenly she felt a small chill of fear and heard an echo of Nanta's voice when the playing cards were swept off the table. Her fingers tightened on Kiaran's.

'What is it, darling?'

'It must be artistic suffocation. All these great master-pieces.'

Outside in the sunshine he said; 'Tomorrow we'll start for home. And then, my girl, it'll be back down to earth, living with a dull farmer.'

Home. Their home. She was impatient to get back to Iniscad.

A few days later they were driving through Derry when a parade of Orangemen marched around Guildhall Square banging their drums. As usual people lined the pavements watching them.

'I think we'll stop here for lunch,' Kiaran suggested and they turned down a side street some distance from the Square to park the car. As they pushed their way through the crowd there seemed to be a change in the people's attitude. They no longer murmured, 'Performing monkeys. Bliddy eejits.' They watched quietly, sullenly.

'Something must have happened while we were away,' Kiaran said. 'We haven't read a newspaper for days.'

'What make you think that?'

'The atmosphere. It seems charged with feeling.'

At that moment, a stone was thrown at the big drum. A policeman grabbed a youth and there was a lot of scuffling; others began to join in.

'Come on, let's get out of here, Cella. We'll stop across the border. Aren't these parades stupid? Apart from the fact that it's damn silly to go about celebrating archaic triumphs, it's bound to antagonize the people. I don't understand why the Stormont politicians allow all that stupid flag-waving.'

'What about the Twelfth of July? The politicians march too.'

When they went to make a move in the direction of the car again, a policeman pushed them aside. 'Sorry, sir, you can't go down there. We want to clear this area.'

'But my car —' Kiaran began. The officer took no notice.

Everyone was pushed back towards Shipquay Gate.

'Kiaran, there's a taxi.'

'What good will that do?'

'I know him. He'd mow down the entire police force for a fare. He'll find a way around.'

Billy the Man nudged Micky O'Kane. 'Business, son. Look smart.'

'I know her. She's stuck up.'

'I don't care where the hell she's stuck.' Billy no longer jumped out when customers approached. Micky said his auld bones creaked and alarmed people.

'I'm afraid we've got a problem,' Kiaran said, approaching the big old-fashioned car.

'Everyone in Derry has the same complaint at the moment, mister.'

'I see . . . well, the thing is our car is no distance away. We can't reach it because the police are closing the way into Foyle Street.'

Billy winked. 'Ye lave it t'me. I'll git ye through.'

'Hello Micky,' Marcella said, getting into the car.

'Ye know m'partner, miss?'

Micky elbowed him and whispered; 'Her's Missus now.'

'Where'd ye say yer vehicle was, sir?'

Kiaran explained. Billy started the engine and saluting a police sergeant, drove straight across the area which had been cleared for the Orangemen's parade. An officer raced beside him like a royal guard. 'Where the hell do you think you're going? Get back. You can't go that way.'

'Sure I'm takin' these grievin' passengers to a funeral. They've just arrived from foreign parts and the lid's about to be closed on the auld father's coffin.'

'Where's the wake? Out on the river?' the policeman asked sarcastically as the car pointed in the direction of the quay.

'Jayus, Billy, yer in trouble,' Micky muttered.

'Double the fare,' Billy murmured from the side of his mouth.

'They're not green.'

'I'm afraid, sir,' he shouted across his shoulder to Kiaran, 'I'll be up afore the courts the morrow. Ah well, all in a day's work. These are troubled times.' He winked at Micky.

Marcella and Kiaran, who had lowered their heads trying to look like grieving people, were choking with laughter. 'I hope you can afford to pay him, he'll be looking for extra,' she whispered.

'Empty your purse. No lunch. The sooner we get out of this damn town the better.'

It was raining when they reached Iniscad. A man from Slievan was cutting the lawn at the lodge house. He came over, shook their hands and wished them all God's blessings on their marriage.

'Not all the blessings just yet,' Kiaran whispered, shutting the door and taking her in his arms.

Chapter 23

Prisca · hurried down Brandywell Road to Eoin O'Donnell's house. It was bitterly cold. The weather had been mild over Christmas, but now a sullen greyness was creeping across the sky threatening snow. As she approached the inner door of the house, she could hear Rosheen Quinn's voice raised in anger.

'You're crazy, Eoin, to even think of it. Let the young ones get on with the Civil Rights march – for all the good it will do anyway.'

'Why don't you give them a chance, Rosheen,' Eoin protested mildly. 'They're going out unarmed. Not even a stick in their hands.'

'And what do you think the Paisleyites will do? Cheer them along the way? Christ, Eoin, you're becoming an idealist.'

'Ah, Prisca Mary, come in my dear.' There was the sound of relief in Eoin's voice.

'Hello,' Rosheen said abruptly, obviously annoyed by the interruption. 'I'm trying to persuade this man not to go on that Civil Rights march. Four days on the road. Is that right?'

'From the first of January. I'm taking my brother Brendan with me.'

'What about the rest of the group?'

'Some of them are going. Others, like you, don't think it will work. The police have been notified. The most important thing it will do, Rosheen, is open up our situation to the world.'

'Huh! Who the hell cares about us?'

'Well, we'll soon find out, won't we?'

Rosheen strode to the door. 'The road for the march is going right through Paisleyite territory. By God, they'll be waiting. And not with empty hands either.' She hesitated, then said impatiently, 'If you're damn fool enough to go, Eoin, I suppose I'd better go with you.'

'Thank you, my dear.' Rosheen replied by slamming the front door behind her.

'That's why I came, Eoin. I thought you might like to accompany me and Bren. We're leaving tomorrow.'

'You know, Prisca, this could be a turning point in the history of Ulster. I've been a Republican all my life with little hope of our voices ever being heard.'

That evening Prisca said to Brian: 'Will you come with me and Brendan to Belfast tomorrow?' She spoke briskly, fearing his refusal.

'No! You should know by now not to ask. I'm not politically minded.'

'It's a Civil Rights march, for God's sake. We're joining students who hope to break through the barriers of religious bigotry and draw attention to the social and economic problems here. Even Rosheen Quinn's going.'

'She'll throw the first stone.'

On that January morning in 1969, a group of people, mostly students, assembled outside Belfast City Hall. They carried banners, one group with the words *Civil Rights*, the other *People's Democracy*. Not far away was a larger group, led by a prominent member of the Loyal Citizens of Ulster. They made no secret of their intentions to harass the peace walkers on their four-day walk to Derry.

'Keep beside me, Bren,' Prisca warned her brother. Though he was a head taller than herself, he was slightly built.

Brendan felt excited at the thought of the seventy-five mile walk. It was the first time his sister had allowed him to take part in any of her activities. Though he felt some of her political fervour, his leanings towards the Church made him cautious. Political hothead, Dominic called his sister. Both he and his mother kept a close watch on

Brendan's after-school interests, frightened that Prisca would influence him. They suspected that she was affiliated to Rosheen Quinn's Republican group. Brendan dearly loved his sister, remembering how she had slaved to bring them all up. It was a miracle she had ever achieved any academic status at all. Only someone with an outstanding brain could have coped with the drudgery and studies as well. That was the cause of the trouble between her and Dominic. He would never forgive Pris for throwing away the chance of going to university.

As the marchers moved off on their four-day march, the Loyal Citizens pelted them with verbal invective and obscenities. 'Ask the Pope to give you a pill,' they shouted.

'Right on that one,' Prisca murmured.

'Paisley . . . Paisley . . .'

'To hell with that one . . .'

Brendan began to laugh.

Later that day, when they were approaching Antrim and heard the ominous beating of the lambeg drum, they knew that trouble was coming. Their leaders had problems with the police who refused to let them go through Antrim. Gradually, the forces of hostility became constant. Despite this, the number of Civil Rights sympathizers increased as the march went along the way. Harassed, but not despondent, they trudged on for the next few days, sleeping rough and eating where and when they could. Brendan had a haversack strapped to his back which had been filled with food and two bottles of water. The food didn't last long, though, because there were hungry people all around them. A welcome awaited at Dungiven, where they were greeted by a piper. Food was supplied and blistered feet attended to.

Finally they came on to Claudy Road, the last stretch of the journey. Approaching Burntollet, Brendan began to get excited when he realized that their progress was being covered by the press, radio and television, but Prisca became alarmed when she saw the crates of empty bottles under a hedge and piles of stones all along the wayside. The march was slowed down when an inspector of police came out in front, twirling a blackthorn stick. Behind him were the riot-equipped policemen.

'Why are they dressed in steel helmets and carrying shields?' Brendan asked.

Prisca linked arms with him and the girl beside them. With head down, she hurried them on.

'Prisca, I'm going to be sick,' the girl said. 'Did you see all those stones? They must have piled them up during the night. They have it in for us . . .'

She wasn't sick, but injured by a stone that came flying across the hedge from the field beyond. That was the moment when the bombardment began. Attackers poured in from a side road and the marchers were ambushed. Young girls and men ran in all directions to escape the stones raining down on them. Some were driven into the icy-cold River Faughan, where they were pelted unmercifully. Their screams and cries echoed across the countryside. Cars came and ferried the injured to hospital. Prisca pushed the girl into one of them then turned to Brendan as a huge piece of rock crashed into the side of his forehead. When Brendan slid to the ground, the last thing he was aware of was his blood splashed across his sister's face, and blood pouring from the head of a television cameraman who had been injured too.

The cars had all departed. Prisca grabbed her brother's shoulders and dragged him into safety. It was then she caught her first glimpse that day of Eoin and Rosheen Quinn. Someone came rushing up to them waving a chairleg, and Eoin was struck violently across the back. Rosheen, with the rage of hell blazing on her face, snatched it from the attacker's hand and brought it down heavily on his head. That was the only violence that Prisca witnessed by one of their own people on that long march, despite all the provocations.

The man, holding his head, slumped away shouting, 'You Fenian whore.'

Prisca and Brendan were sheltered under a hedge where an overhanging bush hid them. To make their bolthole more secure, she broke branches off the tree and piled them along the ground to conceal them better. When she looked down at her brother's face she felt a moment of sheer panic. Gentle Brendan wouldn't hurt a fly. She should never have brought him. But they had not expected this . . . not to be brutally beaten on a peace march. She eased the haversack off his shoulders, pulled out her face cloth, a bottle of water and their first-aid tin. Wiping the blood off his face, she dabbed carefully at the wound just below the hairline, then applied antiseptic ointment, finally putting on one of the large plasters they had brought for blistered feet.

With great care she raised his head and forced a little water between his lips. He came round then and said, 'Ah, Pris, I was supposed to protect you.'

'A fine one you are! Hit by a weedly wee B. Special. Now lie quiet, pet. We're safe here for a bit.'

When Brendan closed his eyes again, fear shook her. What if he had concussion? She would let him rest for a while and wait. Out on the road the screams and shouts were terrible. Then sounds of distress came from the River Faughan. She parted the bushes and looked down. Young girls were in the water trying to scramble up the side of the river bank. Men were beating them back again. One girl fainted and fell face-down under the water. A man came and tried to drag her out; attackers kept beating him across the back with sticks.

Prisca dropped her face in her hands and tightened her eyes against threatening tears. Surely, she thought, this must be one of Ireland's darkest hours. She longed for a gun in her hand to threaten the bully boys. She would like to use it on the policemen, too, who stood by and watched the Orangemen beating the Civil Rights marchers. Thank God I know now how to use a gun, she thought grimly. We can no longer hope for peaceful terms with these people. Even their politicians were out on the road watching the marchers, and doing nothing to restrain the violence. Rosheen was right. At the back of her mind a voice spoke unheeded: *Yes, but now the world knows.*

As soon as another car came she would jump out and

plead for help. Some of the marchers were on the move again. Hurt and bruised, their voices rang out. 'We shall overcome ... some day.' Then the rousing tune of the *Internationale*. The police and the bully boys were after the marchers again. Now might be her chance to get help. She was just about to creep out from under the tree when her name was called. It was Rosheen Quinn.

Together they carried Brendan to the car and placed him beside Eoin on the back seat.

Brendan suddenly croaked, 'Pris, I'm all right –'

'Good boy. Ros, where did you get the car?'

Rosheen crashed the gears. 'Christ, I hope it's not going to let us down.' When the car moved off and gained speed, she answered with her eyes on the mirror, searching the road behind, 'I stole it from one of them big houses. Think the bugger's a member of Stormont.'

Prisca didn't think she was capable of laughing that day. With danger all around them, she couldn't stop.

'We'll take a wee side road I know, then get the men to hospital.'

'The car?'

'Just leave it outside.'

'If we're stopped?'

'A very kind gentleman offered us the use of it, didn't he? He said his man would collect it at the hospital.'

'Rosheen Quinn, you're brazen enough for anything.'

'When you're as old as I am, Prisca McDaid, in this tough old world you can find words to suit any emergency.'

Chapter 24

Marcella was beginning to worry about the tension that hung over their marriage. It was the one cloud in their happiness – the safe period. They had planned to have the first year to themselves and start a family in the second year. How confident we were, she thought, thinking we could plan our lives so well. They observed all the rules of the Church and applied the necessary discipline, but found this rationing of love soul-destroying. They couldn't even hold hands for comfort. Feigning sleep on different sides of the bed was safer.

Marcella often thought angrily about all those women who had no choice and accepted one unwanted pregnancy after another. Surely bringing a child into the world should be a happy experience and not something a woman had to endure unwillingly? Why did everyone meekly accept this rule laid down by the Church? She had to smile. Now she was thinking like Prisca!

Kiaran discussed it with Father McGill but, though the priest was sympathetic, he could not go against the Pope's encyclical. They read and studied the encyclical. No hope there. Marcella began to remember the things Prisca had told her about some Catholic marriages, where men went to prostitutes because another child would have permanently injured the health of their wives. Was the prostitute less of a burden on their conscience than the use of contraceptives?

Oddly enough, it was through Nial the gypsy that she began to sort out their problem in the obvious way. Nial and his wife Tesca's baby was adorable – fat, with brown skin and jet-black hair clustered around its head. She filled a sketchbook with its tiny form. Tesca, like many gypsy mothers, wanted to take the baby with her when she went to sell her wares around the houses, but Nanta wouldn't let her. She and Nial had become very close over the years. He did a lot of carpentry jobs and marketed the things she made.

When Tesca was out of the way, Marcella used to nurse, feed and play with the child. Gradually a longing to have one of her own began to grow. One day when Tesca came back and found her feeding it, she snatched the baby jealously out of her arms and shouted angrily: 'Git a babby of yer own.'

That evening Marcella said to Kiaran; 'I would love to have a baby. Tesca thinks I'm going to steal hers. She could be right!'

He frowned slightly, then smiled. 'Good. Then we can lock up the spare room.' He always slept in there now when it was the 'wrong' time in the month.

'Kiaran,' she went on, hesitatingly. 'After our child is born, I'm not going back to using the safe period. I think the Church is wrong about birth control.'

'Oh,' he said, startled.

'I've thought about it often and my conscience cannot accept something that I now consider to be an unnecessary discipline.'

His eyes searched her face anxiously and she was aware that her words had disturbed him. 'There are many theological principles involved,' he began.

'All right, darling, we won't discuss it for the time being. Things may change completely before we have to face it again.'

Would they change? she wondered uneasily. Millions of Catholics had waited anxiously for the publication of Pope Paul VI's encyclical in 1968. In vain.

The next morning there was a letter from Lisa inviting them to her birthday party. She and Prisca had begun teaching jobs at the beginning of the autumn term; soon afterwards, Brian and Prisca were quietly married. Marcella took the letter and went up to the top meadow to find Kiaran. He and his father were having a heated discussion about repairing some of the workers' outhouses. When Mr Gilroy walked away, Kiaran was quiet and thoughtful, his eyes on the far horizon. 'Father is so out of touch with everything, particularly the people. He expects them to accept conditions which were bad twenty and more years ago. I wish I had more money to put into the estate.'

'So what will you do?'

'Work out a repair plan and do the work ourselves. After the harvest we can work steadily on one property at a time.' As they walked home she listened to all his plans for the future. The land and the people who worked on it were important to him. Marcella was sure he would be able to take all the inevitable pitfalls of farming in his stride.

They were going past Slievan when the aunt came across the lawn in her 'cutting flowers' gear of a garden hat and special gloves. Hanging on her arm was an expensive gardening basket. The staff thought it was a joke and wondered why the woman didn't have the sense to plunge the flowers into a pail of water before torturing them into arrangements that nature never intended.

'You shouldn't be cutting flowers at this time of the day,' Kiaran called.

Urusla Gilroy's lips tightened disapprovingly as she glanced at Marcella and said pointedly; 'You're not very busy, are you? What's this mad scheme for spending money on the farmhands, that your father was talking about?'

'I'm delighted you're interested, Aunt Ursula. Perhaps you would like to invest some money?' He was smiling, charming her. Kiaran said she had the sourest face in Ireland. Marcella knew he felt sorry for her. Apparently the 'royal face', the woman in the portrait at Slievan, had married the only man who had ever shown interest in her money. Just then, Biddy in the brae scuttled past with her head down. She disclaimed friendship when Marcella was talking to the gentry, except for Kiaran. He no longer belonged in that category now he had married her!

268

'Hello, Biddy,' Marcella called. 'How's Ned? Aunt Sarah told me he had to go away for treatment.' Ned had struck a goldmine of poteen somewhere and had nearly drunk himself into the grave.

'He's grand now, Cella. D'ye know what he thought he saw? The Loch Ness Monster sitting on a rock combing a mermaid's hair. As sure as God he was a proper headcase.'

Kiaran roared with laughter. His aunt's lips were invisible with displeasure as she walked past her servant and laughing relations.

When they were having supper that evening, he said: 'I think she's going to help, love.'

'With the farm buildings?'

'Told me to come and discuss it this evening. The materials are going to cost more than I can really afford.'

'If you're going up to Slievan, maybe I'll pay my aunt a visit.' One day, in a magnanimous mood, Aunt Sarah, who was very taken with Kiaran, said if a bit of money was needed for improving the place, they could have it as she was leaving everything to her niece and nephew anyway.

When she arrived at the cottage, Sarah was in the bedroom on her knees, dressed in the nun's habit, reciting the obligatory prayers of the Third Order. She gave a quick glance over her shoulder. There were dark rings around her eyes and an unhealthy pallor on her skin. By the time she came down to the sitting room dressed in her everyday clothes, Marcella had made a pot of tea.

'Are you all right, Aunt?' she asked anxiously. 'You shouldn't be kneeling in that cold bedroom.'

'We should all prepare for the next world.'

'I don't think you get out of doors enough. You're too much on your own.'

'I've never been one to run in and out of people's houses, gossiping. Do you know what that Doctor Johnson said about the Irish? We're a race that never speak well of one another. I don't want to get involved with gossip.'

'For goodness sake, we don't speak well of ourselves at times because we don't mind laughing at ourselves. Samuel Johnson didn't have enough sense of humour to understand the Irish. I'm in and out of all the cottages and I've yet to hear anyone speak badly of a neighbour. Nellie down the road is great fun. All her cows have names and when she goes into the byre and calls them, they turn their heads.'

'It's well for her to have cows with names for that's all she's been able to produce out of that marriage. She's as barren as the rocks on the hills.'

And what have you got, Marcella thought angrily. A nun's habit you put on every evening for your private devotions. A holy woman without charity in your heart.

She was outside the house again before she remembered the reason for her visit. Somehow it did not seem important any more. Sarah would pester her for details that she did not possess.

Over in the lane, pebbles cracked under a heavy boot like rifle shots. She drew back under the fuchsia bush by the cottage. A voice with a Derry accent said: 'We'd better find that other lot even if we –' The voice died away. There was an odd kind of sound. Then, as on the other occasions when something had disturbed her around the cottage, she had the impression that people were somewhere near, yet invisible. Running to the gate leading into the field, she shone the torch over the two acres and up the little lane that led to the windswept hills. There was not a soul to be seen lurking on the long bleak road.

Lurking. The word caught in her mind and for the first time in her life she felt nervous. I've walked these roads since I was a child, she thought, not even considering my safety because I knew I was safe. There was no evil in this place, no attacks on women or children. Even Derry, until the latest trouble, had the lowest crime rate in the United Kingdom.

Marcella returned to the cottage; the door was still on the latch. With carefully chosen words, so as not to alarm her, she told Sarah that in future the door should be bolted, as there were some rough Derry types around.

Kiaran was still out when she returned home. She went straight to bed and fell asleep. By the next morning the incident did not seem quite so alarming and, as Kiaran appeared to have other things on his mind, she decided not to mention it.

'Marcella,' he said, with a sudden lift of his head, 'there's something I've been wanting to say. I'm afraid you're not going to like it.'

'Don't say it then.' The look on his face, that slight frown, nibbling his lips, was always an indication that he was in a serious mood.

'I think I'm going to reclaim Briar Meadow.'

'*What*? You can't,' she protested. 'You promised –'

'It's a rich bit of land compared to other parts I'm trying to cultivate. There are plenty of sheltered barren spots around Iniscad where the gypsies can go. Gypsies – huh!' he said disapprovingly. 'Have you noticed the new generation that are tagging on to the older ones? It's like a modern caravan site now, only three traditional gypsy caravans left. All the rest are cheap modern set-ups. Father's going wild about it, they're mushrooming out and are visible from Slievan.'

'Tell your aunt to pull down the blinds,' she snapped.

'Would Nanta move to one of our cottages?'

'What do you think? She's travelled the roads all her life. She'll never leave Nial's children.'

'Nial. We could do without him and his friends.'

'Leave it for a bit, Kiaran. I'll have a word with Nanta.'

Reluctantly she had to silently agree that the old romantic-looking gypsy camp at Briar Meadow had disappeared. Nanta was furious about some of the people and she hated the modern caravans.

Lisa's home was oppressive, Marcella decided, and her parents seemed quite old. Lisa said they were middle-aged when she was born. They worried unceasingly about her future, particularly whom she would marry. 'Poppa brought home another long-nosed Jewish boy last night for dinner,' she used to complain with a wicked grin. It seemed funny to Marcella and Prisca because their friend's features were strongly Jewish, though attractively so. She joked a lot about her religion; indeed as they often did about theirs.

The birthday table was weighted with heavily crested silver and enormous serving dishes. Dominic arrived late with embarrassed apologies because he was detained at the hospital. Marcella glanced at him covertly. He looked handsome in a well-cut suit and there was an air of authority about him now. 'Hello,' he said casually to her and Kiaran.

The iced soup, made of various fruits, was delicious; and the German wine just right for the meats and salads. Finally the birthday cake was brought in. After the candles were lit, presents were showered on Lisa. Then Mr Schenber proposed a toast in Hebrew and repeated the words in English. Momma wept copiously. When Dominic stood up and spoke some suitable words on their behalf, Lisa's eyes were fastened on him. They drank more wine, then Prisca suddenly jumped to her feet.

'Now let us drink to a united Ireland.'

No one drank; they just stared at her in amazement. Somehow the words sounded incongruous, almost alien, at the Jewish table. Dominic went to interrupt but she began to speak again. She waved him to silence.

'And,' she continued, 'if we cannot achieve this peacefully, then other means will have to be used to remove Stormont.'

'How do you mean, remove Stormont? Emotionally, politically or physically?' Kiaran asked her.

Lisa gave a little titter of laughter. Her expression quickly changed when Mr Schenber rose swiftly to his feet. His face was flushed and his eyes looked sharp. 'Please, no politics. I do not vant such things in my house. I do not vant to have anything to do with political talk. Momma and I have suffered much in the past because of what happens when people get up and make disturbance.'

'Prisca didn't —' Brian began. Dominic interrupted him. 'I'm sorry, Mr Schenber. It was silly of her to bring that up. We don't expect you to be concerned with the things that are happening in this country.'

'Here, why the hell are you apologizing for me? You needn't try to do the big brother act.'

'Don't go on,' Brian said angrily.

'My God.' Prisca looked around the table, her tongue loosened by the wine she had drunk. 'You'd hardly think we had Irishmen here who have lived in a country which has been under the British heel for fifty years and more. And you, Mr Schenber,' she pointed her finger at Lisa's father, 'you'll have to be concerned too because you live here and make your living from the people. You can't simply shut your eyes and pretend not to know what's happening.'

Dominic's anger was palpable. Brian waited for him to say something but it was Kiaran who spoke. 'May I pour you some wine, Prisca? Or have you had enough?'

'It's all right for you, Kiaran. You're a Gilroy from across the border. It's nice and safe over there, so why should you worry?'

'I thought you lived there too. Or is it just a holiday home?'

'But,' she banged her hand on the table making the glass jump and Mrs Schenber to exclaim, 'Mein Gott!' 'You shouldn't be sitting over there unconcerned, turning a blind eye to what's happening in Derry.'

'For heaven's sake, Prisca, be reasonable,' Dominic protested. 'We don't want Free State landowners crossing the border and complicating a situation which might just get sorted out in the near future.'

'I have no wish to come here and get involved in anything,' Kiaran said quietly, 'unless there's a civil war and, if that happens, we are all involved. Just one thing, both sides — Orangemen and Catholics — need the right type of men to lead them. Setting fire to buildings and terrorizing people will never resolve anything.'

'I agree,' Brian said. 'What our people really want is a simple democratic right — one man, one vote.'

'The barest of fundamental civil rights long denied to many Ulster citizens,' Prisca added with a triumphant glow. 'I read that the other day in a newspaper and that puts it in a nutshell.'

'Well,' Dominic said in a quieter voice, 'let's hope that this new Prime Minister will get the electoral system changed and that there will be an end to discrimination.'

'It's inevitable now . . .' The rest of Brian's sentence was lost in a hoarse cry which came from Mrs Schenber.

'*War*.' The word came out in a strangled sob. It was as though she had dropped off to sleep when Kiaran had uttered the word and awakening, remembered it. 'Do not talk to me of wars, you silly young people. You know not what it is like.' To their alarm she began to sob and cry. 'We had to leave our country, flee in the night, all our possessions and dear ones left behind. You play with a word, not knowing the terrible horrors of war.'

'There, there, liebe. Not to worry, not to worry.' Mr Schenber took his wife by the arm and led her from the room.

They were all silent for a moment, then Lisa said in a slightly bored voice; 'Prisca, trust you to stir up the old political pot. Didn't I warn you how my parents have been feeling since the disturbance in Derry? They're frightened, at least Momma is. And Poppa just doesn't want to get involved.'

'For God's sake, Lisa, we were only talking.'

'Only talking was a bad thing to do when they were about our age.'

'I'm sorry about that, Lisa,' Dominic said. 'Of course we shouldn't have gone on.' He gave an apologetic grin. 'I'm afraid it is a failing with us Irish. Like James Joyce's *Ulysses*, we go on and on.'

'It's all right, Dominic.' The full rich mouth was curved in a tender line as she smiled at him. Marcella felt anxious and sorry for her, because the look that Dominic swept over Lisa's face was one of indifference.

'For God's sake, Prisca, why did you have to start all this? I could wring your neck.'

There was a sharpness in Brian's voice that his sister had not heard before. He had always been a quiet, accepting person, but since he married, he seemed to have retreated even more into the background.

'Start what?' Prisca asked with dangerous innocence.

'You know what I mean. It was stupid of you to go and upset Mr and Mrs Schenber like that.'

'Look, Brian, let's face it. If things don't change here, there's going to be real trouble. You know what happens when the civil rights group go out marching. If the Minister for Home Affairs allows the Orange boys to march, why not those people who are simply asking for a fair deal in the running of Ulster?'

'I *know* all that. Why go upsetting the Schenbers, though?' he shouted at her. 'You know what they suffered in the last war.'

She glared at him. 'You're a right lot of laggards, aren't you?'

Marcella pushed her chair back. 'Shut up, Pris. You've always got too much to say. Let's change the subject.'

Lisa clapped her hands. 'Come, we'll go up to the drawing room and have a singsong. Momma and Poppa will soon forget the little bit that was unpleasant. Yes?'

Up in the drawing room Dominic was playing the piano. Mr and Mrs Schenber, restored to happiness, were singing with great pathos a tune of their fatherland; after that, Dominic went on to a selection of popular tunes. Then Lisa's parents said they were tired and were going to bed. The episode in the dining room was forgotten. 'Such a happy time,' Mrs Schenber said repeatedly, kissing each one of the girls.

Lisa suggested they should finish the evening at a pub. They were trying to decide whether to cross the border to the Republic or stay on the Derry side when Dominic announced, 'Make up your minds; I must go back to the hospital for a while. I'll join you later.'

'What about the one just across the border with a flagstone floor and a roaring wood fire,' Prisca suggested, 'or the one on this side with fitted carpets and a fountain in the centre of the floor to encourage the thirst?'

Lisa preferred carpets to stone floors. When they entered the pub they noticed that a piano had been installed in the lounge since their last visit. Prisca dashed over to an empty table nearby; reluctantly the others followed. A pianist with long thin wrists was playing sophisticated tunes from popular musicals.

'Can't you give us some of our own?' Prisca asked him.

He raised an eyebrow. 'Playing what the boss orders, dear.'

Her eyes were glued to the pianist's dangling wrists, longing to play because Dominic had deliberately kept her from doing so at the Schenbers'. When the musician pushed the chair back to go to the toilet, Prisca shot into his seat. With a cheeky grin over her shoulder, she began on a repertoire of nationalist songs. The pianist came back and said: 'Come on, dear, my time's not up yet.'

'Sit down and have a drink. I'll do your job for you.'

'Prisca . . .' Brian called sternly.

'That music won't be appreciated in here, dear,' the man said. 'Why don't you go to the other pub across the border. You can play there to your heart's content.'

'No piano.'

He shrugged his shoulders and with a bored expression went over and looked out of the window. The door leading into the public bar opened and a crowd of yokels, caps firmly planted on their heads, peeped in, devouring the scene of sophistication.

'Man, that wan can play.'

'Jippers, you'd fair get a wet ass if you fell in that wee holey of water in the middle of the floor.'

Someone singing across the heads of the men at the door, made Prisca's hands slow down. She turned. 'Surely that's Bob Sweeney?'

The crowd at the door parted to let through a thick-set, smallish man who entered with outstretched hands, like a tenor in a grand opera. At one time Bob Sweeney had had a promising career on the stage and radio; it ended when drink interfered with his ambition. Now he was just another pub tenor. People showed their regret and pity by showering drinks on him, and that kept him on the downward journey.

Prisca played all the ones he was good at, then to everyone's surprise began 'The Croppy Boy' – a real tearjerker and a rebel song. They all protested. Prisca didn't hear their protests because Sweeney and the cap-chorus were nearly lifting the roof.

The barman called: 'That's enough of that. Cut it out.'

Marcella looked anxiously through the window to see if there was any sign of Dominic. Brian got up and went to the piano. He was very angry. The look on his face stopped Prisca playing instantly. It was too late; without an accompaniment the men, led by Sweeney, went on to one Republican song after another. The barman came across and caught Sweeney by the arm.

'Out the hell you go.'

'I've got a drink,' Sweeney protested.

'I don't care. You're not to come back here again. You've no business in this bar anyway.'

'He's got as much right as anyone else,' Prisca shouted.

When Sweeney reached out for a glass of Guinness, he gave the barman a push, who went crashing into the fountain with a great splash. It wasn't very deep but the sprinkler was drenching him. He tried to turn it off; somehow it went askew and sent sprays of water all over the lounge, soaking the smart customers.

Sweeney's friends roared with laughter as people fled from tables and crowded out to the cloakrooms.

'What a pity,' Kiaran murmured as he went over to help the man out of the water. 'Now he's going to be less tolerant.'

Someone went down the road for the police. When the sergeant and the constable arrived, the dripping figure said: 'It's that lot started the trouble. And that fool Sweeney crying for his croppy boy.'

Everyone's eyes went to Sweeney who was sitting at the table unconcernedly emptying all their glasses. He looked like a peaceful man. When the policeman called him, he frowned, looked up with a hurt expression and said, 'Who? Me?'

'Get up, Sweeney. We've had trouble with you before.'

'Sure we were only havin' a wee singsong.'

'Get up,' the sergeant snarled.

Prisca pushed away Brian's restraining hand and went over to the policeman. 'Look here, officer, we were told to stop and we did stop. If the barman wants to go swimming in that damn-fool hole in the floor and then sprinkle his customers, he can't blame us. And now,' she said, 'if you don't mind we'll go, and that's the last time we'll set foot in this place.'

The sergeant, frowning, looked down at her sparkling brown eyes and neat schoolgirl fringe. 'How old are you?' he demanded.

There was a roar of laughter from the men. Prisca had been doing the pub rounds for years. Brian was about to say something when Sweeney suddenly shouted: 'Up the IRA.'

Everyone looked startled. Even Prisca paled at his rashness.

'Clear that crowd away and shut up the place,' the senior policeman ordered. The front door was locked.

'Oh lord,' Lisa whimpered.

Kiaran caught Sweeney's arm and whispered, 'For God's sake shout "Up the Orangemen" or "King William" or something, else you'll be for prison.'

Sweeney pushed him away. 'What do you mean? I said "Up the Republican Army of Ireland" and I meant it. If I've got to be a martyr for the cause, then I'll be a martyr.'

Prisca rushed at him. 'Listen, you silly devil, some bloody martyr you'd make. What about your wife and weans? Are they going to be martyrs too?'

Her anger seemed to sober him. He looked at her, blinking. 'I'd rather have me tongue cut out than say what that gent suggested.'

'If you spend a year in prison, it will be hanging out.'

Sweeney's eyes moved longingly to the rich black stout in the glasses; he wet his lips with his tongue.

'Up the Orange bastards,' he muttered sullenly, then added resentfully, 'me mouth's forgettin' what me head's tellin' me. I'm a traitor, begod.'

'They're putting him up to something, Sergeant,' the officious young policeman said.

'For goodness sake, Sergeant,' Kiaran protested, 'you're surely not going to take action against a man in his condition?'

'It's an offence to say what he said in this country.'

'In Ulster,' Prisca retorted.

'Yes, I know that,' Kiaran added in a reasonable voice.

'Where are you from? You're not an Irishman, are you?'

'Yes he is – more or less,' Prisca told him. 'He's like some of those you've got up at Stormont; aristocrats educated in a foreign country.'

'Prisca! Stop it!' Brian protested sharply.

Marcella looked out the window again and prayed like mad for Dominic.

'I think you'd all better step down to the station and get this thing sorted out,' the officer said sternly.

When the constable took Sweeney's arm, Lisa gave a piercing scream. 'Oh, mein Gott, it is like the Gestapo. It's what they did to my Momma and Poppa. They were in a beer cellar and they came for them.' She raised two clenched fists at the policeman's face. 'You are the Orange Gestapo.'

The two men looked at her, their mouths hanging wide open in surprise, as if she'd fallen from a spacecraft through the ceiling. Kiaran caught her hands.

'It's all right, Lisa. When we talk to them at the police station we will be able to go home.'

'Ja, ja.' (She sounded more like her mother every minute.) 'Vat about little old Sweeney, what they do to him, eh?'

Marcella glanced quickly at Prisca and saw fear on her face for the first time. Not for herself but for Sweeney.

People were crowding around the window and trying to look in. Then the door behind the counter, leading in from the house, opened and Dominic came through.

The sergeant looked up sharply. 'Dr McDaid.'

When Lisa saw him she began to cry hysterically. Dominic went over and looked at Sweeney as though diagnosing an ailment.

'H'm, how are you?'

'Yer a good lad.' The singer thumped him on the chest and swayed in the policeman's clutch.

'I should duck him in the pool, Constable. Sober him up; never seen him that far gone before.'

Lisa's sobs grew louder. Dominic turned and put an arm around her. She flew into his arms, sobbing against the pale grey suit he had worn for her party. They all stood there silently, watching. The sergeant looked embarrassed. Prisca was clutching Brian's hand; her face had aged in those few minutes. She was thinking of the things Lisa had told her about the Schenbers fleeing from tyranny. About her own people, the Catholics in Ulster, who had to endure gerrymandering. All people caught relentlessly in a political web. She felt inadequate and realized she had not the ability to fight effectively for the cause that had troubled her since the age of reason.

Dominic was able to get everything sorted out peacefully with the police; after that they all went to a café near the border for coffee.

'You should have known better than to get involved with a boozer like Sweeney,' he said to Prisca.

'He's got a wonderful voice,' Prisca replied. 'Singing is part of our national heritage.'

'So is drinking. The Sweeneys of this world are drunken bores and shouldn't be encouraged. At the moment it is not safe to go into bars and get involved with that type of man. The slightest thing can start trouble. Some of us want to get this situation sorted out peacefully. Don't go stirring up the hotheads. There's far too many of them around already.'

'Dominic's right,' Brian added.

'My God, you two have a bloody nerve. I didn't notice either of you on the Burntollet march.' A silence followed her words. Then she started on 'ancient wrongs', sweeping through three hundred years of British imperialism and with a knowledge that astounded them, covered briefly the other countries where England had had to relinquish her hold.

'Get off your soapbox, Prisca,' Kiaran retorted impatiently. 'We know all that.'

She was about to whip back an answer when Dominic said, 'You're a teacher and supposed to be a responsible person.'

'What has being a teacher got to do with it?'

'You could find yourself without a job.'

In an attempt to lighten the conversation, Brian laughed. 'That mustn't happen. You're the wage-earner in the family. When I get my degree you can stay at home in Iniscad and keep out of trouble.'

'If there's trouble,' Prisca clattered her cup deliberately, 'I'll not be hiding away in Donegal. I love the place but I'm a Derry woman.'

Lisa began to look anxious again. Marcella turned to her. 'Don't worry, I'm sure things will be sorted out in the coming year.' She wasn't as confident as she sounded. Derry was beginning to have an ugly look about it.

'It's my Momma and Poppa,' she said anxiously. 'They are frightened of trouble. We were so happy here.'

Kiaran turned to Marcella. 'Why doesn't Lisa come and spend next weekend with us?'

'I would like that,' Lisa said.

'Dominic, would you like to come too?' Kiaran suggested. 'We've plenty of room.'

'No,' Brian said, 'let Dominic come to us. The spare room's ready.' Prisca did not add her invitation to her husband's.

Chapter 25

On the Saturday morning Marcella was in the kitchen baking when Prisca put her head in the window. 'H'm, lovely smell. I'm in the wheelbarrow. Think it will hold me?'

They giggled, remembering their schooldays when Prisca was always doing something mad. 'Coffee?' Marcella offered.

Prisca jumped down and skipped in. 'Marcella, would you mind swopping guests this weekend? After you left last night Dominic and I had another big row. Honestly, it was ridiculous the way he blamed me.'

'You weren't exactly blameless, were you?'

'Don't you start.'

'I'm concerned about Lisa. She's never lost her self-control like that before.'

Prisca was quiet for a moment. 'It's her nerves. I think home is getting her down.'

'And Dominic. She's in love with him.'

'I think that's the way it is. You're a super cook.'

Marcella remembered how, when Prisca was growing up, cakes had been considered a luxury in her home. Margarine was used on bread and not for baking. For a while she paid Biddy in the brae to make a large fruit cake every week because Brian didn't like the shop ones. When Sarah found out she was horrified, and said that Biddy wasn't a bit particular because the last time she opened a sack of flour in her presence there was evidence that a mouse had been through it. Prisca dug a grave at the bottom of the garden and buried Biddy's baking until she found an excuse to stop the arrangement.

'You don't seriously mean that, do you, about swopping guests? What about Dominic? You'll hurt his feelings.'

'Feelings? Has he any?'

'Look Prisca, he's going to be out most of the time. Kiaran has promised to show him around the farm and tonight you're all coming here. Perhaps we might suggest him taking Lisa for a walk tomorrow afternoon?'

'Stop scheming. She might as well go out for a walk with old Ned for all the good it will do her.'

'Come to romantic Iniscad,' Marcella giggled, quoting Miss Boyle's Hotel brochure. 'Perhaps if he sees her in different surroundings –'

'He won't see her. He hasn't got a romantic thought in his head.'

'Was youse wans takin' my name in vain?' Ned in the brae put his head around the door. 'Holy saints alive, youse wee wimin have the fine 'asy times of it now, hasn't ye?'

'Oh Ned,' Prisca exclaimed, 'I thought you were a ghost. What in the name of God have you been doing to yourself?'

'Had a bad turn. Nearly went to m'grave.'

'I thought you'd just got out of it. Come in and tell us what happened. Cella'll make you a nice cup of tea.'

'Sure I wodden like to be troublin' Cella.' He looked at her with a crafty eye and scuttled over to a seat at the table, delighted to get such a welcome after the disapproving glances of Sarah and his sister Biddy.

'Where did you get the mountain dew? You'll have the bishop after you again.'

He looked at Prisca slyly from under the peak of his cap and gave a chuckle. 'The wee still wass up in the Guard's field – the wan he lets to Liam every year. Begob they looked iverywhere, and wisn't us wans crackin' our sides. Sure the priest hisself scoured the hills and niver thought of goin' to the Guard's field.'

'You mean to say it was on the Guard's property, right under his nose?' they asked incredulously.

Ned, forgetting that the deadly brew had nearly cost him

his life, rolled about on his chair. 'Aye, it was a great laugh.'

'You're lucky not to be laughing in a hotter climate.'

'Now, now, Mrs Brian,' he reproved and looked at Marcella. 'Your aunt,' he tipped his cap in a gesture of respect, 'sure she said she was doin' a novena that they wid find the divil's water before it lured us all down to where we belonged.'

'Stick to the Guinness, Ned,' Marcella said, handing him a cup of tea, the way he liked it, with a 'midden of leaves' giving it a bit of flavour.

He poured the tea into his saucer and supped it noisily. Sarah, with her gentility, shrank from the habit but had failed to stop it. His pale blue eyes fastened on the brass handle of the door leading into the pantry; caught in a pencil of light, it sent out myriads of golden circles. Fascinated, he moved his head from side to side, making the points of light whirl kaleidoscopically. They followed his gaze and were silent as though he were a child and his delight in the spectacle must not be spoilt.

'Did you come with a message, Ned?'

Dazed, he moved his eyes from the handle. 'Auld Sarah — beg pardon, Cella — your aunt says wid youse wans come over for tay the morra,' he said and drinking up his tea shuffled off down the path.

'Cella, the poteen seems to be creeping into production again, doesn't it?'

'What's creeping into production?' Lisa had arrived in her Mini, looking very beautiful in a red trouser suit.

'Poteen, darling. If your father gets fed up with the political situation in Derry he can always come over here and try to legalize the manufacturing of it. He'd make another fortune. The rag trade isn't the only one.'

Lisa tapped her playfully on the cheek. 'You leave my Poppa alone. Tell me, what does *Cead Mile Failte Go Iniseoghain* mean? I did not notice the signpost before.'

'One hundred thousand welcomes to Inishowen,' Prisca said, making for the door.

Marcella led Lisa upstairs. The last time she had stayed

with them she had taken a liking to the tiny room next to Marcella's studio; it was painted pale lilac and white, and one day Marcella hoped it would be the nursery. 'Just relax and be happy, Lisa. If you want anything I'm down in the kitchen.'

'You are a nice person, Marcella. You don't say hurtful things. Prisca is very sharp.'

Marcella laughed. 'It's her way . . . she has a quick tongue.'

'I think she is frustrated.'

'Frustrated?' Marcella looked at her in surprise.

'Remember how clever she was at school? I think now she regrets not having gone to university.'

'Lisa, she wanted to get married and live in Iniscad. I can't think of anything more wonderful than to be happily married.'

Lisa gave a hard little laugh. 'For you, yes, it is right. You are an artist, a creative person and Kiaran understands. Prisca, she has got *this*,' Lisa tapped her head. 'Brains, you know, eh?'

'Perhaps she could go to university later.'

'Ha! If she does not have to push a pram.' Lisa curled up on the bed. 'I think she's now involved with many political things in Derry. Since she went on that civil rights march she has become very embittered at what happened. She says they need money, help.'

'She hasn't asked your father?'

'Ja.'

'And he refused?'

Lisa rolled her eyes and threw out her hands expressively.

Later, when they were dressing, Marcella said to Kiaran: 'Isn't that Prisca the limit trying to get the Schenbers involved. Lisa says she asked her father for financial help for some political group.'

Kiaran surprised her by saying, 'I bet the Irish in America are already passing the hat around.'

Marcella shuddered and thanked God they didn't live in Derry. She didn't want to think about the unrest there.

With a flash of guilt she realized it was a selfish thought. 'How did you get on with Dominic and Lisa?' she asked. The two men had planned to go out by themselves but Lisa, who hated walking, said she would like to go as well.

'Lisa's gaudy suit got covered in manure. While we were in the byre she wandered out to the field, met a cow, thought it was a bull, lost her head, ran and slipped.'

'Oh dear! Thank goodness she brought a caseful of clothes.'

'Prisca gave her a pair of Brian's jeans and told her to wash the suit in the stream at the back of the cottage. She wouldn't let her put it in the washing machine.'

'That suit is made of wool,' Marcella said, horrified. 'It shouldn't be washed anywhere, only sponged and then sent to the cleaners.' She had a vision of Lisa bending over the stream and felt a stab of pity. Lisa didn't even wash her own undies. She could just imagine Prisca saying, 'Well, if you've spoilt it, dear, Poppa will buy another one.'

Prisca was sitting on the kitchen table when Marcella went downstairs, a bottle of wine beside her. 'You know, Cella, it might be fun to get Sarah to teach us how to make homemade wines.'

'Didn't Brian tell you the reason why Sarah's wine is so good?'

'Brian tells me nothing. He only speaks when it is absolutely necessary.' There was a touch of bitterness in her remark.

'He's bogged down with work at the moment.' But Marcella remembered her brother's silences. 'The reason it's good is because Ned poured in some of his own concoction when Aunt wasn't looking.'

'Poteen?' They burst out laughing. 'God, Cella, when you think how she goes on about a little glass of homemade wine not hurting anyone, and there she is knocking back the hard stuff.'

'Well, thank goodness she gave up the pledge. Making wine gives her another interest.'

'Hello.' Dominic was standing at the back door. Prisca jumped off the table and as she was leaving, remarked,

'Intellectual conversation coming up.'

'She means these.' Dominic smiled. 'For you.'

Marcella looked at the titles of the three books: they were French novels that they had discussed at one time. How generous of him, and yet Prisca always said he was the mean one in the family.

'Did you enjoy your walk with Kiaran?'

'Very much. How hard he works, there's such a lot of land.'

'You've got tanned, Dominic. It suits you. You should come down here more often.'

He put his hands in his pockets, shrugged, and looked out of the window. 'That's what Brian says. Unfortunately though, Prisca and I always end up bickering. Don't know what's the matter with her these days.'

'The trouble in Derry is getting her down.'

'It's getting us all down, for heaven's sake! I just hope she's not involved in anything damn silly.'

'She was always concerned about the poverty of the Catholics in the Bogside.'

'Why all the secrecy? And every time she opens her mouth she puts her foot in it.'

'You're thinking about the pub scene?'

He turned round, a deep frown on his face. 'Now that could have been serious for Sweeney. What he shouted is a crime in the eyes of the police. When I stopped the car, the little barmaid rushed out and told me what was happening. Sweeney's the type who's always wanting to fight and die for Ireland but never gets past the corner pub. The man's a complete wash-out. The Catholics won't give him a job because they know he'll be drunk half the time, and the Protestants won't employ him because he's a Catholic. So he oils his bitterness with booze.'

'Dominic, come and have a sherry,' Kiaran called from the hall. After a while he brought one in to Marcella.

'Listen,' she whispered, 'try and keep off politics. The McDaids are at loggerheads. The minute I go to fetch coffee, put on our new records.'

They had nearly finished the meal. Kiaran picked up the

bottle and poured the last of the wine. When he put it down, the label was facing Prisca.

'Heavens,' she exclaimed, 'just look at the German name on that bottle. It's the same one as the spy who came over to Ireland during the war to collaborate with the IRA against England.'

'One spy?' Dominic sad sarcastically. 'Records reveal that there were quite a few around the Free State.'

'Yes,' Brian agreed, 'but they didn't get far with the Irish Secret Service at their heels. The government in Dublin was determined not to compromise their neutrality.'

'Most of them landed up in the Curragh,' Kiaran commented.

'That war was our one big chance of being freed from British rule,' Prisca announced.

'Don't be stupid,' Dominic snapped. 'All the Germans wanted was to make use of our ports. They weren't interested in our neutrality or in a united Ireland.'

'Unfortunately,' Kiaran said, 'many English people, and misinformed writers who have written about events of that time, gave the impression that the Irish welcomed the German spies with open arms. Nothing could be further from the truth. As Brian says, they were nearly all interned. Individual people certainly helped them, but there was no assistance given by the government. In fact, the German Embassy in Dublin was supposed to be under surveillance day and night.'

Prisca began to grow moody. She flicked her fringe up irritably. 'But,' she said, jumping right back to the present situation, 'if we must have British rule, why the hell can't it be direct from Westminster instead of having to put up with that monkey-assed Stormont?'

Lisa gave her a quick glance and putting an arm around her shoulder said, 'It will come right one day. Old Hitler corrupted a great country; what was done was bad, evil, but the good God gave him the big kick. That will happen to the Orange Gestapo. One day they'll no longer have power.'

Here we go again, Marcella thought. She gave Kiaran a

pleading look. He was brooding; they were all brooding, twirling empty glasses in their hands, studying them as though they were seeing the future and not liking what they saw.

'Coffee?' she said brightly, and a little shrilly. No one answered. She rose and left the room.

Their mood began to affect her. It was like fear inching into her mind. Why was she afraid? This was Donegal, quiet and peaceful; the people free of religious antagonism. They couldn't be involved with what was happening across the border in Derry nor in any other part of Ulster. They were like another kind of people over there, she tried to convince herself. But the fear persisted.

She had forgotten to put a light under the percolator. Now the coffee would take longer. It didn't matter. Time was needed to shake off the depressing cloak of politics. Opening the back door she went out to the garden. Night lay around her; solemn, beautiful. The moon shining through the trees scattered a mesh of light across the lawn and, in the distance, softly moulded hills seemed like a brushwork against the sky.

As she stood there, Marcella remembered her mother saying that during the war she had often thought of Derry, such a short distance away and held in the grip of war. They had heard an explosion when German bombs fell once – on waste ground – and the staccato sound of anti-aircraft guns. The next day Joyce, the Irish traitor, had apologized on German radio: 'it had not been intended, it was a mistake.' Yet Belfast was bombed to the ground. Now Derry was facing more trouble, worse than war, because the people were rising against each other.

Brisk footsteps came down the road; as they drew nearer, there was a hesitancy in their movement. Who could it be at this time of night? A soft sound of bushes being parted reached Marcella. Whoever it was intended approaching the house by the small woodland skirting the lawn. She went inside quickly, shut and bolted the back door. The coffee was percolating furiously.

An urgent tapping came on the window. Turning, she

saw Nial the gypsy peering in at her. When the back door was opened, he slunk against the wall as if reluctant to reveal himself. His coming to the house like this was surprising, even alarming.

'What do you want, Nial? Come in for goodness sake, it's beginning to rain.'

He stood hesitantly on the doorstep. 'It's the babby. It's real bad. Nanta said the doctor man was here.'

'Why don't you go and fetch Dr Moore?'

His eyes shifted uneasily. Then she remembered Nanta telling her that Tesca had stolen something from the doctor's kitchen when the housekeeper went to fetch her purse. Nanta had been furious. Tesca was considered the black sheep of the gypsies. Her stealing was blatant because she had never learnt the art of the subtle swipe. The doctor, shouting expletives, had sent her running.

When Kiaran walked into the kitchen, Nial made a perceptible movement towards the door. How strange that anyone should be frightened of her husband. When she turned to explain the reason for the gypsy's visit, there was a hostile look on Kiaran's face.

'You'd better go and fetch Dr Moore,' he said shortly.

Nial looked pleadingly at her, his sharp features screwed up with anxiety.

'Ask Dominic to come out, Kiaran – please.'

Kiaran turned away impatiently. Nial shifted uneasily from one foot to the other. 'It won't be bad for you?' he asked anxiously, surprising her by this show of consideration.

'No, it won't be bad for me,' she answered, using the language that he understood.

Dominic looked bewildered when he came into the kitchen and saw the gypsy. When he heard about the sick child, he seemed uncertain.

'Well . . . I'd better take a look at the boy.'

As they walked through the woods (Nial had shot off on his own) he told her that if the child was really ill they would have to go and fetch Dr Moore. It was a matter of professional etiquette. Nanta came to meet them. She looked exasperated. Tesca had just admitted feeding something unsuitable to her baby. Dominic said he would go and make sure it was all right.

When they went into Nial's caravan, Marcella walked on to Nanta's. After a short time, Dominic joined her.

'He's fine. Nanta says you're to give me some wine.'

'Why didn't she come back with you?'

'Pouring oil on troubled waters!'

She understood. Nial adored the child. In his angry relief he had probably turned on Tesca.

'Nice in here,' he said, looking around him. 'Never been in a gypsy caravan before.'

'Try and sit down, Dominic,' she laughed. 'You're too big for this place.'

When she handed him a glass of wine, Marcella found herself comparing him with Dr Moore, the excitable Cork man with the podgy fingers and not infrequent whiff of whiskey on his breath. Dominic was so quiet and controlled. She noticed how the dark hair grew on his strong wrists, though the fingers were long and sensitive.

'You know, Marcella,' he said smiling, 'you look as though you belong here. You're a bit like them, you know.'

Flinging Nanta's large flamboyant shawl across her shoulders and resting a hand on her hip, she said, 'Well?'

He laughed. 'I remember when I first saw you, I was startled to see your ears were pierced. Young girls in our country don't usually go in for that sort of thing, do they?'

'Aunt Sarah nearly skinned me. In a way it brought me good luck – the earrings – because Sarah persuaded my father to send me away to school, out of her way. I met Prisca there, then all of you.'

'We must have seemed an odd bunch. God, that house in Brawn Street. We were desperately poor. I nearly threw everything up to become a clerk in the Derry docks.'

'Your parents managed though.'

'Mother managed, you mean. How hard she worked in that damn shirt factory and piles of outwork to do in the evenings. You'll remember –'

'I suppose you're able to help her now?'

'It's not really necessary, at the moment anyway. Mr Schenber gives Father a generous wage. Still, if things get really bad in Derry, Schenber might decide to get out. One of his business friends has left already. These people suffered so much in the past, having to leave their homes and businesses in Germany. And, as you saw the other night, the Schenbers are frightened. So we might have a financial crisis at home again. I want the younger ones to have a fair chance. You know Brendan wants to do theology? When he goes to the seminary there will be a lot of extra expense.'

'You should marry Lisa,' she said impulsively. 'All that money.'

'Marry Lisa?' he repeated, with one of his disapproving frowns, then looked at her until her eyes dropped.

'She's in love with you.'

An uncomfortable expression crossed his face. 'She's very emotional,' he began, and left the sentence unfinished.

Prisca's right, she thought, he doesn't even see her. Poor Lisa. 'She's very beautiful.'

'Marcella, for heaven's sake!'

'All right Dominic McDaid.' She began to feel unreasonably angry. 'Don't go ending up one of Ireland's bachelors. The pattern is there, you know: heading towards thirty, living at home, mainly concerned about your mother's welfare. Your mother would like to see you married. That I know.' He looked slightly amused at her outburst. 'It's not funny, Dominic.'

His expression changed. 'I wouldn't wittingly hurt anyone, Marcella. What can I do? I'm not in love with the girl.' He spoke quietly, his eyes troubled.

'You could go away and get a job somewhere else.'

'Wish I could. I wouldn't dream of leaving Derry at the moment though. Trouble is building up fast – later I'll probably do that.'

Nanta came in and began to apologize for being so long. 'After it threw up it was fine,' she said, explaining about Tesca's baby.

They left immediately.

Next day Kiaran suggested going to the hills for a picnic.

'What about Dominic?' Lisa asked. 'Would he not like to come too?'

He explained that Dominic had planned to take a packed lunch and go off on his own for a long walk.

'I think I'll go with him.' Before they could stop her, Lisa ran out of the house with a happy, eager expression.

When Lisa returned later Marcella saw by her face that something was wrong. 'Did you enjoy your walk?'

'Not much,' she said shortly, her lip trembling.

'Lisa, what happened – if you want to tell me?'

'Always men fall in love with me, but not Dominic,' she said, with a catch in her voice. 'I told him how I feel. I can't stand it any more, the way he is so aloof. He drives me mad.'

Marcella's heart went out to her. She could see how very unhappy her friend was. At least now she knew exactly where she stood. Later, as arranged, they all met at River House. Sarah seemed pleased to have such a crowd to feed. When she went to get a 'drop of wine' their eyes all met conspiratorially.

'Seems to have developed a higher degree of potency,' Brian told her. 'Should water it down a bit, Aunt Sarah.'

'That's the goodness working in it,' she said knowledgeably.

'Ned's dynamite working in it,' Prisca said in a low voice.

'It's so good this time,' Sarah went on, 'even Ned likes a wee drop. 'Tis a pity he doesn't stick to wine.'

When Prisca began to laugh, Sarah gave her a sharp look. 'There's nothing to laugh about, my dear. The doctor says if Ned gets his hands on any more poteen it'll be the end of him.'

While they were talking, Marcella suddenly noticed how old Sarah had become. She was withdrawn at times, like Granny McDaid. She felt anxious and decided to visit the house more often. Perhaps when there were grandchildren it would give her another interest.

'Where did you say Father went to?' Brian was asking.

'Up to Derry, dear. He said a silly note had been sent to the paper so they're keeping an eye on things.'

'What sort of note?' Marcella asked anxiously, switching her cloud of worry to Conor.

'He didn't say exactly. He was to be back in time for our meal.'

Sarah's edginess about Conor's lateness began to affect all of them as they sat around the table and tried to enjoy the food she had prepared.

'I'll ring,' Brian said. The telephone was in the room. They all heard the efforts of the telephonist, then finally her loud voice saying that the exchange in Derry was having trouble in getting the number. She would ring when she managed to get through. A short time afterwards she came back with the news that there had been an explosion in Derry.

'I'll drive up and see,' Brian said. 'You all stay here.'

Prisca wouldn't remain behind. Dominic said he'd better get back anyway. Lisa was determined to go with him. She was anxious about her parents, she said.

'We can't just stay here and wait,' Marcella told Kiaran.

'You go too, dear. It's your duty to be there,' Sarah declared dramatically, with a look in her eye that said, 'Be prepared for the worst.'

Passing the lodge house Marcella noticed Lisa's ruined suit waving forlornly on the line. The trouser legs seemed to be making slow-motion strides through the air, trying to catch up with their owner. But the suit's short life on Lisa's back had ended; Lisa had already told Sarah to give it to Biddy.

'I wonder what my aunt will say when her cook turns up dressed in that,' Kiaran chuckled.

'It's shrunk on me,' Lisa had said. 'Biddy will wear it, won't she?'

'Will pigs fly?' Sarah implored of the ceiling.

They were a few miles from Derry when they saw Conor's car approaching. The convoy waved him down and they all drew into a convenient lay-by. He didn't wait for their anxious questions.

'An amateurish bomb nipped the lines,' he told them in a tired voice. 'Not much damage was done but there was more trouble again in the centre of the city.'

'More trouble?' They all looked at him uneasily.

'It began yesterday afternoon.'

'Have you got last night's paper?' Brian asked.

Conor reached into the pocket of the car and handed it to him. 'That's a good picture, isn't it? One of our bright lads took it.'

His voice trailed away at the look on their faces. Dominic went pale. Prisca put a hand to her mouth. 'My God!'

'What is it?' Conor enquired, looking from one to the other.

'That boy right in front throwing the piece of brick is Brendan McDaid,' Brian said quietly.

Lisa threw up her hands. 'Little Brendan, such a nice boy.' Almost viciously she turned on Prisca. 'You indoctrinated him with the big talk. He did not get it from his parents. You've . . .'

Marcella tugged her arm. 'Don't interfere, Lisa.'

Kiaran turned to Conor. 'We'll be back later. Sarah's anxious about you.'

'Yes,' Conor replied, 'I'd better move on.'

Without a word, Dominic jumped into his car and shot off into the distance.

'What should we do?' Brian asked indecisively.

'We'll go straight home,' Prisca answered, meaning her parents' house. 'That Dominic will slaughter Brendan.'

Later, when Marcella and Kiaran were walking up the McDaids' path they heard voices raised in anger.

'A person with your intentions should show more tolerance,' Dominic was saying when they went into the house.

'Better to show a bit of intolerance now, rather than later, or he'll be a mealy-mouthed priest,' Prisca whipped back.

'They provoked us,' Brendan protested. 'How would you like it? They were shouting, "Auld Papists with your

Sacred Hearts and Mothers of God and . . ." ' his voice faltered. 'Worse – much worse.'

'Brendan,' Dominic said wearily, 'how many times have I told you that decent Protestants don't go out shouting that sort of thing on the streets? They were louts, you should have ignored them.'

'And you, my son, were a lout too,' Mr McDaid said angrily. 'In future you'll keep off the streets and every minute you're out of this house I want to know exactly where you've been.'

Those were the strongest words Marcella had ever heard the father utter. Mrs McDaid turned to Kiaran. 'It's the young hotheads on both sides that cause the trouble. Just look at that.' She pushed the paper over to them. 'See, every one of them are teenagers.'

'Was it just a scuffle between these youths?' Kiaran asked.

'Scuffle is hardly the word I'd use,' Dominic said grimly. 'They were tearing up pieces of pavement and hurling them at each other. The police used water cannons and women and children got the full whack of it.'

'Cella, would you come here a minute?' She followed Mrs McDaid out of the room. 'Look dear, would you do something for me?'

'Of course, anything.'

'Do you think you could take Brendan back to Iniscad with you? It's a half-term so there's no school. I'd like him to get away from Derry for a bit.' She paused. 'Dominic will go mad if I suggest Prisca's place. You know how she goes on.'

Poor boy, Marcella thought. How was he going to stand the discipline of a seminary?

'He's just a youngster. Oh God, when is this trouble going to end?' Her words stumbled out on a sob.

'Don't worry, Mrs McDaid. We'd love to have him any time. If Brendan brought his homework down at the weekends –'

'Bless you, Marcella. That would be marvellous.' She called to her son.

Brendan looked relieved to get away from the angry faces. His chin jutted out defiantly but there was a glint of tears in his eyes. When his mother told him about going to Iniscad, he broke into a wide grin. 'That's great. I'd like that, Cella. But,' he asked anxiously, 'will Prisca mind if I don't go to her house?'

'Of course she won't mind,' Marcella replied quickly.

He and his mother went upstairs to pack.

'Marcella, I'm not sure it's a good idea for Brendan to go away from home just now.'

She swung round and faced Dominic. 'Why not? It's what your mother wants. Let her be the best judge.'

'Prisca has too much influence.'

'Can't you trust me to do what your mother asked?' she said angrily, the old antagonism springing up between them. 'Can't you believe that Prisca might have some scruples about Brendan's welfare?'

'When it comes to her political involvement, no. A few weeks ago, I was called out to attend to someone who had been taken ill at a meeting, and found my sister up on the platform involved in a bitter political diatribe. That one's clever enough to influence youngsters with immature minds.'

'Brendan's not a simple boy.'

'He was simple enough to get mixed up with that stone-throwing mob. He looked like their leader, if you ask me. Brendan was out in front with a crowd of boys crouching behind him.' Dominic dug his hands into his pockets, turned towards the window and stood staring outside, as though he had forgotten her presence. Marcella had a sudden impulse to stretch out her hand and reassure him: the impulse died immediately. She had never in her life felt so distant from anyone.

It seemed to Marcella that Brian was far more taken aback than Prisca about her mother's decision to send Brendan to the lodge house. After one swift expression of surprise, she looked away thoughtfully and made no comment. It was possibly because her easygoing mother had made a determined decision that in some way held a rebuke for her daughter. Perhaps Mrs McDaid was trying to show Prisca how strongly she disapproved of her political activities. Like all wise women, Mrs McDaid usually held her tongue and kept peace in her family; when it was necessary, she acted in a positive way that evoked no criticism or discussion.

On his last day at the lodge house, Brendan, who was helping Marcella in the garden, turned with a wide grin. 'Mammy's frightened Prisca will talk me out of becoming a priest.'

Cautiously she said, 'You're not being talked into it, Brendan, are you?'

Protesting, he looked at her with a severe frown. 'Marcella, it is *not* possible to be talked *into* a vocation. It's either there or it's not.'

'It's said that Irish mothers are great priest-makers.'

Thoughtfully he answered, 'I know that is said. Surely not so much my mother's generation?'

'Your mother is very devout.'

'Devout like a nun? Never! Her faith gives her a contentment with life that affects everyone around her. *That's* goodness.'

'What do you think of Aunt Sarah?'

'She's very deprived.'

'Deprived?' Her voice rose in surprise.

He grinned mischievously. 'Of hope – joy. Does she ever laugh? You couldn't really say she's content, could you now.'

When they stopped laughing, he said like the wise old Father McGill, 'Ach, God help her.' And remembering what Father McGill used to say, Marcella thought, the boy has the makings of a good priest.

'Brendan, what about the street fight? Good lord, you had a huge piece of pavement in your fist.'

He looked away, not embarrassed by her question but grave, thoughtful. 'I'm sorry about that.'

'Easy to say now.'

'Not sorry that I tried to defend a principle. I would do it again. I'm sorry about the people who got drenched with water cannons and about my father. He wept when he saw the paper. He's such a gentle person. Full of fun, not a serious thought in his head.'

'He was justifiably angry,' she protested.

'Oh, that. I was relieved to see his anger. Before that, he just wept.'

'How did your mother react when she saw the paper?'

'She knows about the other side of my nature. No tears. Only a lovely sentence in Iniscad where I've had space and time to walk and think.'

'Come any time, Brendan. Please don't wait to be asked.'

'I will surely, Cella. I'm off to college soon. Locked up. Away from temptation!'

Chapter 26

The select few who made major decisions at their political meetings gathered in Rosheen Quinn's house. They were Eoin, Prisca and most of the Kindron people – the Curse of Kindron, as they called themselves jokingly. One of the main points of discussion this evening was the buying of arms. The moderates, like Eoin, felt that they should use caution. Rosheen would not agree.

'I don't know what you're worrying about, Eoin,' Prisca said. 'What we've managed to buy so far were dug out of the earth and some hidden in graveyard vaults. By the look of them, I don't think they'd be much use against a dying crow.'

'The situation is not ideal, but it's the only source available at the moment,' someone put in.

Firearms were a sore point. They knew that the other side had shooting clubs which made the holding of arms by Orangemen legal; whereas Republicans had nothing yet. A few guns that some of the men were cleaning had been hidden in their own gardens. If the police raided the house of a suspected Republican and found any weaponry, they would be in serious trouble. Two of the members were going to America soon to contact sympathetic groups there. Funds were alarmingly short and firearms very expensive to buy.

The next point of discussion was 'escape routes'. 'We need another place on the other side of the border, not too far away,' Rosheen told them. 'A place to which wanted men could have easy access later on. Ideally, it should be big enough and comfortable enough to hold men for an indefinite period. And, if possible, capable of storage when things begin to happen.'

'I think,' Prisca said thoughtfully, 'that I know a place that would cover all those necessities.'

'Where? And how far?'

'About ten miles from Derry. It's The Refuge at Ballyglen.'

'The Refuge? You found her difficult, Eoin, didn't you? When Conor Adams got you to run round with thé Kindron list?'

Eoin, who had grown considerably quieter at the meetings, shrugged. 'I offered to do the job, Rosheen. As far as the owner of The Refuge is concerned, she certainly did not want to be reminded of her relationship with Lord Kindron, though her family were the only ones to do well out of the connection.'

'Someone was telling me that she had plenty to say after the Civil Rights march. Maybe she'll be sympathetic now. Let's get in touch with her and find out. Time may not be on our side.' Rosheen turned to Prisca. 'You know her?'

'No, but I'll go. Someone told me about an unusual escape route at The Refuge.'

Prisca borrowed Rosheen's car and drove the ten miles to Ballyglen. In her bag were dark glasses, a scarf and an old raincoat. She had two plans. If one failed she would try the other. About a half-mile from The Refuge, she parked the car in a little quarry, then set out on foot. When she arrived at the inn and asked the barman if she could speak to Oonagh Toland, he pointed to the office across the hall.

'Come in,' a brisk voice called when Prisca knocked on the door. The owner of The Refuge pulled off her glasses and stared. 'Yes?'

In a few carefully chosen words, Prisca explained about the political group in Derry and asked if she would be prepared to help without being involved in any way. *Don't disclose the real purpose of your visit until you can sound out her feelings on the matter.* Rosheen's voice was in her ear.

'Help the IRA? That's what you're talking about, isn't it? How presumptuous of you to come here with such a request. I'm *not* interested in politics. In the past the IRA tried to burn down The Refuge.'

Prisca shot to her feet. 'They tried to burn it down because a tyrant named Kindron built it. *You* know who I mean.'

'*Get out!*'

When Prisca walked away from the inn she could feel the woman's eyes boring through her back. She looked casually towards the lough, then proceeded slowly down the drive to a bend in the road, where she darted off the path into a woodland that ran towards the back of The Refuge. She pulled the headscarf, raincoat and glasses out of her bag and put them on. The clatter of dishes almost drowned the sound of women's voices working in the kitchen. Prisca prayed that Annie, with whom she had been to school, was on duty. A young girl came out carrying a basket of tea towels to hang on the line in the orchard.

'Is Annie in there?' she asked.

'She is.'

'Ask her to come outside for a minute, would you?'

'Under God, who is it at all?' Annie exclaimed when she came to the door.

'Prisca McDaid.'

'Prisca? Sure I thought ye were Greta Garbo!'

'Annie,' she whispered, 'could you meet me over in the woods when you finish whatever you're doing? It's important.'

Her old schoolfriend caught the urgency of Prisca's mood and nodded. 'Well, I'm just preparing something now. I'm assistant cook,' she added proudly.

'That's great. Annie, it really is very important what I've come to see you about.'

'Give me fifteen minutes.'

'Don't let anyone know.'

The assistant cook folded her broad arms, winked and went inside.

Prisca waited over a half-hour before Annie came puffing through the trees. 'Hunger's Mother came into the kitchen wi' one of her lectures.'

'Hunger's Mother?'

'The mistress, Oonagh Toland. Don't waste food, she nags. Never give food to beggars at the door.'

'Did someone tell her about me?'

Annie laughed. 'Naw, she's always goin' on at us. The staff are suffering from starvation.'

'You don't look too bad,' Prisca giggled.

'Och, it's grand to see you, Pris. Ever so clever you were at school. I hear ye got yerself married . . .'

'Annie . . . look, I wouldn't ask you this, but I remember your father was in the IRA and went to prison for it. A brave man. Is he still interested?'

'Red hot. Says he's coming out of retirement to take up the cudgels again. That Civil Rights march put his back up. Under God, did you ever see the likes? Weans nearly murdered at Burntollet.'

'Well . . . students. Would you help us?'

A cautious look came to the girl's eyes. 'I wodden like t'lose me job. She'd have me out in a flash if anything got to her ears. Me doing so well too.'

'No risk. We just need someone sympathetic here on the spot.'

The cautious look increased to alarm. 'On the spot . . . whatcha mean?'

Prisca caught her arm. 'Look, Annie, someone told me there's a priest's hide-away at the inn and a way out to the hills.' Her arm went around the girl's shoulder. 'Annie, dear, we're going to be desperate for a place to hide the odd man if the trouble gets worse.' Prisca was not going to mention the other things that were going to be hidden there as well. 'It shouldn't be too difficult. A man could drop into The Refuge for a drink then disappear. Are you busy in the evenings?'

'Packed out. We're doing a roaring trade. Only pub for miles and a place to come to from Derry for a breath of fresh air. And the trees don't fight, begod!'

'Couldn't be better. What's the set-up when the bar closes?'

'The people staying at the inn go into the lounge and we clear up. She's upstairs by then.' A flush of excited colour began to grow on Annie's plump cheeks. The suggestion that Prisca had made was steadily feeding her patriotism. To help, though not to be involved, if the worst happened. Dad would be proud of her.

'All we need, Annie, is someone here we can trust to make sure the coast is clear when the man gets into the priest's bolt-hole. I know I can trust you. Remember when we were children and you the leader of the secret society at school? You made us wear green, white and yellow ribbons.'

'God, aye. Great times. Listen, me and auld Susan the housekeeper do a final clear around at night. She's getting past it so I'm really in charge. A quiet word at the bar to your man and later I can get him hidden. The entrance to the priest's hole is over by the fireplace. A tunnel runs down to the lough and a boat by the water to get him to the other side.'

'Couldn't be better, Annie. There'll be a bit of luggage –'

'Under the seat in the taproom,' the girl said promptly. 'Pris, I'd better go now. I'm in Derry every Tuesday. Up home.'

'I'll be in touch. Thanks, Annie.'

Well, Miss Oonagh Toland, Prisca thought as she made her way to the car, you're going to help whether you like it or not.

Kiaran managed to get all the work done at the cottages before winter began. It was a harsh season: wild winds beat the coast and the land looked grey and barren. He and Marcella were content to spend the long evenings reading by the fire. Derry, and the occasional sparks of trouble, seemed a long way off.

At the beginning of spring, Prisca came over one day and told her that Lisa was ill and wanted to see her.

'What's the matter?' she asked anxiously.

'Bad temper. Momma and Poppa are up to something.'

'Up to something?'

'Don't ask me. Lisa is like a clam.'

Before Marcella left for Derry, Kiaran said anxiously, 'Take care. If there's any trouble don't go through the town.'

'Ah, Cella.' When Marcella arrived at the house in Derry Mrs Schenber embraced her. There was an excited look in the woman's eyes. 'Lisa, Lisa,' she chanted all the way upstairs. 'Look who comes.'

'*All right*, Momma.' Lisa was sitting up in bed surrounded by glossy magazines, chocolates and expensive jars of make-up. 'Cella knows the way.'

'Ah, la la.' Lisa's sullen scowl did not silence her mother's happy little tune as she went over to the window and banged it shut.

'I *like* fresh air!' Lisa objected, twitching with irritation.

'What's the matter?' Marcella asked when they were alone. Her question was meaningless. Prisca was right, Lisa was just in a bad mood. She always took to her bed when life became difficult.

As she was heaving the window open again on Lisa's orders, the bedroom door opened. 'You can tell Cella,' Mrs Schenber announced and disappeared.

'Lock that door,' Lisa ordered, pointing dramatically.

'Oh no, Lisa.' It horrified Marcella that she wanted to lock her mother out of the room.

A beautifully shaped leg shot out from beneath the bedclothes and her friend spat some Hebrew or German which sounded like bad words. Climbing back into bed again, she said with a tremor in her voice: 'I'm in such trouble. They're going to leave Derry.'

'What?' Marcella was alarmed because she immediately thought of Phelim McDaid's job in the shop.

'Yes, we are going to London. Poppa says it is the only way because of Momma's nerves.'

'What about the factory and the shop? Is he going to sell out?'

'No,' she said abruptly. 'He cannot sell. Who wants to buy places that may go up in flames any minute? Why should anyone get involved in a business here? This country is going down, down . . . You are losing everything. Poppa says Ireland is in for a bad war.'

As she rambled on, Marcella bent her head under the savage whip of words spoken in anger and unhappiness. She felt shame that these people who had been hounded out of their own country, and had been happy in Derry, were forced to move again because they had no faith in the future of Ireland.

'What about Mr McDaid?' she asked anxiously.

'It is good for him,' Lisa replied indifferently. 'Poppa is going to arrange things so that he will keep all our affairs in order here – the shop and factory, I mean.'

With that worry settled, Marcella's concern turned to her friend again. 'London will be exciting. There'll be so much to do that you'll wonder why you ever stuck Derry.'

'It is here I want to be.'

'Lisa, I'm going to miss you. Come over for a holiday any time you feel like it.'

Lisa rested her head against the pillow and tears flowed down her face. Her misery – Marcella could not think of it as self-pity any more – isolated her.

The next time Marcella saw Lisa she looked happier. The Schenbers had been to London to look at houses, and a relation who ran an estate agency had sold them a luxurious flat in Hampstead. That, and the excitement of going to the theatre and some parties, had helped.

'Bet she marries some wealthy Jew,' Prisca prophesied after they left. Sure enough, at the end of July Marcella had a letter; in it was a coloured photograph taken on a yacht. Lisa, looking much slimmer and wearing a bikini, was standing beside a dark handsome man who looked a bit like Dominic, though he was obviously Jewish. On the back she had written, *'He's nice. Momma and Poppa are happy at last!'*

After she had read the letter, Marcella took the photo upstairs to the white and lilac room where she kept her album. Lisa wouldn't sleep there again and there was no sign of a baby coming to occupy it either. She had been feeling anxious and restless for ages, even envious when Tesca and Nial had another child. One day over at Briar Meadow, Tesca narrowed her eyes suspiciously when Marcella took the new baby in her arms. Nanta, who had been nursing it, saw the longing in her young friend's eyes and offered her the child to hold.

'You're lucky, Tesca,' Marcella told her. 'I don't seem able to have a baby.'

The suspicious expression on the gypsy's face changed immediately. 'Aha,' she murmured softly. 'Na baba?' Then added sadly, 'M'sorrow be with you.' It was the first time Tesca had ever shown any warmth towards her.

One day when Marcella was up in the attic storing some canvases she came on the tent they had bought in Brussels, and she thought of the picturesque part of the land near the border which they had visited one day. When he came in for lunch Kiaran laughed at her suggestion. 'Well, the change of air might work wonders!'

On Friday evening they packed all the necessary equipment and set out. 'This is good,' Kiaran said, as they lay in their sleeping bags listening to the gentle sound of the trout stream and the hushing of the trees. The smouldering fire glowed in the failing light and honeysuckle growing along the hedges scented the air. They had eaten a very good supper from the trout Kiaran had caught in the stream and which they baked on top of potatoes.

When the weather was fine they camped there at weekends. And every month Marcella waited for the first signs of pregnancy. Another aspect about Catholic marriages began to occur to her, one she was certain Prisca had not considered. Perhaps some of those women with large families had been in the same situation as herself; longing for a child and having to wait for ages. Perhaps that was why they didn't mind how many they had in the end. Now, she could imagine feeling like that.

They were discussing it one evening, when Kiaran said, 'You're not worrying, Marcella, are you? After all, we both come from small families. My parents were married a long time before I was born.'

'I'm not worrying, I'm . . .' She burst into tears.

'Oh, darling, I didn't realize. You have been anxious.' He put his arms around her. 'Let's talk seriously about it. Look, if nothing happens by the end of the year you go and see a gynaecologist. Goodness, you might end up like Ned in the brae's niece and have three at one go.'

'If my tests are — ?'

'I'll do exactly the same. And if all fails, well, we'll just adopt a couple.'

'What will your aunt say? She's so particular about blood and that sort of thing.'

He raised his eyebrows. 'Of course, naturally, I'll have to ask her permission first!'

They burst out laughing and, somehow, after that she became less tense and bothered.

On their next visit to Derry to do some shopping, they were shocked to see how the situation had developed. Shop windows were boarded up, and groups of policemen and B. Specials were everywhere.

A few nights after that, there was trouble at the border. Someone had attempted to blow up the Custom House. The papers said there would be armed B. Specials on duty in future.

'You know, Marcella,' Kiaran remarked, 'I think that spot of ours is not going to be so comfortable if the trouble continues. Perhaps another night under canvas and we'll pack it up for this year.'

They set off early that evening to make the most of it. The weather was so warm that they decided not to light a fire. Marcella had brought a mixed salad, cold meat and a flask of coffee. After supper, they went for a long walk up through the glen. The country around was beautiful and peaceful. It was difficult to think that only a few miles away trouble brooded over the old town that she loved. Now, she reflected, Derry seemed slightly alien as though characters from its past had risen from beneath the ancient walls and the drums of war were rolling. After their walk they knelt by the burn and bathed their faces in the cool water.

'A swim – that's what I'd like,' Kiaran said enthusiastically.

Suddenly, bursting into the silence of the evening, there came the screaming of car brakes, men shouting, then an explosion. Kiaran jumped to his feet and pulled Marcella with him. Shots were fired, followed by a lot of excited shouting; it seemed to be coming in their direction.

'We'll cross the burn and shelter under the hedge,' he said urgently. 'Something's happened at the Custom House.' Then, out of the night, bullets shattered through the canopy of tree branches stretching across the burn. Kiaran stumbled against her and without a sound fell down into the silvered pool where he had just bathed his face.

Marcella's screams rent the air as she tried to pull him out of the water. Strong arms clasped her and she felt herself being dragged away. People were shouting. Some men were in uniform, others in shirt-sleeves.

'How is he?' a voice asked.

'I'm afraid he's dead,' the other replied.

'He's not dead. He can't be dead,' she cried, trying to break away from the arms that held her.

'For Christ's sake get on the phone quick,' someone shouted.

Marcella broke free from the restraining arms and flew to Kiaran's side. Kiaran couldn't die! A tracery of leaves patterned his face and white shirt. She looked down on his silent face, at the withdrawal of life. She had seen it before on that other face: her mother's.

When she drifted back to consciousness, voices were saying the *De profundis*. 'De profundis clamavi ad te, Domine . . .' A shrieking of brakes came in the lane above the field. Someone was running towards them. 'What's happened?' The man's voice faded away when he saw the signs of death. Unheedingly, the voices went on with the sad lament for the dead.

In a detached way Marcella watched the vaguely familiar figure as he knelt down and lifted up the rug covering Kiaran's face. He curled back in shock. 'Kiaran Gilroy,' he said in a voice split with horror. 'Oh my God, not Kiaran Gilroy killed like that. Not him . . .'

Then his sobs, harsh and angry, silenced the prayers and made the trickling stream sound troubled. In her black silence, she thought. He is doing my crying; someone should be weeping for this terrible night. Now she realized who it was – John Farren, who used to live in the lodge house. Kiaran's boyhood friend, whose father had bought a farm near the border. He had been at their wedding. When the piercing sound of the ambulance came down the road, John Farren stood up and, without looking in her direction, stumbled blindly through the trees away from the horror of it all.

Three days later in Iniscad Church, Father McGill's voice came over her in waves. 'Kiaran Gilroy was killed at the border which divides our country. He is the first Catholic to die in this time of conflict. Killed by an act of violence by unknown hands – Kiaran, the most gentle of men who abhorred violence. His great love for the land –'

Stop! Marcella was shouting in her mind. *Don't talk about him!* She twisted around frantically in her seat where she sat between her father and Mr Gilroy. They looked at her, concerned. Dominic McDaid crossed the aisle and held out his hand. 'Come, Marcella.' Conor rose too. Together they led her from the church.

'She can't take any more, Mr Adams.'

'Take her up to Slievan, Dominic.'

As they drove through the lodge gates, Marcella turned her head away from her home where she had been so happy. She didn't want to look at it ever again. The large house was silent. Biddy in the brae and a maid were putting the final touches to the macabre feast for the mourners.

'When they get back, Marcella, we'll stay a short time then I'll take you back to Bridge House.'

In the evening there was a stream of callers. Sarah hovered over Marcella and fussed around with new authority, as though death had shaken her out of her spiritual lethargy.

It was getting dark when she said to Conor, 'Do you mind if I go out for a short walk? I must be on my own for a while.'

'Let me come with you,' her father pleaded. 'You're not fit to be out by yourself.'

'No, please. I won't go far.'

Reluctantly he let her go with a look of anxiety in his eyes. She walked down towards the shore. It was a quiet road; even so, someone came by and began to pour out condolence. I'll go mad if I don't get right away from people, she thought, looking towards the sea where the island was held in a silver hoop of water. Over there was silence. No one would reach her there.

She ran down to the shore, fighting the strong wind that was whipping in from the Atlantic, and pushed Liam's boat into the water. As soon as she moved away from the beach, the sea took command: it held and tossed the boat around viciously as if the elements had been cunningly waiting vengeance. The oar was wrenched from her hand and the surging waves climbed high around her. Marcella shut her eyes and waited for the force that would end all her terrible pain.

There was a splintering and tearing of wood as the little boat was thrown back on the inlet crusted with small jagged rocks. As soon as her body was tossed out on the shore, strong arms picked her up before the sea could drag her back again.

'Marcella,' a voice said, deep with fear.

'Dominic,' she whispered, stunned and bewildered that death had not snatched its opportunity to leave her in the surging sea. He held her close as though frightened she would run back again into the water.

'Come in through these bushes, 'tis shorter to the camp.' Nanta was guiding him.

When they reached the camp, Dominic stripped off her blouse, skirt and stockings and rubbed her skin hard with one of Nanta's woven towels. Then he pulled off his heavy knit sweater and drew it over her head. His warmth quickly spread through her body.

'I've got a pair of your old jeans here,' Nanta said, as she stirred hot water into a stone jug containing herbal wine. Dominic helped to get the jeans on while Nanta spooned the warming drink into her mouth.

'I've been frightened for her this day,' she said sadly.

'Thank God I went over to her father's house to see how she was getting on,' Dominic replied.

'It was a good thing you thought to look for her here. That island, it's always had a hold on her. Somehow I knew the minute I saw you. After a bit she'll have to get away from Iniscad.'

'Yes,' he agreed in a troubled voice.

'Poor wean.' Nanta kept stroking her hand, as silent tears began to flow down Marcella's face. ''Tis better now,' Nanta said, reaching out for Dominic's handkerchief.

'I'm sorry,' Marcella stammered, 'for all the trouble.'

A little later, when she seemed calmer, Dominic said they should go in case they began to worry at home. He held out his hand for the wet clothes.

Nanta shook her head. 'I'll keep them for now. Mustn't let the auld woman know what's happened.'

'Yes, it would be better that none of them knew about this.'

They were about to leave the caravan when Nanta took their hands and placed them together, as though in preparation for prayer. She pressed them tightly, bent her head and said: 'God go with you. Let the sun always lighten your way and no more sorrow darken your day.' The Catholic and Romany blessing had a strange prophetic sound in the caravan.

Prisca felt inadequate in her efforts to comfort Marcella. For days she had hung about achieving nothing. The reserve that was part of her friend's nature seemed to have built a solid wall of silence around her.

'Let her be for a while,' Brian advised, himself desperately worried about his sister. 'Go off to Derry and see your mother,' he suggested.

It was with a feeling of relief that Prisca stepped on to the Derry bus. As she walked up past the Cathedral, she saw her mother coming down the street. Nora McDaid had been feeling a silent anger in her heart against her daughter ever since Brendan became involved in the Civil Rights march; then the awful scene in the street when the police brought out water cannons. Afterwards she had spoken only a few words to Prisca. 'You're married now and too old for me to interfere in your life,' she said, 'but don't be responsible for influencing your brother or sisters. There's enough bad will and unhappiness going on in this town. Don't bring it into our home.'

Now there she was coming towards her and Nora was heartily glad to see her. They were not a demonstrative family, but in the way of the Irish they smiled and lightly touched each other's arm, making a contact that had more warmth than a peck on the cheek.

'How's Cella, love?'

'Dreadful, Mammy. We don't know what to do with her.'

'Poor wee girl. It'll take time to get over that shock. She wouldn't come up for a while? Maybe a change would be the makin' of her.'

'No, she won't leave the house. She's either up in her room or in the old dairy. Biddy in the brae was very hurt the other day when she wouldn't come down to speak to her. They were always good friends.'

'You say? Poor wean. I've had a Mass said for Kiaran's soul.'

'You could paper the walls of Slievan with Mass cards, I hear. It's a custom I don't like. Where are you going, Mammy?'

'Into town to get a few things for the Misses Thorn, and a couple of messages for Mona's party this evening.'

'Party?'

'She's off to join the Schenbers in London next week. It's all arranged. Must hurry, Pris. Look, I've just slipped down to Mrs Kenny and given her my door key for I won't be back home for an hour or two. You'll see her up at the house.'

'Why is Mrs Kenny going up to our house and where are the others?'

'She's a grand hand at baking – for the party, ye know. I just can't get the hang of it,' she said with a guilty smile. 'The girls have gone to the pictures and won't be back until six o'clock. And Mona's out somewhere. Dom's still in Belfast at the medical conference. Must hurry, love.'

Prisca thought her mother looked years younger. Free from the threat of miscarriages, a good home and a little money to spare had made all the difference to her health. She met Mrs Kenny on their doorstep carrying a bag containing a small electric cake mixer and other things.

'How're ye, daughter? Comin' for the party this evenin'?'

'I'll come in later for a cup of tea, Mrs Kenny, if you're going to make some of your marvellous cakes.' My mother's crazy, she thought. She knows this woman's weakness, yet she gives her the free run of the house. Dominic would go mad! When they opened the door, a blast of music sounded from somewhere upstairs. They looked at each other then made for the stairs. It came from the bathroom where the bath was running, the radio playing and Mona O'Donovan singing at the top of her voice. Prisca shrugged and called out but her voice was drowned by the cacophony.

'What d'ye think of the job yer mam made of the rooms? She's a great hand wi' the paintbrush.'

'Isn't it wonderful, Mrs Kenny, the way she's developed a flair for decorating. Look at the colour scheme she's worked out. I'm hopeless at it.'

The woman nodded towards the bathroom. 'Done hers too. Come and take a look.'

'Well . . .' Before she could protest, Mrs Kenny was opening the room next door. Lying on Mona's bed was the brown plastic bag which she had always been so secretive about. It was empty. The contents were placed in a neat row across the bedspread.

'Wid ye *believe* it!' Mrs Kenny was saying. A Post Office

savings book was snatched up and, once again before Prisca could protest, it was flicked open. 'Look at that date, nineteen fifty-four . . . all those years the mother was saving for her.'

Prisca looked and saw that five hundred pounds had been built up in the account; in recent years, small amounts had been added. Mona was as thrifty as her mother.

'The sly wee bugger and t'think how we had to skin them poor bastards in Brawn Street to bury that Peggy O'Donovan. And yer ma, poor as a church mouse, took her in and scraped to feed her.'

Prisca didn't know what to say. 'Perhaps Peggy wanted to give the girl some security. As you see, she's wisely continuing to save a bit.'

'Ha!' Mrs Kenny pounced again. This time she had Mona's birth certificate in her hand. '*Father unknown*. No surprise there. What's in that envelope . . . old letters? Let's take a look.'

'No!' Prisca protested. 'They're probably her mother's letters. Come on.'

They made their way down to the kitchen. 'Mrs Kenny, I must ask you to do me a favour. Don't tell my mother about that Post Office book. Mona will be leaving Derry soon. It would be better if Mammy could keep that nice warm feeling she has for the girl. You see, Mona has always lied about the contents of the brown bag.'

Mrs Kenny's eyes slid away as though to conceal her thoughts which made Prisca think immediately, She'll tell all Brawn Street — if they haven't already been rehoused. 'It would really be better if no one knew, Mrs Kenny. Mona might come back to Derry again.'

'All right,' the woman agreed huffily.

Chapter 27

There were frequent outbursts of trouble in Derry over the following weeks, then the situation quietened down again. Though Dominic was not able to come to Iniscad, he rang frequently and asked Marcella professional questions with anxiety in his voice. Was she getting plenty of sleep? Did she go to see Nanta often?

One day he arrived unexpectedly. When they were eating lunch he suggested she should come to Derry the following day. She didn't want to go near the place, or shake herself out of the apathy that had gripped her since Kiaran's death.

On the following morning she left earlier than was necessary to get away from her aunt's anxious flutterings. Avoiding the border area, she took the road across the hills, which was used for smuggling. She felt at ease on the journey but as Derry grew nearer a feeling of agitation began to grow. Driving up the Strand Road towards Shipquay Street, she noticed policemen and B. Specials guarding the entrance to some buildings. Near Cassy's house, where Dominic had arranged to meet her, she was startled to see so much rubble on the pavements.

The gardens at Slievan and the cottage were full of flowers yet she had not thought to pick some for Cassy. Parking the car, Marcella walked down one of the side streets to the little florist's shop. When someone bumped into her she found herself staring at a burly B. Special. He could have been at the border that night . . . bullets from his gun could have killed Kiaran. Something beyond her control snapped, and when she rushed at him, one part of her mind looked on appalled, horrified, at her tearing, beating hands.

'The bitch,' a woman shouted, pulling and dragging at Marcella's blouse with vicious grabs. The B. Special, to protect himself, caught her wrist and flung her roughly against the stone wall where the sharp crusted stones tore at her bare arm. She felt pain as the skin broke and with the reality of pain came fear at the man's expression of anger and the woman's look of hatred. What had she done? A minute ago this man had seemed blank, dull, indifferent; now he looked as if he could kill her.

A hostile crowd gathered around from nearby streets. She felt cornered, unable to move away or to enter the florist's because people were blocking the entrance. Then she heard a voice saying: 'Get out of the way, please. I'm a doctor.'

'Doctor?' the woman said derisively. 'It's the polis we need 'ere. Flifin' bitch.'

'Marcella . . .' Dominic put his arm around her and led her to his car.

When Cassy saw them coming, she cried, 'Oh, Mary and Joseph!' The blood streaming down Marcella's arm made it look worse than it was. She kept fussing around them ineffectually. 'Yer room's just as ye left it, Marcella. I made the bed up only yesterday. Dear God . . .' She kept wringing her hands. 'I'll get some brandy.'

'No, make some tea,' Dominic told her.

While he washed and dressed her arm, Marcella cried all the time. 'I'm sorry. As if there wasn't enough trouble here without me doing a thing like that. Dominic, I don't understand why I did it. I lost my head entirely.'

'Hush, it's all right.' He led her upstairs to the room. When Cassy brought the tea, he took some tablets out of his bag and made her sip the tea and swallow them. Pulling up the eiderdown he said, 'Cassy will look after you. I've got to go now but I'll come back later.'

They shut the room door and urgent words passed between them out on the landing. 'Keep an eye on her, Cassy. I'm going to ring up her family then arrange to get her into hospital.'

'Sure, I could look after her here.'

'No, it's not safe. There's too much trouble around this area and it seems to be getting worse.'

'God grant the British Army come soon,' Cassy cried in a loud keening voice. 'Oh God, send the British Army before we're all murdered in our beds.'

'The first lot have moved in. They're manning the barricades now,' he told her.

Marcella couldn't sleep. She lay on the bed listening to the tinkle of the bell on the shop-door ringing downstairs. Nearly all Cassy's customers were schoolchildren. 'A penn'th o'sweets . . . stick o' liquorice.' The shop became quiet. Then the sound of a band playing *The Sash My Father Wore*. A raucous voice shouting, 'Fenian bastards. Orange bastards.' She got up and stood by the window and looked down; it was like a cataclysm. These Christians, see how they love one another, she thought bitterly. What had happened to the gentle people? Had the demagogues destroyed them? And the churches – the churches of holy Ireland? Were they all too busy wading through masses of theology and singing chunks of the Bible instead of giving inspired leadership through the simple message of Christianity? How sadly these men of God had failed.

She remembered the one roaring on the radio the previous night: a vitriolic flow that left no feeling of hope. The man of God who loved only Orangemen. And Kiaran had to die because the wound of distrust was too deep to heal. How many more would die before it all ended? She closed her eyes and leant her head against the window pane, seeing again his face before the metallic rain poured through the trees. Whose bullet had killed him? An IRA or B. Special's? They would never know. She didn't want to know.

Dominic came striding across the room. 'Marcella, come away from that window. A brick has just gone through the one next door.' He looked at the wildness of her face and his concern grew.

'Dominic, I can't go on,' she sobbed. 'I just can't.'

He held her face between his hands. 'You're ill,

Marcella. I'm taking you to hospital now. We'll soon get you well again.'

Avoiding the city walls, where youths were throwing stones, he drove swiftly down to the barricades; painted across a wall were the words *You are now entering Free Derry*. Beyond this area, soldiers on duty clutched rifles in their hands, ready for action: Englishmen, some only boys, with tense expressions not knowing who was the enemy. A tank with machine guns pointed threateningly at the car. When they saw it was a doctor's they allowed it to pass quickly.

'No visitors for the next few days,' Marcella heard Dominic tell the sister at the hospital. This was a luxurious room; a room for a Gilroy, she thought vaguely. The name, without Kiaran to share it, had an empty sound. A young nurse came in.

'Doctor, there's a priest wanting to see Mrs Gilroy.' He frowned. 'He's been waiting a long time. We didn't know when you were going to arrive.'

'Who is he?'

'A Father McGill.'

Father McGill hated Derry; he must have come up specially to see her. 'Let him come in for a few minutes,' Marcella told them.

The old priest sat down heavily on the chair. She waited for the holy platitudes. 'God's will be done . . . mustn't feel hate.' She wanted to scream and bit her lip. There was a long silence.

'Don't pray over me, Father. I'm not in the mood.'

'Pray? You're not dying, are you? Considering you beat the daylights out of a B. Special, you're doing remarkably well, apart from that arm. No child, I'm not in the mood for praying either. The destruction I've seen this day makes me feel like a wicked old man because my thoughts are so murderous. I'll be glad to get back to the peace across the border.'

'Sorry.'

His hand covered hers. 'Marcella, you were one of the lucky people.'

Startled, she sprang out of her lethargy. 'How can you say that?'

'You and Kiaran had a great love. Few people on this earth know the joy of such a bond. It was a rare gift.'

Agonizing grief gripped her throat. She turned her head as tears flowed down her face.

'There was something very special about you two, even when you were children. I used to think, what a pity the social barriers will keep these two apart. All that changed, thank God. Do you know what Kiaran said to me that day he called at the parochial house – the day he was looking for you before he went abroad with his father?'

'What did he say?' The sensation of curiosity stopped her tears.

'He said, "She's lovely and so unusual . . ." something like that. You see, Marcella, he saw the woman in the child; an invisible bond was drawing you together. In that short time of your marriage, you had a lifetime of happiness.'

Lifetime of happiness. These words were ringing in her ears when Dominic and another doctor came to send her into a long, deep sleep. When she opened her eyes again, a bunch of dark red roses was on the bedside table. Their scent filled the room. The nurse sitting beside the bed felt her pulse. She went outside and called to someone to fetch Dr McDaid. There were lines of exhaustion around Dominic's eyes when he came in. He sat down on the bed and smiled – a tired smile.

'How long have I been here, Dominic?'

'How do you feel, Marcella?'

'Empty. I feel as though I've been a long way away. Was it some sort of drug you gave me?' She wanted to talk and talk, at the same time there was a quietness inside her as though the pain of her grief was not so violent. In some inexplicable way, during that long, deep sleep she had come to peace with it. The nurse brought a tray of food. She felt hungry. That too was unusual. She had scarcely eaten a thing in the last few weeks.

After a while, he said, 'Marcella, I don't know what you plan to do in the immediate future, but there's a job going here which I think would suit you, if you'd care to do it.'

'Here in the hospital?' Her voice rang with surprise.

'It's in the children's ward — a mural on the wall. Do you think you could get down to that sort of work again?'

'I don't know,' she murmured, hesitatingly. 'Perhaps I need to do something. Oh dear . . .'

He looked at her distressed expression. 'I know what you're thinking, all the equipment is in the lodge house. Don't worry, I'll get Brian and Prisca to fetch everything up here. The three of us can go down in my car.' He looked at her with a slight hesitation. 'Mother says that if you decide to stay in Derry, she would like you to come and live with us. There's plenty of room and our new house is outside the troubled area.'

Marcella thought of the large Victorian house where they now lived and almost shuddered. She didn't feel up to the gay, happy McDaid family yet. 'Dominic, I think I'd rather go back to my room at Cassy's. I've got used to it.' There was something about the room over the shop that gave her a feeling of security. Also, she remembered how well she had worked there. And dear old Cassy had a comforting, undemanding presence.

She stayed in bed for the next few days. The trouble around Derry raged spasmodically. 'Isn't it dreadful?' a nurse remarked, nodding at the newspaper with news of the latest trouble, when she brought in her breakfast tray. Not knowing what religion she was, Marcella made no comment.

'The police are going mad,' the nurse added. 'The people (meaning the Catholics) have risen against them. There's places in Derry they dare not go any more.'

'Perhaps things will quieten down now that the British Army have come?'

'Aye, maybe.' Her eyes narrowed. She bent down and whispered, 'I don't like some of the things that are going on here. The police are all over the place, taking the names of the people who have been marching. I think . . .'

Marcella didn't hear any more because a sister came into the room. Later that evening she walked down to the casualty department. As she stood in a corner watching, a young Knight of Malta helped in an injured man.

'Was he marching?' a bad-tempered looking nurse demanded. 'Are they still at it?'

'Don't know,' the young boy in uniform muttered through tight lips.

'You know all right,' she snapped.

To Marcella's surprise, a policeman came over with a notebook and tried to get the man's name. She shot out of the corner.

'That man,' she said, 'shouldn't be questioned in his condition. It's a doctor he needs. Imagine asking him where he lives when he's in such a state.'

'He'll get a doctor when there's one available,' the nurse muttered angrily. 'You're a patient. What are you doing down here? Get back to your ward at once.'

'You,' Marcella said in a voice trembling with anger, 'are supposed to be caring for the sick. How can you treat an injured man like that?'

She heard the nurse say to the boy in uniform, 'You'd better get off home.'

The boy limped down the corridor, his face white, his uniform stained with the injured man's blood.

'Come with me,' Marcella whispered to him. 'I'll get you something to eat.'

'Thanks, miss.'

'You're very tired, aren't you?'

'Yes, miss.' His large eyes were clouded with unshed tears. He's far too young to be involved in this situation, she thought. Up in her room, he drank some coffee from a flask and ate the cakes that Sarah had baked. The boy was ravenous as well as exhausted. A few tears escaped down his face and he pushed them away angrily, leaving a streak of dirt mixed with blood. There was a movement at the door. It was Dominic.

'I've just had a bad report about you. Whatever – ?' He looked astonished when he saw the boy. His eyes flicked over her face.

'I'm quite all right, Dominic. Just angry. Do you know what's happening down there?'

Wearily, he pushed a strand of hair off his face. She was startled to see a sprinkle of grey in the black hair. 'I know.'

The boy went over to him. 'There won't be any more marchers coming here, Doctor. Units of the Free State Army are setting up First Aid posts at the border. We'll take them there in future.'

Dominic turned to her. 'I'll be back in a minute, Marcella. Come on, lad, I'll give you a lift home.'

When he returned, she said, looking at the expression on his face, 'You're depressed, Dominic.'

'I suppose so,' he admitted in a strained voice. 'I had such high hopes that the Civil Rights Association and the People's Democracy would achieve something peacefully.'

'They will eventually, now that the world knows what's happening in Ulster.'

'The people who go out marching quietly are moderates: lurking in the background are the extremists. You'll see, they'll take the law into their own hands before we know.'

Her heart went out to him. She began to feel concerned but not for herself. And at that moment too, she realized that her previous indifference about the political situation in Ulster was being replaced by a desire to be involved. The quietness of Donegal suddenly seemed a long way off.

From the day Marcella began to paint the mural in the children's ward, she felt better. The work and the little ones stimulated and fascinated her. The children were aged from about three to five years old; some of them were incredibly tough and coarse. They reminded her of those in Brawn Street.

'Ma's coming,' they shouted every morning after they had been washed and their beds made. A tiny girl with long pigtails and a pram loaded with dolls came slowly down the ward. Wearily, she made her way as though the large family exhausted her. She never spoke or smiled to the others. 'Suffering Ireland' the nurses called her.

'Her ma's got nine weans,' Jimmy told Marcella, who realized that the child's expression reflected the worn-out mother at home who had to cope with nine children. Jimmy was her favourite. He had a crafty little face which looked incongruous under a mop of rusty red curls. He was unable to leave his bed like the other children, so Marcella fetched and carried for him all the time. One day he wet on his teddy. She took it to the bathroom and washed it in disinfectant. As she was putting it on the radiator to dry, Dominic came into the ward.

'Still having the same old trouble, Jimmy?'

'Ach, sure I canna stop leakin', Doctor.' Dominic studied his notes, then he came over and stood beside her.

'You know,' she said briskly, 'you ought to be married. You should have children of your own. You're so good with them.' He gave her a long searching look and turned away without saying a word. For some reason the look disturbed her.

Cassy was delighted to have her back again. Marcella found that with her job at the hospital, helping in the sweetie shop and working on a large canvas of Derry, she was kept very busy. Dominic tried to visit her most evenings. They would sit and talk and drink coffee. Sometimes she worked away at her painting while he stretched out on a large comfortable chair she had bought for the room. He watched quietly, letting the tensions of his day's work ease away. It was strange, she thought, Kiaran was not able to do that, sit and watch her at work. She suspected that Kiaran had regarded her painting as a hobby, something to pass the time and not to be taken too seriously. Yet Dominic looked at it critically. He had an awareness of perspective and colour that surprised her.

'Get it all down, Marcella,' he said one day. 'Derry is rapidly changing. Brawn Street is being pulled down.'

'Good! It will be nice for people to go upstairs to the loo instead of out to a freezing yard.'

'If they're moved to high blocks of flats they won't be happy either. Belfast was a terrible mistake. They pushed people into them there and now they're having every kind of problem.'

The situation had quietened down considerably since the arrival of the British Army. The lull did not last long, however. One night some youths were taunting each other; inevitably fighting began. An elderly man who was passing by tried to intervene and was knocked down. Unfortunately he suffered from heart trouble: before the ambulance arrived at the hospital, he was dead.

'Och, he was a good peace-lovin' man, a good Protestant,' Cassy lamented. 'He'd be the last person to start trouble, may God·rest his soul.'

Then there was another Civil Rights march. When the marchers arrived in Guildhall Square, they were showered with bottles and bricks by a mob behind the city walls. After that everything stirred up again. In the late afternoon, Marcella and Cassy carried out steel shutters, put them on the windows, locked and barred the back door and prayed that trouble wouldn't come through the shop door which had to be kept open for customers.

Most of the time Brian and Prisca stayed in Derry with her family. It was convenient for them as they both now worked in local schools. They were trying to help the people because the Bogside was still in a state of siege. One of the large blocks of flats which had replaced some of the old houses became, to the despair of many people, an 'ammunition centre' – the ammunition being petrol bombs made with milk bottles, and piles of stones.

Dominic did not call so often these days. He, too, became involved with the people behind the barricades. When he came into the children's ward where she was working, the youngsters clambered around him. He did not fool with them like the other doctors, but sat patiently on their beds and listened to their chatter, or tried to make them talk about the books and comics they were reading. He told Marcella that the little girl whom the nurses called 'Suffering Ireland' was a case of 'infant maturity' in the worst possible sense. She had absorbed her mother's unhappiness; the mother's inability to cope with the large

325

family with which nature had so ungenerously endowed her.

Cassy, who was worn out with fear and sorrow, decided to do something more practical than spending her customary hour every day at St Columba's Church praying for peace. She began to help the Citizen's Action Committee. Boxes piled with provisions were loaded into Marcella's car every day, then taken around to the flats where Prisca distributed the contents to the people who needed help. One evening when she was unloading the boxes, Dominic came over and said, 'Marcella, would you do something for me?'

'Yes, of course. What is it?'

'Go to Iniscad tomorrow.'

She went tense. 'What about my work at the hospital?'

'I think you should take a day off, you're looking rather pale.'

And so are you, she thought, noticing the darkness of fatigue around his eyes.

'I don't want to go back yet.' She hesitated. 'Or do you think I should?'

'I think it would do us both good to get away from here for a while and go to the peace and quiet of Donegal. If you drive there in the morning I'll join you after lunch, then perhaps we could go for a walk.'

'You'd like to go, Dominic, wouldn't you? That's different, we'll go then.' He made her feel as though she was doing it for him.

Sarah was delighted to see her. They had lunch early, then Marcella went over to Slievan. Mr Gilroy and his sister were looking much better. Strangely, he had taken Kiaran's death with more fortitude than his sister. Her brisk step had become a feeble pottering sort of movement.

'Don't worry,' Biddy hissed when Marcella went down to the kitchen to see her. 'Any day now she'll be back to normal and cuttin' the bread ration. Wild extravagances have been committed down here and herself past noticing. We're makin' the most of it for it's too good to last. Himself has found great comfort from the cellar. I have a notion he's encouraged his sister to take the same remedy.'

Marcella hugged Biddy. She made the stark emptiness of Slievan less intimidating. The sound of Kiaran's laughter had brightened this house; the echo still lingered in her ears. She told the Gilroys about her work. They showed a polite interest. Like Kiaran, they had considered her career to be no more than a hobby.

'Come into the study, Marcella. There are one or two matters we must discuss,' Mr Gilroy suggested. Looking out of the window with unseeing eyes, he said: 'I think we have both sufficiently recovered to discuss Kiaran's affairs and your financial situation.'

She didn't think there was much to talk about, knowing that Kiaran had put all the money his mother had left him into the estate. Mr Gilroy realized that too, and that was what troubled him; the fact that she had no capital. 'There's the lodge house,' he said. 'You and Kiaran have made it structurally sound. It's in good condition, not like this old place.'

'Could we let it or something, Mr Gilroy? I'll never live there again.'

'Well, it's your property. All that was arranged at the time you were married. Kiaran insisted on it.' He thought for a moment. 'Letting it furnished would certainly be a source of income and we must be practical.'

Marcella looked out of the window. For one brief, bitter second she thought, If Kiaran and I had had a son, he would have inherited all this. What would happen to it now? Her heart ached when she noticed the withered autumn leaves covering the lawn like flecks of gold under the thin sunlight. When she returned to the cottage, Dominic and her father had arrived from Derry. She tried to tell them about her conversation with Mr Gilroy.

'I suppose I really ought to go over and open up the lodge house. I can't keep putting it off. There are things I need to take away.' She had deliberately gone around the back way to Slievan, avoiding the lodge. Now she acknowledged that it was time she confronted a situation that filled her with dread.

'Don't worry, dear,' Sarah said, looking at her with pity. 'Prisca and I went and cleared out the larder and sorted things.'

'Kiaran's clothes?' she said, panicking.

'Everything went to the convent. You know how many needy sources they have. We thought you might feel we did the right thing.'

Waves of panic swept over her again when Dominic opened the door of the lodge. On the hall table there lay a pile of catalogues that had arrived on the afternoon they went camping. Kiaran had said, 'I'll look at those on Sunday evening when we return.' The house seemed withdrawn and cold, resentful about the happiness that had been snatched away from its protecting walls. When she went to go upstairs, Dominic stayed behind in the hall.

'Come with me,' she asked him.

The beds in the main rooms were completely stripped, all the blankets covered in polythene bags. In the spare room, Dominic's eyes went to the pile of farming books beside the bed. She covered her face with her hands and, for the first time in weeks, began to cry.

'He slept here sometimes,' she sobbed, 'before we tried to have a child. And all the time it wouldn't have made the slightest difference because I couldn't have one anyway. The waste . . . We were trying to do what was right and spoiling the happiness of our marriage.'

His arms went around her. For a moment he held her close. She felt the strength and comfort of his body, as though it were shielding her from the pain and loss. 'I understand. Life is like that, Marcella. Nothing is ever perfect.' He led her downstairs, then shut and locked the doors.

Out on the road, she said, 'You wanted a rest and change today, now you've got to put up with my misery.'

The line of his mouth softened and he took her hand. 'Put up with you? Don't be silly.'

After tea they walked over to see Nanta, then on to Brian and Prisca's cottage. They had said they were coming down for the day as well. Prisca was busy typing. A pile of papers covered the table. She told them Brian had been held up in Derry; he was coming later.

'Sit down somewhere.' She waved her hand towards the chairs. 'I'll make a pot of tea.'

Before they could sit on the couch they had to remove a bundle of addressed envelopes. Dominic looked at one curiously, then a deep frown spread across his face. He went through the lot, all the time his look of alarm increasing.

'What is it?' Marcella asked.

He didn't reply. Moving over to the table, he picked up one of the papers. Marcella could see by his expression that something was seriously wrong.

'These are letters,' he said grimly, 'to Irish organizations all over the world pleading for funds to buy guns and ammunition.'

Just then they heard Brian's motorbike outside. Her brother came in and put an arm around her. 'Ah, Marcella, you look so much better. Doesn't she?' He turned and saw the expression on Dominic's face. 'What's the matter? What is it?'

'Did you know what Prisca's doing?'

'Doing? She said she had some typing . . .'

Dominic thrust a letter at him. 'Read that.'

Prisca came in with a tray and placed it on the dresser. She turned and faced them, hands on hips; defiant, ready for battle. 'Don't bother to read them all, Dominic, because they're all the same.'

Brian was now looking as perturbed as Dominic. 'Why did you get involved with this?' His voice sounded unfamiliar, low and harsh. 'What organization is this – the IRA?'

'Let's say we're a more advanced group of the IRA. No old fogeys with rusty guns any more, and no more Civil Rights marches either for our group.'

'You're absolutely mad to have anything to do with these people,' Brian shouted at her. 'You've got no idea where this may lead to. Who are your leaders? Are they going to put guns into the hands of youngsters, like the gang that Brendan got involved with? For God's sake have some sense. Go to the Bogside, help the people. Do something constructive, not destructive.'

'They need help all right, in every way.' Her mouth twisted with bitterness. 'The government up in Belfast doesn't want to know about the Bogside, or the plight of the people in any of the Catholic ghettos.'

Dominic looked at her. 'The people up there are more concerned about getting their Family Allowance. They don't want your guns.'

'*You*,' she said through her teeth, looking at him as though his words were perjurious.

Marcella understood how he felt. Dominic was more concerned about the people's material welfare. The hundreds of children had to be fed, and the Family Allowance provided a stable income.

'Well, tell us,' he snapped, 'what are the aims of this organization you belong to?'

'When we get money, we'll buy guns. We haven't got shooting clubs like the Orangemen. At the moment we have nothing, or very little.'

'Guns. What in the name of God are you going to do with guns?' he expostulated.

'We'll teach the right people to use them, and fight when the time comes.'

'*Fight?*' The word shot out of his mouth. 'That's the very thing we want to avoid. Every time our marchers are stopped, the more impact our cause has on Westminster and the world.'

'Impact.' Prisca hurled the word contemptuously. 'Your peaceful pleas have got you nowhere and they never will. The politicians in Westminster are frightened to offend Stormont. They will connive one or two things, then we'll be back where we started. That's the sort of thing we don't want to happen again.' She looked at them, then rushed at the table and began piling all the papers together. Swinging around accusingly, she shouted: 'You're a lot of bloody pacifists.' Her face was white, her eyes on fire. Then they filmed with tears. 'Christ help Ireland with people like you,' she said brokenly.

'Prisca.' Brian's voice was gentler, with a touch of pleading.

'Let's push on, Marcella,' Dominic said shortly and took her arm.

'See you in the Bogside later,' Marcella said.

Prisca did not reply.

Chapter 28

When Marcella returned to Derry that evening, Cassy asked her to take a box of provisions over to the flats. It was getting late, so instead of putting them in the usual place at the back of the car, she pushed them on the seat beside her and drove off quickly. Dominic was standing in the yard talking to a First Aid worker. When he saw her he came across.

'Do you know, Marcella, I think you and Cassy should plan to come to our house to sleep in future. It's getting too dangerous to be living so close to the city walls.'

'I'll tell Cassy, but honestly I don't think she'll want to move out this evening because she's got a cold and intends going to bed early.'

'All right then, make it tomorrow.' He nodded his head and went to move away.

'Oh, Dominic, could you spare the time to carry some groceries over to Prisca's group?'

'Sure.'

When he opened the back of the car, she said quickly, 'Not in there . . .' The words froze on her lips at the expression on his face. He was silent — almost stunned for a moment. He turned with a look of anger that made her flinch.

'Why the hell are you doing this? I thought you of all people had more sense. Did Prisca ask you to bring them here?'

'What are you talking about? I don't know what you mean.'

'Come here.'

She walked to the back of the car. He drew aside an edge

of the rug. Stacked in neat piles were rows of guns. Marcella couldn't believe her eyes. 'How did they get there? I don't know a thing about them,' she protested. 'Honestly, Dominic, I just don't know how they got into my car.'

He looked uncertain for a moment, then his hand touched hers briefly. 'Sorry.'

'How could they have got there?' she repeated in horror. 'I want to know.'

'Someone put them there when you were in Iniscad. Where did you leave the car? Think carefully.'

'Where I usually leave it, out behind the house by the orchard.'

He bit his lip thoughtfully. 'It was someone who knew you wouldn't come across the border but over the hills.'

'That would be an easy guess,' she said with bitterness. 'Everyone knows I wouldn't go across the border since Kiaran's death – if I could help it.'

'Also, it is someone who knows you come here every evening.'

'Do you think they're expecting these guns?' she asked in alarm.

'Where do you usually park the car?'

'Over there.' She nodded her head at the other side of the flats. 'I couldn't get in because someone else is parked there.'

'Prisca. She's arranged this.' He spoke the words slowly, almost reluctantly, as though the utterance of them made the possibility real. 'After what she was doing today, I would not be surprised.'

'What the hell is the matter with you two?' Prisca came across with a heavy frown on her face.

Marcella was surprised to see her. After the scene in the cottage, they thought she might stay away from them.

'Come here,' her brother barked.

Bewildered, Prisca watched Dominic open the back of the car and carefully lift an edge of the rug. 'God, are you mad?' she whispered in a shocked voice, forgetting that her brother was the last person to bring in guns. 'These people have been through hell; they're not ready for guns yet because they haven't been trained to use them.'

Dominic looked uncertain. Was she pretending, Marcella wondered.

'They're not ready for guns, not yet,' Prisca repeated. 'Later,' she added ominously. 'Back the car to that window.' She pointed to one of the flats. 'Then get out and open the doors and edge the car right up as far as you can go.'

Marcella did this with some difficulty and waited while she and Dominic went inside to the flat. After a moment the lower part of the window was pushed up. Three pairs of arms reached into the back and removed the guns. Prisca came out again and nodded her inside. The door of the flat was locked behind her. She was introduced to a woman with short grey hair carelessly caught in a slide at the back of her head. It was Rosheen Quinn. Silently they began to pull up the lino on the floor and prise up the floorboards.

'We've decided this is the best way to hide them for the time being,' Prisca explained.

What were they planning to do with them later and how soon would they be used, Marcella wondered.

'Silly bastards,' Rosheen grunted. 'They didn't organize that very well. She might have been stopped coming into Derry. They've started searching cars for firearms.'

Marcella disliked the way Rosheen Quinn referred to her as 'she'. The thought also occurred to her, that she could have been in a very awkward situation indeed if the guns had been found in the car, for no doubt the incident with the B. Special had been duly recorded. It might be considered that she had every reason to fight against authority.

'But,' Rosheen went on, 'whoever tried to organize this knows exactly what we're doing. They must've been trailing her all day.'

Could it be a breakaway group trying to work on its own, Marcella wondered. The same thought had occurred to Dominic, as they discovered later.

'The place will have to be well guarded until we can think of the next move,' Prisca said and added tersely, 'there'll come a time when we'll need a few guns around here.'

Rosheen Quinn narrowed her eyes against the smoke of her cigarette and muttered through clenched teeth, 'When the police came rampaging into the Bogside, a few shots in the air might have scared the devils off.'

Prisca threw her head back and gave a harsh laugh. 'A few shots in the air –'

'There'll be no guns used here by anyone – ever,' Dominic said. 'I'll damn well make sure of it, even if it means bringing in the Army.'

'Shut up, Dominic,' Prisca shouted.

'Be careful what you say, young man,' Rosheen snapped threateningly.

He turned away. 'Marcella, you'd better get home. The barriers will soon be up and the Army won't let anyone through after that. See you later.'

As she drove off, Marcella couldn't stop thinking about the guns. Later, when Dominic came to the house, she and Cassy were in the kitchen drinking a cup of tea.

'I'd like a quiet talk with Marcella,' he said.

'Surely,' Cassy agreed. When he followed her upstairs, he threw himself into the chair. She sat on the edge of the bed.

'You didn't stop on your way to Derry, did you?'

'No, Dominic, I came straight from the cottage to this house.'

'There must be an IRA cell somewhere around Iniscad. Where did you say you parked the car? Tell me exactly.'

'Out behind the cottage, near the gate leading into the field.'

'So the guns were placed in the car in broad daylight. It's very secluded back there, isn't it?'

'How could anyone get them around there? Aunt Sarah would know if any cars came near the cottage. The minute one stops or goes up the little lane, she's out of the door like a shot.'

'They must have been hidden somewhere in the field.'

'There are no hiding places in the field; I've searched the place many times.' She stopped, alarm growing on her face.

'What is it, Marcella? You look frightened.'

'It's something that has been happening over the years. I've never mentioned it to anyone because it seemed so ridiculous, like the old fairy tales.'

'Never mind, just tell me.'

She tried to explain the noises, the peculiar sounds and finally the mumbled words spoken in a Derry man's voice.

'When did you first hear these things?'

Her mind raced back through the years, trying to pinpoint the night when she waited for the Inishtrahull Lighthouse to throw its light. 'I'm almost certain it was some time after Prisca's first visit to Bridge House. Anyway, it was certainly not before.'

Dominic frowned. 'Are you sure?'

'I remember the time clearly enough now because she had such an effect on us all. Even Sarah snapped out of her awful moods.'

'Prisca and Brian became friendly almost immediately, didn't they?'

'Yes, from the first day I think. Why are you looking like that?'

'I'm not sure. We'd better have a word with Brian. He'll be back at Northland Road by now. I'll go up there and bring him back here.'

'What's all the mystery about?' Brian asked when Dominic brought him back to Cassy's.

'It's those guns that were stacked in the back of Marcella's car.'

'I wasn't around at the time. What exactly happened?'

Briefly she explained, then they made her repeat every single incident down through the years. Brian sat at the table and rested his head in his hands as though he couldn't bear to hear this new development.

'My God. All those years ago she must have been involved with the IRA and it was I who showed her the perfect place to hide the guns.'

'Brian, what are you talking about?'

'On her first visit to the cottage, I mentioned the project we were doing at school, about underground chambers. Like most people, she was very interested and asked to see one.'

'Do you mean souterrains?' Dominic asked.

'Yes, there's evidence that the one in our field was used during Cromwellian days. In Penal times the priest often said Mass down there.'

'Where is it?' Marcella asked in astonishment. 'I've been around that field so many times.'

'It's in the corner near the lane, behind a group of whinbushes. Sods of earth and stones hide the entrance.'

'Is it big enough to hide a load of guns?'

'It's big enough to hide a load of people; that's where the people around there hid when they saw the Redcoats coming across the hills.'

'What are we going to do about it?' Marcella asked worriedly.

'We'd better get in touch with the Garda,' Dominic suggested. 'They can clear it out.'

Brian jumped to his feet. 'No, that's the last thing to do with Sarah alone in the cottage. Father's not there this evening. I'll go down at dawn and if there is no one around I'll leave a letter telling them to get off my father's land, or else I'll inform the guards. I'll never forgive Prisca for this,' he added.

'Don't be so stupid,' Marcella shouted, angry and frightened. 'If you didn't wrap yourself so much in your own world, she wouldn't get away with half the things she does.' Her anger was really against Prisca. Perhaps she would find her husband not so easy to manage in the future.

'Brian,' Dominic said, 'I'll go down to Iniscad with you. It will be easier for me to get out of the city at that hour. On the journey we'll discuss the best way to handle this situation. We can park the car on the lower road and go up by the fields.'

Brian didn't spare himself, or Prisca, when he called in at his father's office the following morning to tell him what had happened. 'I should have taken more notice years ago,' he said bluntly. 'She tried to get me interested but my lack of enthusiasm for Irish groups or politics silenced her.'

'We're not a politically minded family,' Conor replied carefully, giving himself time to take in the appalling story he had just heard.

'Can you believe it, Dad, I showed her the souterrain on that very first visit to the house and she . . .'

'You can't be sure –'

'Marcella is very sure about what she heard going back to that time.'

'She's never mentioned it to me.'

'Apparently Prisca's friends have stored guns in vaults in the old churchyards.'

'From the last troubles, no doubt,' Conor said cynically. 'God help us, they must be in a pretty rusty state.'

'That's one of the uses they've been making of our place, cleaning them down there. Some very sophisticated high-power lamps have been left behind, also cleaning materials.'

'They'll be back for those. Throw them outside. I'll have the place sealed off right away. Where'd they get the money for that sort of thing, I wonder?'

'I didn't ask. Some questions Prisca refuses to answer. Not that I've tried to probe very deeply.'

Conor shot a quick glance at his son and wondered if trouble was brewing between them.

'Someone around there,' Brian said thoughtfully, 'must be helping them.'

'Liam in the brae. The family are descendants of Lord Kindron.'

'*What*?'

'I'm sure that's your man,' Conor said slowly. 'Ever heard of the Kindron list?'

'Kindron list?' Brian repeated indifferently.

'Did Prisca never mention anything?' Conor asked, puzzled. To his surprise Brian shook his head.

Conor explained briefly. 'They're probably the backbone of this extremist group here in Derry, from what Eoin O'Donnell mentioned to me.' Brian shrugged. 'Maybe,' Conor suggested, 'if we were descendants of Kindron, we might feel the same repugnance and anger in the present political climate, especially with someone like Rosheen Quinn around.'

His son looked surprised. 'Not me. I wouldn't lose a minute's sleep over it.' That was the moment when Conor began to have a feeling of sympathy for Prisca. His son was totally indifferent to Ireland's sad history.

When Marcella started her work the following morning, Dominic came into the ward. She had scarcely slept all night wondering and worrying about what had happened at Iniscad. He shook his head.

'There's not a thing there; everything was cleared out apart from a few odds and ends. Prisca must have suspected something when I went off with Brian and got in touch with her friends. It would seem that someone overstepped their authority when they put the guns in your car. Someone impatient for action to begin,' he added grimly. 'When you see her, don't mention anything, will you?'

'When I see her I'll avoid her,' Marcella said bitterly. 'She pours scorn on the Civil Rights workers and has sided with the extremists. I no longer have anything in common with your sister.'

'Please, for my mother's sake, try and hide your feelings,' Dominic pleaded. 'It would kill my parents if they knew what she was doing.'

'I expect there'll be other families divided before this trouble has ended,' she told him bleakly.

At six o'clock the following evening Cassy said she was leaving the house. 'I'm going up to Northland Road now, though honest to God I'd rather sleep in m'own bed. Are ye sure you won't come as well, Marcella?'

'No, Cassy, I want to finish this painting. Tell Mrs McDaid I'll be up later.'

The elderly woman went around sprinkling everything with holy water, sending a strong dash in Marcella's direction. For further protection, she checked that the Sacred Heart lamp was lit. The little red lamp, with its floating wick in a pool of oil, was always kept alight: the same type of lamp stood before a similar picture in most Catholic homes in Derry.

'Cassy, do you think it would be safer if that lamp was put out?'

'Sure it's only a flicker of flame. Maybe it'll keep the house safe until we get back in the morning.'

The minute she left, Marcella blew it out. The look of the hot oil bothered her. Later, glancing at her watch, she was horrified to discover the time. There were only a few minutes left to get to the barriers. Grabbing her bag, she ran out of the house and jumped into the car. To her alarm nothing happened when she tried to start the engine. There was no time to investigate.

She ran all the way to the Army barrier. Just as she was approaching, they closed it. The soldiers guarding the barrier looked very young and tired, though the guns clutched in their hands made them seem threatening. She walked back to the house again and for a moment considered spending the night there, but knew that Dominic and his family would be worried if she didn't turn up.

Marcella sat down at the table and worked out a rough sketch of the town, letting her memory go back to the days when Prisca took her on exploring trips around the area. Not altogether sure, she decided on a route. She had a rough idea where the Catholic barricades were and the barbed-wire barriers of the Army. These she must avoid, and the trouble spots. It seemed that the quietest, if not the quickest, way was by going down Bishop Street and across towards Brandywell. Here she would have to avoid a barrier but by cutting through the cemetery it would be possible.

It was getting dark. She felt nervous. The hedge dividing the lane from the graveyard was thick with hawthorn bushes. Somehow she crawled through. Scratched and torn, she made her way between the lines of graves.

'What was that?'

The voice came from somewhere near. Marcella nearly fainted with fright. They'll hear my heart thumping if they don't see me, she thought, huddling behind a tombstone.

'Bloody Fenian ghost – this is Papist ground,' another voice replied with a laugh. The low harsh accents gripped her with fear. They weren't English soldiers but B. Specials. Don't let them find me here, she prayed frantically and, lifting her head cautiously, peered around the tombstones.

A B. Special was standing in a bar of light from the lamp outside the burial grounds. If he had just risen out of a grave, shrouded in white, Marcella could not have been more terrified. It was the same man whom she had attacked in the street. What if he discovered her? A policeman came out of the shadows and stood beside him.

'Don't think there's anyone here. Better get back to the gate.'

She didn't look again. Somehow she could feel the man's reluctance to move away. When their footsteps receded, Marcella found it difficult to move, as if fear had frozen her to the spot. The next part of the journey through the cemetery was hazardous because it was newer ground and there were fewer tombstones to hide behind. Every now and then a powerful torch penetrated the darkness. At one point it lingered close. She stood quite still, just like a marble figure at the top of a grave. Thank goodness she was wearing her white raincoat.

Perspiration began to pour down her body as she tried to keep her stance. The light went round and round in wide sweeping circles, then growing smaller, missing the point where she stood by just a couple of feet. Something made her peer down closely at the white slab of marble stone with its black lettering. The name on it made the sweat grow cold on her body; it was Granny McDaid's grave. When she died – about the time of Kiaran's death – Marcella had envied her her escape. Now she could see the old woman in her mind's eye, clutching a rosary, praying away all the time. It seemed strange that in all the cemetery, her resting place had given protection.

Slowly she made her way towards the wall at the other side. There was a part that had crumbled down, she remembered. If only it could be found without delay. Suddenly it was before her. She scrambled up quickly as a triumphant shout rang out across the burial ground and torch light glowed all around her. She jumped. The light followed. All the time the B. Specials must have been quietly coming up through the graves. Now he knows who I am, she thought. He's got a revolver. She stumbled and fell. Then a voice called the man back, warning him not to go any further. She came out to a street with a high pavement and was quietly sick. Exhausted, she sat on the edge of the kerb.

'What's the matter?'

A man and a woman bent down and helped her to stand up.

'Are you all right?' he said.

'No she's not,' the woman told him. 'Come with us, dear. You look shaken. A drink in the pub will do you a world of good. We're just going there.'

'I came through the cemetery.'

'My God! What did you do that for?'

'I was too late to get through the barriers.'

'Well,' the man said, 'there are better ways of getting here. You'd be a stranger in these parts?'

As they walked away, she told them where she was going.

'The McDaid family? We know them well. Dominic, the one who's a doctor, is very friendly with the girl who lives next door to us. We're hoping there'll be wedding bells! She's a lovely girl.'

That news had a startling effect on Marcella. She suddenly felt bereft, as though deprived of something very important.

'Perhaps I ought to go there straight away.' There was a sharpness in her voice. 'They'll be anxious.'

'Ach, come on, have a quick drink first.'

They were now at the pub door which opened welcomingly, as though they were expected. The place was filled with people. Some were talking seriously about various aspects of the trouble; others were roaring with laughter about the antics of the Orangemen and the police, and how they had outwitted them. An old man in the corner was singing a rebel song – *Who Fears to Speak of '98*. Marcella glanced at the clock and was astounded to see how late it was.

'It's after closing time and the pub's still open,' she said in surprise.

The man repeated her words. Everyone, roaring with laughter, turned and looked at the stranger. 'Sure it doesn't matter what time it is,' they told her. 'The bliddy polis can't get past the barriers now. Sure, begod, we're here half the night.'

'A drop of whiskey?' the man offered.

'Yes, thanks.' The glass was filled to the top without a measure.

As she sat quietly sipping the drink, Marcella heard snatches of conversations about the night the police rampaged through the Bogside.

'. . . I was walkin' along like a civil man when one of the buggers from the constabulary crashed his riot stick into m'skull. "Are ye one of the boyos?" says he, his breath heavy with the smell of drink and a baton wavin' in his hand. I didn't have time to say, "I'm a civil man out for a few messages," when he cracked my skull. Sure, I had to have six stitches . . .'

'Sure, I'm an old man,' another said, 'and I was out buying m'newspaper when they beat me unmercifully. I had to have anti-tetanus injections at the hospital.'

The woman touched her arm. 'If you went into the cemetery in the first place, dear, you couldn't have been all that frightened of the dead. When we came on you, you seemed terrified.'

'No, it wasn't that.' She told her what had happened.

'Oh,' she whispered, alarmed. 'Don't say a word to my

man. He's got it in for them. One of them smashed his mother's window in with a riot stick. She's still in a terrible state.' The woman hesitated. 'The trouble is, it's very awkward for me, because my brother's in the force. I'm in a very difficult situation, you see.'

Her remark startled Marcella. It hadn't occurred to her how Catholic policemen felt when they were ordered to charge into Catholic crowds in the Bogside.

When she arrived at the McDaids' house most of the family were gathered in the kitchen wondering what had become of her. Dominic was just about to leave to search. They were horrified when they heard her story.

'Marcella, don't ever do a thing like that again,' he said angrily.

'I'm all right.'

'That B. Special is a surly type. I don't think he'd have seriously harmed you, but who knows what can happen at the present time? Everyone is caught in a frenzy of bitterness. Yesterday some of the teenagers turned on a priest who was trying to get them off the street. Gave him cheek!'

'*A priest*?' Nora McDaid's eyes widened in disbelief. 'God help us, I never thought I'd live to see the day that anyone would turn on a priest.'

They were quiet for a moment reflecting on this new turn of events, until she spoke again. 'Marcella, you won't mind sharing a room with the girls this evening, will you? I'll get things better sorted out tomorrow. I'm decorating up there, so everything is upside down at the moment.'

'Of course I don't mind.'

Dominic's sisters crowded around her excitedly.

'No, I think she'd better go to my room tonight,' he said quickly. 'I'm on duty.'

'Perhaps that's a better idea,' his mother reflected. 'The girls will just chatter away and keep you awake. After what you've been through you'll need a good night's sleep.'

Dominic's room was large, with a desk and rows of bookshelves. The table beside the bed was crowded with books, too: most of them were textbooks, apart from a copy of *The Phenomenon of Man* by Teilhard de Chardin and a biography of Karl Marx. His mother brought up a hot water bottle and a fresh pillowslip.

'I only changed the sheets today, Marcella. Now, if Dominic will give you something to read, I'll bring up a glass of hot milk to make you sleep.'

He went over and knelt beside the bookshelves. Fascinated by the number of books, she sat on the floor beside him as he pulled various ones from the shelves. 'What's it to be? A Scots or English writer? Or would you like one of our own? Kate or Edna O'Brien?'

'You choose. Nothing too heavy!'

He flicked through some. 'Perhaps Edna O'Brien.'

She put out her hand for the book. He placed it on top of the shelves. 'Marcella . . .' There was a note of pleading in his voice which was out of character.

'Yes?' She was aware of his searching look. Suddenly and quite firmly he drew her into his arms.

'I was so alarmed when you didn't turn up this evening. When I went to Aunt Cassy's and saw your car, I was frightened something had happened. Tomorrow evening, if you don't want to come here too early, wait for me and I'll call in on my way from work.' His arms fell away when Mrs McDaid came into the room.

'Now, Marcella love, have this. A wee read then off to sleep.'

Marcella had felt secure and happy in Dominic's brief embrace. His caring and anxiety moved her in some inexplicable way. She realized now that she needed the feeling of strength and protection that he gave her. When he looked at her again his eyes were gentle.

'Come on, Dominic,' his mother said thoughtfully.

Chapter 29

Mrs Kenny, who was looking after her twin grandsons while her daughter went out to work, pushed the pram up Waterloo Street to Butchers Gate where a tall coloured soldier was standing on duty. It was the first time in her life she had seen a black man in the flesh. She stood and stared at him, her mouth wide open, while the two little boys in the pram chewed their way down one side.

One of the children looked up, spat out the pieces of flock stuffed into his mouth and asked, startled: 'Granny, what's that?' The look on his grandmother's face alarmed the child. He dived under the rug in the pram. His brother followed.

'It looks like a man wi' a touch of sun, pet,' she said slowly, her eyes fastened on the soldier's face.

Corporal Brown, irritated by the woman's scrutiny, moved his head in Mrs Kenny's direction. His eyes widened in alarm and, without leaving his post, he pointed towards the pram. 'You come over here, Mam.' The corporal had been warned about the things that could travel in prams in this part of the world. 'You got bombs in that pram?'

'Bombs?' Mrs Kenny shouted, outraged. 'The only two bombs I've got are them two wee devils ye've frightened the wits outa. Where'd the likes of you come from?'

'Take that cover off,' he ordered.

'Go to hell!'

'Missus, I tell you to take d'cover off.'

It seemed to Mrs Kenny that the man's eyes were blazing with fury. Any minute now he might use that gun. The soldier reached out and jerked off the rug revealing two bare bottoms sticking up in the air. Mrs Kenny shrugged at the soldier's expression. The weans were for ever wanting to pee. Nice and handy just to pick them out of the pram and stand them against the kerb whenever they wailed, 'Us wanta go . . .'

The embarrassed soldier dropped the rug. 'You bad mother,' he said contemptuously.

'Christ!' she shouted at him. 'Are you wan o' the wee black bastards I used to save m'pennies for at school? Every week aw put m'money in the mission box for poor black weans.' Furious, she smacked the bare bottoms, sat the children up straight and hurried down Waterloo Street.

The soldier looked after her, his eyes rolling. A nutcase, he thought, not comprehending that the sight of him standing there at the old city gate below the walls had seriously disturbed Mrs Kenny. He stared suspiciously at a group of young women who were peering over the turret on the wall above at a crowd of hostile-looking youths below in the Bogside.

'Look at them askin' for it,' one of the girls shouted. She put a hand in her pocket and threw down a fistful of pennies. 'Go and buy yersels some contraceptives,' she called raucously.

Some of the youths sniggered, while others yelled: 'Buck off ye flamin' Prods,' and began to throw stones.

The soldier, remembering his instructions, ignored the little fracas. At that moment the sound of a band came from Guildhall Square.

'Come on fellas,' a youth shouted. 'The boyos are at it again,' and they tore off down Waterloo Street.

Man, the soldier thought, there's sure more big trouble startin' down there. He tried to remember what it was all about and why he was doing duty in this country.

'Trouble on the way, son,' Billy the Man said to Micky O'Kane, who was driving his taxi. 'Git yousel' into Little James Street and down Sackville.'

'Barricade,' Micky replied.

'Keep on then. If one o' them bastards puts a scratch on m'car I'll be out and at 'em.'

'A right eejit ye'd look. Man, it's not yer car wid git scratched.'

Billy, with his friend and co-driver, Micky, had long since lost his fear of the Bogside area. His Orange friends up Fountain Street talked about the Bogsiders as though they grew green horns. Ach, they were not too bad. Sometimes when he thought of his Catholic mother he felt he belonged; then when he got back to Fountain Street again he felt proud to be an Orangeman.

A volley of shots rang out across Little James Street as a piece of boulder smashed into the taxi. Before Mickey could stop him, Billy was out of the car beating his way through the crowds of rioters pouring down the street. Micky jumped out after him and saw a hail of missiles flying towards a group of policemen who were trying to retreat. Warning shots went into the air. The mob backed up the street again. Just as Micky went to grab Billy, a shot ricocheted and hit his friend who fell to the ground with blood pouring from his shoulder.

Micky went crazy. Billy was killed. He would get the bastards who did it. Screaming with rage and anguish, he picked up lumps of stone and flung them wildly at the rioters and the police. Then he fell on his knees beside his friend, who opened his eyes and whispered: 'What are ye bawling at, ye wee scut? Sure, the taxi's yours now, son.'

Micky beat his head in despair and cried like a child as the old man, who had been like a father, shut his eyes and grew very pale. His sobbing stopped when a hand fell on his shoulder. 'Micky, the ambulance is here. Move out of the way.'

Micky O'Kane looked up and for the first time in his life was relieved to see stiff-necked McDaid. When he went to climb into the ambulance after the stretcher, Dominic stopped him.

'Better to move the car away from here, Micky. It might be used to build up the barricade. Do you feel up to driving?' Dominic asked this with a look of concern, as Micky O'Kane's eyes followed the frail figure being gently eased into the ambulance. 'You don't want Billy to come out of hospital and find his car has been used as part of a barricade, now do you?' Dominic spoke firmly.

'D'ye think he'll make it? Is there a chance?' The youth's eyes had lit up hopefully.

'He's an old man, Micky, but tough as they come. Move the car now and come over to the hospital later.'

Cassy shut the shop early and went to church for Benediction before going to Northland Road. Marcella got down to her painting. The scene of Derry before the trouble was nearly finished. It was comforting to think that Dominic would be coming around later. Nevertheless, she felt depressed. The people who had come into the shop earlier had a tenseness about them. Everyone was expecting things to get worse. There seemed to be no hope any more, and now some people were beginning to revolt against the British Army. That was ironical, she thought, considering how many like Cassy had cried, 'Thank God, they've come. They'll protect us from the Orangemen.' Dominic had told her that Prisca's friends were rapidly gathering followers. They couldn't stand the sight of a British uniform.

About nine o'clock there was a smell of burning. She hurried downstairs and checked through the rooms. Everything was all right in the house, but the smell was growing stronger. Cautiously she opened the front door. At first, the screen of smoke rolling down the street looked like something used by the Army to disperse the crowds. 'The warehouse is on fire,' someone shouted. The fire did not alarm her as much as the hostile mob of people advancing along the street.

She pushed the door shut and prayed that Dominic would not get caught up in that mob. The wind was in their direction; it would not take long for the fire to spread to the houses on this side. She rushed upstairs again and bundled the best of her canvases together. Cassy's money . . . Did she really hide it in the house, or was it safely in the bank? Frantically, Marcella searched and nearly wept with the hopelessness of it. There were so many things Cassy cherished. How could she possibly take them all with her? She would have to wait in the house for Dominic, unless the fire spread too rapidly. He would try to get through somehow. There was a frantic knocking at the back door. No sound of a car. Would she hear it with all that noise outside?

'Who's there?' she shouted, her mouth to the letterbox.

'It's me, Marcella. Open quickly.'

When Dominic staggered in through the doorway, she slammed it shut behind him.

'Stone got me on the leg. Had to leave the car at the other end of the street. Couldn't get it through . . . came down the back lane.'

He looked dreadful as he limped into the kitchen. She ran to the cupboard and took out the brandy bottle. 'Drink some. Thank goodness my car's out in the lane. We'll try to get away in it.'

'Do your best to get right out of town, if we can get through,' he said wearily.

'Wait a moment.' She rushed into the shop and tossed some boxes of children's toys on the floor. She and Cassy had laughed when they unpacked them because there were two large First Aid posters in the nursing kits. She wet them under the kitchen tap.

'Come on, Dominic,' Marcella urged, forgetting about her paintings and all her possessions which she had bundled together. They crossed the yard into the lane. She slapped the posters on the back and front windows of the car and they drove off. Carefully she eased the car out into the street. The crowd seemed to have moved away slightly but stones and pieces of pavement were still flying through the air. A young policeman came over and stopped them.

'Go down the next street, Doctor. Make your way from there. The mob's coming up this way again. They're not able to get past the Army barriers.'

'Look after yourself,' Dominic told him urgently. 'Don't take any chances.' As they turned the corner he said to Marcella, 'That man's wife has just had a baby. She's not very well.'

'He doesn't look as alarming as his fellow officers. Look at them, shouting and charging along in their riot helmets, waving batons and shields. You'd think they came out of the jungle.'

When they smelt the gas they knew it would be better to keep far away from the barriers. The crowds were trying to break through to the Bogside and were being driven back by the Army discharging CS canisters.

'God almighty,' Dominic muttered. 'Marcella, we'll have to take a chance on this. There's a derelict house by Hawthorn Lane with a field behind. If we can get through, there's a lane at the top leading to the road. Heaven knows what it's going to do to your car though.'

She thought despairingly of all the rubbish that was bound to be lying around a derelict house; also she was frightened that someone would stop them and ask for Dominic's help. He looked ill and was exhausted. One blessing anyway, the wind had changed and no longer sending the gas in their direction.

The field behind the house was better than she had expected; hard and not marshy enough to drag down the car wheels. All was silent at the top of the lane when they bumped out on to the roadway. Just sighing trees mourning over the graves on the other side of the hedge. She drove straight out to the country and stopped the car in a smooth, sheltered spot. Silently, they sat there and looked towards the city where the fires and turmoil were changing the lives of the people who had lived uneasily together for many years and now, because of their political inheritance, were overshadowed by the threat of civil war.

He turned in the seat and laid his hand on hers. 'Marcella, you managed that very well.'

'Desperation!'

He smiled and they climbed out of the car where they stood still for a moment, aware of the silence and the scents of the night in the breeze. It was like another world. Dominic limped around slowly, testing his leg. She pulled the rug from the back seat and spread it on the ground.

'Sit down and have some brandy.'

'I must tell you that I didn't get to bed last night. Brandy might send me to sleep.'

'Well, sleep . . . look at those first-aid stickers, don't they look ridiculous?'

He laughed and rolled up his trouser leg to examine the wound. It was still bleeding. She handed him the first-aid box from the car and said, 'Dominic, when you have bandaged your leg, do let's have some brandy and relax.'

They passed the bottle to each other and drank uncomfortably from the lip, then he stretched out on the rug and closed his eyes; there was such a look of weariness about him again. After a while he opened them and let his gaze wander slowly over her face, as if he hadn't seen her for a long time and each feature was being recalled.

She broke the long silence by saying, 'How can I thank you for helping me? This job at the hospital and all you've done, even getting cross at times – it's all been good for me. Sometimes I feel as though I've stepped into another life. Ulster and its problems used to seem so far away. Now I'm here and just as concerned as anyone else.'

He put up his hand, drew her down beside him and buried his head on her shoulder. 'Marcella, don't you know I need you. I don't care how long I've got to wait – months, years, it doesn't matter because I've loved you for a very long time.'

Her arms went around him and she held him close, feeling a strange maturity. He was a strong man, but vulnerable too. She thought about him up at the flats in the Bogside, how he shouted at the parents for allowing their children to fill milk bottles with petrol to throw at Orangemen and police; and now at the soldiers. Even the toughest moved out of his way when he was angry. This was the kind of man people needed to lead them; free of bigotry and hate. He had great compassion and strength.

As they lay there on the hillside, close together with the scent of grass and wild herbs all around them, she remembered the day he had quoted Dostoyevsky: 'Each of us is responsible for everything and to every human being.' If only he could take on the challenge of leadership these people needed before Prisca's extremist friends claimed the right to represent the people of Bogside.

He raised his head. 'What are you thinking about?'

'About your future, Dominic.'

He touched her face and smiled. 'I hope, Marcella, you'll share it with me.'

They sat up hastily at the sound of a car racing along the road, thinking it was an Army patrol or the police. A station wagon passed and stopped. Two men in civilian clothes jumped out.

'Dr McDaid,' the older one said, 'we need your help. We've got an injured man here.'

Dominic jumped too quickly to his feet and winced at the pain as he limped towards the car. 'What happened to him? How did he hurt himself?'

'Shot wound,' the other said laconically.

When Dominic had inspected the invalid he announced, 'This man needs proper treatment. We'd better get him out to the field hospital at the border which the Irish Army have set up.'

The younger one, who had a keen foxy face, muttered, 'He's not going there. Get in beside him.'

'For God's sake, man,' Dominic retorted angrily, 'there's not a minute to lose, he's bleeding badly. We can go down this road and out that way. The field hospitals are well equipped.'

'Get in,' the man snarled, 'and stop that bleeding. We're going to no border. There's a cottage up in the hills.'

Blazing with anger, Dominic reiterated: 'You'll damn well get out to the border. It's probably a better and quicker journey than your den in the hills.'

'Look, Doctor,' the other one said, 'I understand your professional concern, but there could be an Army patrol on that road. We want to cross over to the Free State our way and as quickly as possible.'

Dominic looked pleadingly at him. 'How can I help you? I've got nothing.' He threw his arms out in a helpless gesture. 'This is not even my car.'

'Don't blasted well argue. Get in.' The younger one

whipped out a gun. It was his eyes that frightened Marcella. They were filled with rage and fear.

Turning to the more reasonable one, Dominic was about to make a final plea.

'*Get in.*' There was a movement of the hand on the gun and for one terrible moment Marcella thought he was going to fire.

She sprang to Dominic's side. 'Do as they say – *please.*'

He released her hands gently and, without a word, climbed into the car. The one with the gun took the wheel and prepared to drive away. The other said to her: 'I'll go with you. Just follow close behind.'

They continued up the road for a mile or so, then the car in front slowed down and unexpectedly stopped. The driver jumped out and began pulling away great clods of turf and bushes from a gap in the hedge. He drove through rough scrubland that led to a wood. She went to follow, but her companion ordered her to stop. He climbed out of the car and quickly built up the hedge again. When they were through the woods, there was a rough road strewn with small stones; this road went straight up into the hills.

'If that man is badly injured, the ride up here won't do him any good,' Marcella remarked to her silent companion. He did not reply. Eventually they came to a cottage. Dominic, face white, mouth grim with anxiety, waited impatiently for the door to be unlocked. 'Both of you help here,' he shouted angrily.

They obeyed his order in a subdued manner, as though they were fully aware now of the seriousness of their action in dragging the injured man up to a hide-out in the mountains. Marcella hurried inside. There was a kettle cauldron hanging from a crane over a smouldering fire; warm kindling, peat and wood were piled on the side of the inglenook fireplace. She poked life into the fire as they carried the injured man into a tiny bedroom off the kitchen. Dominic poured some hot water into a tin basin, pulled off his woolly, rolled up his sleeves and, shouting impatiently for Dettol, began to scrub his hands. Anxious now, the two men came up from another room, arms loaded with clean linen and various things.

'Dominic, can I help you?'

'No, no,' he said grimly. 'They're well prepared. There's been other emergencies here. You'd better go down to the room over there and wait.'

The room across the passage was bare apart from a double mattress on the floor, a table and a built-in cupboard. She looked inside the cupboard and saw a shelf piled with odd bits of linen. The other shelf had papers stacked on it and a square wooden box with a padlock. She knew what it contained. Revolvers. There was a box exactly like it at Slievan.

Marcella lay down on the mattress and prayed that Dominic would be able to save the man's life. After a while she went over and listened at the door. There wasn't a sound coming from across the passage. She stretched out on the mattress again, wishing there was a chair to sit on. As she lay listening to the silence of the hills surrounding the cottage, she thought of the things that had happened to her. Kiaran's death. That was 'the dark night' of her mind, body and heart. Somehow, she had lived through it. Her life with Kiaran – that short wonderful life – would always remain a sacred memory. She was a different person now; more aware of other people's problems. Slowly and painfully, she had grown up. What would have happened to her if she hadn't had that breakdown and left Iniscad? The work at the hospital and the troubled people had restored her. How fortunate she was that there had been someone to help after the two crises in her life. First Nanta, when her mother died. Now Dominic, so hard at times, tender and passionate –totally unlike Kiaran.

The door opened. The older man brought in a lighted lamp and placed it on the table.

'What's happening? How is he?'

He turned up the light. 'Thanks be to God, he'll be all right now. The doctor did a fine job. As soon as dawn comes we'll take him to the hospital at Letterkenny.'

'Why don't you take him now? We're in the Republic, aren't we?'

'Yes, but it's a bad road and we don't want to attract attention with car lights. We might run into the Garda.'

As the man left the room, Dominic came in with two mugs of tea. 'I'm sorry, Marcella, that you had to face all this.' She was touched by his consideration for her at that moment.

'You were the one who had to face it. Was it bad?'

'Not anything as bad as I expected. They're amazingly well equipped for emergencies,' he said drily.

'Their car must have been somewhere near that old house. They saw us turning in. Wonder what happened?'

'God knows.'

'When will they let us leave?'

'We go at the same time as them — daybreak. So,' he looked at the mattress, 'we'd better get some rest.'

After they had drunk the tea, she said, 'I must go to the loo. Where is it?'

'At the bottom of the garden. They've left an oil lamp in the hall for us.'

When she went towards the door, Dominic followed. 'I'll come with you and wait by the back door. The one who threatened to use the gun is still in a very excitable state for some reason. I don't trust him.'

Quietly they left the room. As they passed the kitchen there was the sound of a radio. It was the twelve o'clock news. And then they heard: *'A young soldier was killed in Derry this afternoon. The gunmen got away.'*

Trembling, Marcella stumbled down the garden towards the toilet, her feet crushing weeds on the overgrown path, filling the air with a clean aromatic smell. At the door she disturbed a cluster of fully blown roses; the petals poured to the ground in a flow of glacial purity. It seemed strange that a familiar, simple thing like that could happen on such a night when fear and death were so close at hand.

Back in the room, she said to Dominic, 'It must be those men.'

'I'm afraid so. It could account for the state of the younger one. This,' he added grimly, 'may well be the first English soldier to be killed in the present trouble.'

'We didn't believe Prisca when she said things would come to this, did we?'

'It is the beginning of something terrible,' he added slowly. 'The guns have arrived. God, to think it could have been avoided if the Civil Rights quiet protest had been listened to by the politicians of Westminster.'

'Dominic,' she said anxiously, 'you'll be careful, won't you? Don't say anything to these men. Don't lose your temper.'

He pressed her hand. 'Come on, let's lie down and try to get some rest. We'll have to be up in a few hours.'

The mattress was hard and lumpy. Marcella knew that she wasn't going to sleep, but hoped Dominic would be able to. She curled into the side next to the cold stone wall; a channel of cold air separated them.

'Marcella.'

She turned round quickly. He was lying with his hands behind his head, staring up at the ceiling. 'You know, we may be in for a very bad time in Derry.'

It was something in his voice that made her say, 'I'm not going back to Iniscad.'

'There's England. You'd have no trouble in getting a job over there. Would you consider going, just for a time?'

'It would be lonely.' And then before she could stop herself, she said, 'I don't want to be so far away from you.'

She heard the sharp intake of breath. He put out his arm and pulled her towards him. Then, just as abruptly, he swung himself off the mattress and began to walk about the room. Confused and startled, Marcella lay peering into the darkness, wondering how she could feel like this so soon. She got up and stood beside him.

'Dominic . . .' He put his arm around her and didn't speak. 'Dominic, you must rest.' Taking his hand she led him back to the shake-down. There was a shabby bedcover in the cupboard. She took it out and arranged it around him. For a moment she rested her face against his and whispered, 'Now sleep.'

He slept.

When the greyness of dawn touched the window, they brought in mugs of tea and a plateful of soda bread. Dominic went into the other room to see the injured man.

The older one followed him back again. 'Thank you, Doctor. He was lucky.'

'The young soldier who was killed yesterday wasn't so lucky, was he?' Dominic snapped.

The other's face showed no sign of surprise. 'Look, Doctor,' he reasoned, 'when a country is in a state of civil war, it is inevitable that lives will be lost.'

'We're *not* in a state of civil war yet,' Dominic retorted.

With gentle patience, as though pacifying a child, the man went on. 'We stood aside while people with your point of view tried it the peaceful way. We saw people being terrified by police, Orangemen and,' he added with emphasis, 'the world knows what happened at Burntollet when our people were ambushed and driven into the river. You see, Doctor, there'll never be a good life for Catholics in Ulster as long as we're ruled by Stormont. We are a people without hope.'

'What do you think you are going to achieve by using force?'

'This time we're going to fight to the end for a united Ireland.'

'Against a trained army? Christ, man, our people will be slaughtered.'

'We'd better be on our way,' the one with the gun shouted from the hall.

'Right,' his companion answered. He turned to Marcella. 'Finish your breakfast, miss. When we get the patient comfortable for the road, you follow us as far as the spot where we entered the woods last night. You'll know your way from there.'

Silently Marcella and Dominic climbed into the car. They knew now that it had begun again, more determinedly perhaps than ever before, the fight for the dream of a united Ireland. Cautiously she made her way down through the hills. Her eyes were glued to the road, nevertheless she was aware of the grey, violet light creeping up on the horizon.

Another day was beginning for their troubled land.